THE TAKEN

BOOKS BY VICKI PETTERSSON

THE SIGN OF THE ZODIAC SERIES

The Scent of Shadows

The Taste of Night

The Touch of Twilight

City of Souls

Cheat the Grave

The Neon Graveyard

THE
TAKEN

CELESTIAL BLUES

Book One

VICKI PETTERSSON

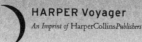

HARPER Voyager
An Imprint of HarperCollins*Publishers*

FIRST EDITION

Library of Congress Cataloging-in-Publication Data has been applied for.

ISBN 978-0-06-206464-6

12 13 14 15 16   OV/RRD   10 9 8 7 6 5 4 3 2 1

For James—for talking me through this book in the beginning, living with me through its middle, and helping me see it through to the end. It's as much yours as it is mine. Ditto the series. Ditto my life.

ACKNOWLEDGMENTS

My gratitude goes out to *Burlesque Beauty, Tattooed Cutie,* ChaCha Velour, for educating me on the exciting and addictive world of rockabilly culture. My Facebook friend Sharon Bond answered newswoman questions, and Kristin Grammas not only told me what a decaying body smells like, she offered to take me on a ride-along to show me one *in situ.* Gee, thanks, Kristin. Pamela Patchet and Joy Maiorana read early versions of the manuscript, and their astute comments and suggestions ended up making me look smarter—always appreciated. Miriam Kriss was a singular force in helping shape this new series from proposal to rewrites, and Diana Gill, as ever, championed it the whole way. My heartfelt thanks to you all.

THE TAKEN

CHAPTER ONE

Here's the thing. Every two-bit Tom and Dick on this glorified mudflat thought prostitution was legal in Las Vegas, but that's never been true.

Least, not when Grif was alive.

Maybe times had changed—plenty on the Surface had—but it was more likely that the johns were too lazy to trek out to Nye County for a sampling from the legal sexual menu. No, there was too much premeditation in that. But score a lay in some trucker-heavy roach-motel, and a man could tell himself he was the victim of impulse. Caught up in the moment. Just a little ol' fly snared in Sin City's glinting web.

Grif knew different. People created chaos, not places, and they were damned good at it no matter where they lived. And when this glittering gem of a city teamed up with the world's oldest profession, fantasy piled atop fantasy; it could convince anyone that impulse was a virtue, not a vice.

Just one roll of the dice, he thought, checking the number on the warped motel door against the entry in his notebook. Just one sip, make sure to tip. Play hard, enjoy the ride, and be certain to take your secrets with you when you leave.

Nicole Rockwell's last john, however, had taken a bit more.

"Help me!" she was yelling as Grif came through the door. Impressive, since she was missing her larynx. "There's been a terrible crime!"

Can't argue that, Grif thought, gaze skimming the hem of her cheap vinyl skirt. "You Nicole Elizabeth Rockwell?"

"Wh-what?" She looked from Grif to the fresh corpse on the bed—her own—then back again. "Yes."

"Right." He shut his notebook, returning it to his suit pocket. "Come with me."

Rockwell took one good look at his quasi-transparent form and promptly collapsed on the bed. "Wh-who are you?"

"Griffin Shaw. I'm here to help." He hesitated, then jerked his head at her remains. "Sorry I couldn't get here sooner."

Her expression, blasted and constricted all at once, made his jaw twitch, but he shrugged it off. Guardian wasn't his beat. As a Centurion, he merely assisted the recently, and violently, deceased into the Everlast. Those who'd been clipped early often had trouble getting there on their own. As Grif well knew.

He explained all of this to Nicole quickly, flatly, hoping it would keep the hysterics to a minimum. Given half a chance, females were always either jawing or at the waterworks. Dead or alive.

"But I can't just *leave*," she protested when he was finished. "I'm going to a bonfire this weekend, the first one of the spring.

And my best friend is waiting outside. We're gonna chill down-town at the Beauty Bar tonight. Unwind a bit, ya know?" She glanced down at Grif's proffered cigarette. A calming tactic. "Oh . . . thanks, honey."

Something stirred Grif as he bent down and lit her smoke. Probably the shake in her voice, though she talked like a lady, too. Not like most of the rabble he'd been picking up this decade. He snapped the Zippo shut. "Look, I'm sorry to be the one to tell you, kid. But you've been rooked."

"What?"

"You know, you got the dust-off. Killed. Murdered. Clipped. It's a rough deal, but you've had some good times, right? Some wild rides?" He gave a little hip thrust to illuminate the point.

"I'm not a hooker," she said evenly.

He let his eyes roam around the sex flop. "'Course you're not."

Blowing out a stream of smoke, Nicole returned his flat stare. "So where exactly is this . . . Everlast?"

"Now you're choosy?" Grif muttered, glancing at his watch. He would've turned away, but the walls were mirrored and their reflections overlapped, her horrified heat wrapped over his impassive ice. Sighing heavily, he motioned her to the door.

Nicole didn't move. "What if I wanna do it all over?"

"What over?" he mumbled, lighting his own stick.

"You know. Life. Earth. Humanity. Come back until I get it right."

"Relax, sweetheart. Mattress time don't count against you."

That got her back on her feet. "I told you! I'm not a hooker! I'm a photographer—"

"Where's your camera?"

"Well, it's not here, but I have this notebook—" She pointed

at the dresser bearing a crappy twenty-inch television and a
Moleskine identical to his. Except for the blood splatter.

"Sure," he said. "A photographer's best friend."

The fight drained from Rockwell then, and she slumped
where she stood, falling so still the only sound in the room was
the soft drip, drip of her arterial blood as it fell from the bed to
the floor. "But I'm not done here."

"Just take my hand, kid. It'll be all right."

She looked at him dubiously. Grif frowned. Sure, his suit
was rumpled, but it was clean enough, and his pomade had
held at his time of death, though it was hidden beneath the
brim of his fedora. A little ginger stubble had sprouted—he'd
been offed after five—but if his eyes were hard, they were also
clear. All in all, not too bad for fifty years dead.

Yet Rockwell remained unconvinced. "How do I know
you're not tricking me? You could latch on and suck my soul
down to hell, like in that movie."

"You mean *Ghost*, right?" A couple of the younger Centurions had explained about that. Some sleeper flick that hit it big
a couple decades ago. Now he had to explain himself to every
corpse that walked his way. "Look, I'm not a demon, and I'm
no ghost. I'm a . . . gentleman."

Nicole blinked.

"Lots of firsts for you today, eh, Ms. Rockwell?"

Eyes narrowed, she crossed her arms. "Piss off, Shaw. I'm
not going anywhere with you."

Grif fought not to grind his teeth. He'd get hell from Sarge
if she took it in her mind to hang out here and haunt the place.
And he'd be damned—figuratively speaking, of course—if he
was going to let her sully his perfect Take record. Besides, she'd

been dead all of five minutes. She didn't yet know what was good for her.

Grinding his cigarette beneath his heel, Grif said, "What are you going to do, honey? Throw down the ménage in this joint for the rest of eternity? Though . . . I guess it does beat sizzling."

"Sizzling?"

"One wrong turn outta here, and . . ." He made a sound, trout frying in a pan. It was a rotten trick but it worked.

Nicole shuddered in her demi-cups, then stood and slowly glanced around. "So, that's it, huh? Twenty-six years of—"

"Twenty-nine," Grif corrected.

"—of mortal struggle, and this is how it ends."

Grif made another show of looking at his watch, while peering at Nicole from the corner of his eye. She didn't look like she was going to leak, he decided gratefully. Instead, she looked like she was going to kick something.

She did . . . then dropped back to the bed, and put her head in her hands while Grif began hopping around.

"Damn it, lady!" He glared, cradling his throbbing shin. "I've had enough of this postmortem crap! Get your lifeless, flabby backside off that bed and follow me!"

Now she began to cry.

The recently murdered were so *sensitive.*

Sighing, Grif lifted his hat and ran a hand over the top of his head. He could practically hear Sarge's barked reprimand. *Patch it up, Shaw.*

"Sorry," he muttered, stealing another glance at his watch.

"Fuck you, Mr. Sensitivity!" she yelled. "I'm not following your washed-out, B-movie, pseudo-Five-O ass anywhere!"

"Careful, peach. Look how you get to spend eternity." Grif showed his teeth, and though there wasn't any blood in her ethereal body, Nicole blanched. Then her outline began to shimmer. Not much time left. "That's right. We're all stuck in the clothing worn when we die. Kinda makes you wish you'd overcome that latex fetish, huh?"

"Oh, God." Nicole looked up at the mirrored ceiling and fussed with her hair, but it sprang back into the deflowered do she'd been sporting at the time of her death. "Oh, God!"

"She's on her lunch break," Grif muttered, but his heart softened anyway. He couldn't help it. He was lucky to have been offed in 1960. He'd watched too many Centurions shy away from mirrors in the Everlast in the decades since.

"All right, I have an idea." It was technically against the rules, but the girl was looking at him with those tearful eyes, and he was looking back, really seeing her for once. Helpless females always got to him. And though Rockwell was a lady of the night here on the Surface, there could be someone waiting for her on the other side. They might not recognize her like this . . . or want to.

Besides, he'd been blood and bone once, just like her. In the end, and that's what this was, they were exactly the same. "All right, listen up. There are some clothes in that dresser over there—"

"How do you know—?"

"I just do," he interrupted, "and you'll move fast if you know what's good for you. You're starting the Fade. I can send you back into your body long enough to change your clothes and do something with that mop on your head. But you gotta keep quiet. Your E.T.D. is twelve fifty. If someone hears you rummaging around at one, my superiors will know I interfered."

Nicole nodded vigorously.

"All right. Get back in."

"In?"

"Your body. You gotta line up those pulse points over your earthly remains. Then I can fuel them."

It wasn't technically necessary, but using her remains was a way to ground her both mentally and physically, giving her the impression of purchase on the Surface even though her spirit was already free. It was like tying a boat to a dock, securing it there even as waves crested around it.

Rockwell did as told, carefully settling her ethereal energy atop her body so that it looked like a shimmering chalk outline. Grif listened for a faint click in the etheric, her final pulse point snapping into place, before echoing the action, positioning his translucent body above hers so their chakras aligned. It required submission on her part, and a smothering of her energy with his own. It was a sensation most loose souls found claustrophobic, but Rockwell didn't even flinch.

Probably used to it, Grif thought, letting himself sink.

Vacuumed silence overran the room, blunting even Grif's celestial senses. Shape and form and sensation blurred as their energies melded as one, and they fell together, burrowing back into skin and cells and tissue and blood. By the time they fully occupied Nicole's body, her life energy was cocooned safely inside of his.

The blood in her core was not entirely still. Her sluggish pulse still lapped like low tide at the shore, not yet aware its efforts were futile. Grif was, though, which was why the sudden explosion of color behind the dead woman's eyelids rocked him. Then the tang of blood and saliva invaded his mouth, followed by the ache of mortal injury—dulled by shock but still keen—

and Rockwell's gaping wounds were suddenly his. Stinging fingertips—she had fought—were also his. The clamminess seeping in to claim the once-warm body made him want to gasp and struggle, and the ache that swelled inside him wasn't from injury but from a long-forgotten, yet familiar, desire.

Life.

Grif clenched his jaw, and felt foreign teeth grind together in an unfamiliar way. Pushing that discomfort away, he forced his energy down, past cells and tissue and the molecules that made everything on the Surface so tangible. An instant later, he was facedown beneath Rockwell's deathbed, alone in spirit, lying in a sticky pool of blood. When he slid out from under the bed, Nicole was already sitting up, literally holding her head.

"I feel like shit," she gurgled.

"Well, keep your eyes on the floor, honey, 'cuz you look even worse."

She did, though glared at him first. "And keep yours to yourself."

"Not a show I care to see," he muttered, but crossed to the window to wait. Clumsy rummaging followed, silence, then exhausted groans and more silence.

Grif needed a moment to recover anyway. Rubbing his aching chest, he pulled back one grungy curtain panel. He'd left the pain of mortality behind long ago, and the suggestion of skin over his soul smothered and burned, like he'd been dipped in hot wax.

How could he have forgotten this?

A movement outside the window caught his eye, and he focused on it like an alley cat spying a rat. He tried to zoom in, but Nicole's humanity blunted his vision. He'd gotten so used to telescopic eyesight—to all the gifts afforded a Centurion—

that he was unaccustomed to limited senses. Yet there was just enough residue from the Everlast to see clearly into the blackened winter night, and when Grif finally focused, he couldn't help but wish for full celestial vision again.

If Grif was a B-movie version of an old-school P.I., then this woman was a full-fledged screen siren. Even from a distance, he could make out silky sable hair pulled back from sky-high cheekbones. They rode a round, sculpted face with lips tucked at the center of it like full, pink cushions. And that shape, he thought, as she stepped from the car. Curves like he hadn't seen on a woman in decades. More hairpins than Mulholland Drive, every sweeping stretch draped in red silk, shimmering in places that made his mouth go dry.

Maybe it was just his imagination, but the outfit looked like a throwback to his time, when women wore clothes that made them look like walking gifts instead of unwrapped packages. Mirage or not, he thought, rubbing at his eyes, she was the prettiest woman he'd ever seen.

Yet even from a distance, even as she angled her head to reveal a neck as smooth and creamy and inviting as the rest of her, there was a sharpness to her, an awareness of her surroundings as she squinted . . . then looked directly at him.

Grif jumped. Did she actually *see* him?

"Shit," he muttered, letting the curtain fall. It was Nicole's humanity. He was wearing her life-force, sharing it, as much as she was his.

"What?" asked Nicole, sounding startled.

"Nothing," he muttered. They needed to move anyway. "You ready yet?"

"Not quite," she said quickly, halting his turn. "You're not peeking, are you?"

Grif just made a sizzling sound through his teeth. The rummaging started up again, more frantic.

"Can I ask you something?" she managed, though breathing hard. Each exhalation jerked at Grif's chest, like someone was cross-stitching his heart. He'd have to return to the Everlast for a jolt of energy before his next Take. "Why can't I remember who . . . My death?"

"Because it was violent," he said shortly. No need to sugarcoat it. She knew, even if she didn't want to say it. "It's the Everlast's way of protecting your soul so you don't relive it over and again. You'll go through a process called incubation, which will rehabilitate you to forget your earthly years." And, he didn't add, forever conceal the horrors associated with her brutal death. "Then you can move on to Paradise. It's all meant to keep you focused on moving forward, not looking back."

"Like you?"

No. Not like him at all. "You done?"

She blew out a breath, causing a particularly hard jerk on his heart, and made a sound of assent. He turned to find her in front of the dresser, leaning against it, looking uncertain. She'd replaced her hooker-wear with jeans and a tee. Both were still too tight in Grif's opinion, but classic enough to defy most eras. Her hair had been tamed into a style that made her look only half-dead, and at Grif's half-hearted thumbs-up, she staggered back to the bed, exhausted from the blood loss.

"More to the left," Grif instructed, squinting one eye as she attempted to resume her previous pose. "Perfect."

He climbed aboard once again, inhaled deeply, and withdrew his own energy, the needle in his heart disappearing instantaneously. Solitary silence reigned inside of him again, though it brought with it an unexpected sidekick: loneliness.

Damn it, he thought, as he stood, wiping at his mouth to hide his shaky breath. He'd have left her as she was if he'd known he'd have to feel *that*. But as he rubbed his chest, the last of the energy tethering Nicole's soul to her body fell away, and she rose again from her deathbed.

"Better?" he asked, swallowing hard.

If she heard the shake in his voice, she didn't show it. "Much."

Then, though she hesitated, she reached out and put her still-warm hand in his. "Thanks."

"All in a day's work." And despite the ache in his heart, and the ghostly memory of all his mortal pain, he shook it off and led her away.

Proof that he really was an angel.

Though ostensibly leading the way, Grif allowed Rockwell to go first. As he'd told her, he was a gentleman, and though he was careful to keep her close—last thing he needed was for the kid to get lost in the moon shadows—he gave her enough space to keep her from feeling flanked, like a dead woman walking.

Another calming tactic: the use of doorways to pass from the Surface and into the Everlast. Or if a door wasn't available, a window. Some sort of passageway a human mind could latch onto to ease the transition. Opening the door to find the cosmos splayed before you like a celestial buffet was shock enough, so it was best if the Take didn't notice it until it was too late. So Grif kept his hand at Rockwell's back, and waited for her gasp as he used his celestial power to will the door open at her touch.

Yet Grif was the one who jolted at the sight of the grungy

hallway. He jumped again when it began to bend, rippling in the same way pinned sheets moved in the wind.

That wasn't right. In fact, it was all wrong.

"Get back," Grif told Rockwell, as the ripples merged across from them to form a giant, diaphanous bubble. Features began emerging in the bulge of that apex, pressing through wood grain and peeling wallpaper until they became recognizable as an enormous face.

Rockwell stared at the emerging face like it was part of a magic show, wonder and delight replacing wariness. After all, it was her first glimpse of sinless sentience. All she saw was a brilliant smile forming in the wood chips. A nod of welcome in the dip of the giant head. A shimmering film of gauzy Everlast to mask the staggering appearance of one of God's most awesome creatures.

Grif saw fangs and a predatory gleam in an incendiary eye. "Get back!"

But Rockwell had already forgotten him. Once a newly gleaned soul glimpsed a Pure—in any form—the Centurion who guided them to the Everlast was just a leaf in the forest of their memory. Utterly forgotten.

"Do you know who I am?" The voice ground deep and low with the sinew of the splintering walls.

"No," Nicole said dreamily, stepping forward.

"Yes," Grif replied and reached out to grip Rockwell's arm, but she'd begun the Fade and merely shuddered as his energy invaded hers. Gaze locked on the Pure, she stepped directly into the undulating hall.

This wasn't right. "Stop, Nicole! It's an angel!"

The hallway cocked sharply at that, casting Rockwell to one bowing side. The face grew more prominent, as if pressing against a thinning membrane . . . and Grif realized that was exactly what was happening. The Pure wanted something, but wouldn't, or couldn't, breach worlds to get it.

Its chin sharpened. "Use my proper title," it said in that slivered voice.

Grif swallowed hard. "A Pure."

"*I* am of the order of the Powers," it hissed. "The first of the created angels, kin to the Dominations and Virtues, controller of demons, and guardian of the heavenly pathways."

"Whoa," said Rockwell.

But the voice, with breath as hot as a furnace, was directed at Grif. So was the fiery gaze. "Do you know who I am now?"

Grif knew only one angel in the order of the Powers. "Anas."

Keeper of the Gates, the chosen Pure who shepherded mortal spirits into Paradise proper. It was said Anas was the first angel that uninjured souls saw after death, though to say she welcomed them into heaven was giving her too much credit. From what he'd seen, she mostly ignored the human souls, chin high and gaze distant as they passed through the Gates.

But Grif wasn't at the Gates. Anas—and her big, bulging forehead—was on mortal turf, so he reached forward to pull Rockwell back.

But the mouth opened, and the Pure inhaled, lifting Nicole Rockwell from her feet. The woman was like a rag doll sucked into a tornado, gone in an instant, jerked into the fanged mouth, and a throat that was black and specked with burning stars.

Grif stepped into the hallway to follow after her.

"Not you."

And the walls shifted with a whipping exhalation. Blown from his feet, Grif tumbled back into the mirrored motel room, and the door rocketed shut.

Heart pounding, Grif just lay there for long seconds.

When nothing else happened, he wiped at his eyes, which were suddenly gritty and dry. In fact, his whole etheric form felt like it'd been sandblasted by the hot, needled breath. Even still, instinct and stubbornness had him stupidly rising to the fight. Rockwell was *his* Take.

Crossing the room, Grif motioned to the door again, willing it open with his celestial power. The door didn't budge. The cosmos didn't appear.

"Fine."

And dropping his head and arms, Grif fisted his hands so that his wings flared with a rip of the silky air. Gossamer-black, dripping dew, sprung directly from the Everlast itself, the wings rose and plunged like a waterfall of spears. He whirled, propelling himself forward until the wingtips caught the door and sliced it from existence.

Anas awaited.

"Disobedient! Child of wrath!" Her face was inches away, contorted with rage.

"No need to get personal," Grif told her evenly, though the membrane between worlds was now stretched so tight she looked like she was being smothered in plastic.

Anas hissed, and her fangs elongated, the sound of wood stretching. "Breath . . ."

"Oh, *that?*" Grif got it now. He was in trouble for joining his energies to Rockwell's, for reanimating her body with his. He shrugged it off. "That wasn't breathing. I was just trying to help."

"You donned the sinful flesh—"

"It wasn't really a sin. More like a lapse of judgment—"

"You have breath!"

"I gave it back."

"And now flesh!"

He drew a blank until he recalled the grit in his eyes when she blew him back. He looked down, panicking. "You gave me . . . skin?"

Her snarl grew to a fanged smile. "You cannot enter the gloaming, Child of Sin. You have no place in the Everlast."

"That's Child of God to you." Grif's eyes narrowed. "And I have wings."

"Ah, that's right." She grinned so widely that wood grain punctured the plastic. "I'll take those."

And she plucked his wings from his body—his *flesh*—then pushed him so hard that decades rushed by, along with burning stars and rioting universes that roiled around him like debris as he fell . . . fell . . . then landed with a jarring thud.

Rockwell's corpse bounced as he landed on his back, on the bed. Unmistakably, *on the Surface*. It shocked Grif into losing the breath he didn't even know he possessed. Then the pounding began in earnest, starting at his shoulder blades, where his wings should have been. It spread like lava through his core and into his limbs, nothing like the lapping low tide of the pulse he'd shared with Rockwell. This was a red monsoon. His veins throbbed and surged as they . . . what?

What?

"Fill with blood."

Grif turned his head and found Nicole Rockwell's eyes fixed on him, though her pupils were overtaken by surging flame as Anas stared from the dead girl's body. His heart leaped again, and his veins pulsed and rushed and, yes . . .

Filled with blood.

And the yearning ache he'd felt while inhabiting Rockwell's

body crested in his chest. Rearing against the pain, Grif felt new flesh stretching over bone. A scream lodged against his unused vocal cords, and he fell still, closing his eyes, trying to hold it all back.

"Breathe," Anas instructed through Rockwell's corpse.

Grif gasped and shivered. This was the animation of skin coupled with life force. This wasn't just the innate desire to live. This was rebirth. This was *life*.

Clamminess lunged to seize the new oxygen in his lungs. It was only the experience of having been alive for thirty-three years once before that kept the confining flesh from being revolting. Maybe when it warmed, Grif thought, he wouldn't feel such a need to run from himself.

But blood still clotted most of the virgin veins, and his heart had to struggle to move it. Its amplified thump hammered like the lead bass in a marching band.

"Breathe."

The word banged like a pot off Grif's competing thoughts. Worse were the spasms ripping through his chest. Fear, insecurity, guilt, and sorrow all huddled in newly exposed corners, naked, cowering things, frightened children trying to pull the covers of the Everlast up to their chins.

But the protective coating was slipping away. He knew it, and it was why—even without a true heartbeat or thawed blood or a sense of self and place in the universe—he began to shake in his new flesh. "No . . ."

"Breathe," Anas hissed again.

"It hurts," he managed, squinting into her fiery gaze.

"Being clothed in sin does, yes."

"I can't . . ." The shake of his head, side to side, set the pots to clanging again. He had no idea how he heard Anas's voice above them, only knew that she said, "It will hurt more when you die again."

And a knock sounded at the door.

He stilled, looking at Anas.

"You must flee," she said, eyes still burning, breath still scalding. Still merciless.

"Why—"

She cut him off. "There's a window in the bathroom. Go while you can."

"But I—"

"But you're lying next to a murdered woman. And you, Griffin Shaw, are *alive.*"

He couldn't comprehend it, but the burning skin, the pulsing blood, the breath in his chest . . . "It's too much."

It was all too much.

Another knock at the door, louder, accompanied by annoyed voices on the other side.

Anas was right; the time for privacy was over.

"Just enough then," Anas said impatiently when he still didn't move. She pursed Rockwell's blue lips. Everlast washed over him in a cooling balm and he could sit, and then stand.

"It won't last." And the burning eyes dulled, then snuffed out completely, leaving behind Rockwell's black, sightless pupils.

Yet the small hint of Everlast had cleared his mind and Grif could see what Anas had, and what anyone else would when they entered this room: a man standing over a woman's blood-splattered body.

Whirling, he darted into the bathroom, and wedged open

the small, single-paned window. He heard the door to the room open just as he clambered through, and reached the rusting ladder right before screams sounded behind him. Half-falling, half-jumping, Grif hit the ground seconds later, and ran from the voices and the building. He ran blindly. He ran until the sliver of Everlast wore off.

He ran until he could run no more.

CHAPTER TWO

Kit had never been to the station house on a Saturday night and found it even noisier and more crowded than during working hours. The irony was that if she had stuck to those hours—if *they* had—she wouldn't be here now. Waiting to be interviewed by a cop. Shivering in a dress meant for cheerful occasions, not sober ones. Mourning the death of her best and oldest friend.

"Kit!"

She looked up, relief washing over her at the voice, strain immediately returning as she spied the tight look marring her ex-husband's always handsome face. He might be able to hide his emotions from an entire courtroom, she thought as he wound his way through the noisy room, but she'd known him too long not to see the irritation bristling from him. The hard-pressed man was one of his best looks, and Kit knew then that he'd only come in case she needed council. The go-to attorney. Another favorite.

Kit chided herself, feeling stupid as Paul neared. But they'd once shared a life and a bed, and Kit needed someone around her who'd known both her and Nic well. Yet as soon as Paul perched on the plastic chair next to her, her loneliness doubled.

And it made her wonder. If *he'd* been the one she'd never see again after tonight, would there be anything left behind to miss?

The shame accompanying that silent question settled next to the guilt already at home in her gut.

Nic was dead.

"What the hell happened, Katherine?"

"Don't interrogate me, Paul."

"Hey, I left a Caleb Chambers fund-raiser for this," he said, which explained his tuxedo, the over-styled hair, and the hint of scotch lacing his breath. No, Kit thought, catching two underage girls whispering from behind cupped palms as they stared at Paul. She wouldn't have missed him at all.

"At three thirty in the morning?"

"VIPs and generous donors to his various charities are often invited to his house for a private party after the gala."

Of course they were. And Kit didn't have to ask which group Paul belonged to. He was always trying to buy his way into something. "Well, while you were brown-nosing the don of the social scene, someone murdered Nic. She's dead, Paul." She blinked. "*I* could be dead."

His brows knit, and he reached for her hand after a brief hesitation. He really was a handsome man, Kit thought, automatically pulling away. His golden hair glinted even under the station's harsh fluorescent bulbs, and his eyes were the color of spring moss. But they were unable to hold a gaze, which meant unable to hold a promise. The girls across from them didn't seem to notice. Nothing but experience could teach them that anyway.

"Let me guess," Paul said, oblivious to the teens, to Kit's fractured heart, to everything but being right. "You came up with some harebrained idea and Nicole ran with it."

Kit looked away, jaw clenched. Paul knew them, that was for sure. Nic had run with it like she always did—blindly, blithely, madly. Like the idea was chasing her instead of the other way around. But this time it'd chased her into the grave.

Kit covered her mouth with a fist to hold back a cry.

"Dennis said you guys snuck into an illegal brothel."

Her head shot up. "You already spoke to Dennis?"

"I need all the facts if I'm going to represent you."

"I don't need *representation*," she spat, twisting the word. "My best friend was murdered while I waited only yards away! *Those* are the facts!"

"Please lower your voice."

"Right," she said bitterly. "Paul Raggio's first rule of decency and decorum. Don't make a scene." Don't make a mess. Don't make a real effort when phoning in an emotion would do.

Yet he surprised her by putting a hand on her knee. "I'm trying to help."

Kit sat back and tried to steady her breathing. When she thought her voice would hold, she looked up. "It wasn't just an illegal brothel. It was a movable operation. Truckers let each other know about it online."

Hearing the explanation aloud didn't make it sound any better. Paul's answering silence made it significantly worse.

"Look, Katherine—" he finally said.

"Kit."

Paul gave her his courtroom look, the one solely responsible for her falling out of love with him. "Truckers tweeting about their roadside lays is tawdry, but hardly breaking news, and if I know you, you were going after a bigger fish. What was it?"

"It" was a Pulitzer. At least, that's what Nicole had said. *Make our mark before we're ancient . . . or at least thirty.*

"Truckers passing time on the road in the most predictable way possible might not be news, but concrete proof that judges and councilmen are passing the same women between them is prize-winning reporting."

Paul leaned forward, the sweeping angles of his face hardening into calculated thought. "What do roadside hookers have to do with Nevada politics?"

"Good question. Though not one I was even asking. Not at first." Kit wasn't interested in politics, but people. What they did and why. Human nature fascinated her, and this had started out as a human-interest story—on johns, their habits, and why they'd even use hookers when they presumably had wives and girlfriends waiting at home. "In order to find out, we put an ad out on Gregslist."

Paul's brows lifted high. "And these guys talked to you?"

"Of course not," Kit scoffed, but that hadn't deterred Nicole and her. It was too fascinating an idea, and Kit was too curious, to simply let it go. Especially after Nic came up with the idea of posing as a hooker just to get a chance to talk to one of them. "But she didn't catch any action until she started playing down in age."

"Gee, what a surprise. Pretend you're a hooker, get a revved-up guy alone in a hotel room, and then ambush him with a camera and a legal pad. That *is* a good way to get killed."

"We're not stupid, Paul," she said, back on the defense. "We weren't meeting a john. Another prostitute answered the listing. She warned us we were encroaching on already staked territory."

"Gregslist has street corners?"

Kit shook her head, remembering. "You should have seen this message, Pauly. It was full-on text-ese. Whoever this girl was, she should've been giggling over school dances, not sexting strangers."

"Underage?"

"That was our impression."

Paul leaned back, crossing his arms. "Maybe she's illiterate. Or just playing the juvie for extra dough."

"We considered both. But then she sent us this." Kit drew a printout from the handbag at her side.

His eyes widened at the names on the list. He'd probably been hobnobbing with half of them just hours before.

"And that's just some of them," Kit said, pleased she'd managed to surprise him. "She promised more if we met in person, but she wanted to verify we were legit first. After that, she swore to give us names that would make fat-cat heads roll."

Paul sighed, and shot a glance at the girls straining to hear the conversation. They immediately burst into an uncontrolled fit of giggles. "Do you really have to talk like that?"

"Like what?"

"Like *that*," he said, straightening his jacket like it'd straighten Kit out as well.

"Embarrassing you in front of your groupies?" she asked,

tilting her head. "Shall I revert to syllables they can sound out?"

"I'm talking about all of it." He let his gaze scan her body. "Your June Cleaver dress, Bettie Page bangs. The Hayworth face paint. The stupid car."

Kit narrowed her eyes. "Watch your mouth, *dear*. That's a Duetto."

He scoffed and flexed. Giggles rose around the room like startled pigeons. "See, that's what I mean. You weren't born mid-century, Kit. Get over it. At your age, playing dress-up should be reserved for the bedroom."

"This isn't dress-up, Paul."

"This" was her lifestyle . . . one that clashed violently with his post-yuppie materialistic drive.

"Makes it hard to take you seriously," he mumbled, looking pointedly at her peep-toed heels.

"People are going to take me seriously, all right. The whole damned country will take me seriously when I bust this case wide open, vet every name on that list, *and* find out who killed my best friend!"

He shook his head and huffed out a dry laugh, no longer looking handsome. Again, the girls across from them didn't notice. "Kit, the men on this list could own you a thousand times over."

Kit clenched her teeth at the dig. She came from money, a fortune Paul once thought would marry perfectly with his ambitions, and he'd married her before realizing the entire inheritance had been poured back into her family's newspaper. He'd even encouraged her to sell once he realized newspapers were worth less in the Internet age than the paper used for printing, but there was no way she'd ever do that.

"I'm a newsperson, Paul," she'd told him. "It's who I am as much as what I do."

"Then go down with your ship," he'd replied. "But you're not taking me with you."

And he'd taken himself right out of her life.

"Being rich doesn't make a person immune to the law," she said now, another familiar argument.

"There's no proof that anyone on this list has broken the law," Paul pointed out.

She knew that. And it would take considerable resources—time, energy, favors, and yes, money—to prove otherwise. For now, Kit had her reporter's instincts. "I saw something."

"Tonight?" He leaned in again when she nodded. "What?"

"A man . . . or his silhouette, at least. He was in the room with Nic. He pulled aside the curtain that overlooked the parking lot. It was like he was looking right at me."

"Did you see his face?"

Kit shook her head. "No. Only his silhouette. But he was wearing a hat—not just a hat, but a stingy brim, like Sinatra—"

Paul leaned back, letting his hands drop. "Gimme a break."

"I know the style, Paul," Kit said, irritated. "Maybe he knew I was there, or just knows of my lifestyle, and he was taunting me."

"Please don't repeat that to anyone. I can see the sordid headlines now: Rockabilly Murderer Targets Street Whores."

"Bravo," Kit snapped. "You just insulted my life and my profession in one breath."

"Voice," Paul reminded her, gaze wandering. The girls across from him straightened, but his expression remained smooth as it traveled the rest of the room.

Kit pulled out her gold cigarette case, mumbling, fighting not to whack it against his pretty head.

"You can't smoke in here."

Kit blew a stream of smoke directly into his face, running her tongue along her top lip when he coughed. The girls gave her a nasty look.

"These are vintage Gauloises."

"Trolling eBay again?"

She shook her head. "Some old coot was storing them in a backwoods cabin for the past fifty years."

Shaking his head, Paul stood. "I gotta go."

"Wait." She put a hand on his arm, panicked but unable to help it. "You're gonna help me, right?"

His jaw clenched as he looked away. He was either considering it or posing for a profile shot. "You got anything else?" he finally asked.

"In my notebook, but I gave that to Nic." She cursed the impulse now. There was little chance of recovering it as it'd surely been admitted into evidence.

Paul opened his mouth to answer, but stopped and jerked his chin at an approaching detective. "Here comes Dennis. He'll look after you. You don't need me tonight."

Kit stared up at him, wondering at what point he thought she'd have ever needed him, if not tonight.

Glancing back down, Paul caught her expression and his jaw clenched. "Look, I'll read the reports. Ask around, see what I hear."

He paused, waiting for a thank-you, but Kit merely took a drag on her stick. He was right, she didn't need him.

Shaking his head, he turned.

"You know, Nicole was once your friend, too," Kit said

loudly, just as Dennis reached her side. "She was killed because someone was hiding something big."

Paul turned slowly, and waited, knowing there was really nothing he could do if she was determined to make a scene. It was just another thing he couldn't control about her—like her hair and clothes, like her lifestyle. Like her emotions.

"I'm going to find out who did it," she told him, chin wobbling but gaze hard. "I'm going to find out what they were hiding. And I'm going to bring them to justice."

"Still the intrepid girl reporter," he said, but the bite had left his voice, and his gaze had softened. It was what he'd called her in the beginning, back when she, too, had gazed at him like those girls across the room. Tears, already close to the surface, welled.

"Give me a couple of days," Paul finally sighed, returning, one hand outstretched for the papers. "I'll look into it in my spare time."

"Thank you," she replied, even though he'd said it like there wouldn't be a lot of it.

Leaning down, he gave her a dry kiss on her cheek. "Get some rest, Kit."

Kit didn't say anything, but watched him go, like every other girl in the room. Then she shrugged at Dennis's chiding look, sucked down the last of her stale tobacco, and rose to be questioned about her best friend's murder.

Kit spent the next few hours in a room with the cold personality of a morgue, giving a statement about the time, hours, and days, leading up to Nicole's death. Some questions could have as easily been applied to a job application as a murder interview, and strangely, these were the ones that tripped her up. How long have you known Nicole Rockwell? What's your relationship to the deceased? Have either of you ever been a part of a murder investigation before?

Oh, Nic.

The hysteria she'd felt at the murder scene was gone, and the resultant shock had dulled into a numbness to rival a visit in any dentist's chair. The indignation at being questioned—no, *doubted*—by Paul had evaporated like boiling water, not too unlike their relationship, actually. All that remained was a faint ring of fatigue.

Dennis, whom Kit had known both personally and professionally, in that order, brought her fresh tea, let her light another cigarette while they were still alone, and put a comforting hand on her shoulder, kneading slightly at her neck before letting his arm drop. Kit looked up with a watery smile, grateful for even that small touch.

"You understand we have to ask you these things," he said, when his partner arrived and she'd been read her rights and informed the interview would be recorded. "Not because we think you're guilty, but because it'll help us put together a picture of the events leading to the crime. Rarely is something like this truly random."

"I know that."

"That's right," said his partner, who was so stiff he could have been pressed into his clothing. He'd introduced himself as Detective Brian Hitchens. She didn't know him, but unfortunately he seemed to recognize her. "You're a reporter, aren't you? The same one who released the name and address of a gangbanger last year?"

She could tell from the way he said it that he already knew she was, and harbored a grudge over it. Kit gave Dennis a wary glance, then answered, "He was sitting on a stash that would make a cartel blush."

"It got one of our men shot."

Her heart jumped in her chest, but she held his dark gaze. "I didn't pull the trigger."

"How's the saying go? The pen is mightier than the bullet? Or the knife." It was *sword*, but he knew that. The intimation was that tonight wasn't the first time she'd put someone in danger.

"Damned straight," Kit said, without apology, but inside she was cringing. She knew her work helped people . . . but did it also hurt them? Kill them? *Had it killed Nic?*

"Let's get back to the interview, shall we?" Dennis said, shooting Hitchens a hard look. "Tell us about Nicole."

Her favorite color was blue. She could dance for hours and never break a sweat. She was a flea market junkie, she could recite every line in Grease, *and she wore beautiful lingerie just for herself . . .*

"We've been friends since junior high. Met on the student newspaper. She was a wiz with the camera, even then." Kit cleared her throat, which had tightened in a painful knot, and took a sip of her cooling tea. "She could tell a story with her photos, or even alter one with a camera angle alone. She was a college dropout, but smart. Edgy, liked to push people's buttons. And of course, she was a billy, like me."

"Billy?" Hitchens asked, glancing at Dennis and back to Kit.

"Rockabilly," Dennis answered with a small smile, and Kit flashed back on an image of desert sun glinting off the pomade in his jet hair, ciggies tucked in his shirtsleeve, and creepers crossed at the ankles as he leaned against a 'sixty Starliner. It'd been a while since she'd seen him that way, but she smiled, too.

"I've heard of it." Hitchens leaned against the wall. His forearms looked like black logs folded across his chest. "You dress
up like you're stuck in the fifties. Took 'Let's Do the Time
Warp' literally."

"It's not just music or dress," Kit explained, though Hitchens's pinched expression told her she needn't bother. She gave
Dennis a look to let him know she was taking one for the
team—rockabilly didn't fit in any better with life on the force
than it did in a federal courtroom. Fortunately, Kit didn't have
to worry about either, as a reporter. "It's vintage cars, hot rods.
Pinup girls. Mid-mod home décor. Cigarettes. It's a way of
living."

It was a celebration of the senses, and it married well with
Kit's theory that life was about the details. She was ever aware
of what she put on her body, how she wore her hair, how she
crafted her cocktails. Despite the effort, or because of it, Kit
had only grown more fond of rockabilly after a decade-long
involvement. In a world increasingly guided by touch screens,
sometimes it seemed nothing touched the mainstream popu-
lace at all.

"It's a subculture," Dennis added.

"A lifestyle," corrected Kit, again pulling out her gold cigarette case.

"You can't smoke in here," said Hitchens. Dennis looked
pained, but nodded. Kit returned the case to her purse, a
square, red Lucite clutch that Hitchens now eyed suspiciously,
like it was a piece of a puzzle he was still trying to fit.

"Let me get this straight. Your friend was involved in a subculture that essentially lives in the past? So maybe it was one of
these weirdoes who offed her."

Dennis stiffened, but didn't say anything.

Kit was careful to move nothing but her eyes. "My friends and I get off on American cars, swing music, and nautical-themed tattoos. We're not murderers."

Hitchens huffed. "It still sounds weird."

"Probably because it demands more of you than plopping down in a La-Z-Boy, sticking your hand down your pants, and plugging into someone else's reality."

"O-kay," Dennis said loudly, straightening as quickly as Hitchens. Kit just leaned back and crossed her legs. "So we've defined Nicole's lifestyle as rockabilly. Boyfriends?"

"Plenty," Kit answered, then looked at Hitchens. "All weirdoes."

"And when did you last see her alive?"

"Twelve thirty. There's a café attached to the motel. Just a hash house serving grease and caffeine to overtired truckers. She did a round there to attract our contact's attention, as agreed, then crossed the gravel lot and went up the motel stairs."

She'd dressed in conventional hooker wear, Kit remembered—too short, too low, too tight—and had shot Kit a pained grimace as she fought the skirt for movement, hating that such a junky item of clothing would even touch her body. Not yet knowing she would die in it.

"She didn't take her camera with her? We didn't find one at the scene."

"She left it in my car. It's hard to fit a Nikon D3 in a tube top, and she didn't want to scare away our source. She took my notebook instead."

The cops looked at each other.

"I could use it back," Kit tried.

"Evidence," Dennis replied, though there was a strange frown marring his brow.

Hitchens propped himself on the table so that he was looming over Kit. "All right, so Nicole entered the room alone, and you stayed in the car the whole time?"

"Didn't take my eyes from that door." Which meant the killer had been inside, lying in wait the whole time.

"We've confirmed with the motel manager that the place was being used as an unofficial whorehouse," Hitchens said, looking through his notes. "The rooms were booked in blocks. One woman picks up all the keys. Then they're returned in a single envelope placed in the drop box the next morning."

"My research confirms the same."

Head still lowered, Hitchens lifted his gaze. "Your research?"

"Well, I don't just make up the stories that go in my newspaper, Detective Hitchens. I fact-check. Double-check. Then I find secondary confirmation and I check again. This was an ongoing operation. Truckers driving through the southern portion of the state, probably through Arizona via the new Hoover Dam bypass, would tweet about it online."

"So you think it was a passion kill? Some trucker snapped when he found himself being interviewed rather than undressed?"

"No. We were supposed to be meeting a girl there, maybe a woman. And she had a list naming some of the most powerful men in this city as clients. I think one of the names on that list killed her."

"I'm sorry," Hitchens said, "but what would Vegas's most powerful leaders want with street lays in a fleabag motel off a stretch of highway best known for being forgotten?"

Kit exhaled. "I don't know."

Dennis leaned forward. "Kit, can you think of anyone who might want to harm Nicole?"

"She was a reporter," Hitchens remarked under his breath.

"But well-liked," Kit countered. "I told you. Vivacious. Happy. Full of life." And now she was dead. "But she was also stubborn, a total pit bull when something captured her curiosity. Even I thought there was a better way to do this thing, but Nicole wanted the list. And she wanted more than just names, she wanted proof."

"And what did you want?"

Kit looked at Hitchens. "To know who this girl was."

Why she was on the streets at such a young age. Why she'd ever consider selling her body for money. For Kit, it was always about the person more than the story. That's why she was working for her family's newspaper rather than running it. "I wanted to help her."

Dennis looked at his partner. "If she was juvie, it could've been a pimp."

"I worried about that," Kit said, "but Nic just said I was weaving tales again. That my imagination was getting the best of me, and that if the girl was defying a pimp by meeting with us, then she must really be desperate."

"But she didn't come. And you waited a full hour before checking on Nicole?"

"She texted me after ten minutes, told me to stay put."

"We'll want to see that text," Hitchens said.

But Dennis looked worried. "So is it fair to assume that whoever was with Nicole knew you were waiting in the car?"

Kit nodded, and told them about the figure that'd momentarily pushed aside the curtains.

"I'll have forensics do a run on those panels," said Dennis, standing. "Is there anything else you can think of?"

A rockabilly lifestyle, a sting involving truckers, young girls, possibly pimps. An anonymous woman who'd written the names of the city's movers and shakers on a list that had drawn Nicole to her death. Was that all?

Wasn't that enough?

Kit shook her head. "No."

But there was more, of course. There was Nicole's family and friends to inform. There were visits to make and a funeral to plan.

"Do you still have this list of names your contact gave you?"

Kit nodded at Dennis. She could print another copy. "So you believe me?"

"It's an angle," he said. "But even without that list, you girls were playing with fire."

It wasn't the first time they'd done so, and maybe that was the problem. They'd thought their journalism credentials could protect them from anything. "We're a great team."

And before she'd realized she'd spoken as if Nic were still alive, Hitchens said, "Then maybe you shouldn't have left her alone in that room."

"Brian," Dennis said.

But Kit lowered her head, knowing he was right. And, somehow, she was going to have to live with that.

CHAPTER THREE

I n the dream, Grif was driving through the desert, waiting for Vegas to rise out of the inky darkness like a neon mirage, just as he had fifty years earlier. Evie was straining forward next to him, as if she could force the car faster with the weight and heat of her body, like she could bend the entire world to her will with her curves alone. She'd always been like that. Taken the not-inconsequential gifts God had given her— beauty, jets, guile—and parlayed them into bigger game than her Iowa roots allowed. More than what her simple family had expected of and for her. Certainly more than what Grif could give.

He felt it when she finally shifted, turning to him, though he didn't dare look back. "Your love should have saved me."

"I know."

"You weren't strong enough."

Grif kept his eyes on the narrow, snaking road. "I know that, too."

"Are you strong enough now?"

Was he? He had a strong title, Centurion, and a strong job, helping others. And even if Centurions were the lowest celestials on the totem pole, he was still an angel. That had to count for something.

But would he be having these dreams if he were truly strong? No. He'd have already healed from the trauma of his death and moved on into Paradise. Tightening his hands on the wheel of his dream 'fifty-six Chevy Bel Air, Grif sighed. Incubation was supposed to have pulled these flashbacks from his mind. Yet they regularly reached up in the guise of a dream or an unintended thought and coldcocked him, like a fighter sprung early from his corner. And in that brief, flashing moment, even in the Everlast, Grif remembered, and felt, it all.

"I don't have to be strong," he finally said, refusing to dwell on it. "I'm dead."

And that's how he got through his days. His job was to escort Takes to the Everlast, that's all. Didn't matter if their deaths had been accidental, if they'd been murdered, or if they'd severed the rip cord themselves. It wasn't his responsibility to figure out how they'd gotten that way. Not anymore.

Evie laughed beside him, like she could read his thoughts.

"Yet you still help people. Never could break you of that soft habit, could I? All the time, helping others instead of just keeping your head down and doing for us. And look where it got you. Look where it got me."

He finally did turn to her, and she was just as pretty as he remembered. Eyebrows plucked into perfection above irises of dipped chocolate, blond hair styled into waves so flawless they were severe. But she was also angry. "I don't know where it got you," he said.

He'd never seen her in the Everlast. She'd probably bypassed *it, went straight into Paradise. That's what the pure angels did, right? And that's what she'd been to him. His angel. His Evie.*

His wife.

But right now she was his conscience.

"Yes, you do," she said accusingly, just as Grif knew she would. He'd had this dream before. And what Evie didn't say, but what still rose in the dark between them, was that if he hadn't died, he could have saved her. And that was really why it was so hard to look at her: all that beauty and life and energy straining forward in anticipation of a future that would never come.

He scrambled for an answer, trying to think of something that would make it better—

"Hey, man."

Coming to with a hard snort, Grif squinted, and tried to focus. Darkness, layers of it, crowded in and he shook his head. He had no idea where he was. Then the marching band took up again in his skull, and he remembered.

"Hey," the voice said again. "Over here."

Bleary-eyed, wiping drool from his chin, Grif turned his head. Dark lumps rose from the ground in uneven mounds, and a brick wall speared up at his back. The sky rose darkly behind that.

"Where am I?" he rasped.

"Man, and I thought *I* was wasted."

The voice found form in the face of a shaggy-haired man who sat up among the lumps on the ground, plastic shifting around him as he peered, too closely, at Grif. The man's breath kept Grif from doing the same. He recoiled. The pounding in his head throbbed.

Breathe.

"Yo, how'd you find this place? This is prime real estate. Usually nobody bothers me out here."

"Ain't gonna bother you," Grif said, the words guttural, and scraping raw. Clearing his throat, he focused on bringing his senses back to life. That's what was happening, after all. He was coming back to life.

His first observation was of the dark. That, and the chill. It was predawn, by Grif's best guess, and nighttime in the desert was notoriously cold. He already knew from the bungled Take that it was winter but hadn't noticed until now. Then he remembered it'd been late winter the last time he'd been in Vegas, too.

A cricket chirped, pricking his ears, and a breeze caught on the plastic bags around him, but the thumping headache was still rattling his brain's pots and pans, making it hard to concentrate.

Breathe.

But he already was. The cold was only pressing in from the outside now, and his insides were beginning to thaw. He willed his hands to move, concentrating on touch as pins and needles shot into his limbs. He tried to sit up.

Never mind, he thought, barely able to lift his head. Though it wouldn't be long. He was already feeling stronger, less panicked, so he settled back to wait. One thing he'd learned in his half-dozen years as a P.I. was when to act and when to sweat out a moment. Most people didn't have the discipline to be still and wait. Grif didn't have a problem with stillness or discipline.

The same obviously couldn't be said for his companion. "You got some funky threads there, buddy. You first come around that corner, I thought to myself, Jimmy, ol' boy, that man is straight up *Dragnet*. Like some old detective and shit."

Two points for the wino. At least the man's babble gave Grif another concrete detail to focus on. He was, indeed, wearing his favorite suit, the gray flannel with give in the sleeves, his white shirt, black tie. For some reason, that had a smile crawling up his face. Material things had no value in and of themselves, he knew that. There was no difference between a diamond and a brick in the Everlast. Only those things God had assigned value to could sustain a soul.

But this was the suit he'd died in, and though he'd worn it ever since, it hadn't *felt* like this in the Everlast. The soft, clean cotton never caressed his skin like a lover's touch while there. This sort of touch was a gift only the living possessed, though most never realized it.

"Missing your stingy brim, though," Jimmy, still babbling, observed.

Grif perked up. Where *was* his hat?

Frowning, he looked up in time to spot a star hurtling across the sky. Grif followed the movement, eyes tickling so deeply in their sockets that he gasped, and for the first time in half a century, he sucked in raw ozone and earth instead of the silky cosmos.

And dust, he thought, choking. And decay, he realized, scenting the trash around him . . . fruit rinds, coffee grounds, half-finished meals that used to be animals. Human waste. The unwashed bum. No wonder the Pures would rather Fall than don flesh.

But then Grif covered his face with his palm, and was reintroduced to *himself.* The hotel soap he'd showered with fifty years earlier, the Sen-Sen he chewed after every meal, the faint whiff of coconut in his pomade, and beneath it all . . . flesh. Warm, gritty, and real.

And it was the flesh—*the sinful flesh*—that finally grounded him. No sooner did he have that thought than *click*. The radio found its signal.

For one brief moment his senses were amplified. He could scent the shadows. He could taste the night. Yet before he could reach out and touch anything, it was all whisked away, the protective blanket of the Everlast ripped entirely from beneath his chin. All that remained was its knowledge, buried in the coils of his gray matter.

Grif sat up, then rose unsteadily to his feet, bracing against the dirty brick wall for support. He had to figure out where he was.

"Yo, Dick Tracy!" Jimmy called, as Grif began walking away. "Buy me a brewski, right? I let you crash at my pad . . . least you could do!"

Grif had no idea what Jimmy was talking about, not until he rounded the corner and caught sight of pumps, a glowing storefront, and a dark-haired man standing cross-armed with his back to Grif. Ignoring the man for now, Grif looked up at the backlit sign. Gas station. Perfect.

On a hunch, Grif checked his pants pockets for his wallet. Opening it, he saw it, too, was as when he died. Same amount of money—and lucky for him he'd just cashed out at the casino cage—and the same photo of Evie that he carried with him everywhere. He took time to study that with his new-old eyes, then tucked it safely away, just like the dream.

His watch was on and working. His piece strapped to his right calf. Lot of good that did me, Grif thought wryly, before frowning. Odd, though. His driver's license was missing. He coulda sworn he'd had it on him when he died.

Grif didn't know if the dark-haired man heard his sigh, or just sensed Grif behind him, but he turned suddenly, giving a startled curse when he saw Grif. "Where'd you come from?"

Grif hesitated, then jerked his head in the direction he'd come. "Checking on the local wildlife."

"You mean Jimmy?" Worry replaced wariness. "He all right? They didn't get to him, too, did they?"

"They?"

"You know," the man said, in an accent that curled in the air like smoke. "The ones who chopped up the woman across the street."

Grif glanced in the direction the man had been staring. In the background a wide sun was beginning its push over mountains wearing robes of dark purple. In the foreground was a truck stop, rigs idling white smoke in the cool morning air. And across from the closest of those was a sagging two-story motel with an even more depressing café riveted to its side. It was littered with yellow crime-scene tape, and what had to be a whole unit of patrol cars.

Grif hadn't run very far.

"Jimmy's fine," he said, heading inside the station. It was brighter, more crowded than in his time and with a security camera straight out of a science-fiction movie, but still clearly a gas station.

"You a cop?" the man asked, following. He slipped behind the counter, pulled down the Luckies Grif pointed to, and tossed over a book of matches. "Or maybe a reporter?"

"A word-hack?" Grif made a face, tossing exact change onto the counter. Six bills for a pack of cigarettes. He couldn't believe it. What was that? A 2,400 percent increase in fifty years?

He'd consider quitting the habit if he thought he'd be here long enough to properly start again. "I'm gonna need a map. And some coffee for our friend out back."

The cashier's eyes narrowed. "You're not from here, are you?"

Grif wondered if it was the map or his concern for Jimmy that gave it away, but considering the man's dark eyes, skin, and curling accent, Grif didn't think he had any room to comment. "A few years since I've been in Vegas."

"Just passing through?"

Grif bent over the map. "Aren't we all?"

The man shrugged, his attention back across the street now that Grif was no longer a mystery. "Coffee's in the back. I'll be outside if you need me."

But Grif needed him even as the door shut behind him. "Who drew this? An amnesiac monkey?"

Because the map looked deliberately confusing. Red lines, yellow ones, blue. A big squiggly in the middle that meant blast-all. The topography made no sense. He couldn't even locate the Marquis, the grand hotel where he'd died, and was considering popping out back and asking Jimmy exactly where they were when a tinny voice swept through the room.

"Griffin Shaw," it boomed, causing the knobs where his wings had been torn from his body to pulse with pain. "Did you really tell one Melinda Childers that a rap on the head was the nicest thing her husband ever did for her?"

The voice had Grif jumping, not because he'd thought he was alone but because it was so familiar. "Frank?"

Whirling, he looked for the Pure who was in charge of the Centurions, but he saw no one.

"Up here."

Grif turned back to the register.

"Up."

Grif's gaze rose to the security monitor behind the counter. Gone were the live shots of the building that'd divided the screen before. In their place was the Pure who appeared to each Centurion in the guise they most identified with authority. For Grif, that meant a sergeant in a detectives' bullpen, something he'd long stopped questioning.

Glaring through blurred static, and a picture that rolled every few seconds, Sarge crossed his great arms and gave Grif a cold stare. His wings, as black as the rest of him, took up the whole of the screen, though Grif could still see the tips, currently gold-tipped with fury. Hard lines drew his mouth down like a thin hook, and his jaw clenched reflexively. He hadn't seen Sarge this mad since Harvey brought home the wrong soul.

Frank leaned back, and the celestial camera—or whatever was allowing Grif to view him in the Everlast—pulled wide to reveal a desk that was as broad and imposing as the Pure behind it. "Childers?" Frank repeated, pointing to some papers on his desk.

Grif glanced outside to make sure the cashier wasn't looking before he answered. "What is that? My folder?"

Sarge just stared. Like Anas, he had no pupils, though instead of her hot open flame, the rounds of his eyes held mist swirling over black marble. "And you told Simon Abernathy he wouldn't have gotten dusted if he'd stuck to shilling fish and chips on his side of the pond?"

"He was an illegal."

"Shaw." Sarge threw down his pen. "You are a Centurion! You are greeting people in the most vulnerable moments of their afterlife. Don't you remember what that was like?"

"Sure I do," Grif said, tapping out one of his smokes. He lit it behind a cupped palm, and exhaled before meeting Frank's restlessly churning eyes. "Though the part right before that gets a little fuzzy."

Frank narrowed his gaze. "We're not having this conversation again."

"Good." Because Grif had been murdered. No amount of yapping would convince him to forgive it. And, for some reason, he couldn't forget. "Then maybe we can talk about what the hell I'm doing on this mudflat. In *flesh*."

"You have sensitivity issues, Shaw."

Despite those, or maybe because of them, Grif just blew out a stream of smoke. "Maybe I could put on a dress. Sing a little show tune?"

Frank just stared back at him from the video screen. With his angelic nature hidden behind this familiar guise, it was easy to forget he was created in and of Paradise. Yet, unlike some of the other Pures, Frank didn't seem to resent the Centurions. Sure, they were celestial misfits; no longer mortal, not truly angelic. But Centurions had still been created in God's image, they remained His beloved children, and Frank said it was his job to see those souls at peace.

Admittedly, Grif didn't always make it easy.

"That it?" he asked, when Frank just kept eyeballing him. "You knocked me back to the mud just to talk about my bedside manner?"

"No, smartass." Frank's curse was cause enough to raise a brow. "You barred yourself from the Everlast when you did this."

And Nicole Rockwell's corpse replaced Frank on the screen. Grif shot a nervous glance out the window, but the cashier was still staring across the street, giving a play-by-play to whomever he was talking to on his cell.

"Come on," Grif protested. "I was nice to the working girl."

Sarge's words were just a voice-over. "She wasn't a hooker, Grif."

Grif sighed. "Yeah. That's what she said."

"It's not what she said, Shaw. It's what she *did*."

And the image fluttered, shifted, and then there was Grif, entering the motel room just as Nicole Rockwell spotted her dead body and began screaming.

"Damn," Grif whispered under his breath.

It looked more incriminating, more premeditated, from a distance. There was no sound, but he couldn't fault the picture. Especially after he'd resuscitated Nicole's body, and she made him turn away so she could dress.

"The girl wanted some privacy," Grif objected, having seen enough.

"No . . . she wanted this."

And Grif watched, slack-jawed, as Rockwell scribbled something on the Moleskine he'd seen lying on the dresser. When his image finally turned away from the window and back to her, she made sure her head was on straight, literally, and that her body was blocking the notebook.

Grif cursed again. "She tricked me."

"You let her trick you." Frank's wide face reappeared on the screen.

"I wasn't thinking straight!" Grif protested, then finally got the nerve to say what was really bothering him. "You sent me to Vegas. *Vegas!*"

Frank's face remained impassive. "It was mandatory. Doing Surface time in the city where you died—"

"Was murdered," Grif corrected.

"Is part of your rehabilitation and healing process."

"I'm fine," Grif muttered.

"Then what are you still doing here?" Frank asked, gesturing at his office in the Everlast.

"You mean *here*?" Grif motioned around the gas station on the Surface.

The swirling eyes narrowed. "You want to see the rest?"

The rest? Grif frowned. What was left?

But Sarge was shaking his head, and Grif suddenly found he couldn't hold the stare. He might be slow on the uptake, but he was catching up fast now. His actions had changed something on the Surface. They'd altered fate somehow, and whatever his interference had allowed—whatever Nicole Rockwell had written in that notebook—was big enough to gain a Pure's attention. No, he didn't want to see.

But Sarge showed him anyway. The static blurred with a wave of his hand, and there was the same dingy hotel room but a new scene. Another woman and her john entering, freezing when they spotted Nicole's corpse on the bed. Grif was already gone, of course, and the woman fled screaming, but the man looked around . . . then pocketed the notebook.

"Who is that?" Grif asked, leaning forward, studying the blond hair, stocky build . . .

"None of your damned business, that's who!" Sarge reappeared, and looked like he was going to come at Grif right through the screen. "You are not a P.I. anymore. You're not even human! Yet you took anchor in a body still pulsing with life, and so that must mean you want the human experience again. Fine. You're demoted, *angel*."

Every instinct told Grif to remain quiet. "What're you gonna do?" he said instead. "Confiscate my halo?"

Frank's gaze narrowed. "Go back to the man outside."

Grif looked at the cashier. He waved when he caught the man looking back.

"The other one," Sarge snapped. "And take the map. You're gonna need it." And the security screen returned to normal.

Muttering to himself, Grif pocketed the Luckies and folded the map, and was halfway to the door before remembering the coffee. When he finally exited, the cashier looked over, scoffing when he saw the steaming cups, one in each hand.

"You're really not from here."

But he didn't follow as Grif headed back around the side of the building, and Jimmy was right where he left him, seemingly passed out, though his head lifted when Grif stopped in front of him. "Here."

But it was Sarge's misty, marbled gaze staring out at him from the mortal flesh. Grif jolted, scalding his flesh with the coffee. "What are you doing? Is he . . . possessed?"

"It's easy to control those who have no possession over themselves," Sarge said. "Now look in his left coat pocket."

Grif set down the cups. "Why?"

"I'm giving you a case."

"Another Take?" Grif asked, withdrawing a file folder.

Jimmy's expression altered, both hard and sympathetic all at once. "Not a Take. A *case*. You think you can do my job, Shaw? Make the decisions and sacrifices required of a Pure?"

What the hell had the Pure ever sacrificed? Grif thought, but Frank didn't give him the chance to ask. "Open it. Find out more of exactly what it is we do."

A black-and-white glossy stared up at him, a rap sheet stapled across from that, but he ignored the vital stats and studied
the face. He recognized her immediately, of course. The pretty
woman he'd seen from the motel window, though pretty wasn't
a word he'd use to describe her up close. Siren would work, and
her baby blues were lit up as if she knew it, and it amused her.

Cherry-cream lips and sable-hued bangs stood out against
pale skin, stark, even in black-and-white. A rose, blood-orange,
he imagined, was tucked behind one ear. He glanced over at
the name—Katherine Craig—then back at the photo.

"I don't get it."

Jimmy's mouth moved. "What's your job as a Centurion?"

Grif cleared his throat. "Secure the Take. Clean 'em up.
Bring 'em home."

Do it *respectfully*, he added silently. Okay, so he'd learned
his lesson.

But Sarge wasn't through yet. "And when do you meet your
Takes, Shaw?"

"When they are most traumatized. Immediately after cor-
poreal death."

Every Centurion knew that, because that's why they existed. They were the losers. The few murdered souls that incubation couldn't cure. Still tethered to the Surface by memory
and regret, they were pressed into assisting others to cross into
the Everlast. The idea was that helping others would relieve
their mental anguish. Then they, too, would be able to enter
Paradise proper.

The bum gave him a tight smile. Grif blinked. For a moment
he thought he saw fangs. "Not this one."

"Sarge?"

Frank's roiling liquid gaze suddenly looked shuttered. "You

gotta watch this one, Griffin. See, you might be back on the Surface, back in flesh, but you're not human. Take away a Centurion's wings, and all they're left with is an intimate acquaintance with death."

"What does that mean?"

"It means you can still see death coming. It also means you're gonna watch that woman die, and you're going to feel the death as if it were your own."

Grif froze. That's what he was doing here?

"No."

He began to shake his head. He might be a misfit in the celestial realm, but everyone knew the only thing keeping him sane was the protective layer of Everlast that lay between Paradise and the Surface. It was a balm, a numbing cream rubbed atop his sore soul. Flesh would scrub off that balm and expose him. Without it he'd wither.

But Sarge knew this better than anyone, so all Grif asked was, "Why?"

"Because you caused it, Shaw." Now Frank didn't look angry, vengeful, or cold. He just looked sad. "Katherine Craig is fated to die because of you."

Grif's newfound breath deserted him, but his mind fired fast.

My best friend is waiting outside . . .

The siren in the car. The way she'd looked up at him in a way no woman had in over fifty years: as if really seeing him. And the blond man who'd pocketed the Moleskine.

Whatever Nicole Rockwell had written in it was going to lead the man directly to Katherine Craig.

Grif tossed the folder to the ground. "I won't do it."

Jimmy's expression, and Frank's darker one beneath it,

didn't alter. "You're going to bring that poor girl's soul home, Shaw. You're going to see that she gets safely to incubation where she can heal from her death, and the grief over a life and family she'll never have."

"No."

"You will do this so that she damned well doesn't end up like you. And, Grif? You're going to do it *nicely*." The bum's nostrils flared, his stare tumultuous and bright. "Keep the map until you get your bearings. You've been navigating by the constellations for so long now that the streets mean nothing. Now, go."

Grif closed his eyes, and the same loneliness that'd run him under when he sank through Nicole's body wracked him again. Lowering his head, he shook it side to side. "I still remember things I shouldn't. And the memories will be stronger if I stay on the Surface. Humanity . . . hurts."

Silence reigned for so long Grif could almost believe Frank was reconsidering. But when he looked up, the bum's gaze was bleary, confused, and pinned on the coffee cup next to him. "What the hell is this? Where's the sauce, man?"

Grif bent, pocketed the folder, and turned to leave. But, just in case, he paused to mutter, "You forgot my damned hat."

"You forgot my damned beer!" Jimmy replied, but Grif was already walking. He was just out of the drunk's view when he spotted it coming fast, like a soundless comet or a falling black star. It dropped directly to his side, sending a small puff of dust into the air, causing Grif to cough.

Yeah, yeah, Grif thought, bending down. It's all dust. We're all dust. I get it.

But he didn't give Sarge the satisfaction of looking back or up, and he didn't give thanks. Instead he dusted off his fedora, settled it atop his head, and kept walking.

Somewhere out there was a woman with powerful blue eyes, a secretive smile, and curves that made him want to cry. A woman he was going to have to face in both this world and the next. A woman fated to die because of him.

Again.

Kit shouldn't have been surprised at the sun's ascendance in the sky, or by downtown's early-morning bustle. Yet she stood at the bottom of the concrete stairway outside the station, shoulders slumped and limbs heavy, as astonished by the urban landscape as she'd be in a foreign country. It was startling that these people had dressed this morning—or not, in the case of the vagrant sprawled to her left—and bewildering that they could now think of coffee, or gambling, or work.

And what the hell was there to laugh about, Kit wondered, anger flashing as a passing woman threw back her blond, perfectly coiffed head—neck white and pristine and unmarked by a butcher's knife—loosing an inappropriate amount of joy into the world. Kit wanted to grab the sleeve of the blonde's suit jacket, or maybe a handful of that carefully styled hair, and say, "My best friend was murdered last night. Why the hell are you still alive?"

Why am I? she thought, tears welling.

Why was anyone?

Kit realized she was causing a scene, looking rumpled, dazed, and literally shaking in the sidewalk's center. Swallowing hard, she wiped her eyes with her cardigan before beginning the long walk to the police lot where she'd parked the night before.

It was still wintry this early in February, but Kit didn't hurry. Her steps were as measured and precise as an army recruit's. She even halted stiffly beneath the bald tubing of an old neon sign to stare into a refurbished café where lawyers and D.A.s and those who made their living off of other people's vices were talking shop and swapping stories. Blue pendant lamps glowed like crystal jellyfish, and the scent of fresh bread and baking sugar rushed out to envelop her when the door was thrown wide.

Kit frowned and stared. The café didn't look inviting to her. Instead, it looked too hot, like a nuclear reactor. Like it would consume and destroy every bit of life that entered there.

Or maybe she was just projecting.

Hurrying the rest of the way to her car, she slammed the door on the sounds of downtown Vegas, and locked herself in the cocoon-like silence. The familiar squeak and scent of leather wrapped around her like a sumptuous throw. The perfume that'd been her latest flea market find, and that she'd been wearing the night before, tickled her nose. Slumping, Kit let her head fall. She should go straight home and sleep, but she didn't dare start the car with her hands still shaking. Besides, sleep meant closing her eyes, and even blinking was a nightmare. She'd rather cling to the raw numbness of her fatigue. She preferred her overheated anger at the world.

Swallowing hard, she dialed Paul's number to see if he'd done any work on the list she'd given him in the station. He didn't answer, no surprise, but it made her want to gore something with her red fingertips. Forget that it was not yet seven and there was nothing he could have done in three predawn hours. Forget, too, that he'd never been available when Kit needed him, anyway.

But Nicole had. Kit glanced at the metaphorical elephant in

the car, Nic's camera, lying lens-up on the passenger's seat, its wide, alien gaze locked on her. Nic loved that camera like Kit loved the Duetto, so much that her predominant memory of Nicole was in a one-eyed squint, shoulders hunched as she held the camera to her eye.

"With my shots and your smarts, we're sure to hit the major wires," she'd said, pointing the camera up at the room where she'd die within the hour.

"Sure you don't want me in there with you?" Kit asked, staring at the window.

"The girl was insistent. She wants me alone."

"I could hide under the bed."

Nicole raised her brows. "And where's the first place you'd look? Besides, I'd blow any trust I'd built once you climbed out from beneath a stained mattress with old jizz caked on your kneecaps."

Kit made a face. "Get me a Brillo pad. I need to scrub that image from my brain."

"Well, do it from within this George Jetson cockpit. I'll text you and have you come up when the girl and I have established a rapport. Until then . . . smile. I'm about to take the photo for your byline."

Nicole snapped a few shots of Kit in profile, the motel sagging like a battered woman in the background, then smiled as she studied the images. "God, I'm good."

She was. She could see everything through her lens. So well, Kit thought, that sometimes she was utterly blind without it.

Kit slid her key in the ignition. She should go home. There

was nothing outside the safety of this car but more bright sky and oblivious people and futile anger. But how was she to be alone with this grief? It wasn't that she wanted someone's shoulder to cry on—her sadness was heavy enough to knock two people over—but it'd be nice to see someone who'd known Nic alive and well, and who'd also feel the loss now that she was no longer either of those things.

So despite the wrinkles in her dress, the bedraggled ends of her hair, and the shadows haunting her eyes, Kit went to work. She would crack soon, she felt it like an animal sensed an impending earthquake, and would have to be home by then. But not yet. Not now. Her grief still hadn't entered the nuclear reactor's core. But she knew from previous experience—her mother's death, her father's—that when it did, the world as she knew it would be flattened, every particle in her life rearranged, her personal universe blown away.

If only there was a way to take a photo of that.

CHAPTER FOUR

The graveyard-shift waitress in the roadside café was bleary-eyed and slow. The short-order cook was uninspired, and more interested in the activity going on outside the attached motel where Rockwell had died. And the vinyl booth was ripped in so many places it was impossible to sit comfortably. But the coffee was hot, melting the last of Grif's cosmic thaw, though he wouldn't have wished the runny eggs and burned toast for anyone's first meal back on the Surface—or their last.

Yet it didn't matter much to Grif. He couldn't taste it. The Everlast must have somehow flash-fried his senses. He couldn't feel the fork in his hand, either—not the way he should, at least. His eyesight was clearer, but after the Technicolor wonder of the Everlast, it was small comfort. Yet his nose worked well enough that he was thankful not to be in Jimmy's trash pile any longer, so he supposed that was something.

But his hearing was hollow and tinny, probably about right for an eighty-four-year-old man.

You're not human.

No shit, he thought, moving his shoulders. The blades still ached where Anas had ripped the wings from his back.

Yet when he finally looked up from his empty plate, the headache dogging him was gone, and he almost felt a part of the world. So, belching lightly, he got down to the business of locating Ms. Craig.

The map alone didn't help; Sarge had been right about that. But a journey was rarely a straight shot from point A to point B. It was the landmarks and details that made all the difference. The bent street sign and the shifty-eyed man leaning against it. The car parked in the wrong direction on a residential street.

The intricate brick face on the Strip-side bungalow where he'd died.

Yeah, details he remembered.

Fortunately, the waitress wasn't so comatose that she couldn't point out the diner's location, south of Sunrise Mountain just off of Boulder Highway. Outside the window, self-storage units rose like tombstones from each side of the street, and trailer parks squatted behind those. So he knew where he was but still not where he was going.

Vegas's streets hadn't changed that much, he thought, squinting at the black-and-white grid. Though there were certainly more of them. And the place sprawled like it could go on forever. He remembered a time when the Boys tried to pay their entertainers in real estate. The talent had laughed and held out their hand for hard coin instead. Who, they said, would want to own land in this glorified litter box?

But according to this map, people did, and there was only one reason Grif could figure the population would sprawl all the way from the Sheep Mountains to the Black: to get away from other people.

The infamous Las Vegas Strip was clearly marked and the major streets leading from it jumped out at him like old friends at a surprise party—Trop, Flamingo, Sahara—but that wouldn't help him find one lone woman.

So he put the map aside for now and pulled out the folder Sarge had left him.

There, still stapled inside was the Polaroid of Katherine Craig. His case. Before Grif could flip the thing over, his gaze caught on the whites of her teeth, a single dimple, and crinkles around smoky eyes. It took a moment before he could shake off the image and focus on the page behind it. Once he did, he found the information he sought.

Katherine Craig, age 29, born in Las Vegas to Shirley and Martin Craig, both deceased. Mother was a homemaker, died of cancer when Katherine was 12. Father was a police officer, killed on-duty while responding to a robbery when she was 16.

So one parent passed directly through the Gates, Grif thought, sipping at his cooling coffee. The other was dumped into incubation a few years later. Shirley Craig would definitely be waiting in Paradise, though her husband might still be in the Tube, depending on how long it took to get over the trauma of his death. Katherine was going to end up doing time there as well, so it was entirely plausible that if she healed quickly and her father did not, they'd emerge at the same time.

"Some family reunion," Grif muttered, and kept reading.

Marital status, divorced from one Paul Raggio. Schooling, private and then UNLV. Occupation: interned in the Sterling Hotel's advertising department, demoted for insubordination. Moved to guest services, same hotel, but fired a month later for insulting a guest. Has since worked as a reporter for her family-owned newspaper, the *Las Vegas Tribune*. A business constantly on the edge of bankruptcy.

So the girl was a native Las Vegan, had a mouth and possibly a temper on her, and a documented history of getting herself in touchy situations. Yet even as Grif thought it, he knew he was projecting. It was easier on him to believe that she and Nicole Rockwell had forged a head-on with death, but Sarge had made it clear Craig's twisted fate was Grif's doing. Besides—mouth, temper, and occupation aside—no one deserved murder.

So there you have it, Grif thought, leaning back. A nosy divorcee who lost both her parents young, and was destined to die in the same city she was born. Those were the facts, and facts were bricks Grif could lay side by side and atop one another until a pattern emerged and a wall was built. Intelligence and instinct were mortar binding it all together, and with enough of both, he would insulate himself from the emotion that was useless in good detective work.

It would be debilitating to someone who could see death coming.

Facts were a damn sight better than a good sense of direction, Grif thought, and—feeling like he had a big enough wall built up now—he went ahead and flipped the photo back over.

Why the hell was she smiling like that? he wondered, his newfound breath lost to the visual kidney punch. Her mouth was blown so wide that the soft insides showed at the corners, like another grin was building in there. As if her laughter tumbled. Like joy was a living thing.

You caused it, Shaw. Katherine Craig is fated to die because of you.

He looked away, gazing out the window at where Craig had been parked, her tiny foreign car dark, her wide-eyed face white, as she stared up at the window where her friend had just died. Directly at him, he remembered.

"More coffee?"

Grif nodded at the waitress, silent. He couldn't taste it but he needed the warmth.

Yet the coffee didn't ground him this time, and it sloshed onto the Formica as he tried to lift it. It was hot enough to burn his new flesh, and should have caused him to hiss, but he didn't. The waitress noticed it, too. He looked back at her and noted a faint silvery outline to her silhouette.

Plasma. He knew what it was, though it was usually gone by the time he arrived for his Takes. This was a shimmering thread, but growing dark at the edges.

You can still see death coming.

So blunted mortal senses, but a celestial sense for death.

"You need to get that mole checked," he said before she could comment on his burn. "It's not too late, but it will be in another year."

The waitress's eyes widened, but he said nothing more, and she scurried away. Sarge was probably stomping around the Everlast, muttering about sensitivity. So what. Those were the facts. Facts were bricks. Now she could do something about it.

Grif, however, needed more facts, more bricks between him and this . . . this . . .

Woman. Katherine.

Case.

Straightening, Grif flipped past the rap sheet until he came to the last page of the report, hoping to find an address . . . which he did. Right across the top of her autopsy report, dated two days from now. She would die at home, he saw, but most people did. Although they didn't usually die from multiple stab wounds—she'd suffer thirty-two in all. He shouldn't be surprised. Murderers were like superstitious ballplayers. They rarely deviated from a play that had worked well before.

Grif hadn't looked too closely at the placement of Rockwell's wounds, but the coroner's notes showed Craig's deepest, deadliest cuts would be precise and controlled, no breaks in the incisions, no hesitation on the killer's part as he stole her life. So Craig's murderer wasn't just skilled with a knife, he'd probably killed even before Rockwell. Could he be ex-military? A hired killer? A butcher?

You are not a P.I. anymore. You're not even human!

Grif gave Sarge's voice a mental shove and kept reading, saw that there were no lacerations on the finger or hands, meaning Craig would succumb easily to attack. So maybe it'll be fast then, Grif thought, then caught himself. How pansy was it that he didn't know if he wanted that more for her or for himself?

Facts, Grif thought, as he started to sweat. He needed bricks. Reason and instinct. Mortar. He needed a wall if he was going to get through this.

I need the Everlast, he thought desperately, reaching for his coffee. But as he lifted the cup, one last word on the autopsy report caught his attention, and the cosmic freeze he'd felt when relearning how to breathe wrapped its cold fingers around his throat again.

Rape.

So not like Nicole Rockwell, after all.

The grease and coffee rebelled in his new stomach, and Grif bumped the table as he rose. Throwing too many bills onto the tabletop, he then stumbled out into the crisp, bright morning, the last of Katherine Craig's life. He immediately turned his gaze directly into the fiery sun. *How?*

How did Sarge expect him to do this? How was he supposed to watch a killer, a rapist, come to this smiling woman's home, and do nothing to stop it?

Take away a Centurion's wings, and all they're left with is an intimate acquaintance with death.

"I can't," he said aloud, earning a look from a bleary-eyed woman just stepping from her room. Not a hint of plasma around her, he noted, panicking.

How the hell was this supposed to help him heal, he wondered, as a crow cawed above him. Grif covered his ears, wincing. The animal was circling for the kill. Grif's death senses caught that.

"Where's your infamous mercy?" he rasped, stumbling out of the lot and onto Boulder Highway, away from the crow, the half-dressed woman now watching him suspiciously . . . toward another who wouldn't see him at all. And still, there was no answer from on high.

In this question, it seemed, there never was.

Craig."

Kit hadn't been in her office more than five minutes before her doorway fell dark. Her boss's tone had Kit glancing up with guilt, but Marin Wilson returned her pale-faced stare with eyes that were grim as well as sharp. Studying Kit's atypically rumpled appearance, she allowed silence to sit between them before gesturing to her office with a jerk of her head.

Kit sighed and stood, ignoring the stares from the main press room, Marin's wake a defensive wall between her and their unspoken questions. When they reached Marin's office, Kit shut the door behind her without being asked, took a seat, and waited.

Marin dropped into an ergonomic chair on the other side of a desk so loaded with papers it belonged on *Hoarders*. She ran a hand through short, spiky hair, newly silver, a side effect of chemo. She didn't care. Marin disdained pretense of any kind. She'd rather apply pressure than lipstick, and found Kit and Nicole's love for fashion so bewildering she often studied them like they were exotic animals at the zoo.

The look she gave Kit now was less baffled, but also a delay tactic. Marin believed most people found silence intolerable, a theory neatly backed up by the existence of tell-alls, the Kardashians, and Twitter. But when Kit only stared back, Marin broke the silence with a sigh. "Time off."

"No."

Marin's nostrils flared. "Ms. Craig. One of our reporters has been murdered while pursuing a story. You need to trust that every person at this newspaper is going to do their best to discover how and why. Rockwell was one of our own. We'll take care of it."

"I want to do it myself."

"You're not a police officer."

And there, in Marin's infamously caustic subtext, was the censure Kit had been dreading. She and Nic had pursued a story without a direct assignment from on high, proof that Kit was irresponsible, in over her head, and incapable of seeing this story—this tragedy—through to the end. Kit fought back tears. "No, but I'm the daughter of one."

"Kit." Seeing the tears, Marin softened. But not much. "Go home."

"Auntie."

Marin rolled her eyes. "Stop. You only pull that 'Auntie' crap when you're trying to weasel out of something. Just like—"

"Don't. Don't make this about my mother." She spoke sharply, but if anyone knew why, it was Marin. In ways, they both lived in Shirley Craig's shadow. But Kit wasn't going to get into that now.

Leaning back, Marin folded her arms. "What do you have?"

"A list of names." Kit handed her the sheet she'd just printed, then told her about the anonymous contact. Marin's expression narrowed further, and Kit rushed on. "I was writing my account of Nicole's . . . of the crime scene when you came in. The lock on the motel door wasn't damaged. The killer was already in the room. He had a key, maybe a contact at the motel, or the simple ability to pick locks. I don't know."

"But you think the person who killed Rockwell is on this list?"

"Would she be dead otherwise?"

Marin tapped her chin. "What else were you two working on?"

Kit shrugged. "She was helping John with a photo essay on the homeless living in the underground tunnels. I just finished an op-ed piece on the city's backlog of rape kits, not exactly breaking news. There was a lifestyle piece on a new gallery opening downtown."

Marin squinted.

"I swear. That's all. I mean, the gallery's devoted to nudes painted in neon and wearing animal heads, but I don't see anyone killing for that."

Her aunt looked at the list, gaze snagging and widening on the last few names. She finally put it down, where it disappeared in the sea of papers. "You're going to run this entire newspaper someday, Katherine."

Now it was Kit's turn to squint. "You only pull that 'Katherine' crap when you want something. And I told you before. Changing the world is more important to me than running it."

Marin sighed. "And now you sound like your father."

She did—because her mother might have taught her how to live, even while dying, but it was her father who'd taught Kit what to do—right up until the very last breath.

Don't just find the easy answer, Kitty-cat! Find the truth!

But this, too, was an old argument, one neither of them had the energy to chase. "Well, you're going to inherit it, in any case. Sooner rather than later, if this latest quack doesn't get my dosage right." She rubbed at the veins in her right arm in what had to be an unconscious gesture. "So you might try acting as you'd wish your employees to do in the future."

"You mean run everything by you beforehand."

"I wish Ms. Rockwell had."

Kit winced, and looked away.

"Oh, Katherine," Marin said, more softly. "Come stay with me. Just for a time."

And be watched over at home as well as at work, Kit thought, shaking her head. No thanks. Her aunt was pragmatic, dogged, kind . . . and a total control freak. "I appreciate the offer. I do, but—"

"I don't want you alone. There's a killer out there. One with the potential ability to pick locks."

Kit lifted her chin. "My locks aren't simple. My security system was installed by one of Dad's old cronies. And my dog has sharp teeth."

"You don't have a dog."

Kit shrugged. "I'll feel better surrounded by my things."

"They'll remind you of Nicole."

"Breathing reminds me of Nicole."

Her aunt heard the crack in her voice and snapped her mouth shut on whatever she was about to say. Tilting her head, she waited a moment, then spoke quickly, sharply. "Your stubbornness is annoying."

"I come by it honestly," Kit said evenly, because now she sounded like her aunt.

Marin tapped one stubby finger on her chair arm. "Fine," she finally said, leaning back. "Then here's how this is going to work, and I won't take no for an answer. I'm still your boss."

Kit tensed.

"Drop everything else you're working on, hand it to John or Ed, and focus that innate stubbornness on winnowing down that list. You find that damned contact of yours." Marin leaned forward, sharp eyes honed. "You write down every damned detail about that crime scene, hound the detectives, and drive this damned story into the ground. Then we bury the murdering bastard that stole our reporter, *our* girl, with it."

Kit found herself unexpectedly smiling. Yes, *this* was what she'd needed. This was why she'd come here instead of going home. She stood.

"Copy me on everything, I don't care how small or seemingly insignificant. I want an update on your work to date, and daily reports after that."

"Thank you, Auntie."

"Don't thank me." Marin stood, too. "I've known Nicole since she was fourteen years old and you dragged her home like some flea-bitten stray. I don't think I ever saw her without a camera under her arm. I definitely never saw her without you."

She looked at Kit like she was wearing one of her more outrageous outfits . . . or nothing at all. And that's how Kit felt standing in this office without Nicole. Naked. Like something vital was missing.

"The thing is," Marin continued, chin wobbling, "if I ever had a child, a daughter, I'd want her to be . . ." She waved one arm, and shook her head. "Well . . . nothing like either of you. But I cared for that girl. I still care. So go out there and get me the goddamned truth."

"I'll get you your truth," Kit swore, with identical familial passion. "And a goddamned murderer."

Marin smiled briefly, eyes turning up at the corners like a cat considering a three-legged mouse. "Have that report on my desk by morning. I'll be your personal research assistant and an extra pair of eyes. Meanwhile, I'd like you to reconsider staying with me. The circumstances surrounding Ms. Rockwell's death are . . . unsettling."

"Your stubbornness is annoying," Kit said, but reached over to place a hand on her aunt's arm.

Marin grazed Kit's knuckles with her own before letting her hand fall away. "Runs in the family."

CHAPTER FIVE

In addition to the death senses, Grif was relieved to find he'd retained his celestial ability to unlock things. He entered Craig's ranch house without even having to touch the keyhole, bypassing the red blink of a security camera with the wave of his hand. Yet he'd already discovered the ability was clearly meant only for use in locating Katherine Craig. The one time he'd tried to open the back door of a gentlemen's club—just to ask for directions, of course—he'd been yelled at and chased by the owner's dog. Briefly caught, too, he thought, scowling at the ripped hem of his pant leg. He'd have given the fleabag a mouthful of feathered daggers if he'd had his wings. As it was, he had to stick to the plan. He couldn't shield himself from attack, never mind Craig.

And though he still felt vulnerable without his full celestial powers, the limitations were also a comfort. Like a rainbow, their absence was an intangible promise. He'd be back in the protective lap of the Everlast in a few short hours' time. Just an angel's blink, really.

Though still long enough for a woman to die.

Pulling the autopsy papers from his breast pocket, he looked up Katherine Craig's time of death. Ten fifteen at night. Just over two hours from now, and not even a full twenty-four since Rockwell's murder. At least Craig wouldn't have to live with her grief for long, Grif thought, tucking the papers away.

He looked up, squinting into a darkened hallway. Outside the home, the chalky white walls had gleamed beneath the full moon, the Spanish tile roof a red convex helmet above shuttered eyes. Inside, the dark wood floors creaked under Grif's weight as he moved out of the foyer, pausing at the entry of a sunken living room with ceiling beams in matching black chocolate. He couldn't put his finger on it, but there was something both comforting and disturbing about the room. He liked it, though he knew he shouldn't.

A chandelier sat in one corner, a cascade of translucent capiz shells falling nearly to the floor, and a floor screen divided the large room in half, though a giant free-form sofa was the real focus. Grif could almost see Craig lounging there, sable curls thrown back against the silk brocade pillows, creamy neck bowed in a revealing arch. But he shook himself of the image as soon as he imagined her smiling, tilting that jet-black head his way.

A boxy television anchored the north-facing bay windows, and Grif crossed to it. How about that? It was the same model he'd bought for Evie right before he'd died. She'd wanted the most modern available, of course. Said it was important to show that he was a thriving independent contractor. Success, she claimed, made people want to trust you.

Because the thought of Evie made him smile, he reached for the knob next to the television screen and gave it a hard twist to the right. Black-and-white static immediately filled the room, but the sound was off, which Grif gave thanks for a moment later when the static cleared and a woman's image popped on the screen.

Grif jolted as Katherine Craig emerged from the same foyer he just had, dropping her bag and briefcase onto the sofa and kicking off her shoes. She disappeared into the room behind him, then emerged moments later with a tumbler in one hand, climbing the short steps with slumped shoulders, then turned in to a hallway.

The shot cut off there, and the next image was of Craig entering a darkened bedroom, but time had clearly passed. She was wrapped in a bathrobe, hair wet, tumbler empty. She was headed back into the kitchen with her glass when the shadow rose up behind her.

The first blow was just to stun. After all, rapists didn't generally want to roll in blood. Craig lifted her right hand, as if to fend off the punch that had already come, but a second fist flew from nowhere and the crystal tumbler shattered. Strong fists ripped at that shining mane of glossy black hair, pulling Craig up even as she fell. Two attackers, Grif realized, as Katherine Craig disappeared beneath a relentless onslaught of grabbing hands and pummeling knees.

Grif turned off the television. He didn't need to see it twice.

He didn't go directly to the bedroom. He couldn't, so soon after what he'd just seen. Instead he crossed to the fireplace, red brick lacquered white, and stared into an antique mirror with scrollwork that swirled up like gold smoke. Unable to meet his own reflected gaze, he studied the snapshots that'd been tucked haphazardly into the ornate frame, a casual juxtaposition that somehow worked.

He was immediately drawn to a woman who reminded him more than a little of Veronica Lake. She had a cascade of glossy blond hair that obscured one side of her face while revealing a long neck that looked translucent. The dim light gave it the blue-white aspect of a still-developing negative.

But it was the wide smile that caught Grif's breath—the smile within a smile, he thought, touching the photo's side—and that was how he recognized Katherine Craig. How many incarnations did she have? he wondered, eyes skimming photos, finding others. Her face was painted differently in all, her hair dyed in colors that defied nature's rainbow. She was even clearly bewigged in some, but in each she still wore that trademark smile, a radiant blast that warmed even the sepia tones.

She had a lot of friends, Grif saw. His Evie had always said she was a man's woman, that boys were simpler and made better sense. "Like solid corner pieces of the world's puzzle," she'd explained, and Grif couldn't argue. But Craig was obviously a woman well liked by other women.

Moving on to the frames housed on the mantel, he honed in on one of Craig with a slim blond man, arms thrown about one another's waists, both of them posing like Egyptian statues. They were close, he thought, though they didn't give off the vibe of a couple.

Not that it mattered anymore.

Grif wasn't surprised to find most of the photos also included Nicole Rockwell—*my best friend is waiting outside*—or that she, too, was a fan of varying appearances. One photo showed her with hair so red he could almost feel heat and scent flame. But by now she was tucked into the Tube in the Everlast, until she could forget enough to heal and move on to Paradise.

Turning away, Grif saw that the adjacent wall was lined from floor to ceiling in rough-hewn bookshelves, the top rows lined in hard covers, spines so cracked they looked like torture victims. The pulp fiction was piled up below that, tilting in dangerously angled stacks. Baskets of magazines filled the bottom shelf: hot rods in one, full-sleeved comics in another, and a name he recognized from the Everlast, Oprah. So that was the woman who kept so many souls from using a disadvantaged childhood as an excuse for poor behavior.

Even without another person in it, the house radiated life. Shaking his head, Grif stopped short of entering the kitchen. Cursing his mortal sight, he rubbed his eyes, but no. It was all still there. Excluding a gleaming white pedestal table perched in the corner, something pink had seemingly puked all over the room. The oven was pink, the stovetop. Even the icebox. Though larger, it was also the same basic layout as the kitchen in *The Honeymooners*. Grif snorted. After fifty years, and a dip in the forgetful pond, that memory had somehow stuck.

One of these days, Alice, he heard Ralph Kramden saying, *and POW! Right to the moon!*

He replaced Audrey Meadows's face with Craig's.

One of these days, Katherine. Pow! Right to the Everlast!

A covered patio sat on the other side of the room, and wincing, Grif slid the adjoining door open for some fresh air. The past and the present were mingling, joining forces to knock the breath out of him. Anas had said he had no place in the Everlast, but he wasn't adapting so well to the Surface, either. He couldn't tell if having been alive once before was more of a help or a hindrance.

It's probably just these fragile new lungs, he told himself, sucking in a deep breath. Yet it was more of the same outside. Loungers with diamond frames cushioned in colorful patterns. A rolling patio cart adorned with pink flamingoes and a coal barbecue that'd been turned into a planter for succulents.

Life so vibrant against the still, dark night that it practically screamed.

You're projecting, Grif told himself, and maybe he was. But the collision of old and new in this house unnerved him. It echoed eerily of the way he'd plowed head-on into Katherine Craig's life, and his stomach roiled at the thought of all this vitality ending because of him. And it scared him how much he wanted to take it back.

Returning to the kitchen, needing this night over with, Grif almost missed the ripple. It slid behind him, like a breeze sneaking into the windless night. He whirled, squinting hard, but saw nothing. Yet the air purled like curtains parting to reveal a new act. As one of the younger Centurions, Jesse, liked to say, *There's a disturbance in the Force.*

A ripple was a forward thrust, the gears of the Universe picking up speed as fate shifted onto a one-way street toward inevitable conclusion. For Grif, and for Craig, it meant there was no stopping what would happen here tonight. It had, in some sense, already happened. So he wasn't surprised at the way the sliding door vibrated when he touched it, sending out an eddying pulse—one attached to everything else in the world.

This was violence's point of entry.

Grif stared at the door. He had no wings, no celestial shields or weapons to prevent the attack. Just the ability to open doors and lose himself inside. But he relocked the door anyway. He'd already made it easy enough for the world to rob Katherine Craig of her smiles.

Finally, he moved down the darkened hallway, and into the back of the house, where he found himself having to choose between rooms. He turned right, into the one with the largest doors, and didn't even need the pulsing force of fate to let him know this was where Craig would die. The bed was made, pristine in the burgeoning moonlight, but Grif could make out the plasma ringing it like an etheric chalk outline.

You gotta watch this one, Griffin . . . and feel the death as if it were your own.

Turning, Grif searched for the best place to do that, deciding quickly on the mirrored folding screen that turned the room's left corner into a Hollywood boudoir. It was a tight fit but he could stand behind it unseen. Lie down, too, because that's what he needed just now.

Sinking to his knees, Grif simply tilted over to drop his forehead to the floor. Yet when he closed his eyes he saw the television screen again, and Craig's mouth, wide with silent cries as her battered body disappeared into a vortex that narrowed and shrunk, until only a diminishing star remained, centered in his mind. It, too, finally disappeared.

Pow, Katherine! Right to the moon.

CHAPTER SIX

The wind had picked up by the time Kit arrived home, and for the millionth time she wished she'd gotten her garage door fixed. The outdoor carport was a charming architectural detail, and one of the distinctive mid-century features that had drawn her to the sprawling ranch house in the first place. Yet when the wind was spitting at you and your best friend was dead, you wanted a bit more protection than four beams and a wooden roof afforded.

I'll start a fire, she thought, holding her swing coat tight as she rushed to the front door. Something to warm her, keep her company, and burn away the night. Shoving her key into the giant teal door, she wondered if she should have accepted Marin's offer to stay in her cozy stacked town house, or at least returned one of the dozens of calls from friends offering to come over. Her father had always said Kit was too independent. That a friendly nature and curious mind was well and fine, but truly living required being known by another soul. In the years after her mother died he'd lamented not giving Kit a sibling, though the wish was likely as much for him as it was for her.

At any rate, the reality of being alone had all seemed more distant in the day. For one thing, she was used to it. For another, a companion had seemed unnecessary fuel when her body still burned at the core, waiting to ignite. But now, with the wind blowing icicles through her veins, it felt like she, too, was in the grave. All her nuclear energy had been snuffed like a match between the night's icy fingers.

A shower would help, Kit thought, shivering. Some whiskey. That fire to watch over her until light appeared again. That was a start.

Kit punched in her code, silencing the alarm before dumping her bag and briefcase on the sofa. Kicking off her ballerina flats, she left the lights off and headed straight for the kitchen. She flipped on the utility light hovering over the gold drink caddy along the right wall, which she'd salvaged from the Dunes right before the city blew the old girl up. Hotel estate sales, now mostly a thing of the past, were the best. Yet the decanter holding the scotch and the full set of crystal tumblers had been her mother's, a garage sale find from the summer before she'd died. It was the only glassware Kit drank from when she was alone.

She poured two fingers, thought a moment, then poured a third, already sipping as she headed back into the living room. Yet something caused her to pause at the doorway. Glass halfway to her mouth, she turned back to face the wall of sliding glass. Outside, the wind roared, a tornado in an inky vacuum.

She crossed to the door slowly, disconcerted but ultimately uninterested in the disheveled woman reflected back at her, then pressed her forehead against the cold pane so the room behind her disappeared. For all the movement outside—branches swaying, bushes ricocheting, the water eddying in the pool—there was no life. Who would venture out on a night like this, anyway?

So why did she have the feeling of being watched?

Because you are surrounded by the dead, she told herself, nose pressed against the glass. Your dead mother's drink, your dead father's voice, your dead friend's camera. The world might be raging outside, but the inside of her home was a crypt, and Kit felt sealed up by all the loss.

Without using her hands, she pushed back from the sturdy glass door, her image again superimposing itself on the chaos outside. It was rare that she didn't care what she looked like. Kit believed a person's way of moving about in the world spoke volumes about them, and to her it was an art.

But she didn't judge herself tonight. Forget the curve of her hips, a too-wide flare in a heroin-chic world. Forget even the clothes that marked her as a devoted lover of another era. Tonight she was the odd one out because of one thing alone: she was still breathing. She was still alive.

That was a relief, right? So why, as she stood there, exhausted and alone, was she thinking that it'd be nice if the wind could reach inside her homey tomb and whisk her away as well?

Living requires being known by another soul.

So why the hell was she here? Because the woman who'd known her best was dead, and the man she'd stupidly wed didn't even know *how* to live. And for all her big talk about the ability of the press to change lives, and the power of living deliberately to give meaning to one's own, Kit was still standing here alone.

Take away this sad woman across from me, she found herself thinking, focusing on her dark, wind-whipped eyes. *Put her in a different place entirely. Please . . . just make her disappear.*

The first thing Grif noted as Katherine Craig broached the room was the shadows under her eyes. He could see her clearly, though he was altogether invisible to her from behind the folding screen. Plasma moved tellingly behind her in a faint shimmer of silver-gray that threaded the room, inching her way. Despite that, all he could focus on were those telling circles, dark as bruises above the apples of her cheeks, as if the day had gone and punched her square. Then his gaze flickered, and he caught a real movement behind her.

And here comes tonight's knockout blow.

But first, the shower. It gave the intruders, which soon materialized as men, time to position themselves in the hallway, not that time was a factor anymore. They'd entered the home almost as soon as Craig left the kitchen. Grif had felt the invasion like a worm burrowing under his flesh. This woman was already dead, he thought, even as she disappeared under the water.

Nervous, or perhaps just impatient, one of the men stepped forward as if testing the room. Grif jolted. It was the blond he'd seen through the gas station's security camera, the one who'd taken Craig's notebook after Rockwell was murdered. He looked to be in his forties, older than Grif if you didn't count death years, but still strong enough that muscles fought against his turtleneck as he moved.

There was a hiss from the hallway, his partner cursing, and a gloved hand appeared, gesturing him back. Instead, the blond slid along the wall in total silence, almost like he was wandering, to disappear in the darkness of the corner opposite Grif. There was nothing after that, and he knew the rest was already planned. The two men were like sparring partners, waiting to come together at the clang of the bell.

Grif felt a headache growing behind his eyes, and forced himself to relax his clenched jaw. He tried to control his breathing, but felt like he was waiting for a bell, too. He needed a corner man to talk him down, help him shake it out, get his head right. If he could just talk to Sarge, he could make him see that this wasn't right. Not for Grif. Not for the woman, Craig, either.

And what about these men? Why couldn't someone talk sense into them? That was one thing Grif had never been able to wrap his gray matter around, crimes against women. To him, it was like lifting a babe from the carriage and smashing its melon on the sidewalk. Easy destruction, just for the sake of it.

And forget about premeditated violence, the unstoppable train that was just minutes away from Craig's station. Even a random, careless act—even bad luck—was too much for most females to handle. After all, wasn't the way Grif had bumped into Craig's life random and careless?

But it was physiology that was really at fault. Even the big girls were easy to put down. Craig wasn't big or small, but right in the middle where a woman should be. She was like that roller coaster he'd loved at Coney Island as a kid, made up of long slopes and wide curves, built for thrills. Something wild, he thought, but also something that made a man just want to let go.

You'd think that kind of natural wonder would engender a sort of awe in all men, but some were the moral equivalent of a smoker's cough. They were a black noise let loose in the world, a cloud heralding illness and death. The two men entering this room were like that. Walking cancer. Destruction, just for the sake of it.

The shower droned on. He glanced down at the wristwatch Evie had given him on their second anniversary, latching on to the memory for distraction. He remembered the way she'd bitten that sweet lower lip of hers, watching him unwrap it, though she'd waited until it was fastened around his wrist to tell him it was a knock-off. Like he cared. Point was, Evie had been thinking of him even though he hadn't exactly hung the moon for her in the previous twenty-four months, and he was both touched and secretly relieved that she still celebrated being his wife. That she still believed in him.

So he accepted the watch, and wore it religiously, never telling her he thought timepieces were silly affectations, never saying that he believed nothing really started until a person got there anyway.

But everyone's here now, he thought wryly, lifting his head as the shower snapped off. At least for fourteen minutes longer.

You're going to bring that poor girl's soul home. You're going to offer her guidance.

But I don't want to, he found himself thinking as the plasma moved like a panther in the air. It peeled away from the hallway, padding silently through the bedroom and into the bathroom.

Propping one creamy, pale leg at a time on the vanity stool, Craig began toweling off. The limbs appeared disembodied from where he stood, but the blond cancer-man could see everything from his corner, and Grif knew he'd be the one to add violation to death.

I didn't cause this, he almost said aloud, and realized desperation had somehow turned the thought into a prayer.

Nicole Rockwell did this, he said silently to whomever was listening. Frank did this, because he was allowing it.

God did it.

There was no reprimand. As with any prayer, no answer at all. Instead, the wind just continued howling outside, while another minute dropped away within.

Bricks, thought Grif, squeezing his eyes shut. Twelve minutes, and this will all go away.

Time enough to change your mind, Sarge, he thought, feeling panic rise, making itself known as an ache in his chest.

A white robe whirled and was wrapped tight. Grif's boxing robe had always been white, too. He'd loved the feel of it, the scent of bleach against the stiff terry-cloth. Not that it ever stayed white for long.

Plasma swirled, wrapping around Craig's legs like shackles as she rubbed her hair dry. Grif wanted to close his eyes.

Then she stepped into the room. The shower had relaxed her, and the booze piggybacked her fatigue so that her empty tumbler hung from two fingertips. But instinct—prey's or woman's—had her suddenly stiffening. She whirled, eyes wide, but the cancer-man in the hallway, faceless beneath a ski mask, was already on her. Grif had already seen this on the TV, but the sound hadn't been turned up then. His death senses were firing like rockets now, and Craig's knifed gasp jolted him. The slap of flesh was a shot fired. The man's growl was feral as he pounced.

Craig strained forward, but it was useless, and only had her robe falling wide. She turned instinctively to close it, and spotted the blond man already reaching for her flesh. But Craig—Grif's Take, his case, the woman—looked away from that oncoming train for a split second, and, with a mixture of shock and horror, focused on *him*.

She screamed, and this time it didn't sound like static from a television. It sounded like a woman. It sounded like his Evie.

It sounded like a bell ringing, calling him from his corner.

Grif rocketed forward, clambering over the bed like he was bounding the ropes. As he entered the ring, he thought he heard an announcer's voice in the static buzz of adrenaline coursing in his veins. It was an audience's far-off roar, and it swelled when Grif rounded the S-curve of Craig's white, naked hip and caught the man holding her, hard in his ribs. The blond stuttered in surprise, allowing a backward step that gave Grif space to pivot, just as the hallway man shoved Craig to the ground.

Rage had him going for the man's throat. There was no training driving him now; the rust of death-years had softened the one-two, one-two-three-four of his youth into an uncontrolled flurry, but Grif knew just what to do when he caught the chin. He might not have wings, but he still had fists.

Fear entered the hallway man's eyes, but then Grif connected . . . and the swirling plasma parted like the Red Sea.

Sure, a part of Grif still knew he was wearing a watch with marching minutes, that fate wouldn't allow a knockout blow. But something had snapped inside him, that same howling something the Everlast had failed to heal, and he half-believed that if he punched hard enough—if he could just send his award-winning, no-holds-barred southpaw hook directly through the back of the cancer-man's no-good skull—he could prevent what was already done. He could turn his timepiece into a stopwatch. He could halt Craig's death.

The murderer's feet caught air, out for the count before he hit the wall. Grif pivoted through the motion and turned, pulling back one of his mitts and letting loose a fist that wiped the *What the fuck?* right off the blond rapist's face. The blow struck home, and Grif was suddenly *there*. Solid on the rock, square on the Surface, sure-footed in the mud, knuckles singing, breathing deep of the polluted air.

The awareness cost him. A fist came out of nowhere to deaden his nose, and he gagged as blood filled his mouth. The blond man loomed for a moment, but then there was a flash, a white tide rolling his attacker to the other side of the room.

Not a tide, Grif thought, staggering. A different kind of natural wonder. He broke through the shock of tasting his own blood just in time. Pushing Craig aside, he took the blow meant for her, and bled some more, but it didn't matter. The blond was suddenly gone, reduced to a shadow dragging his sparring partner from the room. Grif tripped on his own legs before realizing he didn't need to follow. The air was curiously cancer-free. It was also clear of silvery-white plasma, naked but for shadows that loomed in black and grays.

So Grif just bled. Chest heaving, stinging knuckles bunched on his knees, breath straining in lungs that creaked, he squinted at his watch. Then he looked back up at Craig, who stared back at him with open-mouthed horror.

"Ten seventeen," he said, and offered her what had to be an unsettling, bloody smile. But unbelievably, *miraculously*, time had just proven his long-held theory right.

Nothing really started until a person got there, anyway.

CHAPTER SEVEN

Kit wrote about crime, imagined it, was outraged by it, but up until now it was something that happened around her, not to her. Sure, the threat of attack was a reality for any urban woman. Someone stronger and larger than you could always turn on a whim, and there wasn't much you could do about it. But then *life* could turn on you like that, too.

Yet knowing it wasn't the same as experiencing it. That was probably why shock was settling in now, why she'd begun shaking, and why she couldn't quite believe what had happened. She was in the bedroom she loved, yet the objects she'd so carefully collected suddenly looked like props on a Hollywood set. Vibrant and pretty enough, but without any real value or substance.

And while she was wearing her favorite cream robe, soft as snow, it now sported an unfamiliar tear in it that almost looked obscene. And with the wet blood of a total stranger staining its hem, it was. It was.

And don't forget this, she thought, touching her lower lip, already growing fat. But her fingertips were scented with the foreign man, and she jerked her hand away, and began shaking harder.

Kit looked around at her unfamiliar room, her gaze finally landing on the most unfamiliar thing of all.

"Who are you?" she asked the man hunched on the floor.

"Griffin Shaw. I'm here to . . ."

She watched him struggle, as if he didn't actually know why he was there.

"I'm here to help," he finally said, then winced.

"How did you get in my home?" she said. Whose voice is that? It was brittle and half-swallowed. Hard and meek at the same time. One more thing she didn't recognize.

Her defensiveness seemed to fortify the man named Shaw. Slowly, he rose to his feet. "Just be glad I did."

She was. She studied him, the rumpled roomy suit, the tightly razored pomp. His hair was dusky, a light brown that'd probably faded from the cool ginger of his childhood. Kit loved ginger hair. It put her in mind of blue skies and green hills and made her fantasize about French-kissing young, rebellious English princes on imaginary Welsh vacations. Yet this man could bulldoze fantasies with one hard look alone.

"They were going to kill me."

It was another foreign thought, and something else that didn't belong in her home. In fact, she hadn't even known she was going to say it until it was out of her mouth. Shaw lifted the Mies van der Rohe chair that'd toppled when her attacker—his? theirs?—had fled. He sat with a groan, but kept that hard gaze on her.

"Yes," he said, matter-of-factly, and the confirmation was a gut-punch. Kit lowered her head, and shook even harder. "Ever see either of those men before?"

"No."

"No idea who they were?"

Kit shook her head, then realized she was usually the one asking the questions, and wondered why she wasn't doing so now. She looked up, and out came that foreign voice. "Are you some sort of cop or something? A detective?"

Again, that hesitation, a genuine frown marring his brow. "I'm a P.I."

"Who hired you?"

"I'm here because of Rockwell," he said, both answering the question and not.

"Nic?" The strange voice broke on her friend's name, and the tears finally came. Shivering, she pulled her savaged robe tight, then realized the man had moved toward her uncertainly, like he wanted to comfort her but knew he didn't have the right. She looked at him again.

"There's something familiar about you," she said, sniffling. He edged back again in response, leaning into shadows that reached out to obscure his features. Darkness bent over him in a protective arch, almost like wings jutting from his back . . .

Squeezing her eyes, Kit shook her head to clear her vision. She was definitely in shock.

"'Course there is," he said gruffly. "I'm the guy who just saved your life."

She wiped her face. "Something else."

Shaw jerked his chin at her. "Have another drink."

"I'm not drunk," she said, and was happy to hear her voice had some snap back.

"No, I mean it. Have another drink. You're shaking like a leaf." He tilted his head. "I don't feel so hot, either."

Kit had been so worried about herself—not to mention scared and confused—that she'd momentarily forgotten he'd been assaulted, too. "Oh, geez. Are you hurt?" she asked, moving toward him.

He jerked back, and his wings flared. Kit gasped, blinked, but they were just shadows again, surrounding that craggy face, and eyes that knew so much they gave away nothing. Kit shook her head again, and swayed.

"Whoa there."

She felt a steadying hand on her arm. Warm. Real.

Gentle.

"I'm sorry. I thought I saw . . ." How was she supposed to say, while still sounding sane, that she thought she'd seen wings, with feathers the length of her forearm, rising from his back like black smoke? "Nothing."

"You're falling asleep on your feet."

Her lids jerked open. She was. "Pills. I took a couple to relax. I just wanted to . . . go away."

That would explain the hallucinations, Kit thought. Pills plus whiskey plus near-death equaled wings. What an equation.

"Come on," Shaw coaxed, leading her to her bed. "Let's get you settled into this pastry puff."

"No. We gotta get out of here. They might . . ."

"They won't be back tonight."

"How do you know?" Kit asked as her head found the

pillow, amazed by his certainty, amazed that anyone could be certain of anything after today.

"I can tell," he said as he gathered the covers around her, and maybe he could. Maybe men who popped up to protect strange women could sense danger in a way others couldn't. Maybe he'd tracked so many predators as a P.I. that he had an instinct for them.

Still, she sat back up. "We need to call the cops. I have a friend there . . ."

"I'll take care of it," he said shortly, and waved a hand before her face, as if smoothing out her frown. Relief flooded Kit in an almost dizzying rush, and she fell back, nodding.

Kit wondered how many women he'd rescued since becoming a private investigator, but what came out was "I don't want to be alone."

The stranger who'd saved her, who looked familiar but wasn't, who seemed as suspicious of her as she did of him, hesitated. Then he leaned forward, tucked the covers up to her chin, same as her father used to do when she was young, and stared down at her with enough calm for them both. "I will watch over you."

"Thank you," she said, and this time hers was a different strange voice, not brittle but slurred. Neither hard nor meek. A voice that was the sum of the equation of all the day's events.

The man, Shaw, leaned back, disappearing again into the shadows. Where he belongs, Kit thought. Where he can evaporate like he was never here at all.

Her eyes fluttered shut, closing out even the shadows, but his reply chased her into sleep. "Least I could do."

* * *

What the hell *was* he doing?

Grif leaned back in the leather chair, the question dogging him for the hundredth time that night. Well, he was watching a physically and emotionally beaten woman sleep, and had been for hours, just as he'd promised. Unwilling to entertain any more of his own dreams, he was also fighting off his own mortal need for rest. But more than all of that, the real question was, what the hell had he *done*?

I'm here to help. That's what he'd told Craig, which was ironic since it was the same thing he always said. *I'm here to help.*

Instead he'd hoo-dooed her into not calling the cops, waving his hand before her like a second-rate Houdini just to buy himself time to think. Because Katherine Craig was *alive*. She still had flesh and breath, which she'd likely be thankful for when she woke, but the point was that she shouldn't ever wake again.

Fate, he was willing to bet, was pissed.

But the ripple had smoothed out, and the plasma dogging the woman had disappeared. None of his celestial senses picked up a hint of looming death, and even his headache had dulled. And it had all happened at the moment Craig was scheduled to die but didn't.

Pulling out his Luckies, Grif lit a stick and noted his scraped knuckles with odd fascination. Flexing, he wondered what it meant that they were both still alive.

"Means you're in deep with Sarge, that's what," he muttered, slumping on the chair in Craig's bedroom. The lack of communication alone told him that much.

But Sarge had dumped him back on the mud to do a job no soul should have to shoulder. And now that Grif had screwed up his case, what was the celestial response? Silence . . . with the additional bonus of memory and emotion to cement him to the Surface. Now it looked like he was stuck here until Sarge saw fit to reclaim him.

They'll probably send another Centurion to Take her, Grif thought. Maybe even her Guardian, a Pure. Yet, despite it all—screwing up Craig's life and death, along with the pain of breathing and remembering—he didn't regret beating off those men. Craig had been so outnumbered, so helpless, and literally naked, that it seemed unnatural not to help. He couldn't stand by and watch a woman get beaten, raped, murdered. He'd rather be dead.

"I thought for a moment that it had all been a dream."

Grif jolted and, looking over, knew exactly how she felt. Katherine Craig sat up, the covers slipping down the upper half of her body to reveal her bare neck and one smooth shoulder, the skin so flawless it was like a curvy pail of warm, fresh milk. He swallowed hard, keeping his gaze away from the flare of her hip and breasts as she pulled her robe tight, but it was like trying to keep his eyes off the hills framing a sunrise. After all, it was so much more of an event when there was something majestic supporting it.

Yet Craig's eyes weren't bright with dawn. The shadows that'd been beneath them the night before were now deep half-moons, made even darker with knowledge. Oddly, coupled with the cascade of rumpled raven hair and her round bare face, it made her look impossibly young.

"Did you sleep?" she asked, the very question eliciting a yawn. It felt strange. He hadn't been tired in decades. Grif shook his head, putting out his cigarette in a white ceramic vase. Craig's shadowed eyes narrowed at the movement, but she didn't chide him.

"Coffee?" she asked instead, pushing back the covers.

"Please." His voice was as musty with disuse as his manners. He stood, and so did she, which was how they found themselves uncomfortably close. It was odd, Grif thought. He knew what she looked like close to death, close to naked, close to him . . . yet didn't really know her at all.

"Excuse me," she said, lowering her head and skirting him. Grif shoved his hands in his pockets, allowing distance between them as he followed her from the room.

The house looked fresh-scrubbed in the early morning, unfiltered light falling over the dark wood floor like the kiss of a veil. The furniture was even more lacy and feminine glowing with the dawn, and the soft surroundings seemed to revitalize Craig. Until she rounded the corner.

There she saw the kitchen's sliding glass door, marginally ajar, which put a hitch in her step and breath. Cursing himself for not closing it before, Grif crossed to it and locked it shut. By the time he turned around, she was already standing with her back to him, stiff in front of the coffee pot. Though there was no mistaking its use, it was the one thing in the room he didn't recognize from his time on the mud. It looked like it belonged on a rocket ship. Almost immediately the thing began to froth and foam, and Grif's hands were curled around a hot cup in only a few moments more.

So there had been some improvements with the onset of the twenty-first century, he thought, sipping his first decent cup of coffee in fifty years. It was smooth and strong, black and warm, and it made him wonder what else he'd been missing. He'd learned a lot after incubation, things a Centurion needed to know when visiting the Surface, including the objects surrounding his Takes. Cars were different, phones were different, and information flowed through the air now. The Internet. That had been the hardest for him to muscle into his mind.

But many details were considered too small and mundane for the Centurions' purposes. They tapped the mud too briefly for things like newfangled coffee-makers to matter. Instant coffee that tasted like a wet dream was apparently one of them.

Craig joined him at the white pedestal table, where he'd positioned himself in the corner, an effort to appear unthreatening. Craig shifted uncomfortably anyway, pulling her robe tight.

"How do you feel?" It was a question Grif never asked . . . though when you met someone right after a violent death, it wasn't usually necessary.

She stared. "Like my best friend was murdered, I was attacked, and there's a strange man drinking my coffee in my house."

Grif sighed. Served him right for asking. And it had him looking again at the woman across from him, vulnerable in her robe and bare face and mortal body. Strong in her gaze, mind, and will to live.

"How about I ask the questions for now?" she went on, and one slim brow lifted high.

He inclined his head, and slumped into his corner chair. "You're the reporter."

"And how do you know that?"

"Toldja." He pointed to himself. "P.I."

She tilted her head. "But you never said who hired you."

Yep, she was a strong one. Sharp, too. "Someone interested in the Rockwell case."

"She wasn't a case to me. She was a friend."

"Probably why she left you this." He threw her notebook

on the table between them. He'd discovered it in the corner where he'd felled the blond man the night before. Even if Grif hadn't seen the man stealing the journal on the gas-station security cam, this would have been proof positive that he was both girls' killer.

Or would have been, if not for Grif.

Recognizing it, Craig let her cup clatter to the table, sloshing caffeinated gold across the shiny top. The spill looked like one of those Rorschach tests Grif'd had to take when entering the army. He wondered what it said about him that this one resembled a black angel carrying an enormous scythe.

"I found it on the floor." He jerked his chin. "Open it to the last entry."

She did, immediately. It was interesting, Grif thought, the way curiosity wiped away her fatigue. Maybe that was the spine holding her up, the wire threading her resolve. Whatever it was, it sparked the moment she spotted it, the name Rockwell had circled when Grif had allowed her to re-dress for the Everlast.

"This is why they took my notebook!" She looked up, met Grif's gaze, then back down again. "Oh, Nic! You're so smart."

"So smart she almost got you killed."

Not that he could talk.

Kit shook her head, not listening. "We were working on a story. She was meeting with someone who could provide us information when she was killed."

"What kind of information?"

"Powerful men in compromising positions," she said cryptically. It reminded him of Frank.

"You should go to the police."

"You said you were going to call the police."

Grif shrugged. "You fell asleep before telling me your cop friend's name."

Her eyes narrowed, though the notebook still had her attention. "I gave him this list yesterday. But this narrows it down to one."

Grif thought of the plasma seeping into her home, curling about her flesh. "I'm sorry to break it to you, but your friend can't help you. You have to run."

"What?" She looked up, face wide with shock.

"Get out of town," he said shortly. "Change your name. You got money?"

"Yes."

"Use it. Buy yourself a new identity. Invent a new life."

"Wait a minute," she said, leaning over the table that wired strength back. "I'm not the one who committed a crime. I didn't kill anyone. I stumbled onto a story, followed a source, and have clearly found something that's more than what it seems. *I* didn't do anything wrong."

"Don't matter, Katherine—"

"Kit."

"What?"

"My name is Kit. Only my family calls me Katherine."

Grif tapped out a smoke. "They could call you Howdy Doody for all I care. You're still marked for death."

She fell back at that, and Grif sighed. Too harsh. And too knowing. But he needed her to wise up, and fast. "I'm talking about the squiggly your friend drew in that notebook. Whoever killed her, whoever attacked you, saw it. It made you a target."

"Then there's something to it." She lifted her chin.

"Look, I've seen this before. You want to change your

future? You gotta change it now. In this case, alter everything about yourself." The memory of the dooming plasma circling her ankles revisited him. It was gone for now, but he imagined it roaming outside like a wolf, searching for a way back in.

But Kit shook her head. "My life is here."

He shrugged. "Not much longer."

"That a threat, Mr. Shaw?"

"It's Grif," he said, slumping. "Only my family called me Mr. Shaw."

"Cute." She made a face, then crossed her arms. "But I'm not leaving. I'm going to get answers for Nic. I need to find out who killed her, why, and I'm going to make them pay for my busted door. Nobody enters my house without invitation," she said, and looked pointedly at him.

Grif didn't want to look impressed, but it was hard with her staring him down, tough and determined-looking. Like a lion-tamer. Like she'd said . . . cute.

"Guess I'll stick around then, too," he finally said, lifting his cup. He tried to sound spontaneous, but it was a decision he'd come to in the deep, lonely night. He couldn't save her just to allow her to die later.

"I don't even know you," she snapped, as if wielding a whip.

"You didn't know me last night, either. And you still don't know who attacked you."

She frowned. "You think they'll be back?"

"You think they've left?" he said, and she winced again. Best to be straight, though. She needed facts. Facts were bricks. Maybe she could build herself a wall with them, too, one tall and wide and strong enough to keep her alive when he was gone. Knowing Sarge, that would be soon.

Which brought him to the other thing he'd decided in the

long hours where no one on either the Surface or in the skies had been talking to him. Sarge and company had stripped him of his celestial powers, leaving him only with the tools to sense impending death. They'd dumped him here as a freak— neither Centurion nor mortal—with holes in his memory and orders to watch a fated murder.

But Grif had altered fate, and not with wings, but fists. With the part of him that had free will. The part that *was* human.

So Grif had decided to block out his death senses, temporarily ignore his angelic side, and use whatever remaining time he had on this mudflat to take care of a little business. A murder that had been haunting him for decades.

"Ah, here comes the catch," Kit said, studying his face.

"No catch. I just need help with an old case I'm trying to solve. A double murder."

"And?"

"And you're a reporter." And the case was so cold it had frostbite. It would be hard enough for him to get records, reports, and access to eyewitness accounts with no resources or contacts. But with all the newfangled electronics, it was damned near impossible. Still, as long as he was camping out on the mud, why not take a look?

"And you're a hardened P.I.," she replied coolly. "Why don't you lone-wolf your way to the answer?"

"Because it happened here. In Vegas. And I've been away a little while." He showed teeth as he answered, causing fear to move behind her gaze. Good. She should be a little afraid. "Besides, I need some help getting around."

"What? No car?"

He lifted a shoulder. "That, and I get kinda . . ."

"What was that?" she said, leaning forward.

He pushed his cup away. "I said I get turned around."

Craig leaned back, and smiled. So much for being afraid. "A man who admits to being bad with directions." She inclined her head, like that was the deciding factor. "I guess I can help."

She could. Because he'd done more than watched her during the night. He'd also gone through her house. He'd found awards for journalism through high school, college, and even a national one for investigative reporting. He'd found old photo albums with newspaper clippings linking her to the paper she worked for now, one that her great-somebody had started decades earlier. That's how he knew she'd have money if she wanted to flee, and sources if she wanted to stay.

And if Craig—or Kit—stuck around, then Grif would, too.

Besides, why shouldn't he have the answers to questions that'd stalked him on both sides of the grave?

What had happened in the hours leading up to his death?

Who killed his Evie?

Who killed Griffin Shaw?

Kit rose, placed her coffee cup on the pink Formica counter, then turned to address him from the kitchen doorway. "We'll start with this circled name, and my office."

"So we have a deal?"

She gave a short nod, and pulled her robe tight. "It's a Saturday, so it'll be relatively quiet. We'll take my car."

"That fancy foreign number?"

"How did you know that?" She drew back.

Because I saw it from the room where your best friend was killed. I saw you, looking like Hayworth, making me want to pin you up, pin you down, take you for a different kind of ride altogether.

Grif cleared his throat, along with his damned mortal

mind, and shrugged. "It's not exactly a subtle machine. Fact, you might want to ditch it for something less showy."

"I'm not leaving my car," Kit replied coolly. "Wait here while I go change."

Grif decided against telling her to pick something she'd want to be seen dead in, and watched her go, admiring her fragile yet aggressive sway, before rising for more coffee.

Today was the first day of the rest of his life. He could use another cup of joe.

CHAPTER EIGHT

As might be expected of a reporter, Kit had a knack for words. She noticed nuance and inflection, valuing precision in word choice and crispness of tone. Griffin Shaw didn't enunciate half of what he should, she picked that up right away, letting his gerunds and suffixes fall away so that if she were writing them, she'd have to use a lot of apostrophes.

But she wasn't writing them down, and that only partly because she was driving. Instead she kept catching herself gazing over at him, specifically at his full bottom lip when he spoke, his voice lodged deeply in his throat, as if only escaping reluctantly to take flight in the air. He was not a man overly fond of chitchat. Yet she liked it when he did speak. His voice was like gravel rolling around inside a buckskin pouch, and well-suited to his languid watchfulness, the half-lidded gaze, the wide-legged slump. He was like a lion in repose, his strength quiet and coiled until it was needed.

Kit knew. She'd seen him pounce.

And that's really why she agreed to help him. She'd never partnered with anyone but Nic before, and that only because their skills were complimentary, not competing. Kit was something of a lone wolf herself. Yet it seemed apropos to take on a partner who was not only investigating Nic's death, but who had prevented her own. Because even through the drugged haze of fear, shock, and pain, she'd seen her death coming. It'd looked like all the pain she'd ever felt had taken form to rise up against her, as tangible as a tsunami.

And then, because of Griffin Shaw, it was gone.

It was enough to have her overlook the way he'd put out his cigarette in her vintage Zeisel vase, and had obviously been pawing through her things while she slept. And if there was still an unknown element to him—including his mysterious entry into her house and life—well, Kit liked a good mystery as well as anyone.

She was also damned fine at her job. She'd find out everything there was to know about Griffin Shaw. In time.

But first, she thought, hand whipping her glossy wooden steering wheel to the left, who the hell killed my girl?

"Who the hell taught you to drive?" Grif asked, bracing against the door.

"My dad. Parked his car on an unpaved stretch of desert when I was twelve and made me go backwards. I had to perfect it before I was ever allowed to go forward."

"He drive one of these foreign tin cans, too?"

"It was a patrol car," Kit said, smiling slightly. She was used to the scorn from her friends. They all bought American, drove American, bled American. It was her one deviation from her rockabilly lifestyle—forgoing the old Fords and Chevys for this tight, sweet Italian ride. That stubbornness was a trait she'd inherited from her mother, who'd willingly conformed to the things that defined her—cop's wife, professional mother—in all ways but one.

Shirley Wilson-Craig had refused to be domesticated. She'd cook, but only dishes made with fresh market ingredients, most of which took all day. She tidied, but hired someone else to clean. And she'd schedule playdates so Kit would never want for friends, but would never dress down for them, and never, ever carpool.

"Life should be lived as art," she often told Kit, her ubiquitous cigarette dangling from its gold holder. "Everything has its place. Let in only those things that are greatly desired, no more and no less. That's how to make sense of the world, and the only real way to achieve happiness."

Once, over a dinner of lobster salad and roasted lamb, Shirley had reported to Kit and her father that she'd been asked to leave a PTA meeting for wondering aloud why business couldn't be carried out over a two-martini lunch . . . or at least something more civilized than stale cardboard cookies. Yet she was smiling as she refilled her blue-collar husband's champagne glass, and the look said, *I may put myself in this box, but God help the person who tries to force me into it.*

And Kit would never forget the way her father had wrapped his giant hand around that fragile glass and smiled back.

That inherited stubbornness was why Kit worked at her family's newspaper, but, despite Marin's prodding, refused to run it. Ditto the foreign car. She was a newswoman, and rockabilly to the core, but it was those years of formal family dinners with an aristocratic mother, and a father who reveled in his wife's quirkiness, that really defined her. They might be gone, but *she* was not.

"Besides," Kit told Grif now, "this fine automobile is a classic."

"It's Italian."

Kit looked over, impressed, then registered his frown. "You're cranky."

He snorted and gazed out the window.

"And tortured, if I'm not mistaken," she added, using the directness she'd gotten from her father.

Another grunt.

"You torture yourself," she ventured, shooting him a look from the corner of her eye.

The next grunt meant that was true enough.

"You should let it go," Kit said, and still thinking of her parents, added with a laugh, "Let someone else torture you for a while."

His dark brow lifted beneath the brim of his hat. "You applying for the job?"

"Depends on the benefits package," she shot back, playing along. "But I think I could manage it."

"Oh, I'm sure you'd be great at it."

She smiled, choosing to take it as a compliment. The lightness was a welcome distraction. "Well, it'll have to wait. We're here."

Pulling through the newspaper's gated entry, she gave the guard a wave on the way to her regular spot, then took a deep breath as she stepped from the car. The sky was a careless blue, too warm to be dead winter, though lacking the ripeness of full spring. Cool and dry, but still as parched and unsatisfying as a broken sauna.

Heading to the giant brick building's side entrance, Kit gave thanks that she was still around to see it. Too late, she caught Grif's frown, and gave him an apologetic smile. "I'm not really in the habit of waiting for others."

And she led him into the printing rooms where the giant machines were heated but silent. She loved the sound of production and the scent of ink, and inhaled deeply, thankful again that she was here today. Looking around, she thought about all of *this* going away, of the Internet turning the traditional press into an archaic technology. It was enough to make her wish she was a Luddite. Unfortunately, she depended too much on the exact same technology to do her job. Lose her smart phone and she might as well lose her soul.

Kit punched the call button on the elevator, saw the cab was stuck somewhere near the seventh floor, and headed instead for the stairs. It was only three flights up. She had a body. It worked. So she would climb.

They emerged from the stairwell directly into the press room, Grif huffing behind her.

"Does every damned thing in this place have to make noise?" Grif mumbled as they wound their way through tottering cubicles.

"Never thought much about it before," Kit said, though he was right; phones rang, computers beeped, Internet radio streamed from multiple sources, and a bank of televisions stared down at "reporters' row" like a general looming over his troops. She shrugged out of her dress jacket, careful not to bend the scalloped collar as she hung it on the vintage coat rack just inside her office. Whirling without stopping, she jerked her head at Grif. "My aunt has the motherboard in her office."

She waved at the few reporters—Chuck in sports and Sarah in editorial—who were in this early on a Saturday, but kept a brisk pace as she headed toward Marin's office. When she got there, she pulled up short. "You're here."

"Never left," replied Marin, eyes glued to her computer screen. "And before you start nagging me, I took my pills, had a sandwich delivered, and catnapped on the floor. Who's that?"

"Griffin Shaw." Kit shot Grif an apologetic look and said, "He saved my life."

Marin's head shot up at that.

"And before you start nagging *me,* look at this." She tossed her notebook in front of Marin, who immediately flipped to the last page. Her aunt might be controlling and stubborn, but she knew what to focus on, and when, and immediately zeroed in on the circled name.

"Same list I've been working on all night . . . though I haven't looked up *that* one."

"Who've you vetted?"

Tossing the notebook down, her aunt leaned back in her leather chair. "Mark Morrison, the D.A. who thinks you should vote for him just because he *doesn't* wear high heels. Saul Turrets, the up-and-coming Republican who shot himself in the foot by supporting green causes. Caleb Chambers, poster boy for Mormons 'R' Us aka 'We're just like you . . . but with five brides to each brother.'"

"Be fair. Chambers only has one wife."

"That we know of."

Kit shook her head. That was Marin. Always caustic. Always suspicious.

"He's alibied anyway," Kit said. "Paul was at his fund-raiser that night."

"Another one?" Marin rolled her eyes. "Sonja doesn't even note them in the social blotter anymore."

"Dozens of parties a year, yet everyone still wants to go," Kit pointed out, then looked at her vibrating phone. "Speak of the devil . . ."

"Who, Chambers?" Marin sat a bit straighter. Sure, she'd take shots at the man, but he was a local shot-maker.

"No. Paul."

Marin growled, and slumped again.

"Who's Paul?" Grif asked.

"Someone Kit once carried in on her shoe."

Grif snorted, and leaned against the wall. Kit ignored both them and the call. Paul abandoned her at the station in the wake of Nic's death. He hadn't been there when she'd emerged like a newborn into an uncertain world the next morning. And last night . . . well, she could be dead right now and he'd be none the wiser.

He could leave a message.

"I'm confused," Grif said suddenly, half-turning in the doorway, gesturing to the room behind him. "You own all this, and yet you're pounding the street, setting up stings?"

"I don't own it. It's family-run."

"You'll be the only one running it when I croak."

"Marin," Kit chided.

Her aunt merely smiled. "That's why I forced the office on her. She'd be out in the pen with the others if she could, but there has to be some separation marking her for future greatness. For now, she doesn't want to be in management."

"Why?"

"She finds it intellectually numbing and a waste of her pro-digious talent for pissing people off."

"Because I believe in working my way up from the ground floor."

"Here we go," muttered Marin.

"I believe in free press. I believe the world is basically good, and a good journalist can make it even better. In fact, it's our moral obligation to make a difference—"

"These days, we're lucky to make our rent."

Kit shook her head. "No, this place *won't* close. We're not bloggers who don't fact-check, or paparazzi who create drama, then get sued, *then* throw their sources to the wind. We don't just give our readers the easy answer, we give them the truth."

Grif raised a brow in Marin's direction. "She always like this?"

"You got her started."

"Hey," Kit said, catching her aunt's eye. "Knowing the truth is important."

Marin bit her lip, then nodded.

"Anyway," Kit said, clearing her throat and her mind. "The street is where I belong. That's where the stories are."

"Which brings us back to you, Mr. Shaw." Marin swiveled, her eyes again sharp. "What's your story?"

Kit propped a hip on a sliver of cleared desk space, and waited. This man could fight off two armed men with noth-ing more than fists and a molten rage, but how would he stack up under the full weight of the Marin Wilson treatment?

Grif shoved his hands back into his pockets. "Everyone gotta have a story in this place?"

Not answering a direct question from Marin was as bad as screaming a lie. She leaned forward. "It's a newspaper."

"This an interview?"

"Prefer an interrogation?"

He dropped one shoulder. "Not bothered by either, really."

"Then you're either a criminal or a saint."

Grif snorted. "I ain't no saint."

"Grif is a P.I.," Kit interrupted. "He's investigating Nic's murder."

Marin's brows lifted. "How you doing so far?"

"I got you a name."

"And saved my niece's life?"

"Yes."

Marin stared at Grif a moment longer, then turned back to her computer. "So let's see where it leads us." She picked up the notebook and flexed her fingers. "Lance Schmidt. Doesn't ring a bell, which is why I haven't gotten to it yet."

Her fingers danced over keys with missing letters. Marin treated finding information like a battle to be won. Yet she froze unexpectedly, then blew out a long breath.

"What?" Kit asked.

Marin flipped the screen her way. "Please tell me you don't know him."

Kit rocketed to her feet, pointing at the screen. "That's the guy who attacked me!"

Nodding, Grif straightened, too. Marin cursed, then pulled the screen back around, scrolling down. "Lance Arnold Schmidt, forty-two years old, born in L.A., moved here when he was twelve. Divorced, no kids, and . . ." She looked away from the computer, into Kit's eyes. "Vice sergeant in charge of the sexual crimes division."

Shit. Kit looked at Grif. "He's a cop."

* * *

He's the cleaner," Grif said, earning a steely, considered look from Marin, and causing Kit to stare. The image of him flying from the corner of her bedroom flashed through her mind. He'd emerged like a dark knight to beat back a murderer—a *cop*—and he hadn't been scared then. Even with this new knowledge he didn't look scared. "Dirty cop," he muttered darkly, shaking his head.

"He could be the one organizing the prostitution ring," Marin added, thoughts flashing so quickly across her face it was like reading a ticker tape. "But he's not calling the shots."

"How do you know?" Kit asked.

Marin leaned back in her chair. "The powers-that-be don't dirty their own soft palms. Those who can afford it pay for distance from their crimes."

"Let me see that," Kit said, coming around to Marin's side of the desk. Lance Schmidt's hard face, looking into the camera lens so directly, caused an involuntary shudder to run through her. "I'm going to call Dennis."

Marin looked up sharply. "You sure? He's a cop, too."

Kit reached for her purse. "He's a friend."

Grif was beside her so quickly she jumped. His hand was hot on her arm, his fingertips like wires. "No heat."

Glaring, Kit jerked away. "I told you. He's a friend, and there's no way he's in on something like—"

"I don't care," Grif said shortly. "Schmidt is getting away with this, so he ain't working alone. It's like a web. Something touches one corner of it, and the reverberations are felt across the entire network. So no cops."

Kit finally nodded. No cops for now. She leaned back over the desk. "Let's dig deeper, then. But I don't want him to know we're looking."

Marin looked up at her. "You mean the family archives?"

It wouldn't erase their e-tracks entirely, but there was nothing to be done about that. The police had resources.

But Kit had Aunt Marin, who wasn't only the editor-in-chief of the *Las Vegas Tribune,* she was an information magpie. Every story by every reporter in the last thirty years had been meticulously archived, whether it ended up running in the paper or not. There were plenty of reasons the latter might happen—political sensitivity, timeliness, speculation that couldn't be corroborated—but Marin believed knowledge should be preserved, even prized.

Reporters had learned over the years to capitalize on her insatiable appetite for information. A small bit of gossip, properly dated and vetted, could earn a free lunch or a plum assignment, in addition to a byline. A tiny fact, woven in with others, might be rewarded at bonus time. As for the undocumented tips and reports, Marin called those "potholders"—something a preschooler could cobble together and not particularly valuable, but damned handy when the kitchen got hot.

Some journalists called her a gossip, a scandal addict who hoarded secrets and held them over the heads of the powerful and wealthy in order to gain personal favor and exclusive stories. But Marin had never blackmailed anyone, and was the least political person Kit knew. Besides, she knew what others couldn't . . . her aunt came by the habit honestly, learning it from *her* grandfather, who began the secret archives when he took over the paper. Yet no one would ever suggest the honorable Dean S. Wilson, who had a school and a street and a day named after him, was a slanderer. But Marin was a woman, and Marin was in charge. Those inclined to find fault would do so for those reasons alone.

For Kit, Marin's info-hoarding meant only two things. First, she wasn't the one who had to buy everyone lunch. And second, she had access to a treasure trove of information in the family archives that went all the way back to the paper's inception in 1932.

"It'll take time, but a cop isn't squeaky-clean one day and then running flesh the next," Kit said. "Not in an operation of this size. I bet there were rumors. There had to be other lists his name popped on first."

Marin considered it. "My sources at Metro have been a little tight lately, but they were flush ten years ago, about the time Schmidt hit the force."

"So anything from then 'til now," Kit said, then remained hunched over the computer as she peered up at Grif. "Meanwhile, since I'm operating in shades of gray, you might as well gimme one of your names."

Grif backed up a step. "What, now?"

Marin honed in on his reticence like a circling hawk. "What names?"

"He's working on a cold case," Kit said quickly, defending Grif though she didn't know why. "He needs our help."

Marin's gaze narrowed. "Why can't he go to the cops?"

Kit pointed to the obvious, Detective Schmidt's face on the screen. "He. Saved. My. Life." She turned to Grif. "Name?"

Looking down, he shifted his weight, hands shoved deep into his pockets. After a moment, he lifted his eyes and stared at Marin.

Marin huffed and rolled her shoulders. "I'm going to Starbucks. Text me if Mr. Shaw here happens to save your life again while I'm gone. Or if anything pops on Schmidt."

She walked out without looking back.

Grif shifted his eyes. "Breath of fresh air."

"Minty," Kit agreed, settling herself in Marin's still-warm chair. "Name?"

"Evelyn," he said at last. "Evelyn Shaw."

Kit typed it in, aware that he'd grown unnaturally still after moving to stand behind her. *Shaw,* just like him. Was it a sister? Or a wife? Kit wondered as she scrolled through the search results. She'd caught the way his eyes tightened at the corners, which had her automatically leaning toward the latter, and which meant she'd have to put even brief thoughts of his full bottom lip out of her mind.

Yet there was only one hit, and it was from fifty years earlier. Brows raised, she leaned back. "You weren't kidding when you said it's an old case."

Evelyn Shaw, age twenty-four, had died in a casino robbery. The Marquis, one of the oldest, had also been the ritziest in its time. It'd since been demolished, of course. Newer was better, or so the thought went . . . all the way up until it wasn't. Las Vegas had lost much of the glitter and kitsch that'd made it shine, and the unfinished, unfunded white elephant that now stood in The Marquis' stead was proof enough of that.

The article Kit pulled up was just an old police blotter, there had to be more, but the caption alone had her riveted. "Starlet Dies in Botched Bungalow Robbery." And linked to it was a photo. "Wow. She was beautiful."

Slim in a way Kit could only dream of, Evelyn Shaw was also bright-faced and beaming, unaware at the time the photo was taken that her life would be short. And her end was brutal. An attack in one of the hotel's courtyard bungalows that had been so fashionable back then. No witnesses, no leads.

God, Kit thought, looking at the poor woman's dainty features, had someone killed this man's beloved grandmother?

Grif's silence and unnerving stillness prevented Kit from asking, but she wanted to know more—and yes, to help him, too. She did so in the only way she could. Fingers flying over the keys, she said, "Let me go deeper."

But a ping sounded, a flash from Marin's search, and Grif let out a long exhale behind her. Later then, she thought, sensing his relief. Right now, Schmidt . . .

"Ah, so you've had your hand slapped before," she said, as Schmidt's face lit the screen again, less jarring this time. It wasn't solid intelligence, which is why Marin hadn't found it in the official search, just some hearsay by a reporter who'd befriended some runaways and, Kit noted, who transferred to a newspaper in the Midwest shortly after. "Schmidt was forced into paid leave when he was on patrol. A motorist filed a civil suit against him."

"For what?"

"Misconduct of a public officer, coercion using physical force, and oppression under color of office."

"Let me guess. The motorist was female."

Good guess. "Charges were dropped, his patrol term was up, and he requested transfer to the sexual crimes unit."

"Where he used his position to coerce and oppress women who make their living off the streets . . . at least until you and your girlfriend decided to play Nancy Drew."

Kit couldn't even work up ire at the jab. Schmidt's idea of coercion was alive in the bruises on her flesh. "And now he's after me."

Grif jerked his chin at the computer. "Cross-reference the

names. See if there's a connection between Schmidt and any of the others."

"Good idea."

"I know," he said drily.

"Marin will do it," Kit decided, and set about writing her aunt a quick note.

"Why not you?"

"Because I need to do some creative thinking."

Grif shook his head. "Which means?"

It meant her little story on prostitutes, johns, and the motivations of each had evolved into an editorial on a prostitution ring and a crooked cop. There was murder, attempted murder, and a list of politicians powerful enough to destroy a small principality.

And don't forget the sexy stranger who'd assigned himself as your protector, she thought, with a glance Grif's way. One clearly harboring secrets of his own.

"What do you mean?" Grif asked again, impatiently.

Blowing the bangs from her forehead, Kit tossed the pen and finally looked up. "It means, Mr. Shaw, that I need to get my hair pinned."

CHAPTER NINE

It was a relief to get out of the office, and not only because of Kit's aunt, the haranguer who seemed to know there was more to Grif than met her eagle-eye. Maybe she recognized him in a way Kit couldn't. She'd lived through more decades, after all—the Age of Aquarius, the end of the Cold War. She'd probably dined as an adult at Windows on the World.

And she was sick, he could see it. Her outline didn't spark with plasma like those being chased by death, but phosphor was burned around her in a permanent etheric sear, a static etching of how close she'd come to death.

But it was the computers beeping, the printers running, the phones constantly ringing—even in every damned pocket of the people walking by—that was really getting to him. It was nearly more overwhelming than the sensations that accompanied being wrapped in flesh.

What was it about this generation that they needed to be so *connected*? Wasn't there something to be said for autonomy? For holding court in your own head? For putting your heel to the sidewalk and lone-wolfing it until you reached your own damned destination?

And now the word-hound he'd somehow found himself yoked to wanted to put the investigation—*his* destination—on pause so she could put rollers in her hair. God help him, she'd said it helped her think!

At least Marin was going to keep working on a connection between the listed men. Grif had also suggested getting a file going on any of the women Schmidt had busted, going back a couple of years. One of those might be willing to lure a nosy young reporter to her room in return for clemency.

"Here we are! Fleur Fontaine's Beauty Boutique. The best pin-ups for pinups!"

Jesus, the way this woman could turn a simple sentence into bird chatter. He didn't want to see her hurt or dying, but her constant need to look on the sunny side of every sullied coin made him want to punch a blue jay in the beak.

"You coming?" she said, poking her head back in the car when he didn't move.

Grif stared straight ahead. "I ain't hanging out in no beauty joint."

"Aw, c'mon. I want to introduce you to Fleur."

"I'm not going." He should though. He was responsible for her being alive, which meant he was also responsible for keeping her that way. But since he was also responsible for her fated death, the reminder just made him cranky. He folded his arms over his chest.

"She moonlights as a burlesque dancer," she said in the blue jay voice. "She can do things with tassels that will make your mouth water. I bet she'd show you if you asked nice."

"You're off your rocker, lady."

Kit tilted her head. "Why are you mad?"

Why *aren't* you? Grif thought, brows furrowing, which was when he realized he really was sore. "We're supposed to be working a case."

She shrugged. "Nothing to be done until Marin cross-checks those names. Come in where it's warm."

"What about Evelyn? You were supposed to help me find out what happened to her."

"I will," she said, but her softening expression, a mixture of pity and sympathy, hardened him further.

"When?"

"As soon as I don't feel like Medusa."

And at that, Grif climbed from the stupid, foreign, low-slung car and glared at her across the soft hood. "You're supposed to be some modern-day woman, working hard for justice, doing a man's job . . . but you're going to stop to get your hair done?"

Kit tilted her head, then pursed her bottom lip so it looked like a soft pink pillow. Grif tore his gaze away. "Aw, Grif. You're cranky again. Need a hug?"

"I'm a P.I.," Grif replied through gritted teeth. "I need a lead."

Kit fisted her hands on her bell-shaped hips, another part of her anatomy Grif was trying not to notice. Especially considering the subject matter. "Your Evelyn has been dead for fifty years, Grif. She isn't gonna mind two more hours."

But Grif damned well minded.

So he'd turned without another word, and left Kit calling after him on the cracked sidewalk. He wasn't a patsy and he didn't wait for women to tame their updos before working a case. Now, five blocks away—give or take five blocks—he was utterly lost. At least he had his map.

"That thing's upside down, man," said a young man in baggy pants.

"Mind your own business," Grif snapped, and stared until the man scurried off. Then he flipped the map around. He needed a place to stay while slumming on the mudflat, and as sore as he was with Kit, with a rogue cop on her trail, she needed one as well. Problem was, fifty years gone meant most people his age were now dying of *natural* causes, and he hadn't known all that many to begin with. Not in Vegas.

Though there was someone.

"Question is," Grif muttered, squinting up at the street sign, "is the old wop still alive?"

Who's the hottie?"

Fleur was standing at the plate-glass window when Kit entered the salon, and probably had been since Kit pulled her Duetto to a stop at the curb. It was earlier than normal business hours, so they had the place to themselves, the usual chatter and hum of hair dryers missing. Fleur held a steaming cup of coffee out to Kit, cradling a second in perfectly lacquered fingers, tips long and moon-shaped and as red as a stop sign. Her simple, scoop-necked dress matched, though its fishtail hem put Kit in mind of a bullfighter, appropriate as it spoke to Fleur's Spanish heritage and it was how she faced every day— poised, engaged, and ready for anything.

"I don't really know," Kit said, and shook her head. Who *was* the man who'd saved her from death and, if her gut-check was right, rape? Who was this stranger who dressed like all her other rockabilly friends, in a fedora and loose-fitting suit, but one that fit him so authentically it could have been tailored for him?

Who was Griffin Shaw?

Fleur swung a hip, the bullfighter cape flaring, letting out a whistle as she turned away from the window. "Looks like Handsome and Exciting's illegitimate love child."

"More like Terse and Cryptic's outlaw cousin," Kit muttered, following.

Fleur raised a brow as she gestured to her chair. "Sounds like your type," she said, though she didn't say it like it was a good thing.

Kit made a face, but the tension left her as Fleur swiveled her around to face the mirror. Unfortunately, tension was the fundamental ingredient keeping her upright. Kit met her friend's eyes in the mirror, and they both fell still. It was only the welling tears, but the mirror seemed like a water wall, reflecting all the grief Kit had dammed up just to keep moving.

"Nic loved this place," she said, voice breaking.

She had, in fact, been the one to encourage Fleur to open it two years earlier. Fleur had been cutting and coloring their hair since junior high. She'd given Kit her first Middy haircut, and taught her how to do a proper Victory Roll. Making a living was incidental.

"I should pay my clients," Fleur had protested, when approached by Nic and Kit with the idea of the salon. "They allow me to touch them in an intimate way. Lovers are allowed to touch a person's hair and head. Parents and children. Other than that, it's a social taboo."

But Fleur's passion for her art made it impossible not to

think of her as an intimate friend. Even Marin softened under Fleur's loving touch. Kit brought her aunt in after chemo turned the stubble from her once-blond hair to gray ash, and Fleur handled the new tufts like priceless china, saying each strand gleamed with wisdom and experience and strength. Marin sailed from her chair like she had wings of silver, and it was that intimacy and touch Kit needed today.

Too bad there wasn't a way to explain that to Grif.

Leaning forward, Fleur wrapped her arms around Kit, so close to her neck that she tensed for a moment, remembering the violation of the night before. Then she relaxed, the embrace soothing her like a balm. "I didn't want to bring it up first. You were besties. But, oh, I'm going to miss her."

Kit rose at that, and they hugged hard. "Nic's gone, and the whole world is worse for it."

That was the real tragedy, the constant heartbreak that'd remained with Kit in the long night of her undreaming. So they wept in each other's arms, in lieu of the friend they really wanted to hold, and while they did, Kit couldn't help thinking it was their duty to fully embrace this life, if only because Nic no longer could.

And fight for her, too, Kit thought, pulling away and wiping at her face. She sniffled, and looked into Fleur's no longer so-perfectly-powdered face. She sniffled again. "Nic would hate what I've done with my hair."

Fleur pursed pinup lips. "Yes. She would."

They laughed, without humor, before falling silent, each feeling the moment moving away, but neither wishing to leave Nic's memory behind. But that was life, wasn't it? It went on.

Or, sometimes, it was interrupted by Buddy Holly's "It Doesn't Matter Anymore."

Kit wiped her face as she pulled her cell from her leopard-print bag. Fleur leaned over her shoulder, and Kit caught the distaste on her friend's face in the mirror. "Well, now the ringtone makes sense."

Kit shook her head sadly as she sat again, silencing the call and erasing Paul's accompanying picture at the same time. "I actually used to like that song."

She'd picked it for him because it'd annoy him if he ever heard it, a virtual impossibility but a pleasing idea all the same. It also reminded her of the cool, gradual way he'd let Kit—and the rest of the world—know how important he planned to be. Only a few summers ago had they listened to it and other rockabilly songs in what Kit had begun thinking of as the beginning of the end of their relationship. They'd driven down the Strip in her convertible, the hot night whispering against their soft skin, smiling as they ignored the sweat because sweat was what they did back then.

But by Christmas everything had grown cold, and he was telling stories that rarely included her, and making plans that never did. They drove down the same stretch of asphalt with the top up, and he spent the whole time pointing out the things he intended to leave behind, mostly places and memories they'd shared. Then it was on to talk about a law appointment he felt entitled to, a potential summer internship with a political candidate she already found suspect, and a disdain for her clothing, her alternative lifestyle . . . her.

Kit knew he thought he was sharing his dreams with her, but by then it could have been anyone riding alongside him in that car.

"Ah, he loved you," Fleur said unconvincingly, when Kit shared these thoughts with her.

"Please," Kit said, tossing the phone back into her bag. "The only bone in my body he ever loved was his."

"Shh. Not so loud." Fleur held her scissors to the side as she leaned close, voice melodramatic. "Contact shame."

"Was he really that bad?" Kit asked, though what she was really wondering was, Was I really that blind?

"Don't worry, honey," Fleur said, scissors flying like she could snip away Kit's worry along with her split ends. "We've all had judgment lapses that had us tiptoeing toward our own personal apocalypse. Besides, Paul started out all right. Then he was tainted by the lure of zeroes in his bank account."

"A need for obscene wealth is just a symptom of his disease."

"Which is?"

"A profound lack of self-worth."

Fleur snorted. "That's because deep down he knows he gets through life on white male privilege and looks rivaling Narcissus. I mean, what kind of man looks over his shoulder just to see who's watching him?"

Kit thought about the way Grif had walked away from her—back ramrod-straight, steps even and unhurried and sure—never once looking back. "Yeah, well you know Paul. He wants to give the appearance of being 'fiscally sound.'"

"Fiscally sound?"

Kit held up her palms. "His words, not mine."

"I'm fiscally sound," Fleur declared after a moment. "I'm a sound thousandaire."

Kit snorted. "I'm potentially wealthy, but totally unsound."

"And he loved you because of the first part of that sentence." Fleur smiled through the mirror. "The rest of us love you because of the last."

"Unsound is a good adjective. Unfortunately, Paul has other adjectives for me." Stubborn. Irresponsible. Strange.

Sensing the serious turn, Fleur cleared her throat. "Enough about Paul. He's so fake he should have 'Made in China' stamped on his ass. Tell me about Mr. Tall, Dark, and Dangerous. Let this old married woman live vicariously through you."

Kit rolled her eyes—Fleur was both younger than her *and* insatiably hot for her rocker husband—but she went with it, spilling everything about the previous night, how she'd been nearly dead on her feet—too sad, exhausted, and outnumbered to do much more than flail when she'd been attacked in her own home. "One guy was a cop, we think. I'm sure he had some part in Nic's death. I don't know about the other, but Grif drove both of them away."

Fleur, who'd fallen utterly still at the beginning of the telling, came to life, waving her scissors and comb around so wildly *she* looked homicidal. "But you have to go to the police!"

"Did you hear the part about my attacker being a policeman?"

"But your bruises . . ." Fleur touched Kit's neck gingerly now, like she was breakable. Kit gritted her teeth, and shooed her away.

"I'm fine. And Grif has promised to protect me."

With raised brows, Fleur motioned around the salon, empty but for the two of them.

"I'm not in any danger right now," Kit said hurriedly. She hoped. "And I'm sure he's doing something to further our investigation." She hoped.

"Your *investigation*?" Fleur's eyes went round, her arms falling slack. "Kit!"

"You didn't see him, okay?" Kit said, holding up a hand. "He's a fighter, and . . . cranky."

"Cranky?"

"I mean, tough, but gentle enough with me. Well, gentle-ish. Plus . . ." She let her words trail off into a mumble.

"I'm sorry. Can you repeat that?" Leaning over the chair, Fleur looked directly into Kit's eyes. "You saw black wings flare from his back right after he saved your life?"

Kit pushed her away. "I told you I was tired!"

Fleur shook her head, catching herself before she ran her hands through her pin curls. "Gee, honey. Project much?"

"I know, I know." Kit rolled her eyes. "It was the muscle relaxer. The drink."

Fleur winced. "The grief."

"Yeah." Tears threatened to spill again. Besides, if there really were such things as angels, Nic would still be here.

Fleur lifted her scissors, resumed snipping. "The question now is, how'd this Griffin Shaw get in your house?"

"Followed the others, I guess."

"And hid in the bedroom before them?" Fleur said skeptically.

"I don't know," Kit admitted, because the question had been niggling at her, too.

"Kit . . ."

"Don't give me that look."

"The one that says exciting and scary aren't the same thing? The one that says bad boys have *never* been good for you?"

"Yes. That one."

"But *is* he dangerous?"

Kit bit her lip, then nodded. "He wears it like that suit of his. Loose and roomy, like he's always on the edge of a punch."

"Damn," she said, then added, "That is hot."

"I know." But Kit also knew that Grif was somehow broken. She'd seen it when he was talking about his grandmother, that Evelyn woman, and in the way his expression shuttered when she teased him. It was strange, but also intriguing.

"As long as he's not dangerous to you," Fleur said, though it was a question.

"Look, he's helping me when no one else will, so I'm inclined to trust him," Kit replied slowly, then shook her head, which Fleur stilled with her palms, before she resumed cutting. "No, 'inclined' isn't the word."

"Compelled?" Fleur offered, knowing how Kit loved precision in her words.

"Yes."

"Moved? Driven? Fated?"

"Yes. That's it."

"Which?"

Kit offered up a lopsided smile. "All of them."

"Damn it, Kit."

"I know."

It was dangerous to overlook the way he'd slipped into her home. And scary.

And exciting.

"He's helping me," she repeated, more to herself than Fleur. Helping protect her, helping her find out what happened to Nic, helping her get out of bed and keep moving on a day when it would have been easier to just disappear.

But she'd gone that route once before, after her father's murder, and she'd take dangerous any day. That's why she was going to track down Nic's killer. And why she'd go head-to-head with a crooked cop. And why she needed to get her damned hair done. She needed time to think.

She was jolted from the thought by her phone, trilling in her lap with the notes from the past. Kit just looked at Fleur, who rolled her eyes.

"Ah, Paul," Fleur said, as Kit silenced the phone. "You are a bundle of nerves wrapped in a spray-on tan wrapped in a thousand-dollar suit."

"Ah, but he's fiscally sound."

"And a few other adjectives."

CHAPTER TEN

Anthony "The Cobra" Prima was twenty-four years old at the time of Grif's death, but had already been a lieutenant in the Chicago outfit of the Las Vegas mob. Despite being on what was essentially opposite sides of the law, he and Grif had hit it off fifty years earlier, due in part to an incident where Grif had crossed sides to deal with a card shark who was also responsible for early-morning stairwell rapes in the city's most glamorous properties. It was ironic that, of the two of them, Tony was the one to survive the era, but here he was—a spry, if bow-legged, seventy-four-year-old with an irreversible slouch and a bad case of psoriasis.

Prima's digs were in a neighborhood aging similarly to Kit's, with owners clearly obsessed with keeping bygone years alive. The most notable difference was that Tony's wrought-iron fencing was double-enforced, guarded by two Dobermans, and the home iced over with bulletproof windows overlooking a green where Sinatra had once allegedly sunk a hole in one—though the cart girls had never said which of them it was.

His security system would pass muster at NASA, and he had phone jacks in every bedroom closet, each of which turned into panic rooms at the touch of a button. Yet as state-of-the-art as his defenses were, they collectively spoke to the one thing that clearly hadn't changed in the last fifty years: Anthony Prima was as paranoid as ever.

Thus, it had to be disconcerting for the old coot to hear his bell ringing when the community's guard hadn't called, the gate opening when the voice box failed to signal, his perimeter breached when the alarm hadn't tripped, and a knock on the door almost no one ever touched.

I am the prodigal son, Grif thought, marveling at the way bolts gave under his touch. Sure, he was undeniably in the celestial doghouse, but for some reason he had a long etheric leash.

Ringing Prima's doorbell, listening to chimes that would do Liberace proud, he was just about to knock when a blast from above shattered the melody. Hunching, Grif dodged as the ground erupted beneath his feet. Concrete shrapnel trailed him as he fled, and he dove behind a planter as the unmistakable sound of bullets ricocheted to his left.

"Goddamn it, Tony!"

The potted bush in front of him lost its fringe.

Holding up his hand, he hoped the smooth magic he'd used to calm Kit wasn't lost in the frantic wave. "Stop firing, Prima!"

The tommy gun stuttered. Then an equally hesitant voice emerged from the ceiling speaker.

"Hello?"

Prima's voice came through the intercom system, staticky with suspicion and possibly something else. Fear? Excitement? *Agita?*

"Open up, Tony."

Silence. "Step into the outer foyer so I can see you."

Grif hesitated. The tiny rotunda could easily be jerry-rigged for explosives. If so, he might be back in the Everlast sooner than he thought. Straightening, he took a tentative step forward.

"Take off your hat."

Grif removed his stingy brim, and held it in front of him, turning his head up at the camera to give Tony a good, long look.

"Grif?" The static accentuated the disbelief. "Griffin Shaw?"

"Hello, Tony."

There was the scrape of multiple bolts being thrown, then the door gave way to a squinty blue eye and an errant tuft of wiry gray hair. "I heard you were dead," Tony said, with his characteristic candor.

Grif's stomach clenched. So *someone* knew he hadn't just disappeared. "Well, I'm happy to report that as a great exaggeration. Can I come in?"

Tony scoffed. "You *have* been gone a long time. Nobody comes in, Grif."

"C'mon," Grif said, shoving his hands in his pockets. "Old time's sake."

"The only old times we had together involved beating the shit out of some asshole in a urine-soaked stairwell."

"The good old days," Grif said, undeterred.

Tony opened the door wider, but left it bolted. "Then you disappeared, never to be seen again."

"You see me now," Grif pointed out.

"Yeah. You look good, too." Tony rubbed at his eyes. "Damned cataracts. It's like you hardly changed at all."

"Well, everyone's pretty well-preserved where I went."

"California, huh?" Tony huffed. "They didn't offer nothing like that to me. Know what they said when I asked about witness protection? Said I might skate on extortion and embezzlement, but I was still going to take a hit for tax evasion. I got two years then house arrest. Can you believe that?"

Grif just raised his brows. "You gonna let me in, Tony?"

The sole blue eye narrowed. "How do I know you're not here to kill me?"

Because there's not a hint of plasma around you, Grif thought. "Why would I kill you?"

Face creasing further, Tony thought about it. "Look, Grif. I know we go back a ways, but some things don't change. I don't throw good money after bad. I don't believe Joe Pesci just plays a made man on TV. And no one ever, ever comes into my home. Got it?"

Grif nodded. "Well, that's too bad, Tony. It really is."

Tony nodded back. It was.

Then Grif pulled his housewarming gift from behind his back. "Because I brought this."

Tony glanced down and let loose a deluge of Italian curses that would topple the famous tower in Pisa. Chest heaving, he glared at Grif. "All right. But just this once."

Grif handed him the bottle of vintage Sangiovese on the way in. "Don't forget to put out the dogs."

Once Tony got over the novelty of having someone in his home, once he stopped marveling over the way his Dobermans inexplicably turned into lapdogs around Grif—"But they don't like no one!"—and once he opened the bottle of wine and took solitary communion with the first few sips, he actually warmed to Grif's company.

Sitting in a living room wrapped in wall-to-wall shag, Grif looked around and decided the place couldn't be called retro. That was how Kit had referred to hers, but that would imply effort at gathering together items for a space to reflect a bygone era, and from what Grif could tell, the wood paneling and dark stone fireplace and built-in bar had been here from the first. Watching Tony recline on a sofa already molded to his frame, Grif thought of the genie in Aladdin's lamp, a man locked in luxury and a slave to the same.

Tony didn't seem to notice or mind. "Remember that time we set up the unsanctioned fights in the back of Vinnie Covelli's restaurant?"

"Vaguely," Grif said, but he couldn't fight the smile.

"Yeah, you remember," Tony said, pale eyes sparkling. "You won the whole thing, bare-knuckled."

They'd run that racket every weekend for months. It was how Grif had paid off Evie's diamond. "That was the last time I saw you," Grif said, smiling lightly.

Tony's smile faded. "Yeah. Yeah, I guess it was."

Grif leaned forward, casual-like, elbows on his knees. "So you heard I was dead, huh?"

A bony shoulder lifted and dropped, a slight movement that betrayed the gun beneath his sweater vest. "Just hearsay. Not solid, like with your Evie." Tony winced when Grif stiffened. "I'm sorry about that, by the way. She was a real gem. Had a way about her. Coulda given that Virginia Hill a run for her money, that's for sure."

Grif swallowed hard. "Yeah, well. It was a long time ago."

"Yet here you are," Tony pointed out. "Snooping around. Stirring the pot all over again."

He put up his hands at Grif's hard look, then reached forward for the pack of sticks in the middle of the giant coffee table.

"Grandkid?" Grif asked, jerking his head at the world's largest ceramic ashtray.

"Would I have anything this ugly in my house otherwise?" Tony lit up, tossed the pack over to Grif. "Listen, I'm not poking at old pains, or telling you to forgive and forget. I mean, look at me." He waved around the room as if it was an extension of his body. "My kids call this place a glass fishbowl. Say I should start charging people to stand out on the green and gawk at me like I'm in an aquarium. My plaque would read, 'Dago, in his natural habitat.'" He shook his head, his cigarette shaking between knuckles that'd outgrown their fingers. "They tell me the past is over. That it's a new world. But I know what I know."

"And what's that, Tony?"

He pointed his fingers at Grif, smoke trailing behind. "It ain't ever over. You can't have no future if you don't have no past, and the past ain't never done with you." He leaned back, nodding to himself. "At the end of your life, all you have is what you know."

Grif was well past the end of his life, and he knew things Tony couldn't even imagine. But he was right about fingering old pains. Grif wouldn't be here if he'd been able to just let it go. Then again, he thought, looking around at the museum Tony called a home, neither would Tony.

They both dragged on their smokes, neither of them looking at the other, comfortable enough until Tony said, "You really do look good, Grif."

Grif snorted. "Keep drinking, Tony."

But, as he said, despite his failing eyesight and obsession with fine Italian wine, Tony knew what Tony knew. "So what do you want with me? You're not here just to bring me gifts, or fill my ashtray."

"I'm back to find out who did it." Grif lifted a brow. "I could use a little help."

Tony looked down. Shook his head. "Like you said, Grif. It was a long time ago."

Grif felt his jaw tighten, stubborn as flint. "Doesn't make it right."

Tony laughed mirthlessly. "Lots of things weren't ever made right. They won't ever be right again, either. I mean, can you believe this country? You can bust your balls your entire life and have nothing to show at the end of it. Even this town has lost its entrepreneurial shine. And the government called *me* crooked."

Tony looked at him, but Grif wasn't interested in his self-pity. "There has to be someone."

"There ain't." He flicked ash.

"What about the old family?"

Tony licked his lips warily. "What about them?"

"They owe me."

Tony scoffed, voice gone gritty. "What, for saving their dear little Mary Margaret? Let me tell you what happened to that sweet, spoiled little schoolgirl. She took off that Catholic school uniform and it wasn't long before everything else followed. Took it upon herself to sully the family name and pushed her papa into an early grave."

"That's disappointing." Grif meant it. She'd been a cute kid.

"You always were a softie for the females, Grif." Tony blew out a stream of death, and stubbed out his smoke. "First Evie. Then Mary Margaret."

The frown came on slowly, but sank and hardened in his face. "What do you mean, 'first Evie'?"

Tony stiffened, and leaned back, his face carefully blank. "I just mean she was a bit wild before you reined her in. Couldn't do no wrong in your eyes. That's all."

No, Grif thought, studying Tony's poker face, there was more. But whatever he knew, whatever he *thought* he knew, amounted to squat in the wake of Evie's murder. He set his glass down and looked straight into that lying blue-eyed goombah gaze. "She never did anyone wrong, got it? And she ended up dead anyway."

Tony held up his hands. "All right. Don't bust a gut."

But Grif's blood was up, and suddenly he couldn't catch his breath. Without warning, a jutting pain knifed his skull, an arrow behind his eyeballs, and it wasn't just his renegade pulse, his unnatural breath, his unsanctioned life. It was more. It was his past busting in, reminding him he was dead. Walking, breathing, drinking, smoking—thinking and feeling—all without any mortal coil to reinforce his existence. There was a consciousness and a body, but it was flimsy, as if he lacked a spine. Very simply, there was nothing to hold it all up.

"Hey. You all right, Shaw?"

No. His mind was burning.

Tony's voice, worried now, crackled. "I got a white-glove service. The doc comes right to your door. You want I should call them?"

Grif's silence smoldered.

"I really think you need a doctor."

Grif pressed the heel of his hand to his head, like he could snuff the heat that way. What he needed was to get off this mudflat. Get back to the Everlast where the cool plasmic balm could soothe his mental ache. Where he could forget about dying and concentrate on being dead.

You can't have a future if you don't have no past.

Grif waited until his body stopped constricting around him to open his eyes. Breathing deeply, he looked at Tony—whose skin looked loose and lived-in and comfortable—and said, "Look, I don't have anyone else. I have no leads, I don't know anyone here. I don't even have a place to stay. To use your words, Tony, all I have is what I know. Right here," and he punched his own chest so hard that even Tony jumped. Grif's headache momentarily fell into second place in the race for pain, but like a stubborn heartbeat, it sped up again.

Tony said nothing for a long while. He just stared with his gray furrowed brow and for a moment Grif saw his pain, too. Fear lay inside him like a sleeping dragon. That was the real monster that guarded this house. "So what is it that you know, then?"

"Evie died because of me." As soon as Grif said the words aloud, his skull tried to constrict around his brain. He pushed back and the pressure actually dulled. "What I don't know is why."

Tony turned his head and gazed out the window. The golf course stretched before him like a green lake, the sky spun out beyond that, but Tony only stared. The fish, Grif thought, staring back out from the fishbowl. "I have a guest room," he finally said. "It's kinda girly, but . . ."

Grif raised his brows.

Tony looked him straight in the eye, and gave him the death stare that had earned him his nickname. "I'm going to need some more of this Sangiovese."

Grif leaned back with a sigh, picked up his own glass, and let the fine wine pave a cool path through his core. When his agitated heartbeat had settled and his vision was steady, he nodded, then said, "So, backing up. Who told you, all those years ago, that I was dead?"

The hair appointment put her at ease. By the time Kit was back on the curb, the strain behind her eyes from trying not to cry was gone, and the hunch in her shoulders had been massaged away by Fleur's magic fingers. They'd also decided, impulsively, that a fresh look would go a long way to bolstering her energy, so instead of a mere trim, Fleur added a white stripe to the right side of Kit's Bettie bangs, pin-curling it to the left so that it rose over her forehead like a cresting wave. It was a look Nic had adored, her favorite go-to do when out for a tiki convention or car show.

"There," Fleur had said, pinning a matching white flower behind Kit's ear—one she'd crafted herself. "Now you're undercover."

She was put back together at least, Kit thought, catching a movement from the corner of her eye as she slid her key into the car lock. She looked over just as Grif materialized from the alley, sudden and smooth, like some battle-scarred tomcat who'd seen it all. Relief rushed Kit. She hadn't been sure if he would come back.

Stepping up onto the curb, she squared on him, and spent a moment studying his face. His hair was short and razored, but what peeked from beneath his fedora was rust-colored and matched the stubble along his chin. The wide build and bull's neck spoke to an easy masculinity hidden beneath the heavy trench, and the gruff scowl put Kit in mind of scar tissue, as if a hard expression could keep any hard thing from touching him.

Was that right? Did nothing touch this man?

She was still wondering this when she saw something that had her doing so anyway. "What the hell happened?" The panic she felt earlier returned, its strength surprising her, but there was dried blood on one side of his wide neck and face. She looked down, and grabbed his hand. It was there, too.

"I got shot at by a tommy gun. Only hit cement, but the cement hit me."

Gut still kicking, she shot him a look, and cupped the back of his neck. He pulled back, but she held tight, pushing his head to the side. "I'm not kidding, Grif. You're *bleeding*."

He put a tentative hand to his neck. His fingertips brushed up against hers, held for one charged moment, then slid away. "That is strange."

He looked a little unsteady as he backed away, lifting his hat to run a hand over his head, and swaying slightly on his feet. It made Kit want to touch the untouchable again. Instead she wrapped her arms around her middle. "Sure you're okay?"

"Fine," he said, resettling his hat before jerking his chin at her. "Your hair looks . . . different."

"Thank you." She accepted it as a compliment, even with the accompanying nose wrinkle. "I feel better."

Grif shoved his hands into his pockets. "You look like Tonga Lily, but without the English subtitles."

Kit beamed. "I'm impressed. Not many people know their Mexican film history so well, even among us billies."

There was that nose wrinkle again, followed by a frown that Kit had to fight not to reach out and try to stroke from his face. He wouldn't like that, she thought, and it worried her slightly that in spite of knowing it, she still wished to do so. Clearing her throat, she pitched her voice higher. "I got a chance to talk to Fleur about Nic, too."

"Guess that's why you really needed to go there." He gave that hard squint from beneath the brim of his hat again, but this time he nodded. Kit realized it was his way of apologizing and she nodded back, happy to accept it.

"Nic's funeral isn't until Wednesday, but the gang is getting together tonight to celebrate her life. We're going to give her a proper rockabilly send off. She'd like that."

Grif's eyes met hers. "Want me to be there?"

"Of course," she said, realizing she did. She still had reservations about his sudden appearance in her life—her *house*—but not as many as she had about going it alone. Besides, "My friends will love you."

"Yes, I'm very lovable."

Another apology. She laughed, and felt better. One corner of his mouth quirked up, too, and for one dizzying moment they stared. He broke first, and Kit cleared her throat. "Warning, though. My peeps are nosy. They'll ask questions, prod. Relentlessly."

"So they're like you?"

"A lot like us both, I think." She took a step forward, and this time she did reach out, touching his arm. "Look, I'm sorry about before—"

"No, I am—"

Kit shook her head, silencing him. "I was thinking about it. I took a minute to put myself in your . . . well, that woman's,

Evelyn's, position—which, in the end, is the exact same as my Nic's—and I decided that if I were her? I'd want to know who killed me."

Grif fell very still. "You would?"

"Yes." Kit nodded. "I'd want to know why. Why my death was fated to come early, why my life was cut short. Who killed me? What happened to those I left behind?" She lifted a shoulder. "Wouldn't you?"

"Yeah, I do."

"What?"

"I said, yes." He cleared his throat, squinting off into the sky. "Though some say it doesn't matter. Anything we need to know, we'll discover in due time. The rest is not for us."

"Oh, I know those types."

Grif kept his gaze turned upward. "I doubt you know these types."

"But I do," Kit protested. "They came out of the woodwork after each of my parents died, especially my father. Said things like 'let it go' and 'it won't hurt so much with time' and 'you need to move on.'"

Grif's expression darkened at that. Scar tissue, Kit thought. Only loss could put that look on someone's face. Yet it wasn't a look that'd ever fit Kit, despite her losses. Even now, even after what happened to Nic, she still had a need to believe that most people, that most of life, was good. That belief was a sort of strength, too.

"Forgive and forget," she said, trying to lighten his mood. "That's the Christian way, right?"

"Something like that," he said, tone noncommittal. More danger, she thought. More complication.

More to discover.

"Well, if I were Nic," she said, squaring her shoulders, "or your Evelyn, I'd want someone to get those answers. I'd hope that someone would stick around and remember me like that."

Grif surprised her then by stepping forward and placing his own hand on her arm, and when she looked into his eyes, she was further surprised. They weren't hard after all. On the contrary, the blue irises practically pulsed with pain. "You really should run, Ms. Craig."

She blinked, taken aback by the earnest whisper. She didn't doubt he'd seen things she hadn't, but this was different. This was like he knew something she didn't.

"I've been visited by death before, Mr. Shaw," she said, and for some reason that made him flinch and swallow hard. "I told you before, I'm a newswoman, and not as a vocation. As a way of life. I can make a difference in the lives of total strangers. Why wouldn't I do the same for myself? For Nic?"

"Because it's dangerous."

Kit shook her head. "I know myself, and I need to find out who did this if I'm ever to have true peace."

"Enroll in a pottery class," he said, dropping his arm. "Inner peace is one clay ashtray away."

Her arm burned where he'd touched her, but she ignored it and lifted her chin. "The questions that remain after someone close to you dies don't die with them. I don't care what the armchair preachers say, there's no real forgive-and-forget because you can't ever forget. But you already know that, don't you, Grif?" When he didn't answer, Kit offered up a small smile. "She's lucky to have you, you know. Your Evelyn."

He blinked a handful of times, like he was having trouble bringing her into focus, then softly corrected, "Evie."

"Oh. That's pretty." Kit smiled, though some baser emotion moved oddly in her belly. Someone should speak *her* name so gently, she thought, then cleared her throat. "Well, you might be happy to know that I did some work while I was in Fleur's chair. Your Evie's case went cold because there were no leads, except for one. Her husband."

"What?"

Kit pulled out her smart phone, and scrolled until she found the notes she'd taken. "His name was Griffin, too. Your grandfather, I presume?"

Grif really did sway at that, putting a hand to his forehead, pressing like he was trying to still spinning thoughts. "Um . . ."

"He went missing after Evie died. Never seen again." She looked down. "How old would that guy be now, anyway? Eighty-three?"

"Eighty-four," Grif said quietly.

Abruptly, the phone rang again in Kit's hand. She opened her mouth, prepared to curse at Paul's insistent image again, but to her surprise, Marin's avatar popped up on her screen. "Tell me," she said, signaling to Grif to hold on.

"Got a hit."

She smiled and gave Grif a thumbs-up. "So hit me."

"Ran a search on our boy Schmidt, got a little more on his prior infractions. That's already waiting in your inbox, but it's mostly just specifics on what we already knew. Surprise, surprise, he was once named a suspect in a domestic violence charge, though his girlfriend dropped charges almost as soon as she'd filed them. Guess what she did after that."

"Went poof?" Kit said.

The affirmation was in Marin's tone. "I'm looking into it, but the main issue now is that the man seems to have a distinct lack of respect for women. Not a great attribute in someone who holds authority over a bunch of female minors the system doesn't know how to help and barely wants to acknowledge."

"Think he's abusing that authority?"

"I'd bet the paper on it."

Kit's adrenaline kicked in again. With fear, yes. But there was also fury building inside of her. This man had killed Nic. She *knew* it. But he also abused his power over kids who were already hurting and lost and vulnerable. She knew that, too. And now he was after her.

And Kit was going to prove it all.

"So what do you have that I can follow?"

"Bridget Moore. She's twenty-seven years old, but was only nineteen the first time Schmidt busted her. She's been through the system four times since then, the last just eighteen months ago, again by Schmidt."

"Bookended her career?"

"Probably scared her straight."

He'd scare me, Kit thought, remembering the way he'd barreled her way. For comfort, she looked over at Grif. He glowered at her. Comforted, she smiled.

"Wanna take a guess as to where her last bust went down?"

"The Wayfarer Motel," Kit said, already connecting the dots. Same place Nic had died. "I'm on her."

"Contact info is in a separate file, also in your inbox."

"Think Moore knows who's pulling Schmidt's strings?"

"If she does, she's keeping her mouth shut, but she's been

on the streets a long time. Working girls talk to each other. It keeps them alive. Just don't give away that you're sniffing around Schmidt in advance. Instinct tells me that would have her rabbiting before you can look her in the eye."

I'm surprised she hasn't already, Kit thought, and she got an unbidden flash—the memory of his fist flying her way in the dark. The hard fingers pawing at her robe and skin before that. And Grif intercepting it all.

"Is Bogart still with you?" asked Marin, reading her mind.

"Yes."

"Let me talk to him."

Kit held out the phone to Grif, who eyed it warily, but eventually put it to his ear and grunted a few times before handing it back. "What'd she say?"

"Be careful."

Kit lifted a brow. Marin had said more than that, but she could guess the rest. Shoving her hands into her pockets, she looked up at Grif. "I meant what I said before. Evie's lucky to have someone like you fighting for her after all these years. All these girls out here . . ." She shook her head. "No one's fighting for them."

"You are."

That almost brought a smile. "So are you."

"I'm just working a case."

"Don't give me that, Griffin Shaw," she said, jerking her head toward her car. "I'm on to you."

He opened the passenger door. "Are you?"

"Yes. You're cranky . . . but kinda sweet."

He stopped dead and leveled her with a stare over the hood. "Like bitterroot."

"You're sweet," Kit practically sang. She hopped in, and waited until he'd done the same to look over at him. "And I bet you already have a plan for trapping Schmidt."

"Sure." He ignored the seat belt.

"See." She turned to him. "What is it?"

Grif smiled sweetly. "I'm going to use you as bait."

CHAPTER ELEVEN

All Grif wanted was a drink. The headache that'd been dogging him was regaining force, despite the shut-eye he'd managed to squeeze in once he finally convinced Tony to let Kit into the fishbowl. Though that had been another headache altogether.

"C'mon, Tony. She won't break nothing but your heart," he said, edging in and putting out the dogs himself. Tony protested, and Kit took it as a compliment, both of which caused Grif to shake his head as he made for his room. The last thing he heard before slamming the bedroom door was her blue-jay voice asking her reluctant host for Internet access.

Of course, he knew why his headache wouldn't abate. Ol' Kitty-cat had gut-punched him with the news that he was the prime suspect in Evie's death. As if anyone who knew him, or them, could think such a thing. At least now he knew why

Tony initially asked if he was there to kill him, and why he seemed unsure of Grif still.

Five hours later, zipping down Charleston in Kit's foreign tin can, Grif had figured a few other things out. Whoever had offed him in the bungalow all those years ago had immediately moved his body and set him up . . . though knowing that didn't make it any more palatable. He was still dead. So was dear Evie. No wonder Grif's soul couldn't move on. No wonder his head pounded like the ocean crested inside of it.

It was only when Kit sighed next to him that he realized she'd silenced the car. Lifting his head, he caught her gazing at a pink neon sign, her face turned up so that her profile damn near glowed. His breath caught, and another pulsing began inside of him, this one lower.

I promise to protect you, he thought, as if speaking aloud. He watched her chest rise and fall with the breath she was entitled to because she was good and innocent and in his charge.

I won't allow another woman to die because of me.

It was as if she heard him. Slowly, she turned her head, and the warmth in her eyes was like a spotlight, centered on thoughts so deep and feelings so acute that Grif could almost feel them.

"Frankie's Tiki Room," Kit said solemnly. "The only twenty-four-hour tiki bar in the country."

Grif sighed.

"Nic's favorite bar."

Grif canvassed the parking lot for danger, though he relaxed his guard as soon as they entered the bar. The whole joint has been marinated in 120-proof rum.

Lighted blowfish and miniature tiki huts were pinned to a ceiling covered in fishing nets, with a poker-playing tiki god positioned dead-center of the entrance. The bar was directly across from that, wall-to-wall bottles broken up only by a screen at either end, currently showing what looked like old black-and-white Hawaiian porn. To get there, though, you had to cross an expanse of walls made of woven grass mats, bamboo spears, and carved tiki masks. The ceiling was black lava. The music was James Bond.

This was where they were going to celebrate a dead girl's life?

"Kitty!" A high-pitched voice reached out from the crowded room to grab Kit's attention. She waved back, and set off in that direction. Edging cautiously around the tiki god, Grif shot the statue and its base of faux flame an uncertain look, and followed Kit to the bamboo bar. Waiting for him was a coterie of women so brightly dressed and painted that they looked like exotic birds tucked into the tropical environment. Grif had to clench his teeth against the racket of their chirping voices until the greetings were over.

"Girls," Kit said, when the ruckus had died down. "This is Griffin Shaw. Grif, this is Fleur Fontaine, Lil DeVille, Merrily Monroe, and the knocked-up one is Charis."

Charis gave a little wave, then pointed at a car seat next to her. "This one is mine, too. But I figured out how it's done now, so there won't be a third."

Kit put her arm around Charis's shoulders and squeezed encouragingly, then turned to Grif. "Along with Nicole Nouveau—whom you knew as Nicole Rockwell—we are the Pretty Kitty Posse."

The five women beamed. The miniature one in the safety seat—outfitted in a black dress dotted with white skulls—gurgled. Grif frowned. "Don't any of you have normal names?"

"Just Kit-Kat," said Lil, flicking a hand Kit's way before straightening the collar on her blue-and-white sailor's dress.

"Only because I have to play it straight for the byline," Kit said, wrinkling her nose like that was a bad thing. It was then that it finally came together for Grif. The girls were corner pieces in a puzzle that set the whole picture to light: the furnishings in Kit's house, one where Grif felt perfectly at home. Her car, her clothes, her friends and their hairstyles—the likes of which he hadn't seen since he was alive. Even this place, Grif thought, studying the woven grass-mat walls. It was a modern nod to kitsch, to Vegas's heyday, to the South Seas and the world war he remembered . . . yet his time wasn't modern anymore.

"Let me get this straight. You all dress up like you're from the fifties? You—what'd you call 'em, billies?—live your lives in the past?"

"We live nostalgically," Merrily corrected. Grif looked at her, eyes catching on a cherry tattoo peeking from the sleeve of her right arm. "It's fun."

"Fun," Grif repeated flatly, pulling his gaze from her inked arm, only to have it fall on Fleur's, who also had two cherries seared to her arm. They were integrated with a horseshoe, and a row of flaming dice. What the hell?

"It's not just women," Fleur said, amusement lacing her tone as she shifted, revealing more ink. A mermaid flicked its blue-green tail Grif's way. "Plenty of men live the rockabilly lifestyle, too."

Grif looked around, realizing she was right. There were as many men here as women, all greased and suited up, either playing an electric guitar or dancing to one.

"And it's not only the fifties," Kit put in, "though that's my favorite, too."

"You just like crinoline," said Fleur.

"I do," Kit admitted, with a small shudder. "And the capris, the knit sweaters, the cupcake dresses . . ."

"The boys with pomps and high-waisted jeans," Charis said dreamily, chucking her baby under her chin. The little girl smiled.

"Nic loved the music," Kit said. "She always said it was so *alive*."

They were all silent for a time after that. Grif, feeling the pressure to stave off some serious waterworks, huffed and crossed his arms. "Yeah, but none of you really lived it." His assertion was met with dumb silence. "I mean, it's swell that you'd romanticize an entire era, but you don't know what it was really like."

"Excuse me," Fleur said sharply, hands on her hips, "but that's a straight-razored do, if I'm not mistaken, and I can see the pomade greasing each strand. What brand do you use?"

"Pluko."

She smirked, red shiny lips twisting knowingly. "That and no other, I bet. And those are vintage Stacy Adams wingtips, am I right?"

Grif looked at his shoes. She was. But Grif was also the original owner.

"Taking the retro-P.I. thing a bit far, aren't we?" she teased, with a raised brow.

"No such thing," Kit said, mistakenly thinking Grif needed rescue. "I personally find it a refreshing change from all the greasers and swing kids."

"So do I," said a new voice, directly over Grif's shoulder. The faces of the women in front of him soured and he turned to find a platinum blonde poured into leopard print. Long black lashes winged from doe-soft eyes, and her red lips were cushioned in a pout rather than a sneer.

"Bombshell" was the first word that came to Grif's mind. "Calculating" was the second. She edged between Fleur and Grif like the giant cat she was fashioned after. "Though I prefer the pinup period. Neo-burlesque is my poison. Perhaps because I do it so well."

"Grif, this is Layla Love," Kit said, and though she hadn't moved an inch, her voice was tighter than it'd been moments before. "Layla, Griffin Shaw."

Layla's mouth twitched as she inched closer so that her arm was touching his. "So. I hear you're Kit's knight in shining armor. A real hero."

"Not exactly," Grif said, taking a full step back. The woman smiled like it was some sort of battle won.

"A protector, though." She tilted her head, and sent long blond waves swinging. "Like some sort of guardian angel?"

"I wouldn't say guardian."

"Good," she said, and her hand closed over his, and squeezed. "Then Kit won't mind if I borrow you. I love this song. And I'm always looking for a new partner."

Layla commandeered the crook of his arm, but Fleur intervened, and her touch—laid over them both—was less gentle. "There aren't really enough boys to go around, but since my man is busy rocking out, I'll dance with you, Layla. You know how I love to Lindy."

Layla edged back toward Grif. "Well, I don't—"

"And this was Nic's favorite jive," Fleur added with a sigh, and even Grif could tell there was nothing Layla could say to that. They turned arm in arm, Layla shooting one final glance at Grif over her bare shoulder, but tension left the bar like a giant exhalation. Charis promptly groaned. "Good Jesus, look what else the cat dragged in."

"You mean, coughed up," Merrily muttered into her tiki mug, staring at the entrance like she wanted to open fire.

Before Grif could turn, Kit rose from her barstool, putting a staying hand on his shoulder as she edged around him. "Will you excuse me?"

"Who's that?" Grif muttered, and this time it was his voice that was tight as he watched Kit approach a man who was tall, well dressed, and so good-looking he was almost pretty.

Merrily read his mind. "Oh, that's Pretty Paul," she said, painted mouth curled in distaste.

Charis tsk-ed. "Don't let Kit hear you say that."

"Why?" Grif asked, feeling something in his belly grow claws as the two drew close.

"Because digging on him is old sport and she'd rather have moved on to the new." Charis looked at Grif pointedly, then jerked her head. "Paul Raggio is Kit's ex-husband."

Grif did a double take, and the clawed thing in his stomach also grew fangs.

Kit headed toward Paul as if forced at gunpoint. She was annoyed with him for reasons she couldn't name—even though he'd tried to call her back, and she'd been the one to respond with silence. She was also annoyed with herself for being annoyed. Nothing he did should matter to her anymore. He'd made that clear enough last night. "Hello, Paul. Slumming?"

He didn't correct her. Instead, he quirked a perfectly waxed brow and dug a deeper hole. "Can we talk outside, Katherine? The colors in this place are making me nauseous."

His automatic turn toward the door, and unspoken assumption that she'd follow, didn't endear him to her any further. She planted herself next to a wooden island warrior with far more personality than her ex-husband would ever have. "It's Nic's wake, Paul."

He glanced over at her sharpened tone, caught the way her arms were folded over her chest—let his gaze linger, too, on the flare of her hip—then predictably honed his own voice. "I know. I had to convince Marin to tell me where it was."

Considering the way Paul and her aunt felt about each other, it *was* a lot of trouble. Kit softened, giving him a short nod. "Well, Nic would have been glad you came."

"Oh." Paul's brows pulled low. "Yeah."

Kit's hard exhale hugged a silent curse, and she shook her head and turned away. Paul lunged, his hand tense on her forearm. "Hey," he said. "You're the one who wanted my help, remember?"

Yes, she remembered. She remembered begging him to stay with her. She also recalled being left alone to face a night that could easily have been her last. That, she realized, was why she was miffed. He'd walked away again. He'd left her vulnerable. Again.

"Well, I don't need your help anymore," she said, surprising them both. She yanked her arm away, but he held on tight. "Grif and I are working on it."

"Who's Grif?"

"I am." The voice rose over her shoulder just as the shadow stretched over Paul. Kit's back warmed with his body heat, though chills raced over the front of her body—either pleasure at the way he leaned into her or satisfaction at the way Paul straightened. Probably both.

"Griffin Shaw," she introduced, without looking back. "Paul Raggio. Paul, *this* is Grif."

Paul spared Grif the same look he gave all her billy boys, offensively dismissive until Grif also placed his hand on Kit's arm, causing Paul's to fall away. "Who are you supposed to be?" Paul asked, eyes narrowing at the way Grif tucked Kit close to his side. It felt like she was nesting there. Like she fit, and was safe.

"Whoever she needs me to be."

Usually Kit would have worked to smooth over the awkward silence, but Paul's normally placid face had gone puce in the torchlight. His expression also hardened, not dissimilar to a tiki god about to rip the top off of a volcano. But it was Grif who really held her in thrall. His hands were shoved into his pockets, a casualness belied by his wide stance. And he was too still. Like he was waiting. Like he was hunting.

Paul waved Grif away with manicured fingers, and reached around him for Kit again. "Well, can you give us some privacy, please?"

"No."

Paul froze. Grif remained still, keeping him in his sights. Kit wished desperately for popcorn to go along with the show. Alas, Nic's wake was no place for a scene. Sighing, she told Paul, "I was attacked last night after I got home from work."

He was suddenly listening, which was something, but Kit wanted more, and so she added, "Grif saved me."

"Jesus, Kit. Why didn't you—" He stuttered, because she

had called him. He lifted his chin, and stood taller. "Well, you can fall back now, Shaw. Katherine doesn't need protection from me."

"But she needs it all the same."

Paul, slightly taller than Grif, stepped forward. "And you're the man?"

Grif squared up. "I'm just the man."

Kit sucked in a deep breath and held it, slightly high from all the testosterone. But she should stop this.

In a moment.

"Fine." Paul blinked first, sniffing before looking at Kit. "I just wanted to tell you that Caleb Chambers is having another ball."

"You came all the way down here to tell her about a party?"

This time Paul ignored Grif completely, though Kit stayed him with a hand on his arm. It would do no good to push Paul to petulance. Experience had taught her that much. Still she left her hand on Grif's arm. His warmth and strength and presence had butterflies cannonballing into her gut. "You could have left me a message."

"It's a Valentine's Day benefit for children in need of heart and lung transplants," Paul replied, like that explained everything. "Most of the players on your list will be there. I can get you a ticket."

"You'll have to make it a pair."

Impatiently, Paul turned and looked Grif up and down. It was challenging, but Grif didn't wilt. In fact, he seemed to grow two feet under the scrutiny, like a cobra flaring its hood.

"It's a *charity* ball," Paul clarified, his pretty face twisting in an ugly way.

"Oh." Grif frowned. "Then she probably should go with you."

Kit snorted before she could help it.

"I've already got a date," Paul said tightly. "It's Valentine's Day."

"I think we're free. Thank you, Paul," Kit intervened again, but hoped that somewhere, in some other realm, Nic could see Paul getting cranked up about his ex-wife and some moody stranger.

"So have you learned anything else about the list?" Paul asked abruptly.

"Thought that's why she gave it to you, ace."

Though she didn't want to, Kit put a hand on Grif's arm. "Grif, would you give us a minute?"

"Yeah," said Paul, like he'd won the moment.

"Sure. I can do that." Grif nodded, and began to turn away, but paused halfway to level Paul with the same stare she'd first seen, when he'd been bounding from the shadows to beat another man to the ground on her behalf. "By the way," he said, "her name isn't Katherine. It's Kit."

And, mouth half-open, Kit watched him stalk to the bar, noting the way the women there opened up to him, reacting as instinctively to that coiled *maleness* as she did. He glanced back to make sure she was fine, and Kit shivered. She already knew he wasn't a man who normally glanced back.

"What the hell is up with that guy?" Paul said, face twisted like he'd just eaten something sour. But Grif's eyes were still trained on her, even with Layla chatting him up, and suddenly Kit didn't want to talk about him with Paul. In fact, watching Layla gesture animatedly, she wanted to keep him all to herself.

"Do you want to hear about the list or not?" she asked impatiently.

Paul held out his hands, like he'd been waiting for that all along.

Kit chided herself for ever thinking he'd come because of Nic. "I've winnowed it to one name."

Paul's brow rode high. "In one day?"

"The man who attacked me last night is on there, Paul. His name is Lance Schmidt, but he's not a politician. He's a cop."

Paul frowned. "How'd a cop get on that list?"

That was his response?

"I don't think you heard me," she said tightly. "Schmidt attacked me, hit me, and I believe would have killed me if Grif hadn't been there to stop him."

"But he was," Paul said blandly, glancing at Grif like he was the one under suspicion. "Why?"

Oh my God, Kit thought, jaw clenching. How could she have forgotten. It was always, ever, about *him*. "What time does the damned ball start?"

"What, now you're pissed?" He put on his wounded pout, then gave an eye roll when she didn't answer. "Seven sharp."

"Can you get two tickets or not?"

"Sure," he said snidely. "Though I can't promise any cops . . . outside of security, that is."

"No, Schmidt will be there," Kit muttered, staring past him at the bamboo entry. "I know it."

"Whatever," Paul said, turning away. "Just dress appropriately. Chambers lavishes his woman with jewels. And tell Joe Friday over there that it's black-tie only. If he's got one."

And before Kit could form a retort, before he so much as mentioned Nicole's name or death, Paul exited into the night in the exact way he'd exited their marriage. Glancing back only once to make sure she didn't follow.

* * *

Grif watched Kit talk with Paul, wondering how she'd ever gotten mixed up with a piker like that. He was a swaggering suntan. She was a mysterious moonbeam. Their marriage must have been a terrestrial collision.

At least the rum was dulling his headache. As was Charis's second rescue of him from that wildcat, Layla. Though Charis had told the other woman she needed to speak with him privately, and commandeered a low table in the lounge's dimly lit corner, he still glanced over to make sure he was out of Layla's sights before hunching over his weird tiki mug.

"Don't mind her," Charis said, one hand rocking the baby in the seat next to her as she caught his look. "She's a cougar. Or, if you're being era-appropriate, a minx."

"And I bet she's always era-appropriate."

"About the only thing I like about her," Charis grudgingly admitted, leaning forward to tuck a blanket beneath her little girl's chin. The baby immediately pulled it off. "Though she came into a bundle of money, so that helps."

"A little princess, huh?" he said, meaning Layla, not the pixie next to him.

"Oh, no. She worked for it. Not yet out of her teens and she married a man well into his eighth decade."

Grif winced.

"Don't worry," she said, rocking again. "He died within the year, and Layla's not shy in talking about it."

"Doesn't look shy about much," Grif replied, and Charis laughed.

Kit had been right. He liked her flighty hens. But Kit herself was too far away for his liking, too close to the front door. Grif had defied fate in saving her, and now anything could happen. If his gut was right, it would also happen fast. But Kit had asked for some space and he'd respect that.

Didn't mean he had to like it, though.

Leaning back, Charis rested a hand on her belly. "Did you sense a bit of tension between her and Kit?"

"Yeah. I got that." He sipped some more. Rum . . . not his first choice, but it was strong. He could appreciate it for that alone.

"Well, that's why," she said, jerking her head toward Pretty Paul. "Five years ago, when they were still hitched, and Layla's lawyer was still wrangling with her deceased husband's family over his estate, she saw that young Paul's career was on an upswing. Also saw that he'd stopped doting on Kit the way he used to." Her lined brows lowered, and her mouth twisted with the memory. "We all saw it. But Layla hit on him, thinking that if it was a billy girl he wanted, any billy would do."

"And Kit didn't hit back?"

"You clearly don't know our Kit." Charis shook her head, but the smile on her face now was warm. "She's never as curious about what people do as why they do it. It's the questions that intrigue her, the mystery. So she sat Layla down, bought her a drink, and 'interviewed' her about her behavior. Learned that despite a marriage that left her wealthier than all of us put together, Layla believed she was never given a fair shake in life."

"Who has?"

"Said she had to work for everything she's got." Charis huffed, too.

"Who hasn't?"

"And said she had to raise herself to be street-smart. Told Kit she has a 'back-door' education."

"What's that?" Grif asked, sipping.

"My guess? Something her first boyfriend talked her into."

Grif choked.

Charis waited until he settled again, and continued with a smile. "Anyway, long story short, Paul didn't want a billy, and he didn't want Layla . . . but he also didn't want Kit anymore, either."

"So what, he just walked out on her?" Grif squinted at Charis's responding nod, then glanced again at the former couple. "And she can just give him a hug? Chat like nothing happened?"

"That's Kit," Charis said. "She tries to see the best in people, even when they don't deserve it."

"Are you hinting at something, Charis?"

Charis leaned forward to check on her baby. The child's eyes were drooping despite the decibels ricocheting in the air. She sat back. "It's not a hint. *Don't mess with her.*"

Grif frowned. "I don't mess with people."

"Don't mess with this, either," she said, waving around at the room, the people in it. "You were asking us earlier why we live the rockabilly lifestyle, but it's not that hard to understand. Living nostalgically is just one more way to pretend that death isn't going to happen to us. Don't you see? Instead of deferring it with technology, or defying it with babies," she nodded down at her child with a half-smile, "we celebrate the past, keep it alive by reliving the best of it.

"But staying alive, *being* alive, is time mostly spent trying to stave off the Reaper. We work out, take our vitamins, keep looking for the fountain of youth. We choose lovers and careers based on who we want to be in the future, and where we want to go."

"You're not guaranteed a future," Grif pointed out.

"The way Nic died proves that." She looked at her baby and frowned, as if trying to read the future across the child's soft, unlined brow. "You want to know the most horrifying thing about it? Her death wasn't indicative at all of the way she lived. That violence just doesn't fit with . . . all this."

Grif knew what she meant. You expected violence to touch only those who dealt in it. But when it claimed people like his Evie? Like Nicole and Kit? It meant that even if you sucked the marrow from life, your future could be snuffed out at someone else's whim.

"Kit lost the people closest to her at a young age, so she surrounds herself with things that make her feel alive, and yeah, that includes the past. You do, too."

Grif shook his head. "I don't got much left from my past."

"That's not what I meant. I meant you also make her feel alive. I can see it."

"Oh." Grif shifted in his seat, face burning at her words. He looked at Kit, again wished her nearer, then cleared his throat. "So what about you? How do you cope with a cloudy future?"

"I'm Mexican. Same as Fleur and Lil over there. So we were raised Catholic." She pointed to herself. "Under the iron fists of Sister Mary Francis of the Immaculate Conception School. So whatever I do, I do it with unwavering discipline and relentless guilt."

Grif smiled, and clinked his tumbler against her sad-looking water glass. "I'm a product of St. Paul's myself."

Charis sipped, smiling back. "When I was little, I even aspired to become a patron saint. I could recite the Mass verbatim, and Hail Mary myself into a coma. And I saw God everywhere."

Grif narrowed his eyes. "Really?"

She nodded and leaned close. "We were actually pen pals. I'd write Him letters in Latin and leave them in my closet."

"Why the closet?"

She shrugged. "Because He didn't appear after I set my front yard's bushes on fire, so I decided He was shy."

Grif laughed so deeply it stretched his lungs. He realized that despite his recently removed celestial state, this was the most overtly religious conversation he'd had in a long time. Charis shrugged, and resumed rocking her baby one-handed, the other hand draped over her belly.

"Wanna hear a secret?" Charis lowered her voice and leaned close. "A few weeks ago I was dying of hunger. I mean, this little bean inside of me was taking all my energy and nutrients for itself, and I was feeling so hollow I thought I could eat my young."

"Ironic."

"I know, right?" Her eyes flared wide. "Anyway, I was eating a bag of Cheetos, the whole damned thing, mind you, and I saw a Cheeto that, I shit you not, looked exactly like Jesus Christ."

Grif stared at her.

"With his head bowed in prayer." She shrugged when Grif just kept staring. "But smaller. And cheesier." She frowned. "And a snack food."

Grif signaled for another drink.

"Anyway, the point is, I couldn't eat it." Charis shook her head like it surprised her. "I just couldn't bite Jesus's head off, you know?"

He frowned. "So what'd you do with the Cheeto?"

"Oh, I put it up on eBay. Someone might buy it as a relic."

She rocked her baby with a dismissive shrug before stilling suddenly, mistaking his silence for disapproval. "Hey, I'm not crazy, okay? If I don't at least get enough to pay for shipping, I'm just going to feed it to my kid. She'll eat anything."

They both looked down at the Savior-eating child. She was smacking her lips on air as she pacified herself to sleep.

"Hey, can you stay with her for just a second? I really have to . . . you know." She widened her eyes as she stood.

Grif jerked back. "Oh, I don't know. Me and kids—"

"I'll be just a sec, I swear." And she waddled off before he could reply.

Grif realized his head was beginning to pound again. He rubbed the base of his neck, thinking he'd just ignore the little thing. She was sleeping easy, anyway. Why rock a steady boat?

"Cheers," he whispered to the dozing child, before returning to his distant vigil over a woman celebrating the life of someone who was already dead.

Charis took her damn time.

Sipping some more rum, Grif stole another glance at her slumbering child. She looked vulnerable lying there, chubby-limbed, with mere tufts of golden hair giving the aspect of a plucked bird. Yet somehow all the promise of the human race was wrapped up in those fat, milky cheeks, and pretty bow mouth.

Glancing at Kit, back at the bar and hugging Lil, Grif thought of what Charis said about the way Kit surrounded herself with the things that made her feel alive. He could see that. She was trying to recapture a time when things seemed simpler, more stable. He wished there was a way to tell her that even in the fifties nothing was really what it seemed.

The thought sharpened in his mind to the point of discomfort. Instinctively he dropped his head, but the pain struck full-out then, stabbing his skull and severing his thoughts. The left side of his face tingled, and he squeezed his eyes shut. Biting back a cry, he clenched his head, arm brushing against the rocking car seat. The sleeping baby startled.

"Shit."

The child's cries syncopated with the pounding in Grif's head and light sparked like fireworks behind his eyelids. So when the voice sounded next to him—"Hey, Shaw"—he didn't even try to respond. Instead, he rocked himself and the baby.

"Shh . . . don't cry," he said, not exactly sure which of them he was talking to.

"Oh, I'm not the one who's gonna be crying if you don't pull it together. Sit up."

And the pounding miraculously ceased. Lifting his head, Grif realized no one had moved. The girls were still jawing at the bar. The band was still swinging like Jerry Lee was crooning. Charis was still busy in the can.

But the baby was staring at him, eyes large, dark, and hard in the sweet cherub face. Grif leaned closer and the toothless mouth twisted. "Sarge?"

"Who else?"

The words sounded funny when gummed, but Grif didn't laugh, and the blades between his shoulders pulsed, reminding him he lacked wings. "Is the kid going to remember any of this?"

The child's brows lowered so that she really did look like Sarge, though the voice was still undeveloped, making the angel channeling it sound like he'd sucked helium. "Relax.

This'll add ten years to her life and five hundred points to her SATs. Now what the hell are you still doing on the mud?"

"I'm sorry," Grif said lamely. "I couldn't allow it. Craig's a good woman, Sarge. She didn't deserve to die that way."

"It's not about deserving, Shaw." The baby's face hardened further. "And you haven't changed anything. All you've done is prolong the inevitable. Every action she takes, every connection she makes with another person on the Surface is now something we have to work to unravel on this end. It's not natural. She is *not* supposed to be there."

Grif glanced up. Kit was leaning against a carved post, rocking slightly to the upright bass. The thought punched through Grif's brain: *Yes, she is.*

He was the one who shouldn't be here. He'd screwed up. And now a woman who lived in the past and dreamed of the future was going to die because of it.

"Can I ask you something?" he said, peering into the seat. The baby grunted. "Am I really mortal again?"

"Look down, Shaw," the baby shot back. "You are wearing the—"

" 'The sinful flesh.' " Grif nodded dismissively, but rolled his aching shoulder blades again. "Yeah, Anas told me. So I have free will again, right? I can make my own decisions as long as I possess mortal breath?"

The baby's eyes momentarily narrowed, and smoke roiled in their depths. "Don't forget what else comes with that divine gift."

And another shock of burning pain seared the core of Grif's brain. His eyes crossed and tears rolled down his cheeks, but then the pain flashed cold and was cauterized. Yet the first thing he saw when his vision returned was Kit. Talking to her girls. Gesturing animatedly. The brightest spot in a color-saturated room, and exactly what Grif needed to regain his focus.

Eyes glued on her bittersweet smile, he waited for the pain to abate.

"I have blunted the pain of mortality for you," Sarge was saying. "Even now, while what little of your brain is tearing itself apart, I am shielding you from the worst of it. You're not supposed to be alive, and that knowledge lives in every cell in your body. You know those times when you can't catch your breath?"

Grif gave a short nod.

"Well, I'm the one who gives it back to you. You'd spend every moment gasping like a landed trout were it not for me. And you know the flashback you had upon landing on the Surface? That's your memory awakening along with your senses. The longer you stay there, the worse those'll get. But I'm the one who allows you to wake. I alone can keep another from coming your way.

"Now if you want me to stop protecting you from these things, if you want to feel your mind tearing itself apart all the time, then by all means keep disobeying orders. But the only way to find true divine peace is by returning to the Everlast where those unfortunate human emotions are blunted. God is your balm and solace." The baby's eyes narrowed. "But you gotta go through me to get to Him."

"So if I let her die, I can return to the Everlast?"

The infant gave a small nod. "If you walk out and leave her right now."

Grif's gaze returned to Kit. "No incubation?"

"No incubation."

So Grif could go back to the way things were before. Back to working on his guilt over Evie's death in a place where he was safe, protected, and with his mind intact. He'd continue to assist people into the Everlast so they could heal from their stolen, unknowable futures, knowing that eventually every one of them would enter the Gates, and Paradise. To God. To their true home.

The baby put a chubby fist to her lips, looking wise as she squinted up at Grif. "You can't alter fate, Shaw. Katherine Craig *is* going to die. The best you can do now is help her cross into the Everlast."

Like he'd helped Nicole? Was that really the best he could do? "Listen, Sarge—"

"No, you listen. Defy me again and I'll send you dreams you'll never forget. Keep defying me and I will send you a living nightmare. But leave now and all will be as is fated."

"Sarge—"

"Walk out now, Shaw."

Grif tried again, but the Pure was gone. The chubby limbs lost their dexterity, and with a blink, the eyes were once again as light as a robin's egg.

"Oh, look, she's awake." Charis returned, smiling, and lifted her baby with an exaggerated movement, rubbing her nose with her own. "Everything go okay?"

"Sure," he said quickly. "She's, um, a smart one. Might want to aim for Yale. I think she's got a shot."

The infant gurgled agreement, then dribbled spit from the corner of her mouth. Charis wiped it away with a readied cloth and gurgled right back. "That's so sweet of you to keep Mr. Shaw company. But is my little Boo-Bear ready to go home? Ye-es . . . How about just one little dance first? A tiny swing around the room. Gotta show off your onesie . . . everyone loves black skulls and red cherries.

"And," she said, nodding her thanks to Grif, "Nic loved this one."

Whirling away, she held the child high over her other baby bump, still whispering lovely nonsense into the tiny ear. The baby, though, kept her wide eyes on Grif the whole way. She gave him a look that said he could change nothing. That he shouldn't be there at all.

It was a look that said leave while you can.

CHAPTER TWELVE

K it slept like her life depended on it. Even in the home of a former mobster, or perhaps because of it, she fell into a dream state that was a black hole for her thoughts and emotions. Nothing existed for twelve straight hours, and she actually awoke refreshed, and feeling for the first time since Nic's death like it was okay to be breathing.

Maybe that was because Nic had visited her in her dreams, saying she knew Kit would find out who did this to her, and that she really was in a better place.

"Nothing made in China," she told Kit, in a pretend whisper, then straightened with a smile. "Not here. Not in the Everlast."

Shaking her head at her own imagination, Kit took a long shower, dressed carefully in a gray pencil skirt and white blouse, and backcombed the hell out of her hair. By the time she sat down to a hearty breakfast of toast and eggs with Grif and Tony, she felt settled if not totally herself.

But Grif was obviously preoccupied. He kept touching his head like it was tender or he was worried or he'd forgotten something. He snapped at her when she asked if he was okay, and refused to answer when she asked what they were going to do next. The only thing that kept him from sullying her fragile good mood was recalling the way he looked the night before, hanging with her friends, listening attentively as they spoke of Nic's life, and all the while watching the bar door to make sure Paul—or someone—didn't return. She'd even caught him studying her face a couple of times, like she was some sort of riddle he was trying to figure out. When she asked him what he was thinking, though, he just shook his head and turned away.

She was getting to know him, Kit realized, as they set off from Tony's to follow their sole lead. Grif only spoke when he had something definitive to say, then used as few words as possible to do so. She couldn't say she liked his taciturn nature, but she appreciated his directness. It was much more refreshing than, say, the way Paul had once used countless words to camouflage his lies.

And, of course, the way Grif had watched after Charis's baby had been sweet, talking with the little girl as if discussing something important. There was just something about big, gruff guys with tiny, vulnerable babies that was so life-affirming and reassuring. So she sighed, smiling slightly at the road as she drove, while Grif continued being a grump beside her.

"You always this happy when investigating murder?"

"I don't always investigate murder," she said, reason enough to be happy. Yet he wouldn't want to hear that her mood also had to do with him. With all the questions still swirling around his sudden appearance in her life, even Kit wasn't sure how she felt about it. But it didn't stop her from being comforted by the very same.

"Bridget Moore," Kit said, clearing her mind and pulling out her smart phone. "Her first arrest was for solicitation, at nineteen, almost a decade ago. She may have some underage arrests, but we'll never know. Juvie files are sealed, but this one says she was born and raised in Vegas. No listing for a Bridget Moore that matches her age, though."

"So she changed her name?"

Kit shrugged. "And opened the nail salon where we're headed, a year ago. Incidentally, it was an all-cash purchase. Probably her savings."

"Tired of running from Lance Schmidt?"

"Tired of trading her body for that money," Kit guessed. "Else why not head out to Nye County to escape Schmidt's reach and work her trade legally?"

Grif jerked his head. "The legal brothels won't take you if they know you've been working the street. She's got a record. Does she have a boyfriend? Husband?"

"Unknown on the first. Nothing recorded on the second."

Grif made a noise in the back of his throat. "So maybe she found one and he wanted her straight."

"Or she wanted to be straight for him." Kit sighed. "Wouldn't that be nice?"

Grif huffed again, disbelief evident in the sound, his slump, his lidded gaze.

"Everyone deserves a fresh start," Kit said, answering his unspoken skepticism.

"I don't think it works that way, Kit."

And he looked so sad when he said it that Kit almost ran a red light.

They drove the rest of the way in silence. It was ten in the morning, and the streets were steady with local traffic, the tourists confined to the Strip and the airport and the downtown buffets as if held there by an invisible lasso. The street where Moore's shop was located held only a sprinkling of pedestrians, and a roofed bus stop where a man was currently having a conversation with a pigeon. Grif eyed them both warily as Kit pulled into the lot. One car, a late-model Toyota, sat alone.

"Staying or coming?" she asked, turning off the car as Grif continued to stare at the man at the bus stop.

"Coming." Yet even before the sole woman inside caught sight of Grif, her glance toward the door was wary. She'd been disinfecting tools, drying them and laying them neatly across a folded towel on the counter. She was dressed in tight jeans and a UNLV sweatshirt, but even its size couldn't disguise a bosom that'd probably paid dividends in her previous profession.

Kit's gaze skittered over the bleached hair and dark roots. What a shame. Kit could've told her that red lips and dark brows covered a multitude of sins. Then she chided herself. Shadows lay like tiny horseshoes beneath the woman's eyes, and her shoulders were already slumped. Though Kit and she were near the same age, this woman clearly had worries that went beyond the cosmetic.

"Bridget Moore?" Kit asked.

"Appointment only," the woman said in a heavy smoker's voice. But Kit had seen the welcome for walk-ins printed on the door.

"We're looking for Ms. Bridget Moore. Is that you?"

"Let me clarify. *I* only see new clients by appointment."

"I'm happy to make one, but I was hoping just to talk. My name is Kit Craig."

Moore cocked a hand on her hip. "I know who you are."

"How?" Grif interrupted.

Bridget's wariness turned to contempt as her gaze landed on Grif. "I read her paper."

Kit shot Grif a warning look. Angering a source was no way to advance a case, and as a prostitute, Moore likely had less respect for men—and reporters—than the average *CSI*-loving couch potato. It would be hard to do what she did, or used to do, and not be changed by it.

Kit took a step forward, regaining Moore's attention. "So you know why I'm here?"

Bridget considered her for a long moment before looking away. "No."

"My colleague, Nicole Rockwell—" Kit shook her head. "My best friend was murdered three nights ago. She was meeting with someone at the Wayfarer Motel."

Bridget just stared.

"I was hoping you could tell me a little about the place. The way it works. The girls. The clients."

"I don't hang out at the Wayfarer."

Grif rejoined Kit's side. "But you did a year ago."

"That's in the past." She jerked her head to the door. "And I want to keep it that way. Understand?"

Angling herself so she was blocking Bridget's view of Grif, Kit pulled the list from her handbag. "Bridget, please. I have a list of names here. Most of them are local businessmen, politicians with good reason not to be linked to the Wayfarer—"

"So don't link 'em."

"If you could look—"

But she cut Kit off with a brisk shake of her head. "I don't exactly run with the political crowd."

"Well, could you tell me if you've ever seen any of the men listed here at the Wayfarer?"

"No."

And that, Kit thought with narrowed eye, was one of her least favorite words. Inhaling deeply, she made a show of looking around, crossing to run a finger over one of the nail stations. "Nice place you have here."

"It's a business," Bridget retorted, not about to be appeased. She cast a snarling look at Grif. "A *legitimate* one."

Kit smiled. "Clearly. And I could really use a manicure."

"Really?" Bridget asked, crossing her arms.

"What?" Grif asked, crossing his.

"I have a Valentine's Day fund-raiser to attend this weekend. Oh, and the most gorgeous vintage cupcake dress. Red crinoline beneath gold satin. Bought it at an estate sale for twenty dollars, an original Suzy Perette. The woman had no idea what a find it was."

Both Grif and Bridget stared.

"Candy-apple-red fingernails would compliment it perfectly."

"Can I talk to you," Grif said, pulling her toward the door. With his back to Bridget, he whispered, "What are you doing?"

"Being charming. You might try it sometime."

"You're getting your nails done."

"That, too."

"I don't get you! You're this hotshot reporter but you're willing to stop the presses just to pretty-up? After you already stopped the investigation to do your hair?"

Kit tilted her head. "You really think I'm a hotshot?"

"Kit!" Lifting his hat, Grif raked a hand through his hair. "What about saving the world?"

"Oh, Grif." Kit blew out a breath. "Can't you see you're scaring her?"

"Wha . . . I didn't do anything!"

"Besides, the world's a better place when it's pretty. Now take my phone," she said, handing it to him. "Go download an app, and kill a pig with a bird or something."

"Kill a pig with a . . . ?" But he never finished the sentence. Instead he shook his head and left without another word.

"Sorry about him," Kit said, whirling to Bridget when the door had shut behind him. "He's very intense. Tries to hide his soft side."

Bridget just motioned to the nail station farthest from the door.

"I really do like your place," Kit said brightly, as she sat. Bridget looked at her sharply, relaxing when she saw Kit was sincere.

"Bought it with all my own money. And, yeah, I paid in cash."

"Wise," Kit said lightly.

Pulling in tight across from her, Bridget picked up one of Kit's hands. She gave her a hard double-take when she saw they were perfectly manicured, then shrugged and picked up a nail file. A client was a client. "When I'm able, I'm gonna expand to the empty space next door. Add beauticians. Someone who can do facials."

"Sounds real nice."

Bridget nodded, not looking at Kit again until she'd placed that hand to soak, and picked up the other. "Look, I read about your friend in the paper. I'm real sorry. But I ain't been to that shitbox motel since I was busted. I'm clean. I washed my hands of all that shit."

"So you didn't contact Nic?"

"Nope. Don't know who might have, either. I don't run with those girls anymore. They can't be trusted. Most will sell you to the devil as soon as they feel the flame."

Kit lifted her eyes from her hands. "What about Lance Schmidt?"

Bridget didn't look up, didn't hesitate as she removed Kit's old color, but her fingertips tightened over Kit's. "Who?"

"C'mon, Bridget," Kit said softly. "The cop who busted you at the Wayfarer . . . and back when you were nineteen."

Bridget did look at her now, and naked fear warred with anger in the gaze. "I make a point of staying out of Detective Schmidt's way."

"Is he dirty?"

Bridget kept filing.

"Does he blackmail the girls?" Kit persisted. "Make them do things for him in return for not busting them?"

"I know nothing about him," Bridget said stubbornly, buffing harder, then added quickly, "Except that he's mean."

"Mean enough to kill?"

"Mean enough that you don't want to find out," Bridget warned. Her tone also said she wasn't going to risk her own skin—and salon, livelihood, *life*—to help Kit pursue that mad dog. Kit considered telling Bridget about Schmidt's attack on her, but decided it probably wouldn't help. Scared and jaded, she'd likely think Kit naive for not expecting it.

Besides, she might be lying. As Marin said, he'd bookended her career, and could be holding something over her still. He could have used her to contact Nic. She might have him on the phone as soon as Kit left the salon. So as Bridget cleaned and trimmed, Kit tried to think of another angle.

But Bridget surprised her by raising her own question. "That charity ball you're going to this weekend. That wouldn't happen to be the Caleb Chambers event, would it?"

Kit tilted her head. "Why?"

Bridget shrugged, but the movement was stiff. "Is he on that list of yours?"

"Chambers?" Kit nodded. "At the bottom, though. Alibied for the night in question."

And yet, she suddenly realized, his name kept coming up again and again.

"Makes sense. He's a bottom-feeder."

Kit leaned forward on her elbows, staring closely at Bridget, now studiously looking down. A former prostitute who claimed no ties to the political crowd thought the most powerful of them was scum? "Look, if you can tell me anything about Chambers, about what happens at the Wayfarer, anything at all, I'd be grateful."

Bridget's mouth firmed into a thin line. "I can't."

"Not even anonymously? Off the record?"

Huffing, she shook her head. "Who'd believe me?"

"I would," Kit said sincerely.

"I know. I've heard you protect your sources. You got a good rep on the street."

"So what's the problem?"

Bridget stilled and looked at her. "No one even believes you."

Kit drew back but realized Bridget was right. Marin was helping, but Marin was blood, and always on her side. But

Paul had dismissed her claims outright. Even Dennis hadn't yet returned the calls she'd put in to the police station, though maybe he would have if she'd told him her suspicions regarding Schmidt. She'd have to talk to Grif about that later, but for now nobody was asking questions about what happened at the Wayfarer. Nobody but Grif.

"You know," Bridget said, seeing from Kit's silence that she finally understood, "I worked at another salon when I first got my cosmetology license. On the Strip, catering to bachelorette parties and all the bored wives of men who come here to gamble. It was real pricey, real exclusive . . ."

Kit ventured a guess. "Fifth Avenue?"

"You've been there?"

She nodded. "My girlfriends sprang for it when I got married."

"How'd you like it?"

"The manicure lasted nearly as long as my marriage."

That garnered a wry smile. "Well, I saw a lot of women come through those doors, some splurging like you, though most were simply wealthy. They wanted perfect nails to match their perfect husbands and perfect children and cars and homes.

"Thing is, once I started filing away?" Bridget shook her head. "The truth came up quicker than tequila on an empty stomach. Husbands were straying, the women were in denial, all the old clichés and a few new ones as well. But as they talked, and I filed and listened, they all had one thing in common. See, fake nails—acrylics, overlays, gels, tips—all they do is mask imperfection. There's always something else going on underneath a perfect, pristine, glossy facade."

She wasn't talking about nails. "And what's that?"

"Rot," Bridget said shortly. "I scrape under a nail and I pull out dirt. I pull off an overlay and I smell urine. It's the rot of their lives seeping into their nailbeds, you see? They can fix their hair and paint their nails and run on a treadmill until they're anorexia's poster child, but they can't fix their lives . . . lives of rotting perfection."

Kit frowned. "Just because you're rich doesn't mean you're bad, or not deserving of good things."

Bridget shook her head. "I know that. I'm just saying that when something looks perfect, all you have to do is dig down a couple of layers. That's where to find the truth."

A smile began to grow over Kit's face. So Chambers wasn't the perfect businessman. The perfect family man. The perfect Mormon. Pursing her lips, she thought about prodding for more, but if Bridget had wanted to speak openly, she would have. Instead, Kit tilted her head. "So why'd you leave Fifth Avenue?"

The woman smiled tightly, pausing as she pulled the brush from the nail polish. "It seems someone dug down a couple of layers on me as well. Decided that my past made me unfit to render services to such perfect people."

"I'm sorry," Kit said, meaning it, and understood better why it was so important that Bridget work for herself. And why she was so unwilling to talk about Schmidt. After all, who else had the power and authority and *motivation* to reveal such information to her employers?

"And I'm really sorry about your friend." Bridget's fingers tightened on hers again, but this time it was a consoling squeeze. "I'm sorry I can't help you either."

Kit smiled at her, then looked down at her right hand. "These look beautiful."

"Hope your boyfriend thinks so, too."

Kit realized she meant Grif. "Oh, no. It's not like that."

"With that type?" Bridget scoffed and started on the left hand. "It's always like that."

"Type?"

Glancing up, Bridget laughed at Kit's perplexed expression. "Take it from a pro. You know a man by his thrust, and that one's got it."

"I generally get to know the man before I get to know his thrust."

Unoffended, Bridget just snorted, and started cleaning up. "Not physically. I'm talking about a man's drive. Plenty of men are good at acquiring money and cars and things, but only a few have real forward motion. You know. Thrust."

Kit pursed her lips. Paul was certainly driven, but compared to Grif, and Kit had certainly been doing so the night before, Paul had the thrust of a Schwinn. She huffed, surprised she'd realized it only now. "You are so right."

"'Course I am," Bridget scoffed. "And you can lay odds that a man who's driven in his life's pursuits—whatever they are— will be equally driven when it comes to you." Stilling suddenly, she looked up from her work. "You can lose yourself to a man like that."

Kit swallowed hard, and thought of all the questions that remained about Griffin Shaw. She thought of the way her pulse throbbed harder, thicker, around him, too. The way her gut had kicked when she thought he'd been injured. The way it warmed when he'd stood up to Paul.

But the idea of losing herself entirely in another person? Sure, that idea spoke to the romantic in her. But so far it'd done so in a language she didn't know.

"Anyway," Bridget went on. "This case you and your girlfriend cracked open? It's all about ambition gone sour. Sex isn't about power or money."

"No. It's about love."

"No, it's about sex." Bridget laughed wryly, and pushed her hair back from her face. "Sex drives us, love or no love. Power or no power. Money or no money. It's the most powerful drug in the world. Some pay for it. Some die for it."

"And others kill for it."

Bridget held the questioning gaze for a moment, then jerked her head down at Kit's nails. "I'd let them sit for a bit to make sure you don't smudge. Or maybe let your man drive."

Kit didn't correct her this time. She'd been warming to the idea of Grif anyway, backing up to it like it was a cold night and he was a flame. Sex *did* make people do strange things. But Kit would be careful not to do anything too strange—or so she told herself. "Thanks for your time, Bridget."

They settled up, but Kit paused with her hand on the door. "What you were talking about earlier," she said, frowning. "Maybe *that's* what everyone is really after. Not just sex, but a passion and thrust and a love for life that's, I don't know, almost desperate."

"Maybe."

"You think that kind of passion is meant for everyone?"

Now Bridget did look at her like she was foolish. But she also looked wistful. "Ideally."

But they weren't in an ideal world. And it was too bad, Kit thought, exiting the shop. Bridget might have talked to her if they were. Kit might have been able to trust her. And neither of them would have to fear a man with a whole different sort of thrust—corrupted, soured, rotting . . . and seemingly unstoppable.

* * *

She expected Grif to grill her as soon as she was back in the car, or at least chastise her again for getting a manicure while on the job, but he only tossed the phone in her lap and shifted to face her. "Tony called. Guess which little birdie finally flew his coop?"

"No way," Kit said, eyes grown wide. She'd had a long conversation with the old man that morning, encouraging him, aptly, to spread his wings. It just seemed sad to waste what time he had left on this earth hiding from what was both possible and inevitable: death. What kind of life was that, anyway?

"Look, if I can walk around with a killer following me now," she'd said to him, "why can't you go out there after forty years?"

Tony gave her his death stare. "Have you ever had a bomb go off beneath the car you were supposed to be driving?"

"No. Have you ever been attacked by two men in your own bedroom?"

"Three. And more than once."

Kit frowned. "Oh."

Yet he'd done it. He'd left his safe house for the first time in decades and Kit liked to think something she'd said had contributed to that. "So where is he?"

"A coffee shop down on Western Avenue, one he used to frequent when he was still made. He wants us to meet him there. Have a celebratory ninety-nine-cent special."

Kit knew exactly where it was, in the old industrial area now littered with auto shops, XXX movie houses, and a scattering of taco carts. It was closely watched by Metro, carefully ignored by the tourist bureau, and loyally frequented by old-timers despite the unchanging menu and dated decor. Maybe even because of it. One half-expected Lefty Rosenthal to suddenly saunter through the wooden door, and it was one reason Kit and her friends loved the place.

"So is she holding back?" Grif finally asked.

"Who, Bridget Moore?" She nodded at his sound of assent. "Of course."

"Think she was the contact who lured Nicole to the Wayfarer?"

"I don't know." Frowning, Kit turned the possibility over in her mind. "I think it's time to bring Dennis in. I think he can help."

"I told you. No cops."

"I trust him."

"No."

Kit tried on Tony's death stare. When Grif only blinked, she filed his definitive "no" under "maybe" and let her expression clear. "Well, either way, I like her."

Grif looked at her. "Even though she might be hiding something that can help you solve Nicole's death?"

"Yes."

"But . . . aren't you angry?"

"Nah. Who's to say that I wouldn't do the same? Besides, much of the world's problems could be solved if we were all just gentler with each other."

She'd also run into too many reluctant sources to let them get to her now. Sometimes they came around on their own. More often they got tired of her nagging and just fessed up. It was rare that her ability to circle a source and dive back in from another direction didn't create some fissure of opportunity she could crack.

So she'd do so again in this case. Maybe not until Saturday, when she'd hit the Chambers benefit—with beautiful nails and a fantastic dress—but for now she'd fortify herself with a veggie omelet, limitless coffee, and—most important—hope.

"Do you always have to see the best in everyone?" Grif said out of nowhere, watching her face with something close to a wince.

"Yes." She swung into the triangle-shaped lot in front of the hash house.

"Why?"

Turning off the car, she almost laughed at his bemused expression. "You should just be thankful I do, otherwise I'd be obsessing over your presence in my bedroom on a night someone tried to murder me—"

Grif sighed dramatically. "Not that again."

"—instead of thanking you for your help in the days since," she finished, and that shut him up. Kit smiled. "I am thankful, Grif."

He looked away. "I know."

"I'm also still a bit obsessive."

He sighed again, this time resigned. "I know that, too."

Letting it go for now, Kit climbed from the car. "You know, I could ask the same of you. Do you always have to see the worst in people?"

"Yes." And before she could ask why, he jerked his head at the coffee shop. "Case in point."

Kit spotted Tony's head rising like a plucked chicken to peer at them through the window. She frowned at Grif over the hood. "If you don't see the best in him, then why are you staying with him?"

He seared her with a look as he slammed the car door shut. "'Cause we're friends."

And he strode across the lot in that smooth, dangerous gait. *A man with thrust.*

Shaking her head, she followed him in.

Tony was seated in a wooden booth lined with lumpy red cushions, perched at a table that looked like it'd been lacquered in lieu of cleaning. Hunched over a plate of pasta the size of his head, surrounded by a half-dozen other dishes, he glanced up, eyes gleaming. "You gotta try the ziti!"

Kit smiled as she slid into the seat across from him. "It's good to see you out, Tony. How does it feel?"

"I forgot what it was like. So many scents, so many noises." He jerked his head, and Kit saw a waitress coming their way with a coffee pot. "What do you think of her?"

"Long in the tooth," Grif muttered, before the mugs were dropped down in front of them. Kit elbowed him in the stomach.

Tony grinned up at the waitress as she refilled his cup, then leaned forward when she left. "Ah, but she's got all her own teeth. I like that. Here. Try the meatballs. And these pancakes. They're amazing. I tell you, you can't get this delivered."

Grif held up his hand, but Kit dug into the pasta. It really was good. Tony wiggled his brows when she sighed, which made her laugh again. How could Grif not like this guy?

"You're being rude," she told him, and both men stared. "You are. This is a celebration. Tony's first day back in the real world. Here. Eat some ziti."

She held the fork up to his mouth. Grif pursed his lips and glared.

Tony laughed. "You're not going to sway that stubborn old coot with macaroni. If he's determined to be moody, he's gonna be moody."

"You should talk," Grif shot back.

"Respect your elders," Kit hissed so that Tony couldn't hear. She smiled over at him apologetically, and ate the bite Grif had rejected. "His loss."

"'At's all right. Grif and I go way back. Fifty years, give or take." He squinted in Grif's direction. "That about right, Shaw?"

"That's right, Tony," he said, but gave Kit a knowing look. Dementia. She frowned sympathetically, and felt her appetite take a slight dive.

Tony dug around his plate, still talking. "Yep, I used to look up to ol' Grif here. He knew when to hedge and when to move the line back. 'Course, he was working a legal trade . . . and had that stunner of a wife to keep him in line."

Kit's stomach sank further, and she swallowed hard.

"Tony," Grif said lowly.

"What?" Tony looked up, catching the look on his friend's face. "Oh. Sorry, Grif."

There was silence that felt like it would fill the hour, then Tony tapped at the corners of his mouth with his napkin. "Listen, I been asking around for you. Got out the old Rolodex. Used the old number. Actually got ahold of the kid."

"What kid?" Kit glanced up, blinking. "What number?"

Tony looked at Grif, and raised his brows.

Grif gave a short nod. "It's okay. You can talk in front of her."

Tony nodded and resumed eating. "Ray DiMartino. He's fifty-seven now, not really a kid anymore I guess, but I'll always see him running the dice in the back of his dad's liquor store."

"How . . . endearing," Kit said.

Tony chuckled. "Anyway, he owns the old place on Industrial, though they ain't running booze no more."

"What is it?" Grif asked.

"Ever hear of Masquerade?"

"The strip club?" Kit asked.

"Gentlemen's club," Tony corrected, causing Kit to scoff. He pointed his fork at her. "Sorry, missy, but you can't change a man's predilections. It's simple human nature."

Kit waved her perfectly manicured hand in the air. "I don't care about that. There's just no, I don't know, *life* to it. No story to unfold with the dance, no suggestion of magic to come. No nuance to make a boy dream of more. Just body parts swinging around in your face." She shuddered.

So did Tony. "Your point?"

"You should see a neo-burlesque show if you want to see something truly sexy. There's drama, there's kitsch. Winks and nods. It's not just titillating, it's full of life. It's fun."

Tony shook his head. "See what I been missing? Neo-burlesque. Everything old is new again." He dug back into his ziti. "Anyway, the kid remembers you. Said you used to throw him a few bills when he was cleaned out."

Kit drew back. How was that possible if Grif wasn't from here, and was over twenty years younger than the man in question? She wondered again about Tony's dementia, but her phone buzzed with a text before she could follow the thought.

Meanwhile, Tony kept eating, kept talking. "He's grateful for the work you did on behalf of his family and his aunt Mary Margaret, and said you're welcome to meet him at the club. Any night but Monday. That's his night off."

"Thanks, Tony."

Tony shrugged. "Hey, we're friends, right?"

"That's right."

Chewing, the old man nodded for a bit, then stilled. "I gotta take a leak. Don't touch my chow."

"Wouldn't dream of it." Grif waited until the old man had slid from the booth, then turned to Kit. "What just happened?"

Distracted, Kit pulled her gaze from the window, and focused on him. "Sorry. I wasn't listening. What?"

"Not with Tony. With you." Grif almost looked angry as he studied her face. "One minute you're eating like a starved horse and talking sex with a man three times your age. The next you're staring out the window as if you're the one stepping out for the first time in thirty years. Who was on the phone?"

Kit blew out a breath, surprised. She should have known he'd been paying attention. "It was just a text from Paul. Tickets for the benefit are waiting in my mailbox. He thought it best to just drop them off as he didn't have time to meet in person."

Grif studied her carefully, then finally said, "Why do you do that?"

She stopped rubbing her eyes. "What?"

"Give that knucklehead your softest emotion, then let him load it up and fire it back at you." He shook his head, disgusted. "You always look war-torn when you come off a conversation with Pretty Paul."

She didn't chide him for the nickname. "I feel it, too," she admitted, and frowned. Was that the first time she'd said it out loud? Sighing, she leaned her head back, then rolled it toward him. "What about you. Tony mentioned a wife?"

Even now, at the last word, Kit's throat tried to close up. Of course he would have a woman. Probably more than one, looking like that—walking with thrust, taking up all that room.

He didn't wear a ring, but many men didn't. Maybe it was because of his job. She'd read enough detective novels. Letting clients and suspects know you had family could be dangerous. Of course, he might not have worn one for the same reason Paul hadn't. The thought depressed her.

"I'm married to my work these days."

The words lifted her spirits, but the regret shadowing them did not.

"There's more to life than that," Kit said softly.

"That right, Kitty-Kat?"

The way he said it made her heart skip faster, and blood flooded the rest of her pulse points. The mild crush she was nursing over this severe man unfurled, blooming until her breath literally caught in her chest. And when he laid one wide hand over hers, she trembled. Having first seen his hands bunched into fists, flailing on her behalf, she didn't know what was more shocking—the unexpected gentleness of his roughened palms or the pooled warmth as they slid down her fingers, cocooning her knuckles, heating her skin.

"Remember how you said we should all be more gentle with each other?"

"Yes."

"Maybe you should start with yourself."

Kit frowned.

And then Tony was back.

And then, regrettably, Grif's touch was gone.

CHAPTER THIRTEEN

Grif had been fighting sleep for a day and a half, ever since Sarge had threatened him with unforgettable dreams and a "living nightmare."

So when he lay down on Tony's couch while waiting for Kit to finish primping for the charity ball, he told himself he was just going to shut his eyes for one moment. Rest his body for the night to come. He had no intention of actually sleeping, which was why he was already entering the bungalow, hand-in-hand with Evie just as he had fifty years prior, before he even realized he was dreaming.

Of course, by then it was too late.

Defy me again and I'll send you dreams you'll never forget.

This dream picked up where the first had left off, on the final night of his first life. He and Evie had already arrived in Vegas and been driven by golf cart to a room that was a

bungalow in name only. Hidden deep within the thick foli-
age of the Marquis' horseshoed center, these were the high-
roller suites. Evie squealed at the sight of all the white marble
and gold paint, right at home in accommodations meant for a
movie star.

"Everything's comped, Mr. Shaw," the bellboy said, but the
owner had already told him that. *Anything for the man who
tracked down my darling kidnapped niece,* said Sal DiMartino,
clapping Grif on the back. Anything for the P.I. who'd put his
family back together.

"It's like the honeymoon we never took," Evie beamed, once
they were alone. Guilt sailed through Grif at that, but he'd
been working long hours back then, and she had, too, until
a few weeks later, when she quit, saying standing on her feet
behind the counter at Woolworth's was too hard on a woman
trying for a baby.

But she wasn't remotely fragile on this night. They exhausted
themselves with each other in the bedroom, then again in the
gilded shower. The heated water was bested only by Evie's hot
mouth, her need for him thrumming in the tightening of her
thighs around his waist.

"Tonight we'll make a baby," she said, the words wet on his
cheek. Tonight all their greatest hopes for the future would
come true.

And she stared up at him like they already had.

But the Grif that was fifty years older and *deader* knew
better than that, even as the dream-Grif felt his heart swell.

I love her best like this, he thought. Bare-faced, stripped of
clothing and artifice, wet and giving him a look that belonged
to him alone.

But later, when her hair framed her face in tight, gold waves, and she wore a wiggle dress and high heels, he thought her just as perfect. She dabbed perfume at her wrist, a lilac memory that made him pulse, and flashed him a knowing smile. Her nails matched her dress, a blend of dark cherry and glitter left over from the holiday season.

"It's perfect for Vegas," she explained, blowing on the tips, helping them dry. Then they wrapped their arms around each other's waists and traded the privacy of their courtyard bungalow for the action of the clanging casino floor.

Evie went on to repay Sal DiMartino's generous hospitality by chip-hustling her way through the craps pit. She moved like a charmer in a pit of snakes, and Grif was as enchanted as everyone else.

Yet this time he was also aware of the plasma.

He couldn't turn his head, couldn't do anything he hadn't done the first time, but he'd dwelled in the Everlast, and knew what to look for now. The dead could spot death coming, even from the corner of their eyes.

So his eyes remained glued on Evie's wrist, and as time ticked away on his celestial meter, he noted the gambler next to Evie watching it, too. The man, balding and wide, bit his lip as she threw a seven, hooting in celebration even as she slipped a couple of chips out of the rack near his waist. She turned her head away when he tried to buss her cheek in thanks, and fluttered her lashes at Grif, laughing like all of life was a game, and a grift at that.

Behind her, death—the world's greatest con—inched closer.

Grif sipped at an old-fashioned, and then another. He switched to straight whiskey when Evie ignored the subtle jerk of his head and continued to hold the table like she was spotlit in the main lounge of the Silver Slipper Casino. He admired her moxy and style, every red-blooded man at the table did, but he was surprised to realize this time around that he hadn't much liked it on this night.

So Grif drank some more. The Centurion in him, wise with hindsight, screamed for him to stop, that he'd need his senses and reflexes to react, to protect. But the old Griffin Shaw, the dream one—the dead one—kept drinking and silently fuming and watching that slim wrist throw sevens and spirit chips, mending and breaking hearts with fingertips that glittered.

The silver plasma gathering around him was now thick as mercury.

Then, without warning, they were back at the bungalow, and Sarge was right about the moments that followed. They were a living nightmare.

The movement was a blue-black slide from the shadows, too hard and fast for Grif to block, even without whiskey slowing him down. He slumped like a rag doll, but felt the wall, solid at his back, and pushed from it—moving forward, always forward, just like his boxing coach had taught. He didn't yet feel the knife in his gut—the heat lightning of shock masked the severing of tissue and muscle and organs—but this time Grif felt *it*.

The shearing of his remaining earthly years. His mortal coil unraveling like spilled guts.

Then, somewhere, Evie screamed.

And the knife was suddenly in his hand. It was slashing and furious, in some ways more alive than he, and suddenly it, too, was covered in blood. Grif didn't remember this part.

He staggered, catching his balance, watching as the guy he'd gutted twitched but didn't get up. He was dark-haired and olive-skinned, wearing driving gloves that matched his black suit, and Grif had a moment to think he looked vaguely familiar . . . but then there were no moments left.

His skull popped and his legs shorted out, electricity surging through them in a numbness that was oddly sharp, not blunt. A second man, thought the Grif with Centurion hindsight. Why hadn't he realized it before?

Didn't matter. Again. The marble floor was littered with too much, the knife, the gold vase. Blood. His mortal coil. And glittering fingertips, Grif saw. Splayed in the shards of gold, attached to a delicate, crafty wrist now covered in droplets of blood.

He'd never even heard Evie fall.

Horrified, Grif tried to call out, yet his brain was swelling, pushing like putty against the crack in his skull. Baby, he thought as he began to rise and float . . . but there was nothing he could do. Nothing but live out the nightmare, and remember what he'd rather forget.

Nothing but die again and, this time, watch Evie do the same.

Grif!"

Kit had rushed into the room at the sound of the first cry, but froze when she saw Grif writhing and gasping, tears sliding from the corners of his eyes. She thought he was sleepwalking for a moment, but her voice had him lunging into a sitting position so quickly that he fell from the couch. He only hit his side on the coffee table, but he cried out like the wound had gone much deeper.

"Grif!" Kit rushed to his side. "Are you okay?"

But she could see he wasn't. His heart raced beneath her palm, and his fists were clenched and sweaty. He squeezed his eyes shut, but still they moved beneath his lids like minnows caught in a drying puddle.

"God," she said, pulling him close and wrapping her arms around him. "What happened?"

"It was only a dream, just a dream . . ." But he was talking to himself and rocking and still unable to catch his breath. Kit pulled him closer, and this time he clung to her, fingers digging into her back.

"Shh," she said. "Sit. Just be right here, right now. It's over . . ."

She continued to make soothing noises, coupled with reassuring platitudes until his trembling lessened and his grip relaxed. She soothed him as best she could, but fell short of telling him it was all right. She'd never seen anyone wake from a dream so violently before.

"It was only a dream," he said again, and this time he sounded like himself. Kit pulled away and stared at his stricken face.

"You're exhausted," she said, and guilt flooded her because she knew it was mostly due to her. "Let me get you some water."

"I'm fine."

No one this drained of color was fine, Kit thought, but stayed close, still touching him, trying to stroke the nightmare away. "Do you want to talk about it?"

"I don't even want to think about it."

She nodded, and waited. Finally he breathed in deeply. "Sorry, I just . . . it was a flashback. It was a bad time."

"I understand. The good thing about flashbacks is that they're confined to the past. Dead and gone. They can't really hurt you."

More platitudes, she thought, and could see that Grif thought so, too. "You weren't there."

"I'm here now," she said softly. And even with all her reservations and questions about his appearance in her life, she *wanted* to be here for him. Just as he'd been there, and stayed, when she needed him most.

But he wasn't going to make it easy. "It's not that simple, Kit."

"No, I know that. But it can be." Some things, she thought, stroking his neck, should be simple.

He froze under her touch, but this time she didn't let it dissuade her. Her fingers tensed on his neck, neither demanding nor soft, but testing. Grif was trying to catch his breath again, and if she was right, it had nothing to do with his nightmare.

"It's okay, Grif," she whispered, letting her fingertips loosen, stroke, play. "You're safe with me."

He closed his hand atop hers and they both stilled. Tilting his head, he studied her face. "It doesn't hurt as much when you're around."

"What doesn't?"

He didn't seem to hear. "I can actually feel your skin beneath my fingertips."

And he touched her like that was novel, hands moving along her arms, firing nerve endings, and quickening her pulse.

"I can smell you, too. It's been years . . ." And his gaze landed on her mouth.

Pulling her head low, he pressed a kiss to her lips, so that it sat there sweetly, like a gift. Like gratitude and acceptance all at once. He gave a full-body shudder, then slowly pulled away. "Thank you."

But Kit wasn't done. She found that her curves fit nicely to his ridges, and her skin still burned where his hand had found her waist. Her nipples brushed his chest as her mouth hovered over his, just long enough for her to know his breathing had stopped altogether.

Then she pressed with the whole of her body, mouth immediately widening for a deeper taste. Her chin brushed against his stubble as she sought and found soft places on the hard man, causing a needy hum to move in her throat and thread between them. She would have moved in closer if he didn't pull away.

"No."

"Why?" Kit's voice was different, throatier than she'd ever heard it. Needier, too. She swallowed hard, but it was still there, desire rising up so thick in her throat she could choke.

"There's . . . someone else."

She shook her head immediately. "No. You haven't mentioned anyone. There was a wife, I know, but you said that was long ago."

Yet doubt edged in. Could she have missed the signs of another woman? She was normally good about such things. Maybe, she thought, she *wanted* to miss it.

"Don't make me feel stupid about this, Grif," she said, because irritation was better than injury. "Or . . . or like I'm crazy. There's something between us. You know it. You kissed me back."

"It doesn't matter—"

"It does!" Her voice was a shock, a slap, and it surprised her as much as Grif. But she was exhausted, too. Tired of lukewarm relationships, tired of feeling hope only to be let down. She wanted to feel *good*. She wanted to feel desired and cherished and loved.

"It always matters," she told Grif. "At least to me."

"I know that," Grif said, hoping to soothe her. "And it's not that I'm not attracted to you."

"Oh, *I* know that," she shot back, pushing away. Maybe Bridget had it wrong. Maybe Grif didn't have an ounce of thrust in him.

Grif swallowed hard and rose, and she realized it was the first time she'd seen him back away from a fight. "There's something I need to tell you."

Kit's heart dropped like a sinking anchor. Grif almost looked as spooked as he had before she'd tasted those mind-numbing lips. "I'm not a rockabilly guy, Kit."

She sat back on her heels, on the couch, and inclined her head. "I guess I knew that."

"How?"

"You haven't got a bit of ink on you." She'd looked for it, too. She didn't know one man in this lifestyle who didn't, yet Grif was as clean-cut as a Boy Scout. Staring, she asked. "So . . . why?"

"Why what?" he asked, pacing.

"Why pretend? Why . . . me? Info for your case? Something only a reporter could get? Or money? Something only the future editor-in-chief might have?"

Suddenly the danger was back and he halted and pointed at her. "Don't compare me to that knob you were married to!"

Kit threw her hands up in the air. "Well, what would you think if someone just showed up out of nowhere, pretending to like the things you like and—"

"I'm not pretending anything!" he said, suddenly as wild-eyed as she'd found him. "That's what I'm trying to tell you!"

Kit just crossed her arms and waited.

He pointed to his fedora, knocked off during his fall. "That is my hat." He pulled at his suit. "This is really the way I dress. I was murdered in the fall of 1960. I was thirty-three years old . . . nine years older than the man whose house we're in now."

Kit blinked, then frowned. Had he hit his head when he fell to the floor? Maybe when he was flailing?

"And that's how you know Tony? Because you were contemporaries back in 1960?" She spoke slowly, wanting to give him a chance to think about what he was saying.

But Grif just inclined his head, seemingly relieved. Then he said, "There's more."

"More than his being a time traveler from the fifties?"

"I'm also a . . . I'm a . . ." He looked up at the ceiling, cringing like a dog that expected to be swatted.

"A?" she prompted, looking up at him.

"A . . . sort of . . . angel." It rushed out of him and he stood stiffly in place, glancing around the room as if waiting for something to happen.

Kit waited, too, but that was it. She tilted her head. "A sort-of angel?"

He gave her a double-take, like she'd said something crazy. "No, a real angel. A . . . you know. Angel angel."

Kit's recalled the way he'd rushed from the corner in her bedroom, shadows built up around him like wings. It was a good memory to hang on to now that she knew he was out of his mind. "I understand. You saved me from Schmidt and his buddy. You've stayed by my side and even though I'm being chased and I talk too much for your liking and—"

"Kit," Grif cut her off with the sole word. "You're not listening to me. I'm a real angel."

She stared, listening now.

Grif's neck worked as he swallowed hard. "I'm what's known as a Centurion. Angels who used to be human. There are other angels, of course. Pures, born in the Everlast. It's a sort of buffer zone to Paradise."

"Pures," she repeated flatly. *Everlast.* Where had she heard that before? She shook her head. The real question was why was she hearing it now?

He nodded. "You know. Immortal, designed by God's hand, ever in grace. Blah, blah, blah." He waved his hands like she should already be familiar with all this. "They're what humans think of when imagining typical angels . . . but not as cute."

All the warmth Kit had felt while kissing him drained from her then. She remained silent for another few moments and, when she thought her voice was steady, said, "So how many kinds of angels are there?"

He looked surprised that she should accept his explanation so easily. She didn't, but it was the first time he'd volunteered a story on his own, and she wanted to hear him out. It was a doozy. "There are Cherubim, Seraphim, Thrones . . . they comprise the highest order. Then the Dominations, Virtues, and Powers . . . losers, the lot of them. And the Archangels, a breed of their own. Real standoffish, if you get my meaning."

Kit forced a nod. "And where are you on this angel hierarchy?"

This time he heard the doubt edging her voice, and he frowned. "Higher than you, that's where."

"Okay." Kit stood. "Will you excuse me for a moment."

"Where are you going?"

"Kitchen." Rounding the back of the couch, she gave him a tight smile. "Be right back."

She made it into Tony's kitchen, let the slatted half-doors swing shut, then let out a scream that had been building ever since Grif had pushed her away.

He was by her side in a second. Maybe he flew, Kit thought, feeling another scream build. "What the—what the hell are you doing?"

"I. Am. Screaming." She turned toward him coolly. Funny, but it looked like he was mentally redressing *her* in a straitjacket.

"Why?"

Because she'd listened when a so-called professional had talked to her about thrust. Because she'd believed Grif actually had it. But he was just another man with a faulty heart. And the last thing Kit needed was one more of those.

"So. You're a fallen angel." She folded her arms.

"I'm not fallen," he said roughly.

"Then what are you?"

He shrugged. "Busted."

"Uh-huh." Where did Tony keep the hard alcohol in this place? she wondered, bypassing the wine fridge. "And what kind of angelic powers do you have?"

"Now you're making fun."

"No. I really want to know," she said, yanking vodka from the deep freeze and slamming the door shut. "I've never met a . . . what did you call it? A *Centurion* before. This is a first for me." Except, sadly, in many ways it was not.

"Okay," Grif said unsurely, as he watched her fill a tumbler and immediately down it. "I can open doors that are locked."

"So can a locksmith." So could a thief. She filled her glass again.

"Fine." Grif frowned and reached for her glass. "Give me your hands."

She'd have pulled away at his touch but didn't want one more action to give away how much she cared. Slowly, deliberately, he led her palms to his back, where his shoulder blades were bunched tight beneath coiled muscle. For a moment, there was nothing. Then he shifted and widened his back. Two knobs, round and wide, flared beneath her palms.

"Damn it, Grif," she said, jerking away. "What the hell are those?"

"That's where my wings would be if I wasn't trussed up in this flesh." He adjusted his shoulders like it was too tight a fit. "If I were a Guardian, the feathers would grow in like lightning. The Cherubim and Thrones have the downy ones. But the Archangels are the real dandies. They wear the stars in their wings."

Well, he was nothing if not imaginative. And Kit? She was a fool.

Shaking her head, she asked, "Is there anything else?"

"I died in 1960," he said plainly. "I don't need your help in finding out who killed another man named Griffin Shaw. I need your help in finding out who killed me."

Kit looked at him—exhausted, rumpled, irritated with her because she didn't just fall for it when he told her he was an honest-to-goodness angel, and yes, still totally hot. Damn it.

"And the woman?" she asked, reaching for her drink, but keeping her eyes on his face. "Evelyn?"

"My wife," he answered, face grim. "They—someone— killed her, too."

Kit felt another guttural scream building. Tilting back the tumbler, she swallowed, then shook her head.

"You still don't believe me." He shifted so his back was no longer exposed.

"C'mere," she said, slamming down her glass.

Grif frowned, but allowed her to direct his touch. Placing one of his hands on her hip, just because she felt like it, she dropped the other on the top of her head.

"What are you—?"

"Shhh . . ." She turned her gaze up as if that would help as she moved his index finger around, letting the others get lost in her black waves. Let him see what he's missing, she thought, moving that hip. Then she glanced back at his face, and saw the moment he felt it. "My extra brains," she explained, as he moved his hand over the bump.

He dropped his hand and glared at her. "That's a cyst."

"No. It's bonus gray matter. That's why I'm such a great reporter." She shrugged. "And why I usually win at Quiz Night."

"Quiz . . . ?" Grif huffed. "It's a *cyst*."

Smiling, Kit folded her arms, noting he had yet to move his other hand from her waist. "Darling, what's more unlikely? That you've got wings or I've got brains?"

He turned at that. "You are the most infuriating, stubborn—"

"You mean the most awesome, caring, and long-suffering . . . and don't you *dare* walk out that door!" She caught up to him, breathing hard. "Look, I came to you just now because it sounded like you needed me. I kissed you because I thought we both needed it. But what I *don't* need is some stone-cold, emotionally castrated jerk who thinks the past matters more than the present!"

"Oh, that's rich coming from you."

"Shut up! I need your help in finding out who killed Nic, and you need my help, too. But rest easy, because I *won't* kiss you again. I won't even mention this kiss again. It'll be like it never happened, and after we both have what we want, I'll go back to my life and you can go back to the past with your dead wife. But right now *I* am going to walk out of here first. And you know what you're going to do?"

He stared.

Her eyes narrowed. "You're going to watch me go."

And she turned at that, exiting the room first, and she was right. She left him staring after her, watching her go.

CHAPTER FOURTEEN

Grif stood, smoking on the green leading to the ninth hole, shivering slightly in a rented tuxedo, and feeling small beneath the weight of the early spring stars.

Feeling like a snake, too. Kit had snapped back at him—delivered a verbal one-two that he'd deserved, and that rocked him back on his heels, though worst of all was the pain that'd flashed behind the heat. He'd done that to her, and was instantly sorry.

And he'd have lunged after her, had his fingertips entwined in that glossy, sable hair, if only he hadn't wanted to do just that so very badly. But he'd just dreamed of Evie—his darling, his wife—and worse, *seen* her drop to the floor, and death. How could he have woken from that and immediately started pawing at some other woman?

But her touch—oh, her touch. Just like the suit he'd been wearing when he was thrown back onto the mudflat, it *fit*. Even his dream—Evie and him in the shower, the bed, in his arms—hadn't had the punch of power that Kit held in her fingertips alone.

Because she's alive, he thought, mind latching onto the memory of her lips pressed hotly to his.

But you're not, he reminded himself, and pushed the thought away. He wasn't human, not fully, anyway. He wasn't angelic anymore, either.

He wasn't anything.

Flicking ash onto the over-manicured green, Grif turned back to stare at Tony's home. It was a good distraction. Grif could almost pretend he was back in the fifties, with the same desert breeze playing at his back, the same stately homes rising from the earth with their butterfly rooftops and giant windows. Back then, guys like Tony hadn't just run the show, they *were* the show. And they'd been good neighbors, too. Even if they did work nights and sleep days. Even if they did park in their driveways with their Cadillacs' noses facing out. Even if you did have to worry when one of their packages ended up on your doorstep.

Still, they put their hearts in the city, gave it its bones, and kept the town clean even as they wiped away dirty palms. Tony loved it, too. He still talked about Las Vegas like it was his best girl.

Yet these days the town's greatest attraction was Caleb Chambers, who seemed to treat the city like a street whore, tossing money at her, tearing her down, using her up.

A movement at one of the large windows caught his eye.

It was Kit, silhouetted behind the curtain and struggling to hook the back of her dress. She managed it, then smoothed her fingers down in a practiced gesture, obviously facing a mirror.

Turning away, Grif forced himself to stare into the abyss of the course instead. Damn it. What was going on with him? Because it wasn't just the sight of her, the visual punch of her lily-white skin and berry-stained lips. Or the earthy, sweet scent when she stood too close. Or even her taste, though Grif would never loose that one from his mind now. He'd been able to ignore all of that, and thought he could continue to do so, too. She'd already said she wouldn't kiss him again.

But he couldn't ignore what he was feeling, not alone beneath the bare, honest sky. Katherine Craig had slid inside his new skin, nestled right in next to his renegade heart, and he had no idea how. She was nothing like Evie. That woman could hold a grudge like a badge, flashing it as needed.

Kit Craig flashed winks and nods, but if she held anything, it was a smile, the corners of her generous mouth ever curved upward with hope.

"Why the hell is she so chipper all the time?" he muttered into the dark. She'd lost both her parents young. She'd been played by a two-bit sot who wouldn't know a good thing if his life depended on it. Her best friend had been killed practically before her eyes. And even if her fight to keep the family paper humming panned out, she'd already learned that money couldn't keep you safe or healthy or happy.

So what on earth, he wondered, kept that swivel in her step? What made her dust herself off after getting knocked down? Why the hell did she insist on gifting *him* with that damned magnificent smile? Why did she taste like his own forgotten hope?

All Grif knew was that Kit Craig was vibrant and alive and she wanted him in a way a woman hadn't in over half a century. Even with what she called his grumpiness. Even given the way he'd mysteriously barreled into her life.

And he *had* kissed her back. He wanted to kiss her again, too. To go into that bedroom, clasp her face on both sides, and crush his mouth atop hers. He also wanted to protect her.

Yet what he needed to do was let her die.

Looking up into the star-pocked face of the cold night sky, he considered that for a moment longer. "Not a chance," he finally said, and the place where his wings should have been tingled.

Then, turning his back on the darkness of the empty course . . . he ran right into the chest of a Pure.

Angels—Pures—were always depicted as full of light. And they *were* light, comprised of the same particles and elements that imbued the entire universe with color. But the painters and sculptors who decided that "full of light" meant blond, blue-eyed cherubs never properly considered that the spectrum of God's universe was vaster and wilder than anything the human eye could envision. Angels were an untamed natural wonder.

And they were not created in God's image. That was an honor reserved only for his children. It was why Centurions could never be considered true angels. Why true angels, Pures, would never be able to comprehend humanity's plight.

It was how Grif knew this one had been forced to don ill-fitting flesh against her will, against her nature, against the existing caste system of the angelic realm, where even the soulless Pures were divided into orders.

She didn't look happy about it, either.

A perfectly round dark head sat atop shoulders with collarbones that flared. She—unmistakably female—was dressed in black cotton from neck to ankles, so seamless Grif could barely discern where her body stopped and the fabric began. Though it was night, sunshades were wrapped around her temples, perched on a straight, lean nose; she'd have looked severe even without the downturned mouth. She waited until he was done studying her, and had recovered somewhat, before speaking.

"We meet again." She also didn't sound happy.

And Grif recalled these features—not this face, but the underlying features—pressing through a thinning membrane of filmy Everlast and splintering walls. He had to fight not to back away from her, though every renegade cell in his body was telling him to do just that. "Anas."

She looked different than she had when casting him back into flesh and the Surface, though when she whipped her glasses from her face, Grif caught sight of eyes slanted with flame before her true angelic form flashed. Twenty-two-foot wings of downy gold blazed behind her, illuminating the dark body in silhouette. Her close-shaved head prevented singeing, but her neck was suddenly too long, and the air crackled around her when she shifted.

Grif's cigarette fell from his fingers, and he involuntarily stepped backward.

"You will call me Anne," she said, shading her eyes again with the glasses. Her eyes and wings instantly snuffed. Darkness reclaimed the golf green, but this time it sat upon it heavily, like a layer of foreboding smoke.

"Why would I do that?" he asked, blinking hard.

"Because I do not want my blessed name defiled by human lips."

Shakily, Grif pulled out another cigarette. "I mean, why do I have to call you anything, *Anne*? What are you doing here?"

"My job." She lifted her chin, and this time—even with the ill-fitting skin suppressing all that flame—he recognized her. "Unlike you."

Grif licked his lower lip. "Frank send you?"

"You know who sent me." A Pure wasn't to do anything outside of God's express will. Ironically, this made them haughty despite being technically lesser than mortals. It also made them impossible to argue with.

But if Anne was supposed to take him home, why wasn't he already wrapped up in her flaming wings and hurtling toward the Everlast? Squinting, he dragged on his cigarette. "I still have free will, don't I?"

"You are a child of God," she conceded, mouth turning down. "And you are encased in mortal flesh."

"And did you get to choose your outfit?" he said, gesturing to her flesh. "Because you missed a spot right here." He pointed to her eyes.

Her body thrummed with a growl. "Don't mistake my blindness for weakness. The stimulation of all five senses at once would overwhelm one who is Pure. Mortality takes what is Pure and makes it defective."

Grif ignored the insult. "So . . . what? Blind people, the deaf, the mutes . . . all those people are really angels?"

"Don't be stupid," Anne hissed. "They're God's children and destined for Paradise. But, yes, some of his children are closer to the angels than others."

It matched what he'd seen at the Gates, where those who had physical or mental ailments entered the Everlast to find their sight restored, their bodies and minds whole. And while others marched into Paradise like an army of souls, the newly whole ones rocketed past the Gates as if launched from the mud.

Grif grunted. "And all this time I thought God had just gotten His wires crossed."

"Blasphemy," Anne snapped, fists clenching at her sides. "God makes no mistakes. He is divine. Angels are pure. And mankind is—"

"Impure," Grif finished for her. "Yeah. I got the memo."

"This," Anne said, gesturing furiously to her flesh, "is a demotion. Donning human flesh is like being cast out for a Pure."

And she said it in a way that let Grif know she blamed him.

"It's an acquired taste," Grif told her with more boldness than he felt.

"I'd rather Fall." With the deliberation of a hungry python, she came closer. "But I can't return Home until you either kill that woman or let her die. And I can tell you this much, Griffin Shaw, I'm already tired of running into things."

"So kill her yourself."

Anne sneered. "You know I can't do that. The angelic host does not interfere in human affairs. I'm only here to clean up your mess, and preserve other souls from your defiling touch. I've been watching you, you know."

He hadn't.

"It's different this time around, isn't it?" She smiled knowingly.

"The coffee is better."

"And the women?"

"I wouldn't know," he replied stiffly.

"That's right. You're *faithful*. Determined to find your Evie . . ."

"Don't you dare talk about her."

Anne smiled, and jerked her head toward Kit's window. "Let me tell you about these modern-day women, then. They're vibrant and full of *life*. Not like you."

"Not like you, either," he said, because if he was out of place on the mudflat, she was doubly so.

"Thank. God."

Grif crossed his arms, and tossed her own smile back at her. "Make yourself at home, Annie. 'Cause I ain't killing that innocent woman."

Anne growled, flashing teeth like stalactites, and began speaking in tongues. It was like rushing water and roaring wind mashed into one vocal box, but Grif, standing there of his own free will, ignored the babble and lit another cigarette.

"The decision you make here and now will ripple through the tides of the universe," she yelled, when he turned to leave. "The longer you're here, the more likely you are to influence events you have no business touching. I'd think hard about what you're trying to do, Griffin Shaw. And of what you've already done. You've hurt enough people, but you've changed nothing."

That was probably true. Blowing out a toxic stream of smoke, he slowly turned back around. "It's still my choice."

"There is only one right choice when deciding between two courses of action, and that is the will of God."

As if a Pure could understand true moral dilemma. Grif sniffed. "You know, you could help me find out who's trying to kill her. Stop them instead."

"I don't care enough to try."

No, he knew that. She was here on orders alone. Asking a pure angel to help a mortal was like asking a dog to meow. They just didn't have it in them.

So Grif headed across the green, back to the house, and back to protect Kit. His wingless shoulder blades pulsed beneath the Pure's stare.

"I will not assist you," Anne called out, her voice again rumbling like a storm. "But I *will* thwart you. I will block your way. I will take that divine gift of free will and use it against you so that you'll know defeat again in this pseudo-life."

Grif kept walking. "You can't touch me."

"Doesn't mean I can't touch *her.*"

Grif stopped dead, shook his head, and turned with fire in his own eyes. "You know what they say about your tribe, don't you? The other Pures?"

He waited, but she said nothing.

"They say that you're the ones who failed God. You failed to keep order on the heavenly pathways by doing no more than you were told and no less. They say Lucifer and the Third used your rigidity against you. They also say the only reason you were the first of the created angels was because God had to keep going until he got it right."

Anne remained stoic and silent, so Grif exercised his gift of free will and headed back to the house. "See you on the flip side, Pure."

Anne growled in response, but when she called out to him again, he didn't turn around. "Kill her, Griffin Shaw. Kill her, and put the world back in order."

Whose world? Grif wondered, flicking his cigarette butt into the darkness. Because his hadn't seen any sort of order in over fifty years.

CHAPTER FIFTEEN

Kit had never been to Caleb Chambers's lakeside estate before, though she'd read about the fabled parties in the gossips, the glossies . . . even in her own newspaper. Despite his prestige and accessibility, he retained an aura of exclusivity. Do business with Chambers, it was said, and you were practically guaranteed success. He never faltered, never failed. Never a professional misstep, or financial fumble.

"Too good to be true," Kit murmured as the tram ferrying them around the still, glossy lake slid past a looming evergreen and the estate came into view.

"What was that?" Grif asked, tucked in close beside her. The valet had assumed they were a couple, and dropped a fur over their legs before she could protest.

Not that she'd protest. As promised, she hadn't mentioned their shared kiss to Grif, or even alluded to the fight that followed. She wasn't going to lower herself to mentioning that he'd pretend to be an angel just to get away from her touch.

Grif had been tense around her at first, but was loosening up now that he saw she was keeping her word. And she would continue to do so. She had her pride. She didn't chase down men like they were game. She certainly didn't chase moody dangerous strangers who claimed to have wings and dead wives.

But Fleur was right, Kit thought, now that she'd calmed. The bad-boy gene got her motor running. So it wasn't Grif. It certainly wasn't *angels*. It was something faulty in her— something she was going to put a stop to immediately.

Maybe I'll pick up a nice, safe Mormon boy at the charity ball, she thought, as the tram began its final leg up the drive.

"Did you say something?" Grif asked, and she realized she'd been mumbling to herself. Who's crazy now? Kit thought, sighing.

"I was just thinking of our illustrious host," she told Grif, as they rolled past cypresses spaced like sentinels, and torches mimicking the same.

"You mean why his name keeps popping up along those suspected of running illegal brothels."

"Yeah. I mean, why risk all of this?" she said, as they came to a stop in front of a mansion reminiscent of a Tuscan villa.

"Well, what do you know about the man?"

"Facts or hearsay?"

"I'm not picky."

She eyed him in the dark. "It's quietly rumored that he keeps his wives at the lake estate. Or most of them. The first one lives with him at the Trails. No one is ever invited there."

Grif's expression remained blank. "So he's a polygamist."

"Alleged." Kit nodded. "Nothing has ever been proven, and though there are whispers, most of Vegas couldn't care less. Not the most judgmental town, if you haven't noticed."

They followed the other partygoers through an arched courtyard with bubbling fountains, naked statues, and doorways flung wide to reveal a foyer dripping with chandeliers. The noise level rose just inside as guests mingled in a social tapestry of conversation, music, and laughter. Tuxedoed waiters bore hors d'oeuvres, while hostesses in tiny black dresses and two-hour heels offered champagne flutes from sparkling silver trays. Grif accepted two from a high-cheekboned blonde who gave him a generous smile before moving on.

Kit lifted a brow beneath her raven-hued do.

"What?" Grif handed her a flute.

Kit couldn't help herself. "I don't think she likes guys with wings."

Grif gave her a fish-eyed stare. "I was just admiring her dress."

"That's not a dress," she muttered, sipping, "it's a plot summary."

Grif laughed, a deep chuckle that reverberated through his arm where it touched hers, and since Kit immediately wished she could make him laugh again, she discreetly edged away, resolutely turning her attention to the rest of the room.

Everything winked and sparkled against a white marble floor, leaded windows, and candlelight as artfully placed as the paintings on the wall. Chambers favored classical and antiques, which fit the villa, but Kit found them overly precious and twee.

Give me the clean lines of mid-century modernism any day, she thought, eyeing an ugly monkey vase.

"So you came." Paul's appearance was sudden, telling Kit he'd been watching for them, but his expression was drawn, indicating he wished they hadn't.

"Wouldn't waste the tickets," she said, giving a polite smile to the woman he was wearing, one poured into fabric that had more give than the Salvation Army. Everything was so stretchy these days. Where were the butterfly darts? The pleats? The pin tucks that turned clothes into structured art?

"Kit, this is my date, Raven. Raven, this is Katherine Craig, my ex."

"Oh my Gawd," Raven said, in a bubblegum voice that trilled like a string instrument. She looked Kit up and down, eyes gone wide. "He wasn't kidding. You really do dress like June Cleaver. Is that dress . . . old?"

"Vintage," Kit corrected shortly.

"So you wear things that have been worn before? By . . . old people?"

Smoothing her gloved fingertips over the cupcake skirt, Kit replied, "I wear things made in America and made to last, yes. I have a tactual addiction."

Raven tilted her head up, pouting at Paul in a way Kit was sure they both found cute. "What does that even mean?"

Kit smiled cutely, too. "It means cheap textiles make me break out in hives, and that I don't take fashion cues from something called a Snooki."

Grif snorted, quickly covering it with a cough.

Raven straightened so that her breasts nearly popped from her stretch bodice. "How long did you say you two were married?"

"Short enough that it was a long time ago," Kit shot back, before biting her tongue. It bothered her that Paul wasn't standing up for her, and it annoyed her that she was bothered. Besides, how could she blame Raven? Even Kit was beginning to find their marital union hard to believe.

"Some things never change," Paul said, pointedly raising his brows. "Which is why I'm sure you'll understand when I say please, whatever you do tonight, be discreet."

"Darling, everything about me is discreet."

He canvassed her body the way his girlfriend had—from the white stripe in her dark Marilyn do to her Roger Vivier stilettos and her gold beaded clutch in between. Then he looked at Grif. "It's my reputation here."

"Then maybe *we* should be worried," Grif said, and took Kit's arm before Paul could reply. "Come on. Let's dance."

The last thing she saw was Paul's frown as Grif wheeled her away.

"Thank you," she said, as they headed to the makeshift dance floor. "I was about to make an ass of myself."

And she'd already seen half a dozen men in this room that were on her list. She couldn't afford to get wrapped up in what Paul and his walking, talking blow-up doll thought of her.

"Yeah, well. The stench was getting to me," Grif replied, leading her through a particularly dense cluster of the well-heeled.

"I'm happy to see someone else considers the 'Bordello Blonde' scent a bit obvious."

Grif shook his head as he wheeled her onto the dance floor. "I was talking about him. Didn't you smell that?"

Kit shrugged. "I'm immune to his bullshit by now."

Fortunately, if anything could shake off her lingering irritation, it was dancing. And if there was anything that could alter her mood altogether, it was *great* dancing.

Grif apparently didn't feel the same. "What are you doing?"

She slid to the right, the beat moving through the room to syncopate with her heartbeat, moving through her chest, out her arms, and into his. The band was live, she was *alive,* and though she wasn't sure she should be, she was also swinging around the dance floor in a dangerous man's arms. Well, one moment couldn't hurt anything, right?

"Oh. I dunno," she said, twirling, eyes half-closed. "I just kinda like to lead."

"What a surprise," Grif said drily.

The corner of her mouth lifted in reply as she continued to sway, but Grif suddenly dug in his heels. The entire dance floor moved around them, but he just leveled her with a hard stare.

"What?" she asked, pulling his arm, edging right. He didn't budge.

"I know my way." And he swung her to the left.

It took a moment before Kit caught her breath, and another before she allowed herself to relax into Grif's arms. He moved as if he was possessed by the song, his touch sure as he guided her with a mere shift of his fingertips. He anticipated her movements so seamlessly it was like stepping right through the notes, and heat rose inside of her so that she had to force it away.

She *wasn't* going to open to him again.

But, damn, if he hadn't already told her he didn't want her, she would have sworn he did.

And that's why she finally pulled back, dizzy but determined not to lose herself in the music, the footwork, or him.

"So what do you think?" she asked, lifting her head. But Grif's eyes were glazed, and he jolted like she'd awoken him from a dream. "I mean, would you keep all your wives here if you were a polygamist?"

Grif glanced around, making the movement a part of the dance. Again, Kit's heart surged with an extra beat. "Hard to say. I always thought one spouse was enough."

"Funny," she said, spying the back of Paul's head. "I thought one was too many."

"Yeah, because you were married to a total sap."

She couldn't argue that. "Marriage isn't all it's made out to be."

"But being alone is?"

"Being *single*," she corrected, "is about hope. It's about the future . . . the person you might meet at Starbucks or online or in the next aisle at the grocery store. But being married is about the past. How you met, what choices you made early on when there were still choices *to* make. Eventually memories of wonderful things have to make up for all the disappointments since."

Grif almost stopped dancing. "That's . . ."

"Awful, I know." She wrinkled her nose. "Never mind. Marriage and I just weren't a good fit."

"Stop it."

"But it's true."

"No, I mean you're trying to lead again. Stop."

"Oh, sorry."

"Anyway, you're painting in too broad of strokes there, Kitty-cat."

The endearment had been automatic. She saw the regret flash over his face before he could hide it, and clenched her jaws. "Am I?"

He nodded without hesitation. "Same as your reverence for all things fifties."

"Oh, that's right, I forgot. You were alive back then. You *remember*."

"Hey, I don't care if you believe me—"

"Good."

"But you and your friends think things were so great back then, yet there's always been trouble in the world, and enough people willing to cause it."

Kit shrugged. "It was still a simpler time."

"No. It wasn't." And he stopped dancing, though he still held her tight. "A black woman was arrested for refusing to give up her seat on the bus—"

Kit stiffened. "Are you lecturing me? Can we just go back to dancing?"

But Grif's face had taken on a deeper red. "We were battling the Commies on Earth and in outer space—"

"Are angels supposed to call people Commies?"

He ignored her. "The Cold War was the scariest damn thing this planet had seen, and we lived in fear of our own neighbors."

"Yes, and it was before people knew that smoking would kill you," Kit pointed out, "and well before sex really could."

"Yeah, well one thing was exactly the same."

"What's that?"

"Women were still murdered by men who thought they could get away with it."

Kit clenched her teeth. "If you're trying to prove that you're an angel again, it's not working."

"I don't have to prove anything. I know what I know."

"Just like Tony, eh?" Kit scoffed, because the old man had told her the same thing.

Grif shook his head. "No, I know way more than old Tony

Prima. I know something you don't know, too. Marriage ain't about the past. You just chose a man without any drive."

Bridget Moore's words revisited Kit like a gut punch. *A man who's driven in his life's pursuits will be equally driven when it comes to you.*

Tears unexpectedly welled in Kit's eyes.

"Oh, geez." Grif immediately guided her from the dance floor and over to giant bay windows, the center open to allow in fresh air.

You can lose yourself to a man like that.

"I'm sorry," Grif was muttering, but Kit was too busy wondering how a prostitute could know such things, how a crazy man who thought he was an angel who'd died in 1960 could know it. And how she could not.

Pulling a cloth handkerchief from her clutch, Kit waved him off. She'd been right about one thing, at least. This man was dangerous.

"Oh, my. Tears at a charity ball. That won't do."

The voice popped up behind them, smooth as whiskey poured over ice, and Kit turned to find a handsome man with silver hair, a dark tuxedo, and a gaze that was both open and calculating at once.

"Mr. Chambers," Kit blurted, tucking the cloth away. Sniffling, she nodded at the petite woman next to him, and gave a small smile to the young girl on his other side. "I'm Kit Craig. This is my date, Griffin Shaw."

"I know who you are, Ms. Craig. Read your paper every day," Chambers said pleasantly. He then turned his blinding smile on Grif, who managed a sort of grimace in return. "Pleasure, Mr. Shaw. This is my wife, Anabelle. One of my girls, Charlotte."

Though she was chic in black, with golden hair as glossy as her lips, the hand that Mrs. Chambers offered Kit was as insincere and brittle as her smile. Charlotte, who looked to be around thirteen, ducked her head and gave a soft hello. She, too, was in black, and though the dress was age appropriate, she was swimming in it. She wriggled at the introduction, a bit nervous, a bit bored, and it was clear to Kit that she'd been introduced to people all night.

Kit smiled at the little girl. "You have six daughters, if my research is correct?"

"Research, is it?" Chambers laughed, and even that was warm and rich, like hot chocolate. "Actually it's six daughters and two boys now. Another on the way."

"Congratulations," Kit said to Anabelle, surprised. The woman was so thin she wouldn't have guessed. But what do I know, she thought, kicking herself mentally. Mrs. Chambers, who—research showed—had four children by the time she was Kit's age, was the expert. Not her.

The woman placed a hand over the near-imperceptible bump rising beneath her plain tunic. "We're very blessed."

"But why the tears, dear?" Chambers asked, shunting their blessings aside, his voice dripping concern. "I saw you dancing, looking happy enough, only minutes ago."

"Well, she had a friend who liked to dance, too," Grif said, getting right to the point. Kit would have kicked him if she could've done so without being seen.

Chambers's smooth brow furrowed. "Oh?"

Kit cleared her throat. "My best friend, a photographer at the paper, died earlier this week."

"Murdered, actually," Grif clarified, and while Chambers's attention was on him, Kit saw his wife's face briefly crumble, then clear. Chambers, though, remained as implacable as before.

"Oh, yes. I read about that. A lovely young girl, if the photo was any indication. What was her name again? Rocky, Rockson—"

"Rockwell," Kit said, still following Grif's lead. This time she was grateful. "Nicole Rockwell."

Tsking, Chambers shook his head. "Do the police have any leads?"

"No," Grif said. "But we were hoping you might provide one."

Now Anabelle let out a surprised gasp. Charlotte inched closer to her mother and grasped at her hand. A frown appeared between the slim brows, and it was clear she understood there was something else going on here, even if she didn't know what.

A flicker, the slightest irritation, flashed in the older man's eyes. "I can't see how."

Kit laid a hand atop Grif's arm. If he was playing bad cop, she would play good. "Your name was on a list that was delivered to us, that's all."

A silver brow raised in surprise. "Any idea who sent the list?"

"No, but the names on it are rather remarkable. In fact, most of the men on it are present here tonight."

"So let me get this straight," Chambers said, eyes narrowed. "You're *not* really here to support my charity for children in need?"

"Not here for the canapés, either," Grif said coolly.

"Mama," Charlotte clutched at her mother, holding her by the forearms as the woman's face drained of color, and she staggered back.

The look Chambers gave Grif this time was downright hostile. Progress, Kit thought, even as he turned smoothly to his wife. "Please take Charlotte upstairs now. She may have some ice cream before she goes to bed."

If his curt tone or lack of comfort bothered Anabelle, she didn't show it. Instead, she turned on her sensible heels and steered Charlotte stiffly through the crowd. Or was it the other way around? Kit wondered, watching them carefully. They headed directly up the right side of the staircase splitting the room, nodding at guests but never stopping. And if Kit wasn't mistaken, there was a perceptible relief in Anabelle's shoulders, and yes, there it was. Charlotte took the lead, guiding her mother instead of the reverse. Kit frowned . . . but by then Chambers had whirled back around.

"I don't know what you two are after, but that was entirely inappropriate. This is not the time or place for gross accusations."

Grif tilted his head. "There's a time and place for those?"

Chambers grew so still the whole room seemed to hold its breath. Then he leaned close. "Some nosy little girl gets taken out by bad guys in a bad place she had no business being, well . . . I don't see what that has to do with me."

"She was investigating a prostitution ring," Kit said, just as pointedly, if louder. "A source told her that you, and many of the men here tonight, were involved."

"Then maybe she should have been a bit more selective about her sources." He straightened his tux impatiently. "I've been the target of rumor, innuendo, and extortion for too long to get worked up by some young reporter's overactive imagination. But when I've invited you into my own home, for a holiday charity event, then I expect you to bring your manners along with you."

He gestured to someone behind them. Kit had an image of being escorted out into the dark by Schmidt, and her heart jumped.

"Kicking us out?" said Grif, reading at least part of her thoughts.

"On the contrary," Chambers said, as a hostess arrived with a tray full of drinks. He removed two fresh flutes and offered them to Kit and Grif. "Make yourselves at home. Enjoy the festivities while you can."

He turned, but paused in his retreat to stare her down. Kit's mouth dried, her pulse quickened, and she had to concentrate just to hold on to her champagne flute. Had she ever been looked at in such a way before? Like he was seeing her and not. Like she was an object that had been propped in the wrong place.

"If you ever have so-called evidence linking me to a horrific crime again, I suggest running it by the police before you go running your mouth. Or you might find yourself on the losing end of a very large lawsuit. And I don't believe your little family newspaper needs that, do you?" Then he straightened, blinked like he was coming out of a trance, jerked at his jacket lapels, and walked away as if they didn't exist.

"Was that a veiled threat?" Kit asked Grif, ignoring a pointed glare from Paul as he headed directly toward Chambers.

"I didn't see any veil."

Neither had Kit. Sipping from her flute, trying not to shake, she looked around again for Schmidt, but saw only other guests, most now eyeing them warily.

"Notice he didn't ask exactly what kind of list he was on," Grif said. "Grocery list. Mailing list. Prize chump of the year list."

"I did notice. But we still have no evidence linking him to the Wayfarer." And now she was also on the bad side of the most powerful man in the city.

Grif tsk-ed insincerely, jerking his head at Paul, who'd finally caught up to Chambers, though he looked like he wished he hadn't. "And with his reputation at stake, too."

"It's not funny, Grif." Kit whirled to the windows and placed her flute on the sill so she could cover her face with her hands. Outside the wind ripped around trees that had no business being in the desert, the sound as foreign to Kit as an ocean rushing the shore. For a moment, she imagined herself far away.

Then Grif's arm slid over her shoulders, and he pulled her close. "Hey, now. It's all right. I don't think you were going to make his Christmas card list this year anyway."

Kit knew he was right, but was suddenly overwhelmed with the enormity of what she was doing. She really could lose it all—her reputation, the paper . . . her life. Who the hell was she? And what was she trying to prove? "This whole thing is a catastrophe."

"Yes."

"That's it?" A disbelieving snort escaped her. "Shouldn't an angel be better at cheering me up?"

Grif removed his arm, making her wish she hadn't swiped at him, but then he lowered his elbows to the sill and joined her in looking out at the dark. "I can tell you one thing."

"What?" Kit asked, not sure she wanted to know.

"Top-secret angel stuff. Gotta promise not to put it in print."

"Shaw."

He smiled slightly as he lifted his gaze to the stars. "You can't quit, Kitty-cat. You call this a catastrophe, but take it from me, the line between a catastrophe and a miracle is a fine one."

Kit shook her head. "You say the damnedest things, Mr. Shaw."

"Thank you, Miss Craig." Straightening, he offered his arm. "Now, come on . . . there's got to be someone else in here we can piss off."

"Yes." Kit sighed. "We seem to be very good at that."

CHAPTER SIXTEEN

Grif and Kit remained at the ball despite a sudden and clear non-grata status, a state made more apparent when the waitresses ceased offering them drinks. But Kit redeemed herself by participating in the auction, doing brief battle with another woman before winning a spa package for two to some chichi Strip resort, earning an acknowledging nod from Chambers.

There was something about the man, Grif thought, studying Chambers's demeanor as he moved, too smooth, through the room. Ignore the monkey suit, the moneyed air, the constant ass-kissing that Chambers had to practically swivel to avoid. Forget that they'd just met. Grif *knew* this guy. He reminded him of a fighter who'd once sucker-punched Grif in the ring. Neither the largest nor the strongest, the man had a meanness to his eye that Grif had been on the lookout for ever since. Chambers had it, too.

Grif was so focused on him that Kit's low whisper didn't register at first, though her body heat did. "I think we're going to have to split up."

"Not a chance."

"Look around, Grif. There's something else going on here. For example, have you noticed a distinct whiteness to this crowd?"

"Mormon," Grif pointed out.

"This isn't a Mormon function," she returned. "And even the servers are all white."

Not to mention female. At some point the male waiters had all been dismissed, and only the hostesses remained behind.

"And did you notice that the men are disappearing in clumps? Most aren't heading back to the tram, either."

He had noticed. There'd been a slow, intermittent exodus to a doorway tucked beneath the split-V staircase, clearly guarded by a man with an earpiece and battle guns for forearms.

Kit bit her wide bottom lip and narrowed her eyes thoughtfully. "Something else is going on, and I think it's behind that door. But I don't think I can get there."

"Well, I'm not leaving you." Grif had seen the look Chambers had given her. It had him looking for plasma. And for Schmidt.

"Look, I'm too well-known for anything to happen to me here. Besides, we haven't even seen Schmidt. So what do you say I stay here and you go storm the castle."

He eyed her coolly. "You'll stay here?"

"We need to know what's going on behind those doors, and I can't do it."

Grif wasn't even sure he could. But five minutes later, when Chambers completed his final round with the remaining guests, the man's implacable smile slipped as he nodded at the door's guard, and Grif had to watch, frustrated, while he disappeared inside.

"Stay in plain sight," Grif ordered Kit. "I mean it."

Kit saluted as he headed across the ballroom. "You're the alpha angel."

Smart-ass. That's why he was already scowling when he approached the guard.

"Your ticket, sir?" the man said, before Grif had even come to a stop.

"I gave it to the girl out front," Grif said, taking a step forward.

As expected, the guard intercepted. "I mean the other ticket, sir."

Grif had no idea what that meant. "Guess I misplaced it."

"Well, I hope you find it soon." And the guard folded his arms in front of him and looked away.

Grif huffed, and tried another tack. "Look, Mr. Chambers is expecting me."

"Not without a ticket, he's not."

Grif was mulling over his options when the door behind them reopened, and Chambers himself appeared. "It's okay, Trevor. Mr. Shaw is one of our invited guests."

"Of course, Mr. Chambers." Trevor moved aside and Grif resisted patting him on the head as he followed Chambers inside. He shadowed him through a winding hallway, low-lit, carpeted, whispering of privacy.

"Is there a camera in here somewhere?" Grif asked, knowing there was but still surprised by Chambers's easy nod. How else would the man have known Grif was outside the door?

But why did a man need cameras in his own house?

"No women allowed back here?" Grif asked, still probing.

Chambers's glance was smeared with a smile. "What kind of party would it be without women?"

"What kind of party is it now?"

"You'd know if you had a ticket," Chambers said, smile growing.

"Well, I'm an invited guest."

They were circling, taking jabs, feeling each other out. Looking for tells, and waiting for the other to show a weakness. What Grif didn't know was, were they opponents or just sparring partners?

Chambers came to a stop with his hand on another closed door. Music and laughter seeped through the cracks, and Grif relaxed fractionally. "Yes, you are a guest. And as such I expect your utmost discretion regarding the activities behind these doors. If it were to get out . . ."

"Yes?" Grif raised a brow.

Chambers smiled. "Everyone would want a ticket."

Grif inclined his head.

And Chambers pushed open the door to reveal a curtained vestibule holding a dark, gilded podium. A woman stood behind it, wearing slim gold heels, perfume that reminded Grif of citrus on a hot wind, and the most revealing lingerie Grif had ever seen. Grif swallowed hard and she responded with a smile almost as blinding as the jewels around her neck.

One point for Chambers, Grif thought, feeling the man's eyes on him. "Mr. Shaw, meet Melody, your personal concierge. Melody, this is Griffin Shaw. It's his first time at the dance."

Melody couldn't have been a handful of years out of her teens, but slipped to Grif's side with a well-practiced sway. She had large eyes in a heart-shaped face, and a tiny nose with the slightest dusting of freckles. Her dusky hair was shot through with subtle blond streaks, and her firm skin wore a color that could only come from the sun. But that adornment stopped there.

Her negligee skimmed the top of her thighs, and shimmered over the peaks of tight, smooth breasts. Leaning into him, she pressed jutting, gold-tipped nipples against his arm, and linked her slim fingers with his. Her warm, orange-grove scent washed over him again as she purred, "At your service, Mr. Shaw. If you see anything you like, anything you want, you need only give the word. I'm here for you."

Grif cleared his throat in response.

Snorting, Chambers turned toward a wall with parted curtains, and another woman appeared instantly. So the vestibule was also heavily monitored, Grif thought. And this woman was most decidedly *not* Mrs. Chambers. Blond as Marilyn Monroe, with similarly lush curves, she, too, was impossibly tan. Surprisingly, she wore even less than Melody, and she clung to Chambers's arm without reserve, face turned adoringly up to his.

The world's shortest skirt, ostensibly white, skimmed her upper thighs, though like the bikini top, it was utterly transparent. The skirt swirled as Chambers guided her around, revealing red palm marks on her behind as she quickstepped, fighting not to topple over in her heels. Grif got the feeling that Chambers was parading her, trying to provoke another reaction.

Grif was a red-blooded man, so there was definitely a reaction, but he was also a gentleman, so it was involuntary. Chambers still shot him a knowing look, then looped an arm over the woman's shoulders and began toying with her exposed nipple. When Grif just lifted his chin, he said, "Shall we?"

Grif from lunging. "You don't like women much, do you?" he asked tightly.

Chambers laughed, and puffed at his cigar. "I'm surrounded by women. In my work, my family, my church. Outnumbered really. I know women better than most men ever do."

"Really?"

"Yes, and wanna know what most men don't?" Chambers asked, leaning forward. "That even you don't seem to know?"

Grif raised his brows.

"They're just one enormous, intractable problem after another."

He smiled, leaned back, and tilted his head, eyeing Grif from the corner before closing his eyes. "If you'll excuse me for a moment."

Grif looked away, but there was nowhere decent to set his gaze. Nude, intractable "problems" lay everywhere. Was this what the world had come to? There'd been prostitution in his day—any day—he knew that and had never considered himself a prude. But this . . . these men weren't just treating these women as objects . . . they were treating them as *other*.

Chambers finished in utter silence. Grif knew this only because Bethany rose, wiping her mouth with the back of her arm. "Get Marie," Chambers told her. Bethany wobbled away without looking at either of them, and a few moments later another woman appeared. She was still beautiful, but older—around Kit's age, maybe even Grif's—and clearly some sort of authority as she'd been allowed the dignity of true clothing, even if it was skintight leather from head to toe.

"She's a slob," Chambers told Marie.

"I'll see to it," the woman replied, and disappeared immediately.

The ballroom had been grand, the slim passageway private, but this room was opulent and rosy, with a thickly carpeted floor, silk-papered walls, and damask curtains hanging from ceiling to floor. Hurricane lamps offered the room's only light, providing shadowed alcoves and niches where men and their dates could repose in private.

Not that most of them bothered.

Grif now expected the women, scantily clad, but what he didn't figure on was for them to be draped across every surface, vertical or horizontal, some spotlit or uplit, others dripping shadows. Some were dancing, or moving to a beat that matched someone's idea of music, while others writhed on pedestals that looked like blocks of ice. Alone or in pairs, they were all smiling and taking requests from the men who were gathered around in groups—smoking, drinking, even reaching out intermittently to sample the golden, embellished flesh.

The largest platform was located in the room's center, where not one but two women were performing for a cluster of men. The two kissed, sliding their hands up each other's slim wrists and arms, cupping their soft faces and necks, taking turns tipping their elegant heads back to allow access to their lips, necks . . . breasts. One of the women slipped pink manicured fingertips between the other's legs, who arched back in response.

The men applauded.

Grif turned away. Score another point for Chambers, Grif thought, and while the other man didn't gloat, it wasn't because he was beyond it . . . it was because he was already leading Grif to a roped-off alcove with two chairs and a table draped in black silk between them. Once seated—once his fawning escort was kneeling beside him—he motioned for Grif to sit as well.

"So what brings you to Vegas?" Chambers asked conversationally, like there wasn't a half-naked woman sliding a hand over his crotch.

Grif cleared his throat, trying to ignore Melody, who was clinging to him like her life depended on it. "Not this, that's for sure."

All these women. What were they doing here? And why? He could barely stand it for them.

"Fair enough. After all, women are a ubiquitous commodity. You can get this anywhere." Eyes cold, he jerked his chin at Melody. "Mr. Shaw needs a minute to acclimate. Go get him a drink."

"Of course." She leaned over Grif, looming close so the gold-tipped cleavage was even with his nose. "Signal me when you're ready, darling."

Watching her saunter away, Grif wondered if vomiting on his shoes would be considered a signal.

Chambers's girl made to follow, but he stopped her by grabbing a handful of hair. "Not you, dear. Back on your knees. And be discreet."

Though her eyes were watering, and the strain showed in her neck, she managed a tight smile, which widened when she swiveled back around. Only then did Chambers loosen his hold on her hair.

"Always," she managed, and made to kiss him on the lips. But Chambers turned his head, his expression sour, and the woman improvised with a quick nibble on his earlobe before she sunk out of sight. The tablecloth lifted, a zipper sounded, and Chambers held Grif's gaze, unblinking. Then one corner of his mouth lifted in a smile, and he held his right hand out to the side. Another concierge materialized immediately to hand

him a cigar and snifter, before melting away. Without taking his eyes off Grif, Chambers slid lower into his seat.

Grif returned the cold stare. Opponents, he knew now. Not sparring partners.

"You really should try this," Chambers said, puffing away. He wasn't talking about the cigar.

"I'm here to talk murder, Mr. Chambers."

"Hear that, Bethany? You're going to have to work extra hard." A blond head popped up to respond. One-handed, he pushed it back down.

"A woman was murdered after being provided a list with your name on it," Grif continued.

"Among other names, if I'm not mistaken."

"Others in this room."

Eyes half-lidded, Chambers sipped. "And?"

"And she was investigating a prostitution ring."

"Is that what you think this is?" Chambers laughed, a hearty, hard sound. "Look around. Does any woman here look like they'd be caught dead at a shitbox like the Wayfarer?"

Grif and Kit had never mentioned the Wayfarer, and Chambers realized it immediately. "You seem to know a lot about it."

"This is *my* city, Mr. Shaw," Chambers said now, carelessly flicking ash on the floor. "I have a vested interest in everything that happens here."

"Then I'd expect you to be more concerned when an innocent woman is butchered."

Chambers didn't reply immediately. Instead, he slid further back into his seat, eyes glazing slightly. "What's the big deal? Every woman plays the whore at one time or another. Nicole Rockwell just died while doing it."

The cameras, and the beef at the door, were all that kept

Chambers caught Grif's eye. "See what I mean? Always a problem."

Moments later, Bethany was escorted from the room by the same man who'd been guarding the ballroom door.

"Keep hanging out with that Craig woman and you'll see." Grif's gaze shot back to Chambers, who nodded as he finished his drink. "Yep. Her family tree is littered with crazy bitches. Her mother, who loved to fuck the blue-collars. That dykey aunt of hers. Even her father was just one big pussy." He smiled blandly. "Excuse my French."

Grif didn't want to discuss Kit's father or family with Chambers. He didn't want her name to pass this man's foul, profane lips, or the thought of her anywhere near his mind.

But Chambers didn't stop. "If you want to do her a real favor, you'll teach her a woman's place . . . or someone else surely will."

Don't let him know you care, Grif thought, though he'd stiffened at the oily smile, the thin threat, the weighted stare. Instead of answering, he jerked his head toward center stage. The two women had finished with each other, and were now pleasuring themselves with toys tossed from their appreciative audience. "So what's your racket here? You keep your wife, or wives, upstairs while you sell skin to your friends?"

"Selling?" Chambers laughed, zipping himself discreetly. "These little ladies are budding entrepreneurs. I'm just the middle man. I provide the environment and opportunity for consenting adults to get to know each other."

"You're a pimp."

"Don't be vulgar," Chambers shot back, and this time the animal, the *other*, was alive in his eyes. "These are grown men and women. The women are beautiful, the men wealthy. They can all easily find sexual partners for themselves."

"So you just provide access."

"Look around. Does anyone look like they're here against their will?"

No. They were partying like it was the last night of their lives. "It's the same thing if it's their only way to make a living."

"We're all in the business of survival, Mr. Shaw."

"Yeah, well some of us are surviving more notably than others."

"Perhaps you'd like to do a little more than survive? Take one of these ladies for a little ride. It won't cost you a thing."

Grif looked away, and saw that a third woman was now lying atop the center stage. As the men hooted and hollered suggestions, she stripped what was left of her clothing and spread herself wide. Grif thought about slipping into a dark corner with a woman that anyone could have, and his stomach heaved.

"I don't quite understand your beef with this," Chambers snapped, seeing the disgust roll across Grif's face. "Are you of the homosexual persuasion?"

If this was straight, Grif realized, he'd rather be. "I ain't queer. I just don't like taking advantage of women."

"Taking ad—?" Chambers growled in the back of his throat, frustrated. "So some of the women here might need the money. So what? It's an exchange, like any other. Services for coin. That's the way of the world."

"It's *sex*."

"Also the way of the world," Chambers said, his voice brittle and hard. Lifting an arm, he snapped his fingers. Marie materialized instantly. Some of the men behind Chambers stopped and stared. However, he looked nowhere but at Grif's unblinking gaze. "Tell the three centerpieces I want a proper show, and not a tease. I want it raw and I want it now."

"Yes, Mr. Chambers."

"Marie was one of my first acquisitions," Chambers said, as she strode away. "She's worked her way up in my esteem because, like a good bitch, she's learned to take orders. Sit. Stay. Shut up."

But she was currently giving the orders, leaning across the transparent glass to whisper in the nude woman's ear. One of the men behind Marie fondled her ass, but she neither flinched nor appeared to notice. The girl she spoke with looked up, caught sight of Chambers watching, and quickly nodded. Yet Grif caught something else—brief, just a flash—but it looked like regret, or sadness. It was quickly covered with a snaking smile as she turned to the others.

"I'm not watching this." Grif rose, pushing away from the table. He and Kit would get what they needed another night, another way. He wanted no part of this filth . . . and he wanted Kit out of here now.

"Do you want to know what the difference is between sex for money and sex for free, Mr. Shaw?" Chambers's voice twisted across the room to snag Grif one last time. He waited until Grif had turned, to finish. "Sex for money always costs less."

Grif wanted to ask how Mrs. Chambers felt about that, then remembered Kit's words. *Marriage isn't all it's made out to be.* Was it true? Did all these women feel that way? Was it a twenty-first-century development that he couldn't understand because he was out of his place and time?

Had his Evie ever felt like that, even for a moment?

Chambers folded his hands behind his head, sensing he'd

hit some sort of nerve. "Money is the invisible elephant in every bedroom, Mr. Shaw. You'd do well to remember that."

"Marriage is not a business transaction."

Chambers laughed like he was naive. "You keep believing that." Then he rose from his seat, and ran his hands through his hair. "Now if you'll excuse me. I see something I want to fuck."

Grif flinched, and realized too late it was the reaction Chambers was hoping for. He turned away again, but Chambers's laughter chased him.

"Remember your promise," the man called out, and the reminder, along with the laughter, hung on the air like a threat.

After Kit noted the men systematically disappearing, after catching the ripe scent of a good ol' boys club souring the air, she made quick work of getting rid of Grif. There was no sense in trying to gain access to that back room—some doors, she knew, would never be open to her, so instead of beating her head against this one, she turned the mystery over to the ever-capable Grif.

After letting him think it was his idea, of course.

It was the women that she was most interested in, anyway. Thus, Grif hadn't been gone five minutes before Kit was breaking her promise to remain in clear sight, and heading up the big, winding staircase in search of Mrs. Chambers. With Grif no doubt occupying Chambers's attention, this was her chance to talk to Anabelle about the list, the Wayfarer, and Nic's death outside of her husband's overpowering presence.

Besides, she was curious. What kind of woman willingly shared her man not just with other women, but other *wives*? As a reporter, Kit strove for understanding rather than judgment,

The ballroom had been grand, the slim passageway private, but this room was opulent and rosy, with a thickly carpeted floor, silk-papered walls, and damask curtains hanging from ceiling to floor. Hurricane lamps offered the room's only light, providing shadowed alcoves and niches where men and their dates could repose in private.

Not that most of them bothered.

Grif now expected the women, scantily clad, but what he didn't figure on was for them to be draped across every surface, vertical or horizontal, some spotlit or uplit, others dripping shadows. Some were dancing, or moving to a beat that matched someone's idea of music, while others writhed on pedestals that looked like blocks of ice. Alone or in pairs, they were all smiling and taking requests from the men who were gathered around in groups—smoking, drinking, even reaching out intermittently to sample the golden, embellished flesh.

The largest platform was located in the room's center, where not one but two women were performing for a cluster of men. The two kissed, sliding their hands up each other's slim wrists and arms, cupping their soft faces and necks, taking turns tipping their elegant heads back to allow access to their lips, necks . . . breasts. One of the women slipped pink manicured fingertips between the other's legs, who arched back in response.

The men applauded.

Grif turned away. Score another point for Chambers, Grif thought, and while the other man didn't gloat, it wasn't because he was beyond it . . . it was because he was already leading Grif to a roped-off alcove with two chairs and a table draped in black silk between them. Once seated—once his fawning escort was kneeling beside him—he motioned for Grif to sit as well.

"So what brings you to Vegas?" Chambers asked conversationally, like there wasn't a half-naked woman sliding a hand over his crotch.

Grif cleared his throat, trying to ignore Melody, who was clinging to him like her life depended on it. "Not this, that's for sure."

All these women. What were they doing here? And why? He could barely stand it for them.

"Fair enough. After all, women are a ubiquitous commodity. You can get this anywhere." Eyes cold, he jerked his chin at Melody. "Mr. Shaw needs a minute to acclimate. Go get him a drink."

"Of course." She leaned over Grif, looming close so the gold-tipped cleavage was even with his nose. "Signal me when you're ready, darling."

Watching her saunter away, Grif wondered if vomiting on his shoes would be considered a signal.

Chambers's girl made to follow, but he stopped her by grabbing a handful of hair. "Not you, dear. Back on your knees. And be discreet."

Though her eyes were watering, and the strain showed in her neck, she managed a tight smile, which widened when she swiveled back around. Only then did Chambers loosen his hold on her hair.

"Always," she managed, and made to kiss him on the lips. But Chambers turned his head, his expression sour, and the woman improvised with a quick nibble on his earlobe before she sunk out of sight. The tablecloth lifted, a zipper sounded, and Chambers held Grif's gaze, unblinking. Then one corner of his mouth lifted in a smile, and he held his right hand out to the side. Another concierge materialized immediately to hand him a cigar and snifter, before melting away. Without taking his eyes off Grif, Chambers slid lower into his seat.

Grif returned the cold stare. Opponents, he knew now. Not sparring partners.

"You really should try this," Chambers said, puffing away. He wasn't talking about the cigar.

"I'm here to talk murder, Mr. Chambers."

"Hear that, Bethany? You're going to have to work extra hard." A blond head popped up to respond. One-handed, he pushed it back down.

"A woman was murdered after being provided a list with your name on it," Grif continued.

"Among other names, if I'm not mistaken."

"Others in this room."

Eyes half-lidded, Chambers sipped. "And?"

"And she was investigating a prostitution ring."

"Is that what you think this is?" Chambers laughed, a hearty, hard sound. "Look around. Does any woman here look like they'd be caught dead at a shitbox like the Wayfarer?"

Grif and Kit had never mentioned the Wayfarer, and Chambers realized it immediately. "You seem to know a lot about it."

"This is *my* city, Mr. Shaw," Chambers said now, carelessly flicking ash on the floor. "I have a vested interest in everything that happens here."

"Then I'd expect you to be more concerned when an innocent woman is butchered."

Chambers didn't reply immediately. Instead, he slid further back into his seat, eyes glazing slightly. "What's the big deal? Every woman plays the whore at one time or another. Nicole Rockwell just died while doing it."

The cameras, and the beef at the door, were all that kept

Grif from lunging. "You don't like women much, do you?" he asked tightly.

Chambers laughed, and puffed at his cigar. "I'm surrounded by women. In my work, my family, my church. Outnumbered really. I know women better than most men ever do."

"Really?"

"Yes, and wanna know what most men don't?" Chambers asked, leaning forward. "That even you don't seem to know?"

Grif raised his brows.

"They're just one enormous, intractable problem after another."

He smiled, leaned back, and tilted his head, eyeing Grif from the corner before closing his eyes. "If you'll excuse me for a moment."

Grif looked away, but there was nowhere decent to set his gaze. Nude, intractable "problems" lay everywhere. Was this what the world had come to? There'd been prostitution in his day—any day—he knew that and had never considered himself a prude. But this . . . these men weren't just treating these women as objects . . . they were treating them as *other*.

Chambers finished in utter silence. Grif knew this only because Bethany rose, wiping her mouth with the back of her arm. "Get Marie," Chambers told her. Bethany wobbled away without looking at either of them, and a few moments later another woman appeared. She was still beautiful, but older—around Kit's age, maybe even Grif's—and clearly some sort of authority as she'd been allowed the dignity of true clothing, even if it was skintight leather from head to toe.

"She's a slob," Chambers told Marie.

"I'll see to it," the woman replied, and disappeared immediately.

Chambers caught Grif's eye. "See what I mean? Always a problem."

Moments later, Bethany was escorted from the room by the same man who'd been guarding the ballroom door.

"Keep hanging out with that Craig woman and you'll see." Grif's gaze shot back to Chambers, who nodded as he finished his drink. "Yep. Her family tree is littered with crazy bitches. Her mother, who loved to fuck the blue-collars. That dykey aunt of hers. Even her father was just one big pussy." He smiled blandly. "Excuse my French."

Grif didn't want to discuss Kit's father or family with Chambers. He didn't want her name to pass this man's foul, profane lips, or the thought of her anywhere near his mind.

But Chambers didn't stop. "If you want to do her a real favor, you'll teach her a woman's place . . . or someone else surely will."

Don't let him know you care, Grif thought, though he'd stiffened at the oily smile, the thin threat, the weighted stare. Instead of answering, he jerked his head toward center stage. The two women had finished with each other, and were now pleasuring themselves with toys tossed from their appreciative audience. "So what's your racket here? You keep your wife, or wives, upstairs while you sell skin to your friends?"

"Selling?" Chambers laughed, zipping himself discreetly. "These little ladies are budding entrepreneurs. I'm just the middle man. I provide the environment and opportunity for consenting adults to get to know each other."

"You're a pimp."

"Don't be vulgar," Chambers shot back, and this time the animal, the *other*, was alive in his eyes. "These are grown men and women. The women are beautiful, the men wealthy. They can all easily find sexual partners for themselves."

"So you just provide access."

"Look around. Does anyone look like they're here against their will?"

No. They were partying like it was the last night of their lives. "It's the same thing if it's their only way to make a living."

"We're all in the business of survival, Mr. Shaw."

"Yeah, well some of us are surviving more notably than others."

"Perhaps you'd like to do a little more than survive? Take one of these ladies for a little ride. It won't cost you a thing."

Grif looked away, and saw that a third woman was now lying atop the center stage. As the men hooted and hollered suggestions, she stripped what was left of her clothing and spread herself wide. Grif thought about slipping into a dark corner with a woman that anyone could have, and his stomach heaved.

"I don't quite understand your beef with this," Chambers snapped, seeing the disgust roll across Grif's face. "Are you of the homosexual persuasion?"

If this was straight, Grif realized, he'd rather be. "I ain't queer. I just don't like taking advantage of women."

"Taking ad—?" Chambers growled in the back of his throat, frustrated. "So some of the women here might need the money. So what? It's an exchange, like any other. Services for coin. That's the way of the world."

"It's *sex*."

"Also the way of the world," Chambers said, his voice brittle and hard. Lifting an arm, he snapped his fingers. Marie materialized instantly. Some of the men behind Chambers stopped and stared. However, he looked nowhere but at Grif's unblinking gaze. "Tell the three centerpieces I want a proper show, and not a tease. I want it raw and I want it now."

"Yes, Mr. Chambers."

"Marie was one of my first acquisitions," Chambers said, as she strode away. "She's worked her way up in my esteem because, like a good bitch, she's learned to take orders. Sit. Stay. Shut up."

But she was currently giving the orders, leaning across the transparent glass to whisper in the nude woman's ear. One of the men behind Marie fondled her ass, but she neither flinched nor appeared to notice. The girl she spoke with looked up, caught sight of Chambers watching, and quickly nodded. Yet Grif caught something else—brief, just a flash—but it looked like regret, or sadness. It was quickly covered with a snaking smile as she turned to the others.

"I'm not watching this." Grif rose, pushing away from the table. He and Kit would get what they needed another night, another way. He wanted no part of this filth . . . and he wanted Kit out of here now.

"Do you want to know what the difference is between sex for money and sex for free, Mr. Shaw?" Chambers's voice twisted across the room to snag Grif one last time. He waited until Grif had turned, to finish. "Sex for money always costs less."

Grif wanted to ask how Mrs. Chambers felt about that, then remembered Kit's words. *Marriage isn't all it's made out to be.* Was it true? Did all these women feel that way? Was it a twenty-first-century development that he couldn't understand because he was out of his place and time?

Had his Evie ever felt like that, even for a moment?

Chambers folded his hands behind his head, sensing he'd

hit some sort of nerve. "Money is the invisible elephant in every bedroom, Mr. Shaw. You'd do well to remember that."

"Marriage is not a business transaction."

Chambers laughed like he was naive. "You keep believing that." Then he rose from his seat, and ran his hands through his hair. "Now if you'll excuse me. I see something I want to fuck."

Grif flinched, and realized too late it was the reaction Chambers was hoping for. He turned away again, but Chambers's laughter chased him.

"Remember your promise," the man called out, and the reminder, along with the laughter, hung on the air like a threat.

After Kit noted the men systematically disappearing, after catching the ripe scent of a good ol' boys club souring the air, she made quick work of getting rid of Grif. There was no sense in trying to gain access to that back room—some doors, she knew, would never be open to her, so instead of beating her head against this one, she turned the mystery over to the ever-capable Grif.

After letting him think it was his idea, of course.

It was the women that she was most interested in, anyway. Thus, Grif hadn't been gone five minutes before Kit was breaking her promise to remain in clear sight, and heading up the big, winding staircase in search of Mrs. Chambers. With Grif no doubt occupying Chambers's attention, this was her chance to talk to Anabelle about the list, the Wayfarer, and Nic's death outside of her husband's overpowering presence.

Besides, she was curious. What kind of woman willingly shared her man not just with other women, but other *wives*? As a reporter, Kit strove for understanding rather than judgment, but as a woman? She believed in the right to bear arms when it came to her man's body and affection.

Emerging on a landing both quiet and cool, Kit found tasteful but unremarkable artwork adorning the walls, and expensive but unexceptional side tables lining the hall. Antique vases, fresh greenery. Everything stately, and right where it should be. Perfect.

"There's always something else going on beneath a perfect facade," Kit muttered, recalling Bridget Moore's words. So she peered into the first dark doorway she came to, directly across from the landing. It was just a guestroom—also stately, also unremarkable—and Kit shut the door quietly behind her before continuing down the hallway.

And there was more than one hall. All were dotted with doorways, all dark. Where was the life? Kit wondered, looking about. The other alleged wives or women? Or even another child? Because there wasn't one other sound to accompany her footsteps, and the heavy silence eventually smothered even the residual noise from downstairs.

Yet the final hallway felt different, like the center honeycomb in a hive. A sole door sat at the end, ajar and lit from within, and Kit knew before looking that this was where the queen bee resided. Under the dim light of a vaulted ceiling, she peeked inside to find a warm room done in gingham pastels. Anabelle Chambers was tucked into a corner settee, reading a book to Charlotte, snuggled tightly at her side.

Kit flashed on a memory of her mother doing the same, the warmth of her body, hands stroking her hair, but Charlotte must have sensed her there, because she jolted, causing the book to fall from her mother's hands. "What are you doing here?"

It was the child, not the mother who asked, and Kit was so taken aback by the strength in the young voice that she almost retreated. "I could say I'm lost, but I'm not," she said, stepping forward instead. Only then did Anabelle's gaze finally focus on her. "I came to find you."

"It's bedtime," Anabelle said, but she gazed directly through Kit's body, and there was a slight slur to her words. "Time for us to sleep and to dream and all be together again . . ."

"Is she okay?" Kit took another step inside the room. Other than the gingham, the space was unadorned. There was a gilt mirror, but no jewelry or perfume or even flowers lay there. As someone who took great joy in feminine accoutrements, Kit couldn't fathom that Anabelle Chambers, or even Charlotte, really lived here.

Charlotte was up, tossing the throw aside to reveal a Hannah Montana half-gown and legs that looked like a colt's. "You can't be here."

Anabelle continued slurring. "You should come. I know this place and we can all reach it. *She* told me. She said everyone is better there, everyone is happy in the Everlast . . ."

"Hey, did you hear me?" Charlotte crossed to the door and held it wide for Kit. "You're not allowed up here."

Then who was? Kit wondered. Because it was an awfully big house for one woman and a little girl. "She just told me to come."

"She wasn't talking to you," Charlotte snapped, grasping the door by its frame, her tiny brows draw down tight. "She's been ill."

"Yes," Anabelle sighed, sliding down further in the settee. "So very ill . . ."

"Why are you alone?" Kit asked the girl.

Charlotte pointed out the door. "She needs her rest."

"I thought it was *your* bedtime." When Charlotte just looked at her, Kit pressed. "Charlotte, I know something is wrong. Let me help."

Putting her hand on her hip in a move that looked both defiant and jittery, Charlotte said, "You're a reporter, right?"

"Yes."

Charlotte smirked then shook her head. "Then you can't help at all."

"Then how about as a friend?"

Charlotte looked back at Anabelle, who'd curled into herself and was mumbling, fingers worrying the blanket over her legs. "She said they're waiting for me, just beyond those gates, and then we can all be together again . . ."

"She doesn't have friends," Charlotte said, pushing the door shut. "She only has me."

Kit nodded slowly. "And the baby."

Charlotte lowered her gaze, and said lowly, "There's always another baby."

Of course. The Mormon culture valued children like riches. So why was this woman, who'd claimed to be so "blessed" downstairs, curled into a corner, pale and drawn—and apparently drugged out of her mind—being watched over by a sole thirteen-year-old girl?

Glancing at Charlotte, Kit decided to take a chance. "I need some answers Charlotte. I'm looking for a man."

The girl jerked her head, causing her long dark braid to swing over one shoulder. "Men aren't allowed on these floors."

"I think your father knows him. His name is Lance Schmidt. Ever hear of him?"

"No." Charlotte lifted her chin. "And don't bother asking Mother, either. She doesn't do well under pressure."

"Very protective of her, aren't you?"

"That's my job."

Kit looked Charlotte dead in the eye. "Usually it's the other way around."

"Listen, if you don't leave you're going to get me in trouble." The girl swallowed hard, her eyes now pleading. "And . . . you'll be in trouble, too."

"What do you mean?"

"I don't know." Charlotte cast a quick glance over her shoulder, like she expected to be punished. Anabelle Chambers, though, had fallen asleep. "You have to go."

Kit pulled out her business card, and wrote on the back. "That's my number on the front, but this is a friend of mine. He's a cop, and he's always willing to help someone. You know, if you need it. Just keep it close, okay?"

Charlotte looked at the card, then took it uncertainly. Then she looked up at Kit. "You might want to keep it close, too."

And before Kit could again ask what she meant, she shut the door, locking it with a firm snap. And as silence descended on the heels of the warning, Kit realized how very alone she was. She could hear nothing from downstairs, which meant no one could hear her, either, and Charlotte's warning of trouble had her hurrying back through the halls. But then she took the final corner and spotted the light seeping from the room across the hall. She knew she'd turned it off before, and that she'd shut the door as well.

But it was on now, and the door ajar, and a feminine humming rose and fell in the air, drawing Kit close. Once again, she looked in, and this time there was a woman in the rocking chair. The humming immediately cut off, and she looked up.

"Curiosity killed the Kit." The woman smiled.

Kit did not. "What did you say?"

"The cat," the woman said, putting down the Bible she was reading, resting it on her lap. "I meant the cat."

"Who are you?" Kit asked, because she was fairly sure this woman wasn't another guest. She wasn't dressed for a party, for one, covered instead in unrelieved black, including her skin, her close-cropped hair, and the smoky shades shielding her eyes.

Not a wife, either, Kit was willing to bet. People of color weren't traditionally a part of the Mormon Church, and while there was still a lot Kit didn't know about Chambers, she got the feeling that he was extremely traditional in this regard.

"Were you drawn in by my song?" the woman asked, ignoring Kit's question. "'Amazing Grace.' You people are supposed to like that."

So she wasn't Mormon . . . but thought Kit was? "Are you supposed to be here?"

The woman laughed, so that her lips pulled tightly against her teeth. "Of course not. And neither are you."

"Well, I—"

"Time to go home." She rose, thin and taller than Kit initially thought, and crossed to stand before her with an airy grace. Looking down her nose at Kit, she sniffed. "Time for us both to go home."

For some reason, that made Kit's heart skip a beat. Then it sped up again and stayed revved. She didn't like the way this woman was looking at her. Or the way she'd ignored Kit's question. Or her cryptic words. Yet instead of challenging all of that, as she normally would, Kit just wanted to back away.

"Do you read the Bible?" the woman asked Kit suddenly.

"Um, I have before."

"Then you might be familiar with the apostle Paul. He argues in Romans, chapters six through eight, that humans have two competing natures. The flesh and the spirit. The pure spirit follows God. But when people allow their fleshly nature to take over, they follow their lower desires. And that is sin." Her lips thinned in disgust.

"Why are you telling me this?"

"Because I hate sin." The woman looked down at her body, her flesh, like she hated it, before her attention returned to Kit without altering. "Plus, I don't want you to be surprised when you see me again . . . though the competition will be over by then."

"The comp—?" Kit drew back. "You mean, between the flesh and the spirit?"

"Don't look so alarmed," the woman said, careful not to touch Kit as she handed her the Bible. "Even when you lose, you'll still win."

Kit frowned, dropped the Bible onto the bed, and rushed to follow her from the room. "Hey—"

But the woman was already gone, leaving only an empty hallway again, the notes of "Amazing Grace" still trembling on the air.

CHAPTER SEVENTEEN

A promise?" Kit repeated, disbelieving as she and Grif left the Chambers estate's serpentine two-lane road behind, and the neon outskirts began building up around them. "He made you promise not to tell me about the sexual bacchanal going on in the back of his Mormon palace?"

She shook her head, less bothered by the fact that such events existed than she was by not knowing about them sooner.

Grif stared straight ahead as they entered the city, neon swallowing them up as they headed toward its belly. "Not just you. He's hiding it from the world at large, and it doesn't take much to keep the other men silent. There were cameras all over the place. As soon as you walk into that back room you're part of the club."

"Which is why he let you in," Kit guessed. "And I bet some

not-so-subtly-applied peer pressure in the personage of one Officer Schmidt ensures everyone stays that way."

Grif huffed, a sound Kit was starting to anticipate. "I didn't see Schmidt, but most of the men didn't look like they needed much convincing."

"I'll bet." They were silent for a bit, the road sluicing easily beneath the trim car's tires, a sound Kit normally found soothing. Biting her lip, she looked over at Grif. "So what about Nic? What about the Wayfarer?"

He kept his gaze trained forward, but jerked his head. "There's still no proof that Chambers was involved, Kit. And my gut tells me that's precisely why he allowed me back there. Not just to find out what I know . . . but to show me we really know nothing."

"Arrogant jerk." Squinting out at the road ribboning before her, Kit shook her head. "No, there's definitely more going on in that house than musical sex-partners. Why else would Anabelle Chambers have to drug herself into a coma?"

"What?"

Kit tightened her fingers around the wheel as they slid onto Industrial Avenue. "Oh, yeah. I forgot to tell you . . ."

Biting her lip, Kit shot Grif an apologetic look in advance, then told him about her foray upstairs. It was only when she mentioned the strange woman with the Bible, however, that he lost it.

"What the hell is wrong with you? You can't take a simple order, can you?"

She opened her mouth to say orders weren't hers to take, but he didn't let her speak.

"If I tell you something, it's to keep you safe! What's so hard to understand about that?" He sat forward, back, then forward again. If they hadn't been driving, she would have sworn he'd have walked away. "I guess it's just your nature to disobey and do what you want anyway."

"My nature?" The mysterious woman's words revisited her in a whisper. "You mean my *fleshly* nature?"

Grif frowned, thinking about it. Then he nodded. "Yes. Yes, that's exactly it."

Kit jerked her steering wheel so hard that Grif crashed into the door and cursed. She was glad they were at their destination, Masquerade, because she wasn't feeling so calm, either. "Griffin Shaw, you're starting to piss me off!"

"Yeah, well you're not exactly a peach to be around!" And he started ticking off annoyances on his fingers. "You're flighty, girly, impossibly cheerful, and you never stop moving or *talking!*"

"Those are not bad things!"

"And you're stubborn!" he said, trying to name something that was.

"So are you!"

"Don't insult me," he said, climbing from the car.

"It was a compliment," she said, slamming her own door shut. "And what's your problem? I'm doing my best here!"

"The problem," he said, edging around the car, "is that I don't like your cavalier attitude! Not about danger or sex or—"

Kit straightened. "I am *not* cavalier about sex! I take my sex very seriously, thank you . . . not that you'll ever find out—"

"Good."

"Because you're too busy polishing your halo!"

"Hey!"

She took a step forward and got in his face. "Furthermore, *I* am a survivor. I don't need you to protect me. I've gone almost thirty years surviving the death of my parents, the decline of my newspaper, and now there's a murderer on my trail. But I'll survive this, too."

He looked for a moment like he was going to disagree, then tilted his head. "Is that all?"

"No."

That drew a low growl from him. Good. She didn't want him calm when she wasn't. She actually, suddenly, wanted to annoy the shit out of him. So she took another step forward and poked him in the chest. "You. Are not. An. Angel."

"Fine, honey. I'm not."

"Those are not wing . . . *lumps* on your back."

"Wing lumps?" he asked, with one raised brow.

"They're cysts!" She poked him again, but there was less heat now. She was calming down.

"Just like the bumps on your head."

"No," she said, turning away. "Those are extra brains."

"Of course they are." And at his exasperated sigh, she felt instantly better.

Looking up at the Masquerade sign, with enough flashing bulbs and faux gold scrollwork to melt even Trump's iron heart, she calmed her breathing. "Glad we got that settled. Now can we go inside, please? Because a man and a woman arguing outside a strip club in Vegas is such a cliché I want to slap myself in the face."

"Uh-uh." Grif grabbed her arm as she reached for the door. "You're not going in there."

"Why not?"

"Because you dress like a princess, act like a lady, and are just nosy enough to get us both in trouble."

"Oh, Grif. You say the sweetest things when you're being a

total sexist pig." She fluttered her lashes and made a long face. "But I'm scared to death to wait all alone in my conspicuous car in a dark lot of a sketchy part of town with a murderer hot on my trail."

Grif's eyes narrowed. "That's a low blow, even for you."

"So are you going to walk in with me, or do you want me to grab some tassels and sneak in the back?"

Grif answered by crowding in so close his body heat warmed her through his clothing. "I still don't like your cavalier attitude."

But Kit smiled to herself as he held open the door to the club. The argument had invigorated her, and seemed to set them back on solid ground. Besides, she'd seen the look in his eye when she'd stomped her foot and held her ground. He didn't *like* her cavalier attitude.

He loved it.

The DiMartino strip joint was old, practically an institution in the Las Vegas nightclub scene, one Kit claimed got by mostly on its reputation for a management that turned a blind eye to its employees' "extracurricular" activities. It couldn't have been anything else, Grif thought, wincing at the music that assaulted them as soon as they walked through the door. It didn't look like the carpeting had been replaced since he'd been offed, and the only thing recommending the furniture was that it was too dark to show stains. Even the bar was dodgy, a mere frame for the flat-top video poker that stole quarters instead of bills, though he supposed all that mattered was the one thing that *had* been kept up to date. The girls.

It felt wrong to bring Kit here, and he regretted being browbeaten into it as soon as they entered. Yet when he turned to tell her so, he found her bent over, head tilted to the side, staring at the center stage. "Oh, wow. She can do the Helicopter. Do you know what kind of muscle control that takes?"

Grif looked over, actually considered the question, and by the time his attention returned to Kit, she was moving away.

"Go find your friend," Kit called back, waving him away. "I've got to see this up close."

So while Kit sat front and center, by all appearances trading critiques with a group of college boys at a nearby table, Grif was escorted to an elevated booth at the back of the room. It was flanked by an in-house phone and a small console bearing video images of the adjoining rooms. He was offered a drink, which he accepted, and two lap dances, which he did not, then made to wait another ten minutes before the club's owner joined him.

In the meantime, he watched the dancer Kit was currently applauding. The woman was certainly flexible, Grif thought, tilting his head the way Kit had until the woman flipped back to her feet. And he supposed she was strong as well. Hard to tell with gals, though. They mostly held their strength inside, like a coiled spring. His Evie had been like that. He'd once watched, shocked, as she hauled off and clocked a man she thought had patted her behind. Grif wouldn't have thought her capable of it, but that night, when she rose above him in bed like a smooth hot wave, he made a point of testing the muscles beneath her sweet skin. The strength he found there heightened his climax in a way he hadn't known possible.

He couldn't imagine Kit popping someone like that. Not because she wasn't strong, though he didn't think she'd ever really tested it before, but because in the past few days she'd shown him a different type of resilience. A spirit that refused to be crushed. A heart that seemed to expand when, by all reasonable accounts, it should contract. Even in the parking lot outside, standing toe to toe with him, she had squared up and told him what was what. It was remarkable, damned feminine . . . and uniquely Kit.

Realizing he was smiling, Grif averted his gaze from Kit—currently waving bills at the stage—and immediately spotted the man beelining his way from the other side of the crowded room. Ray DiMartino looked uncannily like his mobster father, though if Grif remembered correctly, it was Theresa DiMartino's sculpted nose and pointed jaw that made the kid not unhandsome now.

And not a kid, either, Grif reminded himself, doing the math. The last time he'd seen Ray, the kid had been a hair under eight years old, but he was fifty-seven now, and the tousled-haired boy was nowhere to be seen. Still, his bloodshot eyes momentarily lit up when he saw Grif—no doubt thinking there was a striking resemblance to the man he thought was Grif's grandfather—and the dimples the kid had sported at seven flashed against thick stubble as they shook hands.

"Thanks for meeting with me," Grif said, as Ray slid into the booth. Ray lifted a finger, earning a nod from the waitress, and settled back with a contented sigh.

"Well, a call from Tony Prima was enough to pique my interest. The guy isn't exactly known for his social skills, know what I mean?" He laughed, a throaty growl that also reminded Grif of Ray's dad. That man had been a bull, and though there were obvious similarities, the son had a hunched look. This DiMartino had been castrated before he'd even grown horns. "But once he said Griffin Shaw wanted to see me, hey. It was a no-brainer."

Waiting until the waitress had put down their beers and left, Grif lifted his with both hands and inclined his head. "Thank you."

"Yeah, well your grandpops was real good to me," Ray said. "The other guys always treated me like some sort of pet, but Shaw took time for me, you know? I remember wishing for a while that he was my real pop, or at least a wise guy, you know? I didn't know he had a kid, though. You look just like him, man."

Grif cleared his throat, and changed the subject. "So how's your aunt Mary?"

Ray's brows lifted in surprise, before his expression softened. "Of course your grandpop woulda told you about her. My family was out of their mind about her, you know, the way she just disappeared. But he brought her back. She's still nutso if you ask me, but every family has their oddballs."

"Well, life didn't lean easy on her," Grif said, remembering how mentally frail the girl had been. "Even when she was young. She'd have to work real hard not to look over her shoulder after being kidnapped like that."

"He tell you all that?" Ray gave him a sidelong look, then turned to watch the girl writhing center-stage, gaze distant, eyes narrowed against the strobing lights. "Well, a lot of the girls here are the same way. Broken homes, abusive fathers. It don't take a genius to see how they'd start to think this," he motioned at his flesh, "is their only worth. They're lucky they have me, actually."

Grif raised a brow.

"I look after them," Ray explained. "They come to me if some punk's pounding on them, you know, if they need a place to stay." Ray pursed his lips, beetle brows drawing low. "Never really thought about it before, but I guess that's because of what happened to Mary. Your grandpop protected her; she was lucky. A lot of these girls don't have any luck in 'em."

Grif looked at the girls in question, thought of the ones he'd seen at Chambers's place, and couldn't argue that.

Lifting his bottle, Ray waved it in Grif's direction. "You know, Mary still talks about your grandpop. Says he was one of the finest men she ever met. Between you and me, I think she took to him like a baby chick seeing the first being around. Get the feeling she's been looking for one like him ever since, too. But . . . you know."

Grif shook his head. "Know what?"

"What everyone else said about him."

"No. I don't."

Ray took a long pull on his beer before answering. "It's just that your grandpop was married. Once. Obviously before your grandmother." He glanced over to see if Grif did know, saw his face carefully devoid of expression, and leaned close. "Evelyn Shaw. She died. Was murdered, actually."

"I did know that." When Ray only continued staring, Grif stared back. "And he didn't do it."

Ray either caught the hardness to Grif's voice, or spotted the expression that shifted over his face, and pulled back. "Of course not, man. Not Shaw. I mean, they did speculate about him for a bit. You know, she was last seen alive with him. And he did go missing the same night of her death—"

"He didn't do it."

Ray stared out over the room, nodding. "Yeah, it was a long time ago, right? A different life for everyone. I mean, my old man would have a heart attack if he saw me now. A DiMartino running a skin joint instead of the numbers. But you do what you can, right?" He glanced at Grif like he was looking for approval, then frowned, as if realizing it. Shrugging, he held up his hand for another beer. "Anyway, from what I heard, that Evelyn Shaw had it coming."

"Who told you that?" Grif said carefully.

"No one told me shit. I was just a kid. Seen and not heard. Those were the rules in my house. But," and Ray leaned closer, licking his lips, "I heard my pop talking about the case a few years later. Mention murder and what kid's not going to listen, right? So I snuck into the living room where I could hear him and my stepmom arguing."

"Your stepmom?"

"My mom died in sixty-one. Not too long after your grand-pop . . . disappeared."

"I'm sorry," Grif said, though his fists were now bunched beneath the table. With a deep breath, he forced them to relax.

"Me, too. Barbara—Pop's new wife?—was a real bitch. Moved in quick, and tried to get Pop to ship me off to boarding school. As if Italians ever really let their kids go." Shaking his head, he made a face. "No love lost between her and me, tell you that much."

"So what'd they say about Evie?"

"Evie? Oh, you mean Evelyn Shaw." Ray nodded as the waitress sat down his extra beer. "Barbara said that both Shaws got exactly what was coming to them, and that if my pop was a real man, he'd make sure history didn't repeat itself."

Grif jerked a shoulder. "What does that mean?"

"You know women," Ray said dismissively. "Always shooting off for no reason, using words like weapons. Besides, it was like the pot calling the kettle black, if you know what I mean. Barbara wasn't no angel."

"But she knew them? Evie and . . . my granddad?"

Ray shrugged. "Guess so. Town was smaller back then, though. Everybody knew everybody."

Grif pursed his lips. "Think she'd talk to me?"

Ray scoffed. "If you can find her. She moved to Cali right after my pop passed. Sat me down for one lame conversation about a mobster's life and how dangerous it was, then looked me square and said the apple didn't fall far from the tree, whatever that means. Point is, she couldn't get out of Vegas fast enough . . . though she had time to take all the furniture and Pop's savings with her. Believe that shit?"

"Think she'd remember anything at all about that time?"

Ray smirked. "She don't even remember my name."

Grif leaned close to the other man, and stayed there until Ray's eyes had fully focused on his. "I'm trying to clear Griffin Shaw's name here. I want to set things right for him and for his first wife, Evie."

"Righting old wrongs? Watching out for the ladies? Guess *that* apple didn't fall far from the tree, either." He laughed, but stopped abruptly when Grif didn't join him. "What does it matter anymore, Shaw? It was fifty years ago. Town has changed since then. The world has changed. And everybody's forgotten that business with Evelyn and Griffin Shaw."

Now Ray looked exactly like his old man. Defiant. A tad angry. And ready for a fight.

Grif stiffened then, very slowly, leaned forward. "It matters because he mattered," he said, holding Ray's gaze. "And so did Evie. And so did your dad, who might have been made, yeah, but he was one of the true architects of this city. The whole shining thing sits perched on his bones, but people don't remember that, either."

Ray listened, rapt.

"From the way my granddad talked about old man DiMartino, your stepmom was dead wrong. He was gristle and bone and unyielding firepower, and he was bound to his own moral laws. My granddad respected that. Sal DiMartino was a formidable man."

Grif leaned back, and Ray remained silent for a long time. Watching with disinterest as the woman on the center stage tucked loose bills into her panties, Grif waited.

"Last I heard, Barbara remarried," Ray finally said. "Who knows, she may have remarried again after that. She might even be dead. She never contacted me after she left."

Grif had to fight not to drop his head. It'd been the first decent lead he'd had, even if it concerned a woman he didn't know, and who thought he and Evie deserved to die.

"But listen, I still have some of Pop's old stuff. His files. His Rolodex." Ray glanced over, nodding once. "I'll look through it. Let you know if I come across anything that might help."

It was the best Grif could hope for. "Thanks."

"Hey, no problem. My pop liked Shaw, too." Ray blew out a hard breath. "Besides, it might be nice to revisit the past for a bit. The present is wearing on me."

Looking back over the room, thinking back over the night, Grif felt the same way.

"Excuse me."

Grif turned to find Kit staring at them both, frowning. He wondered just how long she'd been standing there.

"And yet the present is looking better all the time." Ray straightened, throwing an arm over the back of the booth as he turned toward Kit. "Here for a job, beautiful? We normally audition in the afternoons, but I could make an exception for you."

"She's with me," Grif said coolly.

"Oh. Sorry, man. No offense." But the smile he flashed Grif was damned offensive.

"Aw, you're so sweet," Kit said, grinning so sincerely that Grif wasn't sure she didn't mean it. "And I'd love to talk to you at some point about incorporating more sensuality into your repertoire of acts—"

Ray's face scrunched. "Wha—?"

"But right now I seem to have a bit of an emergency." She held her cell phone out to Grif, revealing a text displaying 911, followed by an address. "It's from Paul, but when I tried calling him back, there was no answer."

"2856 Mockingbird Place. Where's that?"

Kit shrugged. "Let me MapQuest it."

"You trust him enough to just show up to an address he texts you?"

"I wouldn't trust him with my pet goldfish," Kit replied, studying her phone. "But he would never hurt me, and I know I'll be able to get him to tell me more if I can just get him alone. I always have."

Grif's jaw clenched as he thought about that, but Ray's sudden exclamation had them both glancing over.

"What was that address?" he asked, leaning forward over the table. Kit held her phone out, just as the crossroads popped onscreen. Whistling lowly, he leaned back and shook his head. "That's one of Caleb Chambers' properties. Talk about a dangerous man."

"That little ol' Mormon businessman?" Kit leaned close, forearms on the table, face open, inquiring. Beautiful. "How so?"

Ray didn't answer right off, clearly distracted by her nearness, as well as the heat and scent Grif was picking up even from the other side. Funny how quickly he'd grown used to it. Less funny that he wanted to knock Ray from between them just for the thoughts he knew were playing in his mind.

Ray, unaware of all this, leaned on the table, too. "It's different from my pop's day, you know? Not that anyone went around saying they were made, but no one had to. If you didn't want an ice pick in the ear, then you shouldn't mess with the guy holding it, know what I mean?"

"Words to live by," Kit said, nodding.

"Right?" Ray said, missing the ironic note to her tone. "But Chambers ain't like that. No, that man is stealth. He would never bother with me, of course. My family's history keeps me well clean of his lily-whites. But the white-collars in this town? They gotta watch out. And after he's moved on to someone else? They still gotta watch out."

"So maybe Paul is tired of watching out," Grif said. "What is this property?"

"Officially? A horse farm. One of the biggest ranches in southern Nevada."

"Settebello," Kit said, nodding now. "I know it. But that's not one of Chambers's places. I've covered stories there before. It's a city-funded ranch. It gives disadvantaged children the chance to play cowboy."

"Right," said Ray. "*Officially.*"

Kit straightened, frowning like someone had just told her there was no Santa Claus. "And unofficially?"

Leaning back, Ray crossed his arms over his chest, his face

as grim as his father's had ever been. "That's something you should ask your friend Paul."

Kit drove quickly, her silence a testament to her nerves, though her hands were steady enough. They couldn't be sure there was a problem yet. There'd been no follow-up to the text, but that wasn't unusual for Paul. Their conversations were usually one-sided.

So why had her heart sunk into her gut when she'd gotten his text in the middle of that tasteless club? And why was it still caught there now?

"You sure you trust Paul?" Grif asked again, out of the blue.

"Yes," Kit said, grateful for the distraction from her own thoughts. "I mean no . . . but he'd never put me in danger, if that's what you're asking."

Not physically anyway.

To distract herself from *that* thought, she asked, "So what was all that about?"

"You mean Ray DiMartino?"

She nodded.

"Ever hear of the Desert Dukes Gang?"

"Sure." No one could truly call themselves a lifelong Las Vegan and not know someone who knew someone who knew where the bodies were buried. Most rumors led back to the Dukes . . . and most weren't rumors. "They haven't held any sort of power in this town in a long time, though."

Not since Howard Hughes overtook the Strip. Corporations turned a light on every shady place after that, and the town was different for it. Better, most argued . . . but those generally weren't lifelong Las Vegans, either.

But Grif knew his local history. "They ran the city back in the 1960s. Tony started working for the family when he was only seventeen. That means his loyalty is endless and his memory is even longer. He told me Ray's father knew for a fact that one Griffin Shaw was killed on the same day as Evelyn Shaw."

"There are no official reports of that," Kit said tightly, turning onto the long street that led to Settebello. She'd checked after he claimed he'd been killed in 1960.

"Exactly," Grif said, like that meant something.

"And how did you say you knew the family again?"

"I brought back their little girl, Mary Margaret. That'd be Ray's aunt. They thought she'd been snatched, and accusations were flying between them and their rivals from New York. Bullets were about to follow." He looked out the window like he was really remembering it. "Turns out, she fell under the spell of some early New Ager with a funny accent. Australian or something like that. Ran away to a compound with no indoor plumbing but a lot of vegetable gardens. I brought her home."

Kit didn't feel the need to lash out this time. Instead, she wanted to cry. He really believed this—she saw it in his eyes—which meant he really believed he was an angel, too. Swallowing hard, she said, "And you're wondering if Sal DiMartino had you rubbed out despite what you did for his niece?"

"Tony's words do make a man wonder. Besides, power and money have always ruled this town, and gratitude only runs skin deep. They could have easily allied themselves with someone more powerful than the lone wolf who'd found their little girl."

Kit bit her lip, and fought back tears. Dangerous had been bad enough. Now she'd have to tell Fleur that Grif was crazy. Blowing out a breath, Kit decided to play along. "So why don't you ask her?"

"Who?"

"You know. Mary Margaret."

Grif shook his head. "She was just a kid."

"Not anymore."

Grif frowned as they turned onto Mockingbird Street. Kit had never been so grateful to see a dark, spooky street in her life. Yet, looking up, she frowned, too. "This block is far darker than the others."

"You said you've been here before," Grif said, noting how she'd slowed.

"Not for some time. And not at night. The streetlights are out, too." She pulled up in front of a gate with a giant, decorous S—more beautiful than it was functional. Kit turned off the car. "I don't see Paul's car. In fact, I can't see a thing."

"I can," Grif said grimly, opening the door. "Stay here."

"The hell I will."

Grif cursed under his breath as she followed but said nothing more.

The air was even cooler than the previous hour, and Kit shivered, glad she'd brought her vintage fur capelet. Grif assisted her as she ducked beneath the gate, gravel crunching beneath their feet as they headed toward the barn. The faintest light shone between the slats of its front-facing window, though nothing else moved in the night.

"Must be expensive to hold and run this sort of place in the middle of a city."

"Chambers can afford it," Kit murmured, stepping over a suspiciously dark pile. These shoes had taken her from a gala to a strip club to a horse ranch in one night. One thing was sure, Griffin Shaw got around.

Yeah, and he thinks he has wings to do it. Kit rolled her

eyes, but stilled when Grif stiffened, palm tensing over her own. "What was that?"

"City boy," Kit whispered, pulling him forward. "Don't you know a horse when you hear one?"

But the noise sounded again, and this time it drew out like a long, low foghorn pushing its way through a thick mist.

Holding her a little tighter, Grif started again toward the barn.

The whitewashed stables were pristine and impressive beneath the full beat of the day's sun, but ghostly in moonbeams that sliced through the clouded night.

"Paul?" Kit called out, earning a glare from Grif, but the door wasn't only unlocked, it was slightly ajar. Her eyes quickly acclimated due to a light in the long room's farthest corner. Given the sounds, it seemed a groomsman or trainer was still working there. Maybe a horse was ill or giving birth. The barn's center was covered by a thick rubber matting that absorbed the clack of Kit's heels as they walked, but that only heightened her sense of heading into an abyss.

"Get behind me." Grif's voice was low and tight as they advanced past the pine-paneled stalls.

"The breezeway doors are open," she whispered, recalling that the exercise yard was on the other side. All she saw was a sliver of moonlight peering inside like a curious visitor. Meanwhile, the dark figures moving through the stable windows looked like shadows shifting in another world.

"What is that smell?" she asked as they rounded the corner. Then her gut—holding her nerves, which were holding her heart—registered the visual like a punch. It also registered the scent as fresh blood.

"What is . . . ?" she tried to say, but her voice was airy with the loss of breath.

The body was strung up along the front of a giant treadmill, a way to exercise the horses when the Vegas heat grew too extreme. She recognized that much. She tried to add, "Who is . . . ?" but she knew that, too. After all, she'd seen Paul only hours before, and his face—as always—was pristine. So instead of asking questions with unfathomable answers, her mind locked onto the one fact she could actually grasp.

I gave him that watch.

Then she screamed.

Next thing, Grif's hands were under her arms, his voice insistent but nonsensical in her ear, his breath rising and falling, it seemed, for them both. He pushed her back around the corner, but it was too late. Kit had seen the extended reins holding Paul's arms wide, a second pair securing his legs against the giant treadmill. An iron bit pulled his mouth into a macabre grin, and a bloodied whip lay abandoned in the pool of blood at his feet.

But the shallow movement of his tattered chest told her he was still alive.

"Get your phone," Grif was saying. "Call the police."

But then the sound came again, slipping around the corner to steal her focus, and the coolness fled the air as the world blurred. The horse in the nearest stall stomped its displeasure.

No, I just saw him. He's at a party. He's with a girl . . .

Grif's arm moved around her waist. Nearness and support. She would have liked that . . . except that it meant that what she'd just seen was true. That it'd happened. That, like Nic, Paul was also dead.

Almost dead.

I have to call the police, I have to call, I have to . . .

But she couldn't move. Why couldn't she move?

And then, suddenly, she was at her car. Grif was rummaging in her purse; wide, strong fingers jerking at the delicate cloth. He found the phone, dialed, then he took her face in his wide, warm hands.

"Look at me." His hands were so hot they almost burned her cheeks, and she felt fevered as she stared into his face. "I'll take care of this. Get in the car. Stay warm. I'll need to see if I can . . ."

Help, he was going to say. He was going back in there to help Paul.

Kit nodded, a motion that seemed to unlock her teeth. They began an uncontrollable chatter.

"Help will be here soon, and we'll show them the text. It'll all be . . ."

He was going to say "okay." She saw the words forming . . . and saw them melt away. That's when the thought that'd been chasing her since Nic's death finally caught up, and when it hit her, it wrapped its unrelenting grip around her heart, and began to squeeze.

It was never going to be okay again.

CHAPTER EIGHTEEN

Paul died before the cops even arrived. But the first police officer on the scene, Dennis, was an obvious friend, and he folded Kit into his body like he was the one with wings. He also told Kit what Grif couldn't, that it was all going to be okay, and snapped at his partner, a Detective Hitchens, telling him to take a walk, though he glanced at Grif when he said it. Grif nodded once, then hung back as Dennis swung Kit around. She needed an old friend right now, not him. He'd let the officer get her settled, warm her up, and calm her down, then rejoin them later.

But the wail that Kit had let out upon seeing Paul's mutilated body followed him as he disappeared back into the dark. It'd sounded brittle and ruined, like something had fractured inside of the woman. And while she might not yet be able to accept her ex-husband's death, Grif knew she was already blaming herself for it.

I'll take care of this. That's what he'd told Kit before calling the cops . . . but he hadn't fulfilled the promise yet, and he could at least try that. Because Paul's death, he knew, lay on his shoulders, not Kit's.

So, hugging the high property wall, he surveyed the white brick to see if there was an easy point of entry to return to the barn. His impromptu plan was to hop it and approach from the back. If Paul's charming personality held true to form, his Centurion might still be arguing with him over his passage into the Everlast. It sometimes happened, even when the newly deceased wasn't a total heel.

Grif found a delivery gate about a third of the way along the wall, but it was padlocked, and the lawn beyond it dark. Neither deterred Grif, and he crossed the sprawling estate in a silence so absolute even the horses couldn't hear him. From this angle he could see what he'd missed before. A carriage house sat only yards away, white and pristine under the full moon. That's where he'd drag a reluctant soul if he couldn't convince it to leave before the police came. Some Centurions let the souls squat near their own remains while the police and medical examiners did their thing, but he'd found the medical jargon and black humor either depressed or angered the dead. So he liked to draw them away, if possible.

Yet his approach to the carriage house stalled when a throat was cleared directly behind him. It was the cop who'd been eyeing Kit and him from the patrol car, the one Dennis had called Hitchens.

"Going somewhere?" The steel-lined voice belied the thumbs tucked casually in his front pockets.

"I'm with Kit," Grif tried, wondering if her friendship with Dennis extended to his partner.

Those thumbs twitched and Grif knew that it didn't. "I know."

Since Hitchens had the look of someone who wanted a chase, Grif joined the man on the darkened lawn, pulled out his Luckies, and let one flare in the dark.

Hitchens decided to chase anyway.

"We've been keeping tabs on that weirdo. She was present at the scene of a murder. Two, now." He raised his dark brows like he expected Grif to elaborate. *In the billiards room, with the candlestick* . . .

"She wasn't present here."

"She is now."

"Right." Grif nodded, as if mulling that over. "Well, keep up the good work, Detective."

Then he headed toward the barn.

"You can't go in there," Hitchens called after him.

Grif turned and looked at him like he was crazy. "Why would I want to go in there? There's a dead body in there."

But their voices would have driven away any Centurion in the carriage house, even if Paul had to be dragged kicking and cursing into the Everlast. On to Plan C. Slowly, staring into the bushes and night-shrouded trees, Grif headed to the rear of the barn, well clear of the chaos.

"What are you doing?" Hitchens wasn't going to let up, which was fine. Grif hadn't expected him to.

"Looking."

"For?"

"Doves."

"Doves?"

He spared the man a glance. "You know, little birdies? Feathered symbols of peace and purity."

Hitchens's expression soured further.

Grif almost smiled. "Mourning doves in particular, though a white one will do in a pinch."

Hitchens placed his hands on his hips. "It's the dead of night at the ass-end of winter."

"I know," Grif replied, and turned back to the nearby bushes. "Should make 'em very easy to spot."

Okay, so he was just messing with the guy now. Yet Guardians didn't exactly play it straight, either. Most of the angels in that tribe appeared to their assigned mortal soul in the form of those sweet, winged messengers of peace, thus most people couldn't spot the celestial heralds if one dropped a turd on their heads. Grif, though, knew how to look. If a Guardian had been here, then Paul Raggio's death had been preventable. If not, that meant it was long predestined that he would die today, and Grif wouldn't be held accountable.

So he worked his way across the lawn, the individual blades still illuminated by the remaining angelic strength in his cornea. He scoured the ragweed and underbrush while Hitchens followed a short distance behind. "See one yet?"

"Nope," Grif said, ignoring the man's scorn.

"And what does that mean, Sherlock?"

Grif turned so abruptly he actually startled the man, who'd gotten too close. Hitchens took a large step back, covering the uncertainty in the gesture by placing his hands on his hips. Grif, though, stepped forward and stared him straight in the eye. "It means the heavens are closed. It means the angels have abandoned mortals to our folly. It means Raggio doesn't get a fast pass through the Pearly Gates."

"That right?" Hitchens gave an indulgent smile. "Well, I doubt that's where the guy was headed anyway."

Grif lifted a brow. "What makes you say that?"

Something slithered behind Hitchens's gaze, but was gone before Grif could name it. "People who die with their bowels falling from their bodies usually aren't Boy Scouts," Hitchens said, watching Grif carefully. He shouldn't have told Grif that, but he was after a reaction. And something more. "Besides, the kid was a lawyer. He's probably already taking briefs for the damned."

Grif gave the surrounding darkness a final visual sweep. "Nah. There is no hell. Mortals who have proven themselves unfit for Paradise have to join the Third."

"The Third?" Hitchens asked, mouth immediately turning down.

"That's the percentage of the angelic host who followed Lucifer in mutiny against God."

Hitchens's lost swagger turned into outright contempt. "What are you? The resident Jesus freak?"

Grif told himself to stop talking. He should return to Kit and try to console her. He should save his voice for someone with the capacity to listen. But there was something dark and small about this man. Something combustible that lived inside him, like it was just waiting for a match. If Grif could warn him away from that fire, help him avoid whatever mental ember that would send his life down a destructive path, then it might help right the wrongs Grif himself had already set into motion. Sarge might still say he was meddling where he shouldn't be, but it wasn't as if that condescending old angel was doing much to make the world a better place.

In other words, Grif had to try.

"The Third are still alive, active, and angry. They're like invisible rabid wolves. They inhabit a vast forest as dark as the earth's core. That's where blighted souls are sent when they leave this stinking mudflat.

"But the Third doesn't just wander the eternal forest like the souls of the damned. No, instead they *are* the forest. They move like a gust through the trees, like old leaves lifting from the decomposing floor. They place themselves at strategic points in the woodland. The damned can't ever gain their bearings, much less navigate the place. It's said that if a soul were to reach the other side of the eternal forest, they'd be able to find their way into the Everlast . . . and, of course, the Third—the fallen angels—can't allow that."

Hitchens was captivated despite himself. Outside of soft porn and Monday night football, it was probably the first time he'd allowed himself to be carried away by someone else's narrative. "But they're angels," he protested. "God made them to protect mankind."

The man's interest, and engagement, gave Grif hope.

"And they violated their angelic nature by turning against God. If you're against God, you certainly harbor no love for his most beloved creatures." Grif looked up in the sky and the blades that had once supported his wings shuddered. "Remember, angels are not God's children. They're not Chosen. They're not made in His image. They're just winged monsters who are there to serve Him."

Hitchens stared at Grif for a long moment, then shook his head. "Let me see if I got this straight. All the assholes who should have taken a tumble into a fiery pit are instead walking around in a forest with fairies jumping out from behind the trees?"

In that moment, something flared, twin flames of white-hot fury located directly behind Hitchens. Grif took an involuntary step back, but stopped there. Anne wouldn't confront him with Hitchens present. Still, he corrected: "Angels. Not fairies."

Flame erupted in Anne's gaze as she shot him another fiery warning, but then the glasses went back on, and she melded again with the night.

"And they don't jump out at them," he continued, eyes fixed on the place he'd last seen her. The itching between his shoulder blades now thrummed. He felt his wings like phantom limbs and knew it was because the Pure was near. "They ambush them. They ride herd. And every time they catch a soul, they do to it whatever that soul did to earn their spot in the forest."

Anne growled, a sound too broad and loud for the human ear, though the horses in the barn behind them began whinnying in unison. A crack sounded, hooves on wood, and a half dozen others followed, along with alarmed shouts and a particularly sharp cry. Hitchens glanced over nervously. At least that spooked him.

"They torture those souls that way again and again. They do it endlessly. They do it for lifetimes."

A whip of wind slapped him, and he stumbled back as the Pure rocketed straight into the air, but Grif already knew Pures hated it when mortals discussed them, their world, and their true natures. He'd been prepared. However, Hitchens had not.

Offering a hand, he helped up the now visibly shaken detective.

"Don't know about you," Grif said, shoving his hands into his pockets, "but I think I'd rather burn."

And, shooting the wide-eyed man one last smile, he headed back across the lawn.

Hitchens's voice rang out a second later. "You're a sick fuck, you know that?"

"Not as sick as you," Grif muttered, knowing as only someone with a healthy dose of celestial eyesight could, that he'd flat-out wasted his breath.

By the time Grif returned to her side, Kit had mostly composed herself. Dennis had the unpleasant task of informing next-of-kin as to Paul's death, and since she had once been his next-of-kin, she convinced Dennis to bring her along. Though relations between Paul's parents and her had iced over after the divorce, they still exchanged Christmas cards and the occasional phone call. It would help, Kit thought, for her to be there.

Either that, or they'd blame her entirely.

God knew she blamed herself.

Grif knew that, too. He rejoined her side in that stealth way he had, though Kit knew the moment he arrived. Her world warmed a bit with his presence, but Kit wrapped her arms around herself anyway, and looked out into the darkness. Right now her world was operating at a few degrees below the arctic chill.

"It wasn't your fault," he tried, as she knew he would. She continued to stare into the unyielding night.

"You keep saying that."

"Dennis said it, too."

She gave him a look that was more wry and despondent than any she'd worn since her father's death. "It's his job to say that."

"As a cop?"

"As a friend."

Grif studied her face, those expressive brows drawing now, and even though he didn't move, she felt as though he inched closer. "I'm a friend."

"Thought you were an angel?" she shot back before she could stop herself. She held up a hand immediately. She didn't want to injure anyone else. She certainly didn't want to argue. "I'm sorry."

"It's okay."

No. Kit shook her head. "Look, I know that you've been there and done that as a P.I., but I've spent my entire adult life investigating these sort of stories as well. Sordid tales about murder. Stories that invite people into lives they'd never lead, or want to. But they weren't just stories." She shook her head, and slumped against the cool wood of the white ranch fence.

"When I was sixteen I had to read the headline blaring the news of my dad's murder over the front page of my own newspaper. When I was twelve my mother's obit took up a whole page inside. They were more than just stories then, and the same goes for all the bylines since. Same goes for now." She looked directly up, and though close, Grif's expression was blurred by her tears. "But I think I've started something here that I can't stop. And I have a bad feeling about how this story is going to end."

"No, Kit," he replied lowly. "As long as you're alive, it can be stopped."

"But *they're* not alive." Kit wiped at her eyes. "It's too late for Nic and Paul."

"It's too late because someone else decided to play God." His gaze didn't waver from her face as another emergency vehicle edged by the already crowded entrance. "It's much easier to destroy a life than it is to live one."

Kit laughed bitterly at that. "You don't have to tell me. Every time I create something good in my life, someone else comes along and sideswipes it." She sniffed. "Maybe it's a sign."

"Don't say that."

She sounded bitter and hopeless, a combination she found repulsive in others and intolerable in herself. But tonight, with her ex-husband's blood so thick in the air that the horses couldn't settle, she found it fit like a vintage glove.

"Kit." Grif spoke more softly than she'd ever heard him speak before, like she'd break if he raised his voice. "God gave us this life, and one of its cornerstones and greatest gifts is free will. Unfortunately some people use that gift to harm others."

Kit gave a half-laugh and straightened. "Yeah? So where was my mother's free will? Because the last time I saw her she was a bag of bones gagging on her own saliva. She weighed so little her body seemed hollow, and she couldn't breathe without the help of a machine.

"*Mankind* didn't do that, Grif. A murderer didn't do it. God did it. He set her up, and then he sideswiped her just to watch her fall." Steeling her jaw, she lifted her chin. "So as far as I can see? People are just following in His footsteps. Guess we really are made in His image after all."

Then she whirled, and strode away. Eyes were on her as she walked to the far fence, and not just Grif's and Dennis's. She cut her gaze left as she leaned again against the cool wood, and saw that awful Hitchens eyeing her like she was his next meal. Ignoring him, she looked back into the empty pasture and wondered what she was really upset about.

The words about her mother had surprised even her. Of

course, she wasn't foolish enough to think she'd recovered from that loss. But she'd survived it, then lived with it, and thought she was doing well . . . at least until recently.

Now her life was under attack, and she was shocked to find how fragile everything she'd built really was. She was dumbfounded, too, to find that while people were being ripped from her life like paper dolls from a chain, she longed to be the one who'd be gone first.

I, she thought on a pitiful half-laugh, want my mommy.

Yet all she had was herself.

Then Grif rejoined her side. Kit shot him an annoyed glance. Even when he was trying to be sweet, she thought, he was damned contrary. Tucking her arms around her body again, she turned to him. "Not exactly the Kit Craig you're used to, is it? Don't worry. The dark mood only hits when someone close to me dies. It'll pass soon. Until the next time, that is."

This time his hand closed over her arm when she tried to turn away. With the mere pulse of those fingertips—tensile, she thought, fighter's hands—he drew her back. But what kept her there was the bruised intensity of his gaze.

Grif cleared his throat. "I don't have a lot of friends. Those I once counted as close are long gone, but I was never an easy man to know. I was a loner as a kid. I played only in my mind. I chose individual sports over team. That's how I got into boxing."

Grif gave his head a little shake, like he hadn't meant for all of that to spill out. "Anyway, I made sure anyone had to work hard to get to know me. As if my friendship and company is some great gift, right?" He chuckled for them both, but Kit was listening now, and caught the self-consciousness in the way he moved his shoulders.

"Anyway, it's no coincidence that I married the one woman who did work to get to know me. I mean, when someone looks past the rubble of all your faults, digging to find the good in you, it's . . . appreciated." Grif squinted into the empty meadow. "I asked her once why she didn't just leave when I was surly or distant or, you know. Too talkative."

Kit huffed. Was there anyone less talkative than this man? "What'd she say?"

He shrugged, and the accompanying self-consciousness this time was sweet. "She liked my way. She said there was magic in how I moved around the world, my every action so tightly controlled that when I finally did relax—when I turned that energy in her direction—it was like being spotlit."

He paused a moment before his small smile shifted to a frown. "She also said I was like a lone island that would be there long after the buildings and monuments other men had built turned to dust. She thought it was a compliment, but how could she know? It's all dust."

Kit pursed her lips. "I'm sorry . . . is this your pep talk?"

Grif shrugged.

"That's it? You're done?"

"Pretty much."

Kit was suddenly furious. "Then what's the point? Why bother living or loving at all? Why set yourself up for inevitable heartache?"

Grif didn't even change his expression. "Because it's still worth it."

Worth it to watch everyone around you die? she wondered, screaming inwardly. Worth it to know you could be next—no telling when or how? Worth it when some asshole could take the gift of free will and turn it into a weapon, a curse?

"You're wrong," she said, furiously wiping a rogue tear from her cheek. "I'm beginning to think it doesn't matter at all."

Then Grif put a hand to her cheek, and the magic he'd referred to before stole the breath from her body. "It always matters, Kit. Didn't you tell me that?"

"But—"

His fingers stroked her cheeks. "Trust me. Even if you die today, and never step foot on this mudflat again, love always matters."

She shook her head until his palm dropped away, then immediately wished it back. God, she thought, tears filling her eyes. She didn't want to want him and she damned well didn't want it to matter. "I don't think you understand, Grif. People drop from my life like flies. And I don't know if I'm just used to it by now or just fucking stupid, but I've kept spinning my stories, working hard to live deliberately—in print, in the way I dress, in the actions I take, all the way down to the damned car I drive—like doing all that would give me a say in the whole process. But I don't have a say in anything, do I?"

He swallowed hard, and she knew she was right. Even the man who pretended to be an angel couldn't deny that. No one had any say in their fate at all.

This time she was the one to lay a frigid palm over his. "If God wants to smite you dead, He can. If a murdering cop wants to sneak into your home, he can, too. I mean, if you— Griffin Shaw—wanted me dead," she shook her head, "there wouldn't be a damned thing I could do to stop it."

"But I don't want you dead," he said, in a low, fierce voice. "I don't."

Yet there was little he could do about it if someone else did. She let her hand drop away. "Maybe you should just go, Grif.

Two people have been murdered in the span of one week. My gut tells me it's precisely because of their proximity to me."

"I've been closer to you than anyone else this whole week," he countered hotly. "And my gut tells me that's exactly what's keeping me safe."

"That's a very strange thing to say."

He shrugged. "That's my way."

And, despite it all, she liked his way, too. But she couldn't say that now. Dennis was walking toward her, which meant she'd soon be standing before Paul's parents. If she wasn't strong, their grief would mow her down. "I know I'm not supposed to care about this. Paul was an asshole throughout our marriage. He was an asshole to you. He was an asshole tonight. But no one deserves murder. And . . ."

When she only shook her head, mouth still open, Grif finished for her. "And you loved him, once."

She nodded. So maybe Grif was right. Maybe love—even an old, discarded one—did always matter.

"Ready, Kit?" Dennis said, joining her side.

Nodding, she leaned into his embrace and let him wheel her away. Yet they hadn't taken three steps before Grif's gravelly voice rang out behind her, louder than she'd ever heard it before. Loud enough that even Hitchens turned and looked, all the way from across the lot.

"I'm not going anywhere, Katherine Craig. I'll spend every waking hour of this life helping you find out who's really responsible for these deaths. 'Cuz it's not you. It isn't even Paul Raggio's fault, no matter what else he's done."

Kit put a hand on Dennis's shoulder, asking him to wait. "Do you think Chambers is responsible for this?" she said lowly, when she was again square with Grif.

"What part of this case have we touched that doesn't have his name on it?"

Kit dragged her fingers through her hair. "And yet he remains untouchable."

"Nobody's untouchable."

She considered that for a moment, then lifted her hand to his stubbled cheek. It had the island of a man swallowing hard. She gave him a small smile. "You remember that, Griffin Shaw."

Because even though keeping him near had Kit questioning her own mental health, for some reason he, too, very much mattered.

CHAPTER NINETEEN

Dawn was tugging at the skyline by the time Grif headed back to Tony's, carefully navigating the wide streets in Kit's precious car. If what remained of the night had a scent, it'd be heavy ash and cheap perfume. If it had weight, it'd be a hangover. If it had emotion, it'd be regret. The whole damned thing—from Chambers's party and Ray's skin club to the call that'd led him and Kit to death—had left a bad taste in Grif's mouth. It was the taste of humanity's underbelly, and he wished there was some way—other than the obvious—to wash it away.

On top of it all, Anas was stalking him. Grif couldn't see her, but he'd have known it even without her appearance at the stables. The ability that allowed him to open locked doors and communicate with the Pure and feel the combustible heat in Hitchens's heart was also an instinct. It was an inborn lightning rod, giving him advanced warning, if not protection, from an oncoming storm. The angel was near, she was furious, and she was making it clear she still wanted Kit dead.

Which put her and Grif at absolute odds. Because Grif was no longer here just for himself, or even for Evie. His wife was long dead, and whatever restitution he could give her would be a cold, unknown comfort. However, Kit was warm and alive, and if she were to perish now, he wouldn't feel mere guilt.

He'd want to die, he realized . . . and then he'd want to die again.

The thought pulled his chest tight. If he wasn't careful, his headache would return. Sarge might be controlling the strength of his fierce mental attacks, but it also seemed the longer he was on the mud the more he could do the same.

But he still couldn't find his way around this damned city. Where the hell was the entrance to the Country Club?

Grif turned his mind back to Chambers as he searched. He believed, though he couldn't prove, that the man was behind the murders of those closest to Kit. He also believed and couldn't prove that those murders were linked to the list initially acquired by Kit and Nicole. More than that, he thought as he finally spotted the club's exclusive entry, the man's openness with Grif about the sexual frat parties, and his willingness to host them at his personal property, meant he was also unconcerned with the world at large discovering his little secret. And why would he be? All those men gathered in one room like powerful little lemmings . . . and not one of them was talking.

And people love to talk, Grif thought, cursing as the road dead-ended before him. Backing up, he wondered what sway Chambers held over the powerful politicians, entertainers, and judges. The cameras in those rooms were part of it, but that wasn't why Nicole Rockwell had died. Like Kit, she'd no idea about his estate parties.

So back to the Wayfarer Motel. To something connecting the two sexual enterprises. But what? Grif thought, finally spotting Tony's long horseshoe entry. And who?

Pulling the car to a stop at the top of the private drive, Grif inwardly patted himself on the back for seeing Kit's little treasure safe, and stretched into the night. Exhaustion was etched on his insides. Fatigue was something else he'd forgotten about his mortal years.

And the bone-weariness cost him. Grif had already shut Tony's front door when his intuition caught up with his thoughts. The dregs of the weighty, ash-strewn night weren't ready to be washed away after all.

A shadow lunged. Six feet, one-ninety, favoring his right. Grif leaped left . . . right into Lance Schmidt's iron grip.

"You're not as pretty up close," Grif gasped, right before Schmidt blew out his kidney. He folded with the bolt of pain, immediately hobbled. The fist that rocked his jaw corrected his posture, and the headache he'd been dodging all night splintered his brain.

Booted feet caved in his stomach, cracking ribs, then a thud, and he was flipped, his mouth blooming with numbness and blood.

"Not so pretty, either . . ." he heard, right before steel-tipped toes found his head, his ear. Then he heard nothing.

His breath wouldn't come. He was dying—he suddenly remembered it from the first time, and couldn't help wondering if Sarge would send another Centurion or if he'd be expected to trudge back into the Everlast alone. Probably the latter. It wasn't as if he didn't know the way.

Unfortunately, he wasn't dead yet. Grif opened his eyes— about all he could manage—and immediately regretted it. He'd only suspected that Hitchens was headed down a violent path, but Schmidt's cold, marbled gaze told Grif that he'd killed before . . . and he enjoyed it.

Grif almost wished the man *would* torture him. Then, once Schmidt's time was up on this mudflat, his soul would be shipped directly off to the forest. He'd have to endure every moment of pain he'd ever caused, and do so at the hands of the relentless, single-minded Third. And, oh, how they'd love to destroy this cruel soul again and again and again.

But Schmidt pulled out a gun instead. So it was to be silent and fast. Without another word, Schmidt compressed the trigger in a slow-motion squeeze that still lasted too long. Braced for death, Grif could only watch in frame-by-frame increments as the bullet left the chamber.

Then Grif's shoulder blades flared with pain as Anne intercepted.

No. Not Anne. That was an unremarkable name meant for mortal lips. The creature who caught the fired bullet with the sharp edges of pointed teeth was Anas—the Pure, created by God, numbered among the Powers, tribal kin to the Dominations and Virtues, the first of the created angels who controlled demons and guarded the heavens . . . and who, self-admittedly, wouldn't help a mortal even if her own soulless life depended on it.

Spitting the bullet back at Schmidt, who flinched, wide-eyed, when it burned his skin, she checked on Grif with a side-long gaze and a growl.

"Your eyes are healed," Grif slurred . . . or maybe he just thought it. He couldn't be sure his larynx wasn't crushed. He couldn't be sure of anything, because that was when all hell broke loose, though Grif was no longer conscious to see it.

Memory. Teeth and wings, fire and full-throttle screams. It was all that remained of the chaos following Anne's rescue. Or maybe he'd dreamed his second death, the blood slowing, the tissue dying. Even Grif's beaten and bruised flesh merely echoed with the abuse, like a sad note lingering on the air, though paralysis had settled in his bones. When he tried to lift his head, nothing happened.

"A few more minutes," Anne said, a giant shadow passing above him. Memory flashed again and he saw her bending, lifting, *healing*, but then she, and the thought, disappeared. "You'll never even know it happened."

Untrue. His memory had proven intractably stubborn . . . though his flesh was proving as weak and fragile as ever. Yet Anne's healing touch worked. He was sitting up within five minutes, standing unassisted in ten. Even his back, where his wings had been ripped away, felt strong, solid, and whole. "You saved me," he said, wobbly as a newborn deer in the middle of Tony's wide, wood-paneled living room.

Anne cut him an annoyed look, and his breath caught. Her eyes were blue from corner to corner, and roiling like storm clouds beneath tightly curled lashes. She waited until his heartbeat had settled, then went back to staring out the window as the sun rose over the dewy green.

"Did you kill them?" Grif asked.

This time she looked at him like she wished she'd let him die. "Kill a child of God?"

"Right." Stupid question. He cleared his throat. "So . . . ?"

"They left," she said, back to him. "Ran. Though your

would-be assassin accidentally drilled a hole in the side of his partner."

"Must have seen a ghost," Grif said, stretching. That was better. "So how's his buddy?"

"Couldn't you tell? He'll be dead within the hour."

Grif froze mid-stretch.

"Come on, Shaw," Anne said with undisguised disgust. "You're a Centurion. You can still sense death coming for others."

Grif shook his head. "I blocked it out."

He'd been working so hard to ignore his angelic side, to use the time left on the mud to clear his name, that he'd missed death coming for *him*.

Yet Anne's words jogged another memory from Chambers's gala.

"Didn't you smell that?" he'd asked Kit after they'd walked away from Paul, but she'd waved the question away and Grif let it go. But he recognized it now. Paul had reeked of postmortem plasma.

"Use it or lose it," Anne said, without sympathy.

That must be why Grif hadn't perceived the swirling mist, the sign of impending death he'd relied on most, though in retrospect even Paul's voice had sounded tinny, the echo of the hourglass running out. "It was the same smell that was stalking Paul earlier tonight."

Anne merely continued gazing out the window. Grif joined her, staring until she was compelled to turn his way. Up close, the eyes roiled like an azure cyclone. "Why'd you interfere?"

Now she sneered. "Because I know what you're trying to forget. You're not human, Shaw."

"So why help me, Anne? If I'm gone, Kit dies, and you're back in the Everlast. That's what you want, isn't it?"

Glancing down at a rip in her silk blouse, Anne stroked the soft material with her fingertips, and frowned. "Katherine Craig will die anyway. But I can't return to the Everlast unless you, the man who bound her to that fate, escort her there. She's your Take, Shaw. And you're mine."

And he couldn't Take Kit if he'd already been shipped back to incubation to heal from the trauma of yet another death. So Anne needed him alive and near Kit, but they couldn't order him to harm her . . . and couldn't stop him from protecting her, either.

"Of course . . . now you owe me."

Grif tilted his head. "Which means?"

"If you were to speed things along, I wouldn't forget the deed." She tried on a smile, but it looked like a puzzle on her face, and Grif didn't smile back.

"You mean kill her myself so you'll play nice with me in the Everlast."

"You've already killed her," Anne said coolly. "You need merely to put her out of her misery."

Grif turned away, but Anne was there, too, and Grif hadn't even seen her move. "Don't walk away from me."

So he leaned against the thick bulletproof glass. "Were you trying to scare her at Chambers's house?"

Anne smiled, mouth unnaturally wide. The flesh she was so regrettably trapped in wasn't a perfect fit. She wore it like a sweater that was too tight and so her expressions bulged in places they shouldn't. "To death."

Grif began shaking his head. "No, I—"

"Kill her!" Anne yelled, and she lashed out with her fist, not at Grif—no, she couldn't do that—but at the barrier that'd protected Tony for the last fifty years. The glass wall fell in a shower of sharp drops, and Anne jerked away, as surprised as Grif by the outburst. More surprised at the blood welling in her palm. She jerked back at Grif's touch, but when he held firm, she allowed him to take hold of her arm.

"You catch bullets with your teeth," he said quietly, "but you bleed when you break glass?"

"It's this flesh!" she cried, the sound of mourning doves in her voice. "It's a handicap! I am dying in here, can't you see?"

Welcome to the club, Grif thought, releasing her arm. "That's the human condition, Anne. As long as you're alive, you're dying."

Shooting him a squalling, blue-stained glare, Anne pinched together her wounds. The skin melded where it touched, and she massaged it like clay until it was once again smooth and the blood was wiped away. However, Tony's fishbowl was a mess. He's gonna be pissed, Grif thought, huffing as he looked around.

"Nice job . . ." he began, but when he looked back at Anne's face, a lone blue tear slid over her cheek, trailing wet stardust.

"This is not my nature," she said, her powerful voice a mere whimper, a child's despair carved on her smooth, perfect features. "This is not my way."

Grif had never even heard of a Pure in need of comfort, much less seen one. But he understood.

"Come here," he said, holding out his arm. When she only looked at it, he moved to her side, and drew her close. Anne stiffened, then suddenly slumped. It was the first human empathy she'd ever known. Grif guided her to the half-moon sofa, settled her back with a chenille throw across her lap, and a pillow tucked behind her neck. Telling her to wait, he raided Tony's beloved wine rack, choosing the bottle the old guy had pointed out as his favorite, one he'd been saving for decades.

"It's for a good cause," Grif muttered apologetically, pulling the cork from the bottle. Only the best for a Pure. Yet he hesitated in handing the glass to her. "You said you couldn't bear all five senses at the same time. Your eyesight is back . . ."

"My touch is gone," she said, running her fingertips along the chenille, and then back up to the rip in her silk. Fingering the material, she looked genuinely sad. "I never knew a material thing could be as soft and cool as the wind."

Blinking, she lifted her gaze to Grif's, and nodded as she accepted the glass. Holding it on her lap, she said, "My sense of touch was acute when I arrived, but then it just went blank. It wasn't just that I couldn't feel things anymore, it was like they didn't even exist. That's when the colors flooded in."

Anne leaned her head back and closed her eyes. "Now I know why a rainbow is a gift. Oh, and the glorious dimension of everyday objects. I spent this entire morning studying a single rose." She raised her head, and the blue depths of her eyes were wide with the memory of her first rose. "Did you know that life thrums through the veins of every petal? It's so alive that humans try to wear its secrets."

Grif lowered himself to the lounger across from Anne, and shook his head. He hadn't known any of that.

"But the touch is gone. Textures mean nothing to me anymore." She stared wonderingly at her palm, then said as if to herself, "And somehow . . . they mean more than before."

"Because you can't unknow your life's experiences," Grif said. This was *his* area of expertise.

She looked at Grif. "I must go home."

Sighing, Grif leaned back in his lounger, then held up his

glass. Staring at Anne through the dark cranberry stain, he said, "Do you know why people drink this? I mean, wine instead of beer or scotch or vodka? Or anything else?"

"I do not know why one would drink at all."

Nodding once, he continued, "It's because wine tells a story. If a bottle is properly stored, and this one was, you will taste a juice that is changed only in age. The rest remains the same as when it was bottled. All the choices the winemaker made in picking the grapes, and blending them, and storing them are in the bottle. You taste the fruit, but you also taste the wood of the cask as if it were a living thing—and, of course, it once was. You taste the storm that hit right before the grapes were picked, and whether it cooled them too quickly. You taste the earth . . . the way it was fed, when it was watered, and if it was healthy.

"All these things come together in a simple bottle, and when you drink it, a climate and a man you never knew, and a bit of mud you never actually stepped foot on, reveal themselves to you. It's the personal history of the world recorded in a bottle. This one is the record of the year Tony was born." He jerked his head. "Taste it."

It was fascinating, watching a Pure experience sensation for the first time. She tried to hide the foreign emotions, but there was no controlling her surprise when the first drop of wine hit her lips. As her eyes fluttered shut and her throat hummed, Grif could almost follow its path as it rolled down her tongue, igniting the sweet and sour taste buds, before sliding into her throat, disappearing in a mysterious heat of knowledge in her belly's core.

"Now that's a story," he said, lifting his glass in a toast when her eyes finally refocused.

For a moment, Anne didn't move at all. Then, just as he spied more blue tears filling her eyes with liquid stardust, she opened her mouth and screamed. A raven's rabid screech ripped the air, accompanied by bared teeth and bulging eyes. The cry blew through the room, elongating until there should have been a hesitation. Yet the moment when any man would have to draw breath passed, and the weight behind the spine-scraping pitch only increased. Lifting, the tonsil-ripping howl reached another crescendo, then snapped like a band into a numbing silence. Feeling a pressure grow above him, Grif looked up.

Lightning cracked through the ceiling to arrow between him and Anne. For an eye's blink, Grif caught the origins of the unnatural fire bolt. Through the rooftop, past ozone and sky, a grainy membrane lay ripped like skin. A tangle of color rested behind that—the rainbow God unfurled onto the Surface, bunched up like ribbon in a box. Anne's cry ripped the seams of God's promise, allowing an even briefer view of what lay on its other side.

Paradise.

Grif's cry joined Anne's at the sight, and he reached up toward the wonder, both everything and an abyss. Every element of the universe was mashed together in undulating effervescence; flame burning behind frost, velvety clouds roiling over gold sheets of evaporating water, peaceful pockets of darkness, inflamed and full, like bulging black hearts. Grif listed toward it like a sailor toward the siren's call. Yearning rose in his chest like a wave, followed by an ache that crashed in to lay him flat.

All of his losses—his life, Evelyn's, the unknown future of their doomed past—they all reached from inside to choke him.

Yet the beauty above spoke to him, as if *only* to him, and his mouth opened to form a reply from his heart. Across from him, Anne was speaking in tongues. Even with tortured minds and broken spirits, even bound to the Surface, they ached for God's presence. It would be like being drawn back into the womb. It would be rest. It was the only real redemption there was.

It took Grif longer to recover from the sight of Paradise than it did from the attack. But it left Anne even worse off than before. After she'd stopped screaming—mending the rainbow, sealing the membrane, stitching the sky, raising the roof—the beautiful chaos disappeared, and the world was normal once more. But Anne was curled around herself and looking about blankly, wide-eyed at the room, as if she couldn't remember how she'd gotten there.

Then, azure eyes blazing mad, she said, "Kill her."

"No."

A bolt shot into Grif so quickly he was smoldering before he realized her fiery wings had flared. Now he was the one forced into the fetal position, but she didn't allow him to remain there, curled around his burning belly. A long arm forced his gaze up and the dusty scent that had stalked Paul, as well as tonight's attacker, blew into his lungs as Anne hissed.

"Then I leave you both to your fates."

And she hit him so hard his mortal senses fractured, and darkness spun to claim him, and the blue-eyed Pure was instantly gone.

CHAPTER TWENTY

Y our love should have saved me."

"I know."

It was that old dream, Evie and Grif in the 'fifty-six, racing through the bleak Mojave, except that this time they weren't. Evie wasn't there, the car was missing, and there wasn't even a sense of space, much less the expansive desert around him. Grif was alone, and the surrounding darkness was matched only by the nothingness in his heart.

"You weren't strong enough to save me." The sweet voice turned into a hiss.

He answered as he always did, his words reverberating into the void. "I don't have to be strong. I'm dead."

"Not anymore," Evie's not-voice returned, altering the script. "Better wise up, tough guy, or you'll have to feel it all over again.

I told you to keep your head down, but no. Look where it got you, wearing skin again. And look where it got me."

Grif squinted, searching for her. "Where, Evie? Where did it get you?"

"Same place as you, Griffin," she shot back, tone as glittering and hard as a gem. "In the dark. Alone. In this cold place where no one comes, no one sees me. No one cares."

"Evie, I'm trying to get to you. I want to help. But I need to know where you are."

"That's rich, Griffin." A bitter chuckle rose up to choke him. "Because you don't even know where you are."

And Grif tumbled out of the darkness, rearing into wakefulness in time to see a woman's approaching shadow. His first thought was, *Evie,* but he knew her body like his own, and this wasn't it. *Anne,* he realized, as a room began to take shape around the approaching form. He could label the objects—couch, table, light—but the names were devoid of meaning, attached to shapes his spinning thoughts couldn't hold. Fear reared as the woman reached his side, and he fell back, trying to escape.

"Grif." Kit touched his arm. The room flipped, and suddenly he knew which way was up. His greedy gasp for air was what told him he'd forgotten to breathe, and he tried to make up for the lack by sucking in great gulps of air. Meanwhile Kit perched next to him, palms cool on his face and neck.

"It was another nightmare, sweetie," she said, treating him more gently than he had any right to be treated. Swinging his feet to the floor, he braced them there like that would anchor him firmly in this time and place, but the movement had Kit's hands sliding away, and the darkness threatened the edges of his vision again.

Growling, Grif punched the couch. "Damn it! Why can't I locate myself on this rock?"

"Shh," Kit soothed, and reached for him again. Her palm against his forehead had the room stilling. The other lay supportively at his back. "You bumped your head. You're not making sense."

But despite the bump and the fading dream, everything suddenly made perfect sense. Schmidt knew where he and Kit were staying. Anne, crazed with the need to return to the Everlast, had attacked. People were still dying.

And it was all his fault.

"Where's Tony?" he asked, just before he noticed the glass wall was once again erect, as thick and indestructible as before. A sidelong sweep of the foyer told him that was cleaned of blood splatter and wreckage, too. The red eye of the alarm showed it was engaged. No wonder Kit was so relaxed. Anne had cleaned up before she left.

How thoughtful of her.

"Haven't seen him," Kit said, handing Grif a glass of water. He accepted it with a murmur of thanks.

"Yeah, he has a reputation for disappearing when things get rough," he said, sipping.

"So, what happened?" Kit asked, propping herself on the coffee table in front of him. He wished she was closer, then immediately wished that thought away. "One of his old cronies come by and try to shake you down?"

He almost told her. She'd met Anne, so she might believe him. Then again, she might not, and he didn't want her open expression to close to him. And it would, the moment he said the word "angel."

"How are *you*?" he asked instead.

"Oh . . ." She deflated a bit, like lifting his spirits was the only thing keeping her up. Circles rode undercurrent beneath her eyes, and her shoulders sagged as she nodded. "I've been better. Paul's parents were kind, though. I think they were too shocked to blame me for his death, though I don't doubt that's coming. His mother blamed me for a lot of things."

"The divorce?"

"The marriage," she answered wryly, then shrugged. "For now she needed a shoulder to lean on."

And Kit had given it, Grif saw, even knowing it would take something from her.

And because of that, Grif reached out slowly and took her chin in a light grip, fingertips sliding over her jawline. Kit froze, caught by the intensity of his stare. Then she finally shuddered. "Grif—"

But he took her mouth, and her, by surprise. What surprised him was how gentle the kiss was, and that he suddenly wanted it so much. Yet if her touch had grounded him before, it unraveled him now. All the senses he'd tried to bury flared like fireworks. She was so warm, so soft. So alive.

But Kit pulled away. "Didn't we try this one before?"

"Not exactly this," he replied, pulling her atop him.

"I'm not sure we should." But she wanted to. He could feel it in the press of her thighs. He could even scent her, female and musky, warm like the earth.

"But you want me." For the first time in fifty years, someone had a need for him. He ran his finger along her bottom lip, and Kit swallowed hard. "I want you, too. And do you know why?"

She shivered as his calloused hands roamed lower, then shook her head.

"Because the taste of you sits round and ripe on my tongue. It's like a promise." He tasted again, eliciting a moan.

"Your touch," he said, lifting his hips. "It ripples through me. Makes me realize how long I've been still."

His eyes moved to her cleavage, down the length of her, gaze caressing her curves.

"And just the sight of you—"

"I'm a mess."

"Shh . . ." He placed a hand over her mouth, hard enough to hush her but loose enough to play. When he felt her protest drain from her, he slid his hand to the back of her neck. "I swear, this face is carved in marble somewhere. In Italy or Greece or somewhere goddesses once roamed."

"Jesus, Grif . . ."

"But none of that's why I really want you." He stilled, and she did, too. "All this rockabilly stuff . . . you wear it like armor. I get that. It protects you. But you're strong in your own way, and you don't need any of it. Fact, I think I'd prefer you in nothing at all."

And he let go of his fear, his need for control, the distance he was trying to keep between him and his humanity and, pulling her into his embrace, finally allowed his full angelic sense to flood him again.

He saw her with his Centurion gaze, a white halo circling her body, with lavender hooks spearing in as she looked at him. "Your soul is magnificent," he gasped.

Kit rose, specter-light above him, and pulled him to his feet.

Then he lifted her from hers and crossed the room with her in his arms. No way was he going to let go of her now. "Someplace without windows or light. I want to disappear in you."

He carried her back to her bedroom, the one he'd once studied from the golf course with the flaming eyes of a Pure boring into his back. But Anas was gone, and it was *his* blood and his flesh that were currently heated—not a burden, but a gift now that he was alone with Kit.

Kit freed him of his jacket, and tugged impatiently at his shirt. Her blood was up, too, evidenced by her swollen lips and heavy lids and all those human signals he hadn't even known he'd been missing in the Everlast. Fifty years since a woman had looked at him this way. It felt like forever.

More important, the haunted look that'd been in Kit's face just moments earlier was gone. Now she looked aggressive and demanding and strong. He'd given her that with his need, he knew, and was doing it still. Grif slid the straps of her dress from her shoulders, blindly working the zipper from her back, wanting to do it some more.

Bare skin found his, and simultaneously their hands grew rough. Grif's mouth dropped lower, lips tugging so that this time Kit arched back of her own accord. A low moan moved from her body into his, and his legs quivered. One of them dragged the other to the bed, Grif wasn't sure who, and it didn't matter. They found it blindly and there they fused.

Nothing like it in the Universe, Grif thought. Those born into the Everlast had no idea what they were missing. If they knew, he thought, as her hands raced over his body. If they knew . . . they'd bow down before *us*.

A hard nip from Kit had him grunting, then reversing their positions, though their limbs immediately tangled again. Wild

suddenly, needing her female heat and taste and scent everywhere, Grif pinned her arms to her sides hard enough to bruise,
then went lower. She cried out, she struggled, but it wasn't in
pain. It made him ravenous, and he hadn't even known he'd
been starving.

Minutes later, she took someone's name in vain. He finally
looked up and found her chest heaving, head turned up to the
ceiling, eyes unfocused. Grif wiped his mouth over her belly,
then felt her jolt as he again caught a nipple.

"God." Her hands braced his shoulders. "Wait . . ."

"No." And he slid his hands beneath, cupped her, and pulled
her onto his lap, entering the wetness that was already his.
Her release was almost immediate, but Grif held her steady,
wanting more. Though his own breath was ragged, though
his vision threatened to blur, he kept his gaze hard on her face.
He'd been in the Everlast, he knew what it was to be akin
to air. Now that he had every sense at his disposal again, he
would damn well use them. Levering back, he thrust forward
even more.

Her cry, he thought, would outshine the angelic choir.

And her voice—that insistent, cheerful, nonstop voice—
was how he found her rhythm. He waited, giving her a series
of slow glides on which she could catch her breath, then rose
above her, still holding her thighs, and sent her cresting again.
He felt wild now, like some sort of animal driven by desperation and an instinctive need to shatter inside of her. The quake
moved from her body into his and back again, and she bucked
for and with him, also an animal, wholly his.

He waited, quaking and moving and building and thrust-
ing, until the cry was in his sightline, until it pulled back like
a cocked arrow in a bending bow. Then he braced himself over

her, her thighs still lifted over his hips, and plundered. Heads close, cheeks pressing, breaths strong in each other's ears, they rode each other in tandem, and let need turn to greed. Kit pushed him to climax even as she fought to get there first. Then the arrow flew and Grif was free, emptying into her as she disappeared in him, and both cries found their targets before spiraling off into the raw, violent night.

CHAPTER TWENTY-ONE

What just happened?" Kit murmured sleepily. Her head was nestled in the crook of Grif's left arm, but her gaze was tilted up, soft on the side of his face.

"Honey," Grif replied, without opening his eyes. "If you don't remember, there's no sense in me repeating it."

She slapped at him lazily. "I mean what just happened to put that frown between your brows. You look like a grumpy bear."

Grif shook his head. "Just the opposite. This is the first time since I've been back on this mudflat that I haven't woken up totally disoriented." He did look at her now, brows drawn so low it was as if he was confused to find her there. "You're like an anchor somehow. A steadying force as the rest of the world just spins."

Kit smiled. It was the nicest thing anyone had said to her

in a long while. And on the heels of an orgasm that'd shaken her inside and out, it was also the steadying force *she* needed to believe that maybe, just maybe, things might turn out all right yet.

Of course, that's precisely when Grif had to open his mouth again. "I think we should leave. Get out of here. It's not safe anymore."

"Hmm . . ." Kit said, because it felt safe to her. "Think we can wait until morning?"

He was silent for a long time. "I think so. I don't see anything . . . I mean, any reason why not."

"Good," Kit said, nestling in close. "Because we can't follow our new lead until then anyway."

"What lead?"

"The one I was going to tell you about right before you seduced me."

"Oh. That one."

Kit smiled into his chest.

"Wanna tell me now?"

No. She wanted to disappear under the covers and taste him some more. Yet Grif was going to need a couple of minutes to rest up for what she had in mind anyway, and truth was, so did she. So she gathered the sheet around her waist, and stood. "Be right back."

But she wasn't surprised to feel his eyes on her from the doorway as she strode through the house. I could get used to being looked at like that, she thought. To being looked *after* like that.

The thought worried her, so she pushed it aside and put a smile on her face as she returned to the bedroom, bag in hand. "I found something after leaving my former in-laws' house.

I didn't want to go anywhere public, but I didn't want to be alone, either. So I drove."

The wide, empty streets of a Vegas night always calmed her. She could order events in her mind while driving, as if they, too, were on a map.

"It's strange, but it's the old landmarks, the ones with the most inconsequential memories—Laundromats and burger joints and theaters—streets I haven't been down in years, stores I've never even been in, but have seen a million times . . ." She looked at him. "These calm me the most. They've outlasted . . . lives."

Grif placed a hand on her arm when she swallowed hard. She gave him a watery smile. Yes, she could easily get used to this. "Anyway, I was driving by this pizzeria I used to go to with Paul—greasiest pie ever, I swear—and, of course, I was thinking of him, the good and the bad, when I remembered something else that was just plain strange."

"What?"

"The night of Nic's wake, when he stopped by to tell us about the gala. I was so irritated with him that I wasn't listening to half of what he said, but I remember one thing. He said Chambers lavished his 'woman' with jewelry. But when we saw Anabelle Chambers at the gala—"

"She looked like a nun," Grif said, sitting straighter in bed.

Kit nodded. "Same thing when I talked to her upstairs. There was no jewelry chest in sight, no perfume bottles. Nothing . . ."

"Fussy?" Grif provided, as she searched for the word.

"Pretty," Kit corrected, and made a show of fluffing her hair. They shared a brief smile. "So I thought, what if the rumors are true? What if Chambers really has half a dozen wives, and what if one of them is pissed about it? I mean, it can't be a good feeling to share your wedded husband with other women, right?"

"You think one of Caleb Chambers's other wives anonymously gave you and Nicole that list in order to get back at him for, what, not being his favorite spouse?"

"It's a theory," she said, shrugging. "A woman scorned and all that."

"Maybe it's Anabelle," he reasoned. "Maybe she found out about the parties and girls downstairs. She could tolerate him having his own personal harem, but not mistresses."

"No," Kit said, shaking her head after thinking about it for a moment. "You didn't see her. I like the other wife scenario better." She lifted a finger, holding off his scowl. "So I went to the office and got on dear Auntie Marin's precious private computer."

"The family archives?"

"The very same." Kit smiled, seeing she had his interest. "Turns out the illustrious Chambers clan can trace their ancestry all the way back to Joseph Smith and his fancy spectacles."

"His what?"

She waved his question away. "The point is, Mormons are fastidious about their family histories. One of their core tenets is that the dead can be baptized into the faith so that the whole family can exist together in the afterlife. Therefore they're the best collectors in the world of all things genealogy. Good thing for us, too."

Kit reached into her bag and pulled out a black-and-white photocopy of a girl with limp pigtails and a freckle-spattered nose. "Because otherwise we'd never get the chance to meet one of Caleb Chambers's daughters."

"We already met one of Chambers's daughters."

"Yes. But this is his eldest. Ms. *Bridget* Chambers," Kit said and waited. Even recovering from a bump on the noggin, it didn't take long. "Yep. That Bridget."

Grif took the photo and studied it closer.

"Use your imagination. Erase the freckles and bleach the hair into chopped layers. Then drop a veil of distrust over that schoolgirl gaze."

"Bridget Moore."

"Funny," Kit said, curling into his side. "But she didn't mention the family connection when I was getting my nails done."

"Seems neither of them want to." Grif absently placed a palm on her thigh. "So what leads a nice Mormon girl into the world's oldest profession?"

"Maybe an early influence," Kit said in a way that suggested probability rather than possibility. "Maybe Daddy."

"I can see the man running hookers. But his own daughter?"

"He didn't exactly appear to be overly solicitous of women," Kit replied wryly. "And Bridget was clearly afraid, though that could have been because of Schmidt."

"So you think Bridget sent the list. It was the lure, Schmidt the catch."

Lips pursed, Kit shook her head. "No. It's her father. He's family, so it's more personal."

Grif nodded after another moment. "So now we have our connection between Chambers and street hookers."

"But still no clear evidence linking him to the Wayfarer."

Grif's hand returned to her head, stroking her hair before fisting around it, tugging so her head was forced back. "You're right. Tomorrow."

"So we're not leaving tonight?" She grinned to show she wasn't afraid, and voluntarily opened to him further. His eyes flared with heat, and he tightened his grip while his other hand traced her collarbone.

"There's something you and I still need to discuss."

"Discuss, is it?"

"It's about your attitude problem." He trailed his index finger down her cheek.

"Oh, that's right. I'm . . . what was the word?"

"Cavalier."

"Right." She smiled as his palms moved lower. "About sex."

"And danger."

She lifted her hips. "Am I in danger now?"

He accepted the invitation. "Absolutely."

Who's cavalier now, she thought, smiling as his mouth found hers.

Whereas there'd been no thought before, just movement and need, Kit honed in on this moment, noting his gentleness with the precision of her reporter's mind. It was almost as if he'd been a line drawing before—a very good, complicated one—but still sketched in black and white, single dimension, and as untouchable as a painting on the wall. But now, with his touch and desire funneling into her, he was a riot of color. The boldest thing she never knew she wanted.

Wanting, needing, to drop deeper into his warm flesh and raw strength, and away from the horrors of the entire week, Kit shifted closer. His heart beat strong as she slid her palm across his chest, and she noted that his earlier solemnity was gone. Whatever haunted him had been shut out of this room. Here there was just the two of them. Just life, not death. Strength, not weakness.

Hope, and none of the despair that lay outside this home and this moment and these arms. And then, just as her eyes were slipping shut, she saw his wings flare. She gasped, blinked, and they were gone. Who's crazy now? she thought, relaxing again.

"I feel like I'm underwater. Not drowning, but immersed." Biting her lip, she recalled what Tony had said about his home. "Submerged in this old fishbowl."

"Everyone needs a fishbowl." And, gaze fastened on her mouth, breath steady, Grif took them deeper. Warmer, wetter, one eight-limbed creature instead of two separate beings. Kit wrapped her limbs around him, and when he entered her again, driving deep, she gasped, then gave a little laugh. "Wings," she said, on a rasping breath.

"Brains," he said, chuckling, too.

And then, aligned in the unblemished moment, despite all those that lay so imperfectly outside of it, they rolled, comfortable in each other's skin, if not their own. Together, Kit thought. And, joined, they were perfect in their deformities.

CHAPTER TWENTY-TWO

Grif was wrong. *Danger didn't lay in his arms, but in Kit's dreams. She heard the voices raised in argument in the kitchen, and thought for a moment she was really awake. But no, Grif's voice rattled like pebbles in a tin can, and the other curled around syllables like wind, a rise and fall that held a threat of fury.*

"What did you think would happen, Shaw? One night in a mortal woman's arms is supposed to erase fifty years in the Everlast?" A laugh, the wind gaining force before dying down again. Kit froze. She recognized it. The woman from the Chambers estate. The one who'd handed her the Bible and told her to go home.

"You might have your precious free will while walking this mudflat in human flesh, but you're still a creature of the Everlast, just like me."

Kit edged closer, and peered around the corner to find Grif with his back to her, staring out the small window over the kitchen sink. "What does that mean?"

The woman paced behind him, circling like a wolf. "It means that every day, at four-ten in the morning, you will return to your exact state of death—that clothing, that watch, the loaded gun at your ankle. Four bullets. And, of course, the photo of that pretty little wife tucked deep into your wallet."

"You leave her out of this," Grif said lowly.

The woman smiled, and Kit saw fangs. "You can strip it all off again in the next minute—you can put on a top hat and tap until your feet fall off for all I care—but everything will be back twenty-four hours later. Same as when you died. Same as what happened just now."

Grif said nothing.

"You can't escape it, Shaw. And, no matter what you told yourself while burying your flesh in that female, you will never unknow being dead."

"Are you done?" Grif asked, voice tight.

"I won't be done until I'm home again," the woman said, echoing what she'd told Kit at Chambers's estate. Kit frowned.

And the woman turned with blue smoke swirling in her eyes. "Oh. Hello, dear."

Kit jolted awake. "Jesus," she said, placing one hand over her thumping heart, the other automatically searching for Grif in the bed. But he wasn't there.

Biting her lip, Kit wrapped the sheet around her body, and slowly stood. It was just a dream, she told herself. Her mind's way of trying to make sense of everything that'd happened in the past few days.

But she headed straight to the kitchen anyway.

He was leaning over the kitchen sink, arms splayed wide, head down, and yes, fully clothed. He must not have heard her come in, because he jolted when she wrapped her arms around his body.

"Shh," she said, as he'd done with her, but he shivered despite her warmth, and didn't press back into the embrace.

"Want to hear something amazing?" Kit said, trying anyway. Her voice was only a little strained, but she forced it lower, huskier, like it'd been when she cried out in the middle of the night. She wouldn't let one bad dream sully all that had come before it. "It's something I forgot in the chaos of the last few days. Especially last night after . . . you know.

"When I first saw you, when you saved me from Schmidt. You zigzagged from the shadows, and for a moment I imagined I saw . . . well, wings. They were black, like an onyx river falling from your shoulders. They flare like rising smoke, right? And dissipate the same way at the tips?"

Now Grif did turn. "How did you know that?"

One corner of her mouth had lifted with the telling, but now it fell. *Shit.* She thought indulging his angel story would make him laugh and bring them closer. Instead, though he'd joked about it during their night together, he was again serious. Dead serious. "I don't *know* anything. I told you, I was just seeing things."

But his expression had grown far off. "Because you were so close to death. Because you were supposed to die."

Kit retreated a step, pulling the sheet tighter around her. "Well, that's what angels do, right?" Kit tried again, with a forced laugh. "Protect the innocent from a wrong, untimely death. Knowing that, knowing you did just that for me, I feel . . . different this morning. Like I might just get through this, you know?"

Grif met her gaze, and for a moment he looked like he was going to touch her. But then he turned away, and there was no danger of them touching at all. Not looking at her, he said, "We made a mistake."

Kit's pulse jumped in her chest. "No, we didn't."

"You slept with me because I fit in with your rockabilly lifestyle."

"No, that's why I was first attracted to you. I slept with you because . . . because . . ."

"Because?"

Because you said I was beautiful and strong. Because you said you saw my soul, and because I've always believed that life requires being known by another soul.

She refocused her gaze on Grif. "Because I'm an idiot."

Grif looked down, and shuffled a foot against the peeling linoleum floor.

"What are you doing?" Kit's low, husky lover's voice was gone.

"I need to tell you why I'm really here, Kit. I *am* a Centurion. I really am an angel. I meet murdered souls in the moments after their death."

Wrapping her arms tightly around her body, she jerked her head. "Don't do this. You know my best friend was just murdered. And my ex-husband."

"Nicole was my Take, Kit. I was the one who was supposed to see her home."

The dream-woman's voice popped into Kit's mind again. *I won't be done until I'm home again.*

"Stop it," Kit hissed lowly. "This isn't funny."

But then the thought of Nicole and Grif caught hold, and

the blood drained from Kit's face. "You were there," she whispered. "I saw you in the window. I . . . I saw your hat!"

She saw him consider lying, but Kit knew what she'd seen. Like Tony himself had told her, she knew what she knew. It had been Grif.

"Yes," he finally said, voice clipped and hard.

"You killed her." She backed up, knocking into the kitchen table.

"No." Grif took a step forward.

She held out a hand, like that could keep him from coming near. "I saw you up there. I saw your silhouette! *You were there.*"

He shrugged impatiently, and shoved his hands into his pockets. "I already told you that. But I didn't kill her."

Her eyes narrowed. "Why should I believe you?"

"I saved you, didn't I?"

It was a good point, and Kit tilted her head. "Did you talk to her?"

"Nicole?" Grif nodded, but Kit waited for more. "She said you were supposed to go to a bonfire last weekend. And some bar of beauty."

The Beauty Bar. All her girlfriends met there once a month. Tears blurred Kit's vision, and she hastily wiped them away. "Why are you doing this?"

"I can tell when death is coming from someone," he said, pressing on with his crazy, horrible story. "I can smell it like a hound scents blood in the air. I can see the plasma of world matter, of fate, gathering in the moments before death, marking the end of that soul's Surface time."

"Like Paul?" she asked, one brow lifted in challenge.

But Grif continued to lie. "Yes."

A harsh laugh ripped from her chest. "So you knew he was

going to die? And you did nothing?" She shook her head. "What kind of angel is that, Grif? What kind of *person* is that?"

"It was fated," he replied quickly, defensive. "There was no stopping it. Besides, he wasn't my Take. I was with you."

Kit thought for a moment, tried another angle. "All right. What about Marin?"

Grif didn't even blink. "She's got a stew of drugs inside of her that'll probably have her outliving all of us."

Oh, he was good. Lying with such a straight, sincere face.

"She'll be happy to hear it." Kit crossed her arms. "So what are you doing here, Grif? You don't want me, that's obvious—"

"Kit—"

"So who's your next so-called Take?" She made finger quotes in the air, and nearly lost her sheet. She grabbed it, angry, and spun to leave . . . but froze. Stilling, looking at him, she asked, "Who *is* your next Take, Grif?"

Clearing his throat, he held out his hands. "Look, I screwed up. I did something I shouldn't. I helped Nicole extend her life by minutes after she was already dead. She circled Schmidt's name in your notebook, and that changed everything. Schmidt found it, and that's why he's after you. I let that happen. I . . . killed you."

"I'm right here."

"But you're not supposed to be."

"You saved me," she pointed out. That had to mean something.

"I only prolonged the inevitable."

"What? No . . ." She looked around the kitchen like it was the moon, frowning and shaking her head, then zeroed back in on him. "Bullshit."

"What?" Grif drew back.

"I call bullshit on your black-winged angelic ass, that's what." Securing the sheet, she placed her hands on her hips, advanced on him like she was the one who was dangerous. "You're just scared. You allowed yourself to feel something for me that you hadn't felt in a long time, and it spooked you. You're . . . chickenshit."

"I'm in love with another woman!" he roared, causing her to flinch. "The woman you're researching. Evie . . . Evelyn Shaw. She was my wife. They . . . they killed her. Right after they killed me."

"You have had a total psychotic break with reality," Kit said evenly.

"Really?" Grif used his anger as a counterpunch. "You're the one who said you saw wings on my back. Tell that to your shrink."

"They were shadows, I know. Don't change the subject." Don't remind her of what she thought she saw during their lovemaking. It'd be just her luck if *crazy* was catching.

"So you *don't* believe me?"

"I don't even care!" she yelled, and then pulled at her hair in a way that probably made her look crazy. Grabbing at the sheet, she yelled, "All I know is that you've been there for me in the biggest shitstorm of my life, and there have been quite a few, Shaw! But you've stuck with me and helped me and we just made love for an entire day, and there's something real between us and don't tell me you didn't feel it, too!"

Breathing hard, he opened his mouth, but nothing came out. Yeah, he'd felt it all. She took it as a concession, and moved close, forcing him to look her in the eye. "Look, I understand about losing someone. There's no real getting over it. No one can replace a mother or a father or take a wife's place in your heart. Those places forever belong to those you first loved. But you can carve out new places for new people. Love *matters*. It's greater even than your Everlast."

"The Everlast you don't believe in."

Kit crossed her arms. "Honestly Grif? I don't care if you play the harp and shit stardust. But even if I did believe you, and you *were* a legitimate blast from the past, your Evie is long gone."

"Not to me."

She shook her head. "This is not cheating."

He flinched like he'd been slapped, and Kit knew that of all the thoughts roiling in his mind, that was the one he hadn't allowed to bubble up. "I am here because I want to know who killed me and my wife. That's all."

"You need to move on, Grif."

Turning his back, he pressed his palms against the tiled countertop. "You wouldn't understand."

"What wouldn't I understand?"

"You don't just dispose of love, Kit. Not this kind."

Sucker-punched, Kit was silent for a long moment, then let out a gutted exhalation. "Wow. That hurt even more than hearing that I'm destined to die."

"I didn't mean it that way," he said, turning to her. But of course he had. "Look, this is the only thing I've cared about for the last fifty years. And she's the only woman I cared about before that. If pain can go on throughout lifetimes, then love can, too. When I get this information, when I find out what happened to Evie, and where she ended up, then and only then will I move on."

But Kit was done talking, listening, *understanding*. "Jeez, Grif. The way you talk about her you'd think she was the fucking angel."

"Watch your mouth."

"You're a dick."

"I told you that."

"Not that kind of dick."

"Hey, I'm helping you."

"Your help hurts!" she screamed, bent over herself, holding the sheet tight. Then she growled, whirling away, whirling back, all her anger turning in and around on itself. Finally, eyes stormy, she pointed at Grif. "I don't want to hear another word about your wife and your wings and your lying mid-century ass. You're just another man who's afraid of commitment. Truth is, Grif, you don't have any thrust!"

"Yeah? Well, I'm calling bullshit on your pseudo Lois Lane rockabilly self. How about that?" he shot back, then hit himself in the chest so hard that Kit winced. "Because I *was* there, I know what it was really like, and it wasn't all Lindy Hop and circle skirts. It wasn't different from *anything* you've seen in the past few days. It was just more of the same. Evie was the only good thing I had in that life, so—"

"Oh Evie this and Evie that . . ." Kit blew out such a hard breath the curls lifted from her forehead. "I swear to God if I hear one more thing about the perfect and precious Evelyn Shaw, I'll kill *myself!*"

Grif stared, then narrowed his gaze. "You're not going to have to hear another word about her, Kit. Guaranteed."

"Get out!" Kit pointed to the door.

"It's not your house."

"I meant, get out of my life!"

And Grif stared. And then he turned.

And then he left.

CHAPTER TWENTY-THREE

K it didn't know why she was surprised. It wasn't like she hadn't been left before. But Grif's abrupt departure was at such great odds with his actions the night before, and the silence so deafening in the wake of the previous night's love-making, that she stood in the kitchen long after the front door had slammed shut, shaking with mental vertigo.

An angel.

"More like a walking plague," she muttered, forcing herself to put one foot in front of the other. She couldn't stay here now. So she headed unthinking, unseeing, back to the bed-room, tossing the sheet on the bed that had barely cooled from her and Grif's intertwined bodies, and quickly dressed.

"I am not the crazy one," she whispered, as she packed her toiletries. "And I don't chase after men who don't want me,

I don't allow anything in my life that isn't greatly desired, I don't . . . I don't . . ."

I don't know what's wrong with me.

Letting her toiletry bag fall to the sink, Kit stared at her reflection in the mirror. Her eyes were shadowed from too little sleep in too many nights, and the lids themselves were low and hooded . . . sexy, she thought. Or would have been minutes earlier. Now she just looked tired.

Leaning toward the mirror, she pulled her hair back from her face until it hurt, then let her fingertips trail over her cheeks and chin. Pursing lips still swollen from kisses, she then shook her head and turned away. The answers she sought wouldn't be found in her unadorned face. Something small and unseen inside of her had her choosing men who just couldn't seem to choose her back. Shaking her head, Kit left the bathroom, picked up her bags in the guest room, and headed back through the quiet house.

But then she spied the rickety computer cart. Biting her lower lip, Kit only paused a moment before dumping her things on the sofa. Seating herself before the desktop computer, Kit shook the mouse, bringing the machine humming to life from sleep mode. "The truth, Kit," she told herself. "Not just the easy answers."

She typed in "Centurions." Nothing. "Everlast." Nada. "You get points for creativity, Shaw," she mumbled, then went back to her original search, back to the fifties.

Back to Grif's stated reason for having entered her bedroom, her life—her *heart*—at all.

Kit's stomach rolled at the image that popped onscreen. There she was, Evelyn Shaw. White-blond hair swirled just above her shoulders in a pinup pose that Marilyn herself would have coveted. The brows were penciled dark, and her eyes shone deeply as well—with color, with secrets, and with the knowledge that she absolutely stunned. Her body, slim yet still lush in a V-neck sheath, slimmed tightly at waist and neck, and her round, soft chin edged up into a full, red mouth. She was authentic, not retro.

Everything, Kit thought, that I'm not.

Kit frowned, and focused on the text. She'd missed this article on her initial search, either because it hadn't been on the search engine's home page or because she'd only been skimming. Of course, she'd believed she'd been looking for a long-dead grandmother. Not a wife. Not Grif's . . . beloved.

But it wasn't only that. She hadn't really been taking Grif seriously. While happy to accept his help in solving Nic's murder, and his protection in preventing her own, she'd put his request on the back burner, deeming its expiration date long overdue and therefore of little importance.

But it suddenly *was* important to Kit, and here was proof that the woman had lived—age twenty-four back in 1960, with a ring winking off her left hand, which Grif claimed was his. "I can't believe I just got in a lover's quarrel over a dead woman," Kit muttered, but she kept scrolling, and reading.

And Evelyn Shaw was long dead, Kit saw, as the police report was quoted. She'd been found in a bungalow at the Marquis Hotel and Casino, with her beautiful throat slit ear to ear. Eyewitnesses said she and her husband had been downstairs gambling all night, and that her actions in the craps pit must have led to an armed confrontation in the lush, shadowed courtyard.

"Sure, blame the chick," Kit said, scrolling until she found mention of said husband—just one line in this article, and only two words: Griffin Shaw.

Of course, it was a different Griffin, Kit reasoned, though her stomach knotted. The same man she'd already found mention of before, the grandfather that Ray DiMartino had cited at the club, and the man Tony thought he knew.

Grif and I go way back. Fifty years, give or take . . .

Tapping her fingers against the desk, refusing to accept that, Kit started a new search. This time she entered Ray DiMartino's name, and a slew of articles came up, mostly commentary on the family's dubious connections, and their infamous mobster past. Too broad, Kit thought, then added Mary Margaret DiMartino's name to the mix. That limited the search a bit more, and leaning closer she began to scroll.

It didn't take long. Mary Margaret's disappearance back in a day when young girls didn't disappear had been big news in this small, dusty desert town. That she was the niece of reputed kingpin Sal DiMartino made it even more remarkable. Both the *Trib* and *Sun* had covered the case extensively, though the reportage verged on gossip. What had happened to Mary Margaret? Who would be stupid enough to mess with the reputed don of Vegas's underworld? And who would be brave enough to bring her back?

Kit followed that question to the end of the long article, written by a man named Al Zicaro, who'd apparently considered himself an expert on Las Vegas's shady side. "Blah, blah, blah—associates, contracts, bada-boom, bada-bing . . ."

She scrolled to the last page of the article, and that's when she saw it. Ginger hair, a hint of freckling, eyes lined with a perpetual, considering squint. The same gaze she'd stared into so deeply the night before, that'd loomed above her, giving and taking and making her forget everything but his name.

Griffin Shaw.

He stared back at her from an image taken fifty years earlier, making Kit feel like she'd been thrust through time, all reason and sense obliterated in a headlong rush into the past. When she caught her breath again, she leaned closer to the screen.

That was his suit jacket. That was his hat and tie. That was the five o'clock shadow she could still feel sliding against her slightly raw cheek. Barely breathing, Kit read the whole of the article again. Then, putting her hand to her mouth, she looked up and stared out the bulletproof-glass windows.

"Well," she said, talking to herself again, no longer sure what was crazy. "How about that?"

Then she was grabbed from behind.

Grif was so unsteady, his breath so tight in his chest, that he could barely locate a direct thought, much less orient himself once outside Tony's house. It didn't matter. He was in Vegas. He just looked up, spotted the telltale neon spires, and headed in that direction. But his mind kept going in circles.

Already regretting the things he'd said to Kit, or—if not precisely that, then how he'd said them—he shoved his hands deep in his pockets, tucked his head low, and sighed. She'd treated him more gently than he had any right to be treated, then opened to him with earth-shattering trust. It wasn't her fault she'd been marked for death. It also wasn't her fault she was so damned beautiful and feminine and *alive* that he'd forgotten every damned reason he was here, and had gone to bed with her.

God, he'd gone to bed with her!

Grif couldn't wait to hear what Frank had to say about that. That thought alone kept him from turning around and going back. He'd sworn to Kit that he wouldn't leave her side, but that might just be the best way to protect her. Literally, starting with the moment he'd laid eyes on her, outside the window of her best friend's death chamber, he had been Kit Craig's worst enemy. Besides, there wasn't even a hint of the rotting, algal, postmortem plasma stalking her when she'd wrapped her arms around him this morning. Not an ounce of the death scent that'd hunted Paul at the Chambers estate.

Kit, Grif knew, was safe for now.

But she was wrong in thinking he could just *choose* to move on from Evie's death. She was the reason he was here, after all. The reason he couldn't move on in the Everlast. He didn't know who he was, or where he'd be, without that reason.

So Grif headed back into Vegas's core, hoping the chaos there would help order his thoughts. Though it was not yet full dark, the city was already a visual scream, and as Grif turned onto the boulevard, he caught it mid-shout. Tourists traipsed across intersections like colorful soldiers, moving in platoons, the city itself in command. Instead of guns, yard-long plastic cups were strapped across shoulders. The uniforms were anything but that—the pedestrians sported both glitter and jeans, and everything in between. Grif observed it all with casual disinterest, and he'd traversed the full of the Strip before realizing he was wandering with even less purpose than the slot zombies around him.

Breathe, he reminded himself, coming to an abrupt halt. The yelp behind him skittered into a curse, and he caught a glare from a couple using each other to remain upright. Grif sucked in another lungful of air and ignored them. As long as he kept breathing, he could figure this mess out.

Spotting a coffee shop across the street, Grif headed there to pay an exorbitant amount of money for a great cup of joe, then sat outside on a metal bistro set, pairing the java with a smoke. Breathing *that* in, he felt better. Now . . . what next?

Obviously he couldn't just leave Kit wrapped up in the mess he'd helped create. Even were he inclined to let her die, as Frank and Anne wanted, he'd get no thanks for it. They'd ignore whatever obedience he'd shown and rap him about all his other mistakes instead . . . which included telling Kit who and what he was. As for Kit herself—well, she'd know him for a liar if he just stood by and let her die. He'd promised he wouldn't, and he still meant to keep that promise.

But what was that old saying? About a woman scorned? She had her mad up now, no doubt about it. She might get over it eventually, but she wasn't going to help him find out what had happened to Evie—or him—any longer. However, she'd given him an idea. He'd look up Mary Margaret's whereabouts, go back to Ray for her address if he had to, and find out if she recalled anything about what had happened after he returned her to safety fifty years ago.

Yet thinking of a young Mary Margaret had his mind swinging immediately to another young, vulnerable girl. Someone else whose family should have taken care of her, but didn't. Bridget Moore, born Bridget Chambers, should have lived a more charmed life than even a mafia princess. Chambers certainly seemed to dote on the daughter he'd been parading around the Valentine's Day gala. So what had caused him, initially, to turn his back on his eldest?

Or had it been the opposite and *she* didn't want anyone to

know they shared the same blood? She'd changed her name and not mentioned the Chambers family connection to Kit, even when she had the chance. She could just be forgetful— maybe forgive-and-forget-ful?—but she could also be afraid.

"But afraid of who?" Grif muttered, earning a concerned glance from the beggar slumped against the coffee shop's brick wall. Her estranged father, or the cop who'd bookended her illicit career?

"Let's find out," he told the beggar, who just nodded as Grif flicked away the cigarette and flagged down a cab.

Bridget Moore was closing shop as the cab pulled up, and her shoulders sagged as she turned toward it, like she already knew she wouldn't like what spilled from inside. Frown deepening when she saw Grif, she pocketed her keys and began walking away. Grif overpaid the driver and rushed to catch up. "We need to talk."

"I don't need to talk," Bridget said, not slowing.

"People are dying," Grif told her.

"People are always dying."

"You can stop it."

"Sure," she scoffed, showing him her cool, disbelieving gaze. "And then I'll stop time itself."

"Look, Bridget," he said, not letting up as her pace quickened. "We know who you are. We know your father is controlling the most powerful men in this town using blackmail and a lot of high-class hookers." When she only walked faster, Grif stopped and shoved his hands into his pockets. "What we don't know is how he's controlling you."

Bridget whirled, finger pointed like a weapon. "Nobody controls me!"

Grif lifted his chin. "Prove it."

Defiance and fury popped into her eyes, but she drew her hands together and twisted. There were words building up inside of her like a storm, but something was still keeping them bottled up.

"I believe you when you say you're not tricking anymore," Grif told her, advancing slowly, giving her time to think it through. Her eyes darted from side to side, making sure no one had heard, but she didn't bolt. "I also believe you're your own woman and you make decisions for yourself these days. But you know what it's like to be bulldozed. You can stop that from happening to others."

Now she scoffed. "And I don't believe that."

"Because you've tried to stop it before."

She shook her head, refusing to confirm it. "There's too much money involved. Too much power. And I ain't got any of it."

"You got me," he said, tilting his head as he shoved his hands deep into his pockets.

She huffed again, though her eyes softened. "And?"

"And I'm willing to listen to your story."

Biting her lower lip so that lipstick stained her top teeth, she looked away and rolled back on her heels, as if rocking herself. Finally she looked back at Grif and crossed her arms. "How much you willing to pay for my time?"

"You get paid for every minute in your day?"

"You wanna know my story, Shaw? Here's the Cliff Notes version. I was the original Daddy's little girl. And when I was fourteen, Daddy decided that my use, my purpose in this world, was to provide sex for his friends and power for himself. He made me into an object and a commodity, so do me a favor and don't judge me now if I happen to do it so fucking well."

Grif thought, then reached into his pocket for a hundred. "I got a bill."

She jerked her head at the bar. "And a drink."

So Bridget and Grif left dusk outside and embraced the canned, smoky dimness of the neighborhood bar. It was perfect for their needs. People looked up at their entry, then quickly away, all complicit in not truly seeing each other. A bored but efficient server threw down coasters and took their drink orders, and they listened to a couple at the bar competing with the television for attention until she returned, and left again.

"Where's your girlfriend?" Bridget started, stirring the ice in her glass.

"She's not . . . that," Grif muttered, then glanced at his own glass. "And we had a . . . disagreement."

Bridget looked amused at that. "Let me guess. Your disagreement was about her not being your girlfriend." She laughed when he tossed her a bland look, and pointed her glass at him as she raised it for a sip. "Oh, I read the two of you like the world's oldest, most unoriginal book the moment you stepped in my salon. She's half in love with you, but you're what's popularly known as the strong, silent type."

"Well, I'm not very popular right now," Grif said, stirring his own drink a little too hard.

"Just stubborn and sullen, then," Bridget said, setting her drink down. "And you've ended up exactly where you wanted to be because of it. Alone."

"This analysis part of the hundred-dollar charge, or you just throwing it in for free?"

Bridget snorted at that.

"You got it wrong, chickie. Fact is, Kit Craig would have been better off if I'd never entered her life."

"You're probably right," Bridget agreed, offering up a toast he didn't meet. "But you're here now, and you sound like you're trying to justify your actions."

"Look who's talking," he said, toasting her.

"I got good reason for staying silent."

"Tell me."

Bridget looked down, fiddled with her straw, then tilted her gaze over at him. "You like women."

Grif lifted a shoulder, then dropped it. "What's not to like?"

"Yeah, you like them," she said, nodding on a half-smile. "I can tell. After a while you can dissect a guy's insides like a pinned frog—this one has mommy issues, this one's a user, this one's just an asshole." Huffing, she shook her head. "My father doesn't like women. It's a testament to his entitled nature, and what he would call his 'extreme bad luck' that he's surrounded by them."

"Marrying multiple wives is bad luck?"

She glanced over at Grif with a small smile. "Would you call it good?"

He thought back to his conversation with Kit on the dance floor. "I'd call it excessive."

Bridget leaned on her elbows. "For my father it was expected. His father's side is an extremely traditional Mormon family. There's a branch of Mormonism that has never given up polygamy."

"Was there also a family tradition of pimping out their daughters?" Grif asked lightly.

Bridget's gaze flashed, but when she saw there was no bite or meanness to the words, softened again. Shaking her head, she sipped. "No. That was Caleb Chambers's own personal touch. He pretty much ignored me when I was a child. Seen and not heard, that was his motto. Left my mother alone to rear us." Gaze far away, she frowned. "Left *her*, I think, without ever leaving her.

"So the other wives came, the other children, too, and then I hit my teens. That's when he suddenly took an interest in me, and oh, it was heady." Bridget smiled bitterly at the memory. "Daddy wanted to hang out with me? Read me bedtime stories? Sit and stroke my hair and shoulders as we talked about everything and nothing at the same time?"

She sighed with the memory, but then her face darkened. "The night I had my period he came into my room, said my mother had told him it was a special day, and that he had a present for me. He gave me a beautiful silk dress, pure white. He said I was a woman now, and a woman had a duty to obey her father and honor her family."

"And so he honorably passed you around to his friends?"

"And waste a chance to benefit from the transaction?" She jerked her head, and paused to sip, more deeply this time. "No way. No, instead he held the first of many dinner parties, where I made a guest appearance in my new, wholesome dress. Then he proceeded to auction off my virginity."

Grif's stomach turned.

Bridget didn't look at him, her voice hollowed of emotion. "He was pleased afterward. Pleased with me for shutting up and taking it. Pleased with himself for thinking up what would become his most successful, long-term business plan to date." Bridget's jaw clenched as she stared into her glass. "The next time he came in my room, he told me I was a good girl and I'd made him proud. He left without touching me. He never bothered with me again."

"And your mother? Did she know?"

Bridget scoffed, and the anger he expected her to show for her father now flared. "My mother was the first wife of *the* Caleb Chambers. If she were to know such a thing—if she were to acknowledge it—she'd be that pitiable woman who married a polygamist, let him marry other women, sell his daughters, and raise whores. So she turned a blind eye, kept baking cookies, and we all went on with life as usual."

Grif hesitated, not knowing what the situation called for, finally giving in to impulse and instinct. Gently, he closed his hand over hers. "Except it wasn't."

Bridget was fighting the instinct to jerk away. He could see it in the startled look she gave him, but ultimately she gave his palm an almost imperceptible squeeze before sliding hers away. "I put it behind me as best as I could. Bundled up the white dress and shoved it in the back of my closet. I tried to forget, pretend that it'd happened to someone else, somewhere else.

"And then one day, I was walking home from school, and a car sidled up next to me. It was fancy—long and sleek and black—with crystal bottles inside and plush velvet seats. The back window rolled down and suddenly there, in my real world, was the man who'd bought me. He said he'd been thinking about me a lot since our night together, that he liked me, and did I want a ride?

"Of course I knew what he really wanted, and what would happen if I got into that long, dark car. And then I thought, it had already happened anyway, and everyone had walked away with something—that rich man, my father, even my mother because her ignoring it enabled her lifestyle— everyone but me."

Grif frowned, but gave a short nod. "So you got in."

Her mouth pursed sourly. "After I told him what I wanted

in return. He agreed, and we began having what he called our weekly 'dates.' He was fifty-nine. I was fourteen."

"So fast-forward five years," Grif prompted, because she was a bit unsteady now, and he didn't want her to stop. But it seemed Bridget didn't want to stop either, and she took a fortifying gulp, signaling to the waitress for another as she slammed down her glass.

Shifting to stare directly into Grif's eyes, she studied his reaction as she spoke. "Fast-forward five years and I wasn't just getting into limousines on suburban streets. I'd graduated to casino bars. And I dressed how I wanted. I was less discreet than before. My whole family would gather for Sunday dinner and I would drop innuendos and hints that my father would stew over and my mother would carefully ignore. Nineteen years old."

"Nineteen years young," Grif corrected, as the waitress arrived.

"Yes. But older than ever before." Then, inexplicably, she shuddered. "That's when Schmidt got into it. My father sent him to bust me, I think to scare me straight. He laid into me hard, said I'd do jail time, said he would see to it personally because I needed to get off the streets. He said I was . . . tainted."

She looked into her fresh drink, winced, then threw it back. Grif found that now he could say nothing.

"So I went home, and I thought about it like he told me to. I considered going back to school, getting my degree, maybe even cooking school. I was good at that." A wistful smile passed over her face only to be replaced a second later with a frown. "But then I got to thinking about Chambers—I stopped calling him Dad by then—getting rich off my flesh, and how he thought he could just roll me with this crooked cop. Once again, he told me to take it, and then just assumed that I would.

"Then I thought about Schmidt, and how that fucking pig didn't know me from Adam, but for some reason he was acting like I was the most important thing on his to-do list. That's how I knew."

"Knew what?"

"How to get back at my father." Bridget lifted her chin, her face masked with the same stubborn look she'd shot him in the parking lot. "I reconnected with our old buddy from the limo, the man who wanted me so badly he outbid them all. He had since, unsurprisingly, turned into one of my father's best clients. This time I was the one who drove up in the fancy ride. I told him I'd been thinking about him. That I liked him. That I wanted to take him for a little ride. He got all nostalgic on me, right in the golf course parking lot. He went on and on about our first 'dates.'" Narrowing her eyes, she mimicked him. "'Remember when you were young and fresh and tight' and so on."

She shook her head in disgust, then smirked. "What I re-membered was to turn on the video recorder so I could send copies of what he really did on his golf outings to his wife, his business partners, the world at large. I made sure my mother got a copy delivered straight to her doorstep so she couldn't ignore what she'd allowed me to become. I did the same at Chambers's offices and had it queued up for his secretary's viewing pleasure. By that time I'd learned what I was worth . . . but I still gave the old bastard that ride for free."

Grif whistled under his breath. The little girl with no voice and no choice had taken the sexuality that'd been prized and used against her, and turned it into an A-bomb. "And did your father send Schmidt again?"

Bridget's bravado fell away as she nodded. "But not to arrest me. Instead, he delivered a message that I was to change my name and to cease contact with his family, effective immediately. He said I was free to whore myself to anyone who'd pay, but that I would never talk to him or my mother, my family, again. And I haven't."

"But you still know what's going on in that household."

"Some." She shrugged. "But again, I have no money, no power. No one would believe me because what's my word—a prostitute's—against a cop's? A judge's? A Mormon businessman who owns them all?" She shook her head. "No, I'm no threat to any of them. But," Bridget added, staring into her drink, narrow-eyed. "I know that it embarrasses him."

"That you were a hooker?"

"That I was a street hooker. Did you and Craig go to the gala last Saturday? Did you see the girls?"

She shook her head when Grif nodded. "They're not bad girls. In fact, their very goodness is why Chambers can command such coin. They're told to be good girls, big girls. They're given champagne and caviar when they should be enjoying burgers with their friends. They dream of prom dresses but are given Herve Leger instead. It's both heady and totally disorienting for someone barely graduated from playground politics.

"I can't believe he's still getting away with it." She shook her head again. "Never underestimate the power of tight, young flesh on old, loose wallets."

"Never underestimate the power of raw blackmail."

"That, too." Bridget nodded. "Craig and her friend were on

the right track, of course. Chambers annihilates every person he sees as a local up-and-comer, anyone who might threaten his king-of-the-mountain status, and he does it by luring them to his parties. If he's playing it like he used to, he's friendly at first, gets them off guard. Then locates a weakness—alcohol, drugs, anything to loosen them up. Before they know it they're in a darkened corner with one of his 'girls.'"

"And he's got it on tape." Must have learned that one from his daughter, Grif thought wryly. "Okay, so why is Schmidt still in the picture? He provide the girls?"

Bridget looked at Grif like he was crazy. "Schmidt works the street, and regular johns can't score prime, green flesh. But the glitterati don't want skin that's been passed around too much. Even among the chosen, a few months go by, the girls' faces become known, they get a little too familiar with the local councilman, maybe call him by his first name one time too many, and they're gone. You think Chambers pulls a mind-spin on the men, it's nothing compared to what happens to the women."

Grif had to fight not to down the whole of his drink. "And what happens to them?"

"He sells them to Schmidt."

He stared hard at that. "Sells?"

"Sure. In return for sending out little 'legal' reminders to Chambers's clientele, and making sure the heat is always directed elsewhere, Schmidt gets the castoffs for his own burgeoning illegal brothel. The girls are usually strung out by then, or else they've been made to feel like they've got no other use. Told no one with real class would want them anyway. And what are they supposed to do, go back and seduce their school's star quarterback?"

"They could quit and walk away."

Bridget sneered. "You've clearly never had a pimp."

"That's true."

"A girl can't walk," she told Grif, leaning forward. "She has to run, and even then she'd better have wings. Better yet, a false identity and a crash pad far, far away."

Grif understood now. "Because Schmidt sets them up. Arrests them for nothing, charges them with something. Guess he feels like he owns them."

Bridget inclined her head. "And unlike my father, he's never finished with them. It's work for him or do jail time. Period."

"He can't be working alone."

"Oh no. There are other cops in on it." Leaning back, she blew out a breath. "Even the girls become complicit at this stage. And, of course, the judges and politicians and lawyers they balled back at Chambers's place. Everyone has a vested interest in keeping those women quiet and on their backs."

Grif looked at her. "So what'd they have on you?"

"You mean when I got busted at the Wayfarer?" She shook her head. "I wasn't working for Schmidt. I was trying to get the girls out. I was sick of it. It was eating at me, and I thought, in some ways this had all started with me so maybe I could end it, too. One of the girls rolled me, though. She thought she'd earn points with the 'Old Man' if she told him what I was doing."

"Is that why you didn't tell Kit that Chambers was your father?"

Bridget slumped wearily. "Schmidt cost me my job before. After I was fired from the Fifth Avenue salon, the bastard had the nerve to call me up. He didn't say his name, but he didn't have to. He said if I messed with his business, then he'd mess with mine. He didn't care whose daughter I was."

"And you think he would?"

"Schmidt can do anything he wants. So I decided to keep my nose clean and mind my own business. If they're smart and want it badly enough maybe some of the others will, too."

Grif studied her face. "So why contact Kit and Nicole with the list?"

"I didn't."

Grif drew back at that, because he'd been sure she had. Yet there was no reason for her to lie now. Not when she was being so honest about everything else. "One last thing, then."

She lowered her glass.

"Where is Chambers getting all these girls in the first place?"

She looked at Grif like he was impossibly naive. "He's a bishop in the twenty-ninth ward."

Grif shook his head. "What does that mean?"

"The Mormon Church. He's essentially the head of his own congregation."

Grif felt his face drain of color. "He culls little girls from the church . . . and turns them into prostitutes?"

Bridget smiled bitterly. "Makes priests look downright old-fashioned, doesn't it?"

"But why wouldn't the girls tell someone? Their families, their mothers?"

"There's a system you have to go through. The same person, a man, who takes complaints for the church . . ." She trailed off, looking at him pointedly.

"Takes them directly to Chambers," Grif finished for her.

"One big, happy family, right?" But the scorn was quickly replaced. Soberly, she said, "I actually told at first."

"Told on your own dad?"

She nodded. "I agonized over it for days—prayed over it actually. I thought if God was on my side then someone would listen and . . . save me. So I went to church. Went to the elder like we're told. You know what he said?"

Grif shook his head.

"He said, 'God will help you out of your sin, child.'" She winced with the memory, her face momentarily caving in on itself. "I seen a lot and done a lot since then, but I have never seen anything so cold as that man, who sat before a kid who'd been sold and raped, and told her that her only hope of help was God."

"You know God's not to blame for that, right?"

"Oh, He's not the one I blame." And sighing, Bridget signaled for another drink. "Anything else you need to know? Any other old scars you want to poke at?"

Rising, Grif shook his head, and pushed in his chair. "Thank you for your time, Bridget."

She shrugged, and he began to walk, but paused, and returned to put his palms down on the table's center. "You know, I kinda have a sixth sense about a person's true nature, and well, whatever you've done in the past, whatever was done to you, you're still walking and breathing and making choices for your own life. And you're worthy of a good life, Bridget."

Tears shimmered, and Bridget swallowed hard.

"Oh, and Schmidt was wrong," Grif said, straightening.

"About?"

"You," Grif said, staring directly into her hard-soft face. "You're not a damned bit tainted."

Tears fell unheeded from her eyes as she stared. "Be careful. He's powerful."

"You be careful, too."

Wiping her face with one hand, she lifted her glass with the other. "Don't worry. Chambers can't ever touch me again."

Grif shoved his hands in his pockets. "You should let someone touch you, though."

Bridget shot him that too-knowing half-smile. "So should you, Shaw. So should you."

CHAPTER TWENTY-FOUR

The cab that'd dropped Grif in front of Bridget's shop was long gone, and he was forced to walk back the way he came. Not that he minded. He had a number of thoughts to chew on, and the almost-fresh air did him good. Again, it didn't matter that his personal navigation skills told him no more than which way was up, he just lit a Lucky, tucked his head low against a pushy breeze, and headed to the bright bulge in the middle of the desert night.

As he walked, he reassessed Kit's chances of survival against what Bridget had told him. He'd already known Schmidt was involved in the events at the Wayfarer, and his attack on Kit marked him as enemy number one. He'd assaulted Grif again at Tony's, and, in all likelihood, killed Paul Raggio as well. He had partners—all nameless and faceless thus far—though one had taken a bullet at Tony's, courtesy again of Schmidt.

Which brought him to Schmidt's other partner, Chambers. The oil greasing the wheels. Question was, how was Grif supposed to clear Kit Craig from all these men's sights? Was it even possible at this point? Could fate be altered a second time, or was she in so deep that it'd be like throwing a floatie to someone in the middle of the Atlantic?

Bust the lid off the Chambers-Schmidt connection, Grif thought, nodding to himself. Even in Vegas that was a scandal. But because power and muscle lay entirely with them, proof had eluded the light of day for over ten years. Chambers had it, of course, but he certainly wasn't going to let it be used against him.

"Has to keep those tapes somewhere," Grif muttered, flicking his cigarette butt into the gutter. It'd take time to find them though, and Grif couldn't even be certain of the next ten minutes. Free will or not, Sarge could yank him from the Surface at any moment. So how the hell was he going to score enough time to reveal Chambers's dirty little secret, much less save Kit?

Find out who sent Kit and Nicole that list, he thought, cutting across a vacant commercial lot. That's what started this whole thing, so maybe it could end there, too. But how to find someone who had less interest than ever in being found? And as Bridget had no idea who was behind that initial list, where the hell was he supposed to start?

Exhaling a hard breath, Grif rounded the corner, felt one painful pulse from where his wings once were, and instinctively threw up his hands in defense.

Anne stood there, stoic and unmoving. "If I were going to strike you, you'd already be down."

Straightening, Grif jerked at his jacket's hem. "I knew that."

What he hadn't known was that dark skin could look so ashen. Gone was the glorious sheen that made the Pure's features gleam like polished marble. Her eyes were dull and sunken—they almost looked human—and her structured clothing looked like it was holding her up instead of the reverse.

"You look terrible, Anne. And . . . blue." He took a step back as she lifted her chin, but he struggled to see the vengeful Pure who'd knocked him cold before. "Have you taken a real breath since you hit this mudflat?"

Her jaw clenched, the bones underneath appearing brittle, like they would pierce the skin at any moment. "Air is for the weak."

Grif watched the old disdain flash in her dark gaze, but it had no real heat this time and was banked an instant later. Besides, she might be a mighty, immortal Pure, but he was the expert here on the mud. "Yeah, well you have to breathe."

"Breathe, eat, move—all these necessities and actions." She jerked her head, and it swung back unnaturally, like it was on a spring. "I can't even catch my thoughts anymore. They swirl and swirl and just when they're about to coalesce into something of use, I'm attacked by a sensation—a scent or texture or sight . . . sometimes all at once. It's overwhelming."

She shook her head again, this time swaying with the movement, then stilled like she just remembered Grif was there. Grif might not be in danger of physical assault, but he wasn't sure he liked this neutered, unhinged Pure any better. "Come here, Anne. Sit. You need to take a minute."

Anne allowed herself to be led to the back of the building, where Grif upended a paint bucket. She plopped down with a jerk, and running long fingers over her smooth skull, sighed.

"This is why He did it, of course. I never understood it before, but I do now."

"Did what?" Grif asked, leaning against the wall.

She gazed up at Grif dazedly, like a child. "Made you. Mankind. Why he formed you in His image. It is the perfect vessel to experience life to its full—feelings, emotions, senses . . . all of it piled atop an everlasting soul. Being human . . . it's incredible."

Grif had never seen it that way, through an angel's eyes, before. "Yeah. I guess it is."

Lifting her hands in front of her face, Anne studied the backs of them, then the palms, and back again. "You know, angels were made in a state of grace. It's not prideful to say that we are perfect—it merely is what it is. We are strong, powerful, fearsome, and good. Even those who followed Lucifer are still instruments of use to God, but . . . feeling things the way humans do, the way God does, that is not our nature or our right. Those that forgot that, the Third, were ever ruined."

She looked up at Grif, then surprised him by taking one of his hands in hers. Swallowing hard, he felt her fingertips, curious and caressing, exploring his. It wasn't like Kit's caress . . . or any other person's. Her alienness was palpable. Electricity, not blood, soared in her veins, and vibrated in her touch. She was a different breed even bound in flesh.

"And so," she continued, stroking his palm, sliding her electric fingers along his wrist, "as magnificent as those of us in the Host are—as much as that should be enough—we are not His most beloved creation. How ironic that we have more power in a thought than humans have in their entire bodies, and yet we are not equal to even the lowest of you."

Grif didn't know what to say. To apologize for that would

be an insult to God. To not apologize seemed heartless. Grif might be stubborn and broken, but he was not that. Yet just as he was about to speak, she rose, both of his hands in hers, and stepped so close that he could see the storm clouds roiling in her eyes. Grif swallowed hard.

"I did not give you enough credit," Anne whispered, drawing even closer. Her foreign heart thrummed as she pressed it to his chest. "Wearing this flesh has taught me what you must endure while traversing the Surface. The Pure feel emotion, yet without donning the material of God's exact image, nothing sentient can ever know true passion. I see this now. Even pain is impossibly exquisite."

Grif tried to slide away.

Anne's fingertips tightened like steel.

"You don't look well," he said, swallowing hard. The knobs in his back throbbed.

"Because I am being poisoned by the perfect impurity of the human condition. And yet . . ." Her storm eyes fluttered, unfocused. "I cannot help wanting more. Did you know that strawberries taste like they've been dipped in sunbeams? Did you know that a child's sweat smells like an old oak's strong, wet roots?"

Grif shook his head slowly, not daring to say a word.

"It's your fault." Her gaze refocused, hard upon him, and her grip tightened to the point of pain. Grif tried to jerk away, but he could have been chained in the electric chair itself, and Anne's face was suddenly inches from his. Hissing, she leaned so close they were aligned and touching head to foot. "I wouldn't be here if it weren't for you."

Grif fought to keep his voice and heart steady. She would feel it if his body temperature were to spike, if he were to take even an extra shallow breath. She was, very suddenly, sensing everything. "You'll leave soon," he told her evenly, "and you'll never have to touch the Surface again."

Tears welled—relief or regret, he couldn't tell—and her already stricken face crumbled. Then her legs gave out, and Grif had to embrace her just to keep her standing. "Why won't He call me back?" she cried, body sagging, voice breaking. "My mind is cracking. The impurity is profane."

"I know," Grif said, stroking her head, wiping the tears from her face.

"And yet . . ." Steeling herself, Anne pulled away, then licked her lips while she stared at his. "I can't help . . ."

And suddenly Grif's back was against the brick wall, the overwrought angel pressed against him, her lips probing and bruising. Her tongue flicked out like a snake's, and her nostrils flared to take in his scent. Her eyes rolled, not with pleasure but like a machine cataloguing knowledge, and her tongue clicking rhythmically in his mouth, like she was counting moment after moment. Repulsed, he shuddered and had a horrifying thought. Was that what he'd looked like to Kit?

Grif managed to turn his face away, then pushed at her hands, which seemed everywhere at once. "Stop it! Anne!"

Yet his head hit the brick with a crack that made him wince and Anne seized the opportunity, mouth fastening over his, tongue probing, taking more. "Stop it!"

Using all his strength, he pushed, and Anne rocketed back, body skittering on the jagged asphalt of the alley. She was up again, standing in front of him, in the blink of an eye. "So the bull hasn't been castrated," she said. "It was a good try, though. I almost believed it."

"Believed what?"

"You, trying to fit in on this mudflat. Ignoring your celestial nature. But now you see . . . you're still a freak. Like mine, your celestial nature is bound in flesh. It's like an A-bomb wrapped in rose petals. Feel it, touch it, taste it . . ."

And again, she was there, mouth fastened on his, arms wrapped around his back, and this time he couldn't shake her loose. The power to call thunderheads from the sky filled Grif's mouth, and his veins bulged with ozone. The earth's lava flowed through her lips, and color streamed in sharp blades behind his eyes. Then Anne grabbed his shoulder blades right where they ached, right where his wings should have been, and raked them until he bled.

Screaming, Grif tried to pull away, but her nails were deep inside his flesh, ripping and probing, searching and . . .

"What is that?" Grif staggered away, suddenly free. Yet he felt chained, bound, too heavy in his flesh, and he reached for his back, and found . . .

"Feathers. One each, from my wings." Anne giggled, too girlish and high, and she gave him a lopsided grin. "You can't fight your angelic nature now, can you? Now you have to go back. Now you are also Pure."

She cackled again.

"No." Grif clawed at his back. The phantom pain that'd been stalking him was gone, but the feathers were burrowing under his skin like centipedes, like snakes. Like a pure angel's wings.

"But first," she said, in front of him again, "you are going to kiss me. And then you will move inside me. And then I will know what it really is to be alive."

She lunged again, but this time Grif used her own power—*his* power now—to push her away. She stumbled back, chest heaving, and winced like she'd been slapped. Lowering her head, she slumped and muttered to herself, "Sharp and sour. Acidic and cold. No one told me." Her eyes arrowed up, full of blame. "Now rejection has entered my emotional repertoire, too. And I can never unknow it."

Grif winced, but still backed away. "I'm sorry."

"That's what men always say, isn't it?" She laughed without humor, and licked the taste of him from her lips.

"I just . . . I can't kiss another woman."

A low chuckle rumbled in her chest, and Grif felt it echo in his shoulder blades. Shoulders bunched, she swiped her arm across her mouth. "Do you know what's hilarious about this whole debacle? What's so absurd?"

He shook his head, not daring to say a word.

"You, Griffin Shaw, are under the illusion that you've stopped living." She bared her teeth, the smile gone macabre. "And Katherine Craig is under the illusion that she still is."

Grif shook his head. No, that wasn't right. There had to be a way. Kit was still breathing, they both were. Besides . . . "I wasn't talking about Katherine Craig."

"Oh, you meant Evelyn Shaw?" She bit her lip consideringly, accidentally drawing blood, and her eyes rolled again. Then *his* voice, the desperate nightmare voice, sprung from Anne's throat. "Evie . . ."

Anne straightened, dispassionate again, and nodded once. "I see," she said, in her own voice again. "You desire to know what happened to her, your old love. But do you want it more than anything?"

Grif wiped his mouth, but her taste, the ozone, the Everlast she'd buried inside of him pinballed through his core. "Yes."

"I can give you that."

He stilled and looked at her.

She smiled. "If you let Kit die."

Grif closed his eyes, let his legs give, and slumped on the paint bucket he'd placed there minutes before. Picking up his hat from where it'd been knocked when Anne lunged, Grif settled it on his head, and buried his face in his hands. She learned quick, he thought wryly. He had to give her that.

"You look torn." She knelt before him, then reached out and gently—but insistently—pulled his hands away. Tilting her head, she peered up into his face. "Does it hurt?"

"Yes," he said tightly.

She leaned toward him. "Let me taste . . ."

Grif rocketed to his feet. "Don't touch me!" he thundered, and there was power in his voice, there was pain. There was Everlast.

Anne heard it, and straightened with surprise. Was that concern furrowing her brow? Did she regret planting power inside of him? Maybe she only now realized that in trying to make him more alien, she'd actually made him stronger.

"Then choose," she said, lifting her chin high. "Weigh your need to know what happened to your old love versus your need to save the new. Do you want that old knowledge, or do you want Kit?"

"She's not a new love—"

"I tasted it on your kiss! It's there, like a hint of Paradise!" she screamed, and the building behind him shook. "Why else would you still be here? Why would I? You love her, Griffin Shaw! You love her without willing it or wanting it, and that is the most exquisite pain of all."

Do I? he wondered, wincing.

Anne crossed her arms. "Choose. Two loves, but you can

only have one. Do you want to know what happened to Evie, where she is? Or do you want to stay here and try to save Katherine Craig?"

If he said his wife's name, the mystery that'd haunted him through the last half century, and throughout the Everlast, would be solved. Who killed his Evie? Who killed Griffin Shaw?

Thinking of Evie, drawing the memory of the way she'd looked that last night—dazzling in blood-red—he rose unsteadily. *I might even be able to find her in the Everlast.* He'd apologize, they'd reunite. And they could remain together forever.

Standing, Grif swayed under the weight of the feathers buried beneath his flesh, and gave Anne a baffled half-smile. Tipping his hat, he backed away. "I need to find Kit."

But when he turned, Anne was there, her face inches from his again, blank with shock. "But the knowledge is here! Right on the tip of my tongue."

"The past is dead." Evie was dead. But Kit, and yes, his sudden, unexpected, baffling love for *her,* was very much alive. Using free will, not power, Grif circumvented Anne, and kept walking.

"You can't save her."

But he would try.

"You can't save her!" The Pure screeched again when he kept walking, her fury fully returned. Grif didn't need to turn around to know her eyes were roiling. "Everyone around you is in danger! Kit is. Tony, too! You can't even save yourself, Centurion!"

Grif halted at that. He waited for Anne to come to him,

knowing she would, and tilted his head sideways when she did. "What did you say?"

"You're a Centurion. Your job isn't to save, but to Take."

"Not that. You mentioned Tony." He jerked his head. "That man you saved me from yesterday, Schmidt. How did he know where I was staying?"

Anne said nothing.

"I thought Paul told him." He'd thought Paul had died because of it. "But it wasn't him, was it?"

Anne watched him closely, studying his shifting expressions and emotions with bald hunger. But Kit had never told Paul where they were staying after her house had been broken into. As far as Grif knew, only one man alive knew they were at Tony's. Grif looked at Anne. "Where is he?"

But the Pure had reverted back to her stoic, contained self. It was like her emotions were rubberized. They elongated, but always snapped back into their original form. "Just let her go. Then we may shed this flesh and go, too. No more pain. No more grief or guilt or anguish."

Grif shoved his hands in his pockets and nodded. "Incubation would wash away all my problems."

"Yes."

"No more worry over whodunit. Or anything at all."

"That's right."

"But Anne?" He reached up suddenly, and slid his fingertips along her cheek and behind her neck. Anne, shocked by his touch, didn't answer or move. "Anne," he repeated, "if she dies there won't be any more of this, either."

And Grif kissed *her* this time, allowing the thought of Kit to coalesce in the front of his mind. He thought of her insistent smile and chatter and refusal to be cowed by life, and how it made him want to drink her in so that he might feel that hopefulness, too. He brought to mind their night together, how her body was white silk and hot curves and the only exhilaration he'd felt in half a century, and he poured that knowledge into the kiss. He let Anne in on the secret. He gifted her both with a vulnerability she'd never known and the only thing that would protect against it, which was one and the same. He let her feel love.

He let her know what she was missing, and this time he was prepared for the scream. But it wasn't enough. Covering his ears, he cowered low and squeezed shut his eyes, feeling the cry thunder through his flesh. It pounded at him until he fell to the ground and sent his wingless back to throbbing all over again.

When the street was finally silent, when the aftershocks had faded and the car alarms were silenced, and when Grif was alone and finally able to pick himself up from off the ground, he hobbled down the alleyway and into the street, slamming his hand atop the first taxi he found. He had to get back to Tony's home. He had to find Kit.

He just hoped it wasn't too late.

Kit!" Grif bolted through Tony's home, heart racing after finding the door unlocked, all alarms disengaged. Had he left it that way? Had she? "Kit!"

"She's not here," came Tony's voice from the kitchen.

Relief whooshed from Grif in a gut-emptying sigh, and he strode across the living room where Tony already had a bottle of wine open and waiting. "Oh, Tony. Thank God. I thought . . ."

"Heyja, Grif."

"Jesse." Grif's heart sunk at the sight of the Centurion . . . then leaped when he saw the other one. "What are you doing here?"

Leaning against the wall in a black turtleneck, with combat boots poking from beneath a long flowered skirt, Courtney shot him a disinterested look, then returned her attention to the view outside the open glass door without answering. The maimed souls from the nineties had just begun trickling in from incubation, and Courtney was his district's greenhorn.

"She's just tagging along," Jesse offered, shoving hands in pockets that flared almost as wide as the wings on his back. Parachute pants, Grif remembered. Offed in the eighties, the kid had gotten stuck with the rawest deal in fashion history.

"I have some time before my next Take," Courtney countered coolly, because the only thing she hated more than talking was Jesse talking for her.

Finally, Grif's gaze landed on the old man crumpled on the kitchen's linoleum floor, blood pooling around his head from the back half of his skull, which had been caved in with an equally blood-soaked rolling pin. Grif's shoulders slumped. "God. Tony, I'm sorry."

Tony, already in the first stage of his plasmatic fade, sidled up to him. "You kidding? I'm relieved. I don't have to walk around in that broken-down flesh no more. Who knew my arthritis was acting up that much?" He rolled his shoulders, then shrugged. "Guess you just get used to things, huh? They sneak up on you over the years, and pretty soon you forget you ever knew any different."

Shaking his head as he stared at his destroyed body, he then turned to Grif, bushy brows arrowing up. "Hey, did you know you have wings?"

Grif shrugged. The dead, at least, saw him for who he was.

"I guess you did know," Tony said, then jerked his head at the back door. "No wonder my dogs liked you."

Two furry lumps could be seen through the glass door, one piled atop the other, where they'd dropped after being shot in the head. Their ephemeral forms joined Tony, one at each side, and he absently scratched them behind the ears.

"Where's Kit?" Grif asked, swallowing hard. If she were here—if she were dead—he'd know it. He was her Centurion, after all. Plus, she'd already be at his side, probably yapping about how she knew she'd seen his wings.

"Wasn't here when I got home," Tony said, and Grif couldn't help but heave a relieved sigh. So she'd fled after their fight. He'd check her house. Next to him, Tony scratched his own head. "I called to her, to you, even the dogs, but no one answered. Then, I was bent over the wine fridge, looking for a second merlot, when . . . when . . ." He looked over at Jesse. "What happened then?"

"Your head was smashed in like a rotted watermelon."

Grif lit a stick with shaking fingers. "Jesus, Jesse."

"That's all right," Tony said, putting his right arm directly through Grif's chest as he tried to pat his back. Tony jerked back, and Grif shivered with the plasmic intrusion, and took in another grounding puff of smoke. "I guess the only real surprise was that it didn't happen sooner. You can't live like I did, and make as many enemies as I made, and not expect it to come back 'round."

Nodding, Grif let that sit for a moment, and they stared

together at Tony's cooling body before Grif said what he was really thinking. "Can't rat me out to Caleb Chambers and not expect some fallout, either."

Tony said nothing.

Tilting his head, blowing smoke into the other man's face. "Why, Tony?"

Frowning, Tony stepped away, then gestured to his body with one hand, the house with the other. "Because I wanted out of this fishbowl for good, Grif! Ever since you and that broad busted in my pad, I've felt more alive, and freer, than in years! It made me realize that life was just passing me by! I was as much in prison as old Frankie Alessi!"

Grif snuffed his Lucky out in a crystal ashtray, and shoved his hands into his pockets. "Well, like you said. You get used to things and pretty soon forget you ever knew any different."

Tony looked angry at that. "Yeah, and you made me remember. I thought I'd been safe all these years, but really? I wasn't any more alive than you. So, yeah, I went to Chambers. The old family might own me, but he owns them. He owns everyone."

"And you thought that if you turned me and Kit over to Chambers, he'd call the soldiers off you once and for all."

"It was stupid. It was wrong," Tony admitted, before pointing a bony finger at Grif. "But you drank my most expensive bottle of wine!"

"Oh, stop. You ratted me out before that. Besides, technically, I shared the juice with a Pure."

Tony's nose scrunched. "A what?"

"You'll see," Grif muttered, turning to Jesse. "How's Sarge?"

Jesse, who'd been listening to the conversation as closely as

Courtney had been pretending to ignore it, snapped to, and regarded Grif with a smirk. "How you think, homes? He's pissed and calling for your head."

Grif looked at Courtney, who just nodded.

Jesse stepped forward, grabbing Tony beneath one scrawny arm as he began to wobble due to the fade. "You should just come back with us, G-Man. Everyone knows your old lady is floating around the Everlast somewhere. And you got eternity to run into her, right? You'll find her eventually."

Grif jerked his head. "I'm not here for Evie anymore."

Surprised silence filled the room. Even the dead Dobermans looked up at Grif with quizzical expressions.

"What, the other betty?" Courtney scoffed. "She'll be along soon enough, too."

"Courtney!" Jesse yelled.

"What?" She spread her hands wide. "So what? It's Grif!"

"He's wearing flesh!" Jesse said it like it was a disease.

And Courtney, realizing her mistake, covered her mouth with her palm. "Shit."

He had free will while wearing flesh. He could change things on the Surface. Grif's gaze darted from her to Jesse and back again. "Your next Take . . . is Kit?"

Jesse and Courtney just stared.

"Man, I'm sorry to hear that," Tony said, with a frown. "I really only meant for them to whack you."

"Shut up, Tony."

"Oh come on," Jesse finally said. "It's not like it's any real surprise. You can't change fate, Grif. She's destined to die."

But he'd changed it once before. "Where is she?"

Jesse crossed his arms. "Like we're going to tell you? And get Anas all up in our asses? No way."

"Who's Anas?" Tony asked. "Is she cute? Better tell her to watch out. I'm feeling frisky."

"What are you doing?" Jesse asked, following Grif as he stalked from the room.

"Don't you have a soul to deliver to the Everlast?" Ignoring the semitransparent dog trying to nudge him into patting its head, Grif picked up the phone and dialed the number he'd memorized the day before.

"Fine." The other Centurion gestured to Tony, but he was busy trying to pick up his wineglass. Sighing, Jesse finally crossed the room and grabbed the old man's arm.

"Hey!" Tony said, trying to pull away, but Jesse just ignored him.

Halting directly in front of Grif, Jesse raised his brows. "Just so you know, Sarge plans on sending you straight to the Tube the moment you step foot in the Everlast."

"Then I'd better work fast," Grif said, but cursed as his call went to voice mail. Hanging up, he tried again.

"You coming, Court?" Jesse asked, flanked by two dogs and a dead mobster.

Courtney kicked her heels up on the coffee table, causing Tony to scowl. She ignored him. "Nah, this is the most interesting thing to happen since Paulo tried to start a soccer league in the Milky Way. I'll be there by morning."

"Not if I can help it," Grif told her.

"But you can't, Grif."

This time they all turned, and listened, to Tony. He shook his head, the old mobster gleam back in his dark, watery eyes. "Chambers runs this town from end to end. He makes the rules, and takes what he wants. Just like the family did back in our day."

"Uh-uh," Jesse said, clamping a hand over Tony's mouth. "You can't talk about his old life. Sorry, Grif. Sarge's orders."

"Shut up, Jesse," Grif snapped back.

"Well," said Tony, "I wish you luck, anyway. That Craig girl is a real peach." Then he shrugged. "For a nosy, relentless ink-hound, that is. I liked her."

But Grif loved her. He knew that now. So he gritted his teeth, and dialed Bridget Moore's number once more.

CHAPTER TWENTY-FIVE

Y ou're going the wrong way," said Grif's backseat driver.
"No, I'm not," he told Courtney, as he squinted up at
the street sign, blew past a yellow-ish light, and steered through
a section of downtown that looked better at night than on any
given day.

Courtney huffed and slapped a combat boot up on the dash.
"The map is upside-down, loo-sah."

"Watch your mouth, sweetheart." And he slapped her leg
back down. Kit would keel over dead if there were boot prints
on her dashboard.

"Don't call me that," Courtney muttered, staring out the
side window. Black hair fringed her face in spikes so all that
was visible of her face was one pert pale little nose.

"No one else will," Grif muttered, hesitating before adding,
"'cept maybe . . . Jesse?"

"What? Shut up!" Courtney straightened so fast she would have hit her head on the roof, if it were possible for a Centurion.

"Relax, doll." Grif hid a smile that hid his nerves. "I don't care about your little postmortem crush. Got it?"

Courtney regained her slump and crossed her arms. "Well, I don't care about your Surface-skimming crush getting offed. How 'bout that?"

"Feel free to leave." He motioned to her door.

Courtney smirked. "Feel free to take a right at the next corner."

Grif cursed under his breath, but swung a quick right. His jaw clenched when the street he'd been looking for swam into view, but Courtney—probably sensing he was close to his edge—stayed silent. After another few blocks, she glanced over. "So why won't this Bridget girl tell you where Kit is?"

"I don't think she knows."

Bridget had sounded genuinely sorry when Grif finally had gotten hold of her, and explained quickly that Kit was missing. But she'd also sounded scared. He could almost hear her mind ticking, making contingency plans for her own safety. Yet after their conversation in the bar, he was sure she'd have told him if Kit was in danger. If she knew, that was.

"And you really think *this* is going to work?" Courtney said dubiously as they wheeled into a dirt lot next to a high brick wall.

Grif threw Kit's car into park, and shot her a hard look. "I got no other way of keeping death from touching this woman."

Another woman he loved. Dead because of him.

With that thought Grif clambered out of the car, onto its hood, and jumped the wall leading into the Rose Lawn Memorial Cemetery. Courtney, who merely passed directly through the brick, smirked at him from the other side.

"Find me the fresh ones, Fido," Grif ordered, and took some satisfaction at watching her smile fall.

Yet she slipped easily through the plots, navigating the pitch-black night without a misstep. Grif might have some remaining powers from the Everlast, and Anne had certainly shot him up with a mouthful of something, but it was nothing compared to Courtney's full Centurion senses. She stopped once to crack a joke—pointing at a headstone and exclaiming, "Oh, hey! I know him!"—but a pointed stare from Grif had her continuing on until they reached an obviously fresh grave.

"Now dig."

Courtney shook her head, but faced the grave and waved her hand in the air in a quick windshield-wiper motion. It was a necessary skill—some Takes were buried alive—and the ground in front of her shifted like it was being raked to the side. "You know, if this works, I could get in trouble for helping you. They'll send me back to the Tube and force me to forget shit, too."

Grif considered the fights he'd overheard between Courtney and Sarge, booming from the Pure's office like they were being blared on a blow horn. She thought she needed more time in incubation. He always countered that that was the easy way out, that a Centurion had to work for the most important life lessons, not simply be handed them. So Grif frowned at Courtney as she continued flicking her wrist, flinging dirt. "Haven't you been trying to return to the Tube since you reached the Everlast?"

"Yeah." She nodded, eyes wide. "This might actually do it!"

And with that, she leaned forward, took a deep breath, and

blew away the last of the dirt. When the enormous burst of dust had settled, Grif looked down and found a still-gleaming mahogany casket.

"And this is where I bow out," she said, leaning against the trunk of a nearby oak. "All yours, Shaw."

Grimacing, but resolute, he leaped down onto the casket. There was no room to sidestep or straddle, and he struggled for a moment to figure out how to open the thing.

"Got it down to a science, don't they? You can practically knock on the casket next door," Courtney called, from above. "If they only knew, huh? They probably wouldn't bother."

No, thought Grif, tugging at the casket. They'd bother. People did crazy things for those they loved. As evidenced by Grif's actions now. A quick tug and simultaneous hop, and he managed to get one foot wedged in the opening. A little more maneuvering and he finally wrestled the lid open.

The first thing that hit him was the smell. Like overcooked barbecue and soured sauce. Not decomposing exactly, but sickly sweet. In return—and defense—Grif blew the breath he'd been holding directly back at the corpse, visualizing the electric coil given to him by Anne going with it. She'd been right about one thing, at least. It was time to stop fighting his angelic nature . . . especially when the power rushed through him like a river. The power—even just two feathers' worth—of a Pure.

There was a flash, then a whiff of smoke, and the corpse jumped. Then, for an even briefer moment, the face of the Pure flashed over the bones of the dead. Grif waited as the smoke dissipated, and silence suitable to a graveyard once again blanketed the ground.

Then, a twitch.

And Paul Raggio's body rose from the grave.

"Jesus Christ, who the fuck put me in this get-up?"

"Yo mama," Courtney called down.

Paul looked up, neck cracking unnaturally with the movement, before falling immediately to one side as he squinted. His eyes pulsed in their sockets twice, and then he grimaced. "Aw, man. Not you again. I thought I saw the last of your stuck-up, grungy ass when they stuck me in the Tube."

Grif looked up at Courtney, sucking in a deep breath while his head was tilted that way. "You didn't tell me you knew him."

Courtney made a face. "Contact shame."

Grif could only nod. Death tended to accentuate a person's more distinct character traits, and since Raggio had been a total ass prior to death, all that getting whacked had done was remove his conversational filter.

"Shaw!" Raggio's head swung sickly to the other side. "You got wings!"

"I know." Grif dug around in his jacket pocket for a stick, trying to not be unnerved that all the dead people could still see them, while he could not. The cigarette smoke would also help with the smell.

"Holy shit. You're a Centurion?" Paul propped his wrists on his hips, though with no life force, no mortal coil to hold them up, they immediately slid back to his sides. "Well, I'm not impressed. We've already covered what happens if I don't get over my traumatic death before my time in the Tube is up. Believe me, I've got no problem putting my past behind me. I mean, beam me up, Scotty. Paradise is totally where I belong. I'm not going to let regret and sentimentality keep me from my rightful place."

"No," Grif said, blowing out a long stream of smoke. "Those particular emotions would be the least of your issues."

"That's an insult, right?" Paul laughed, spewing a fly, which surprised them all. Grif cringed, and Courtney groaned, while Paul wiped the side of his mouth before his arm fell again. "Well, I don't fucking care. You and Kit can get your rocks off at my expense, but I . . . What's that fucking smell?"

Courtney sat, legs hanging into the side of the grave. "Is it kinda like a jack-o'-lantern left on the stoop 'til December?"

"Yes."

"Or a diaper that hasn't been changed in a week?"

"Yes."

"That's you, dude."

Head reeling all the way around on his neck, Paul's panicked yelp trailed off into a gurgle. "What the hell? Get me out of here!"

Courtney rolled her eyes. "It's your body."

Paul scrambled, looking like he was literally trying to pull his head from his shoulders, but his arms kept slipping away. The energy Grif had given him was only enough to coil around his spine. He was upright, his body worked . . . but it didn't work very well. "Get me. Out. Of. Here."

"No."

The dead eyes pulsed again with true terror as he looked at Grif. "Please, Shaw! I take it back. You and Kit are great, a perfect couple. Happily ever after, all that. Please!"

Grif lifted a shoulder. "Maybe."

Paul stilled, head dropping to the right, eyes wide. "You want something. What do you want? Raven's number? She's hot, right? I only bagged her, like, half a dozen times, but those were all the freebies she had in her anyway. She dropped the B-bomb on me," he said, and mouthed the word "boyfriend," and then his jaw cracked. "Ouch. Why am I telling you this?"

"Because your mouth and your thoughts are like your body. Falling out all over the place. There's no mortal coil to hold it in. So you're going to tell me what I want to know about Chambers and his little cabal so that I can find Kit before it's too late."

"Kit?" His alarm quickly turned skeptical. "Chambers would never want her. She's too old, too opinionated. Besides, he was furious with her for upsetting his wife at the gala. I told him I'd happily escort you two out, but he said he'd take care of it himself." Paul frowned, and his brow stuck in that position. "Shit. Why did I say that?"

"Tell me what happened to you."

"Now you're talking! Solve a real mystery!" Paul lifted a fist in the air . . . and it dropped like a deflated balloon. "Um . . . I don't know."

"I know you don't know," Grif said impatiently. "What happened right before you don't know?"

Paul's furrowed brows unstuck. "Well, there was the gala . . . and Caleb was pissed at me for getting you and Kit in. How was I supposed to know you two were going to bring up murder in front of the missus? And then, after we came to an agreement on some things, Raven said she wanted to take me for a little ride. We ended up at some horse stables and . . . Shit, you think that bitch rolled me?"

"Guess she was done with you, too, Romeo," Courtney called down.

Grif flicked ash on dust. "You never thought she might be one of Chambers's girls?"

"Ravie? No way, man. She was good, but she wasn't like, professional-good."

"Couldn't fake the O, huh?" Courtney shot from above. Grif and Paul both gave her a withering look.

"And you'd know the difference?" Grif prompted Paul. "Between a rookie and a pro?"

"Hell yeah! I was banging betties at thirteen. Why am I saying that?"

"Because you're an asshole," Grif reminded him. "What's less obvious is why Chambers would want to kill you for it."

Paul grimaced, the rest of his face scrunching up as tightly as his brow had. Someone was going to have to smooth that down for him to get it back to normal. It wasn't going to be Grif.

"Caleb Chambers didn't kill me. No way, man. I was playing him tight! Everyone knows about the parties. But me? I got into his *inner* sanctum. Usually you need a whole lot of money to do that, but I bought my way in with knowledge. Figured it all out myself. He's powerful, but he's not God. As we all know."

Grif ignored the arm Paul held out for a fist bump. It fell after another second anyway. "So how'd you play him?"

"I took the list Kit gave me the night Nicole was killed. I combined it with what I already knew of his predilections— the parties, the young girls. I went out on a limb and shot off an e-mail that said I knew what he was doing, where the girls were coming from and where they were going. That got his attention. It also got me the invitation to his Valentine's gala. I think he wanted to see if I knew as much as I said I did."

"And was he satisfied you did?"

"Satisfied?" Paul laughed, threw his head back, and gurgled. After he'd righted it, he said, "You mean scared. I scared the shit out of *the* Caleb Chambers, and that's what got me an invite to the *real* auction."

Grif stilled. "Real auction?"

"The new girl. Didn't you see her?"

Grif flicked his cigarette away. "There were more than a few women there, Paul."

Paul shook his head. "Everyone wants this one, man, and they're willing to pay top dime for her. I figured, why them? Just because they're rich? Just because they got connections? No, if she was going to be taken by someone, it might as well be me. It might as well be free . . . in exchange for keeping his little secret."

Grif wasn't getting anywhere with this. "Authorities have been covering up the Chambers parties for years, Paul. It's not that great of a secret."

"The parties, right. But not the auctions. Not the virgins."

Grif's blood iced over.

"You still have those down here?" Courtney asked.

"It's not funny, Courtney," Grif whispered.

"Hey, you all right, man? You look like you've seen a ghost." Paul laughed at his own joke, unbalancing his head again.

Bridget's words from earlier that evening came back like a gut punch. *He's a bishop in the twenty-ninth ward. He's the head of his own congregation.*

"You're not talking about the women in the back room, are you? You're talking about . . ." His mind raced, searching out the name. "Charlotte."

One of my girls, Chambers had said.

"The galas are a way of showing off the new merch to interested buyers," Paul said. "That's when the bids come in. The auction, though, isn't until the following week."

Chambers wasn't controlling powerful men using high-class professionals. He was luring them in using sex, yes, but used his position in the Mormon Church—an institution rife with a host of virginal girls—to do it. He was using the church as his cathouse.

He was turning babies into hookers.

"I feel sick," Grif said, and began to climb out.

Courtney edged aside for him, calling down to Paul, "Told you you're rank, dude."

"Hey! Hey! What about me? You can't just leave me . . ." He motioned down at his own body. "Here."

Grif whirled, pointing at the man who'd been rotten even before death. "You know, it's sad that you left a good woman to go running with hookers. It's beyond pitiful that you then got turned by one of your playthings. But to sleep with a kid because you figure it's going to happen anyway is so far past tragic . . ."

"Even the Germans don't have a word for it," Courtney finished for him.

"When is this auction?" Grif asked, glancing at his watch. Today was Saturday, a full week after the gala. Charlotte could already be gone. No, Grif thought. *Taken.*

But Paul said nothing.

Slowly, Grif lifted his gaze and pinned it on Paul. "I will keep you sentient inside that body long after your skull is hollowed out by parasites and your eye sockets squirm with maggots."

Paul's larynx dropped, and didn't rise again. "It's always midnight, a week after the showing," he croaked.

The showing. A memory of Charlotte's open, trusting face

as she gazed up at Chambers flashed, striking Grif so squarely that he almost missed what Paul said next.

". . . in the casino Chambers was building. His pet project—he's gonna splay his name across that big tower. Or he was until the financing fell through. That's why . . ."

"That's why he runs women and blackmails men. It's how he plans to raise enough capital to finish it. Bribing, selling, killing." Grif swore. "You said midnight?"

Paul nodded as best he could, but the Pure energy was fading. He wouldn't be of any use much longer. That's okay. It was just after ten now. Grif still had time.

"But the pre-show starts an hour earlier."

"Pre-show?"

Paul's careless shrug had his shoulders drooping low. "Yeah, you know. Like a warm-up act. Girls who might be a little used up but have volunteered for kink—tie 'em up, tie 'em down. It lets the Richie Riches play out their S&M or rape fantasies, the girls get extra coin, and no one gets hurt."

Unless they were being tied down against their will.

You should teach her a woman's place . . . or someone else surely will.

"Where, Paul?" Something in Grif's tone snagged Paul's wandering attention.

"Wait a minute . . . you think Kit . . . ?" Paul tried to access more of his maggot-laced brain, but quickly gave up. "No way. Why would anybody want her . . ."

"Where, you rotting meat suit?" Grif's breath was full in his chest now, heart throbbing so hard it felt like it'd rip right through the flesh. "Tell me now or I'll slit you back open, pop that bag of organs sitting in your stomach, and let the coyotes feed while you watch."

"Jay-sus, Grif," Courtney whistled, but Grif's sight was red. Red as the blood that had once spilled from his body. Red as his wife's nails had been when he'd allowed her to die. He wasn't going to allow it to happen again. He certainly wasn't going to allow this dead guy to damn Kit to death.

"At the old white elephant sitting in the middle of the Strip, man. The lot where the Marquis used to be."

Grif didn't hesitate, just growled at Courtney as he whirled away. "Re-bury him. Or don't. I don't care."

"Wait!" Courtney called after him. "You'll need me to navigate. You don't know where you're going!"

But Grif just broke into a run. He knew exactly where Chambers's pet project stood. After all, he'd died there once before.

CHAPTER TWENTY-SIX

How long had it been since she had been taken?

Kit turned her head from side to side, like that might help her see. Only hours. Not days. Not yet. But it was full dark now. She couldn't see the sky, not inside what sounded like an empty warehouse, or from behind the folds of the sleek, thick blindfold, but she could sense the night lying atop the city like an opaque veil. Yet unlike her midnight drives along Vegas's bowl-like rim, there was nothing comforting in this darkness. This was both an abyss and a dead end. It felt as if she didn't get out of here soon, she'd be trapped in blackness forever.

Be positive, she told herself, lifting her chin and swallowing hard. It helped that they hadn't hurt her. After she'd stopped shaking, after she'd muted the panic that threatened to crawl up her belly and through her throat in an inhuman scream, she'd heard Schmidt tell his partner that there wasn't to be one mark on her. So maybe Chambers just wanted to scare her out of pursuing this story. To force her to back way off, and warn her of what would happen if she didn't.

Yet when they were left alone, Schmidt's anonymous partner had run rough hands along her limbs, too intimate and too long, claiming with a smile in his voice that he was just making sure she was in good health. She knew then that this was the same man who'd accompanied Schmidt to her home and attacked her the first time, and she shivered with the memory, though she knew that it could have been worse.

It might be worse yet.

As if she'd voiced these worries aloud, the door to her prison opened, and he was suddenly there. She knew his boot steps already, the same way a trapped mouse might know the slithering sound of a snake's belly. She sensed his movement like she sensed the night. The man approached, footsteps deliberate and heavy, and stopped too close, his hot breath and cool attention squarely on her. Kit felt that, too. But if she could just get him talking, it might buy her time. And if there was a person alive that Kit couldn't get to talk to her . . . well, she hadn't met him yet.

However, just in case this one had more on his mind than talking . . . "I have to pee."

"I don't care."

Despite the ice in his voice, Kit rose from the chair she'd been ordered to sit in and said, "Seriously, I really have to go. I don't know how much longer I can hold it."

"Fine."

An immediate shove, like he'd been planning to do it anyway, and she crashed into a wall, hunching there until she was sure that was all he was going to do. Silence met her attempts to right herself and she fought the urge to scream. Instead, she patted at the wall, looking for a door, yet rammed into a table, and elicited a curse from behind.

"No bruises, you idiot." Another shove and her blindfold was lifted. She blinked, though the light was dim, and peered up into a hard, stubbled, and *familiar* face. "Hitchens."

No wonder she hadn't been able to get the police to help. No wonder even Dennis had seemed deaf and mute to her pleas for prompt assistance and investigation. Was he in on it? Had he been party to Nic's death? "Where's Dennis?"

Hitchens laughed. "Dennis is too soft to be of any use to us."

"But . . . he's your partner," she said feebly. She was having trouble ordering her thoughts amid all the latent panic and adrenaline and fear.

"*Chambers* is my partner," Hitchens shot back with such vehemence she immediately knew he only wished it to be so. He also knew she knew it. His round jaw clenched. "I thought you had to piss."

Swallowing hard, she looked around. A trailer, double-wide, uninspired. Typical. The bathroom was behind her. She'd run into a fold-out table.

"Oh, this is for you, too." Hitchens pulled his other hand from behind his back and threw a wad of black material at her. Kit looked down at the strips of fabric in her hands, wondering what she was supposed to do with them. Wipe?

"Put that on when you're done. Do it quickly and quietly or I'll put it on you. And you won't like that."

Kit couldn't help it. Her chin began to wobble.

"Don't worry, I wouldn't enjoy it. Your type isn't even close to appealing to me."

"My type?" she parroted.

"Yeah, you know . . ." The depths of his eyes lit, a bare bulb of meanness shining right through to spotlight her. Kit expected the vulgar and the familiar—sluts, whores, bitches—so Hitchens surprised her entirely when he said, "Weirdoes."

Slumping, Kit looked down at the "clothing" in her hands. She didn't have to think now because there was nothing to figure out. She knew exactly what was happening here, and could pretty well guess what would happen next. In case there was any doubt, Hitchens held out a pair of black stilettos, too. Taking them, Kit bit her lip. She'd always told herself, and believed, that knowing was key because knowledge could keep you safe from harm and all the things you didn't know. Not the easy answer, like her dad had said, but the truth.

The truth was that she might not ever step foot outside of this trailer again.

Tears welling, she looked back at Hitchens. "You killed Paul, didn't you?"

"He was an asshole."

Her fingers tightened against the thin silk. "And Nicole?"

"Nah, that was my bowling night." Tucking his hands into his jeans pockets, he rocked back on his heels, and smiled cruelly through his lie.

Slumping, Kit swayed. "That's awful."

"Only if it happens to you," he replied coldly, because they both knew it would never happen to him. "Now shut up and take your piss. And make it fast, weirdo. You're up next."

Kit entered the small bathroom, dull glaze moving over the dingy linoleum and dirty sink. No lock on the door, of course. No other exit but the . . .

Window.

It was tiny, glazed, but also half-open. Problem was, Kit could practically hear Hitchens breathing on the door's other side. She looked around, gaze dropping to the sink's press-and-hold faucet. Then she looked at the cheap shoes in her hand.

Hell if these were going on her feet, she thought, and pressed the heel against the faucet, pushing down, and wedging the toe against the wall, forcing a steady stream. If she were quiet, this just might work.

She thanked God for the winter chill, which had forced her into cigarette pants instead of a pencil skirt. The argyle sweater would also keep her warm once outside, provided she could get out of the tiny, rusted window.

"Hurry up in there!" Hitchens yelled, as she climbed onto the toilet.

"My tummy hurts," she said, raising her voice to hide the window's squeak. She only got halfway. "And I'm being careful not to put a run in the hose."

There. But only her arms and torso were through the window when Hitchens's voice rang out again. "I didn't give you any hose."

Kit pushed, the sharp steel scraping her hips as the door rocketed open. She squealed, pushed harder, and was falling before she could right herself. Hitchens's face appeared above her, brows drawn down hard over his eyes. "Fuck!" He disappeared.

Kit fought to sit up, and against the stabbing in her chest. No time to relearn to breathe, she thought, wobbling to her feet. There was barely even enough time to run.

Running had left Grif breathless, nerves had him shaky, and if he didn't already know where the Marquis had stood, he'd have bypassed it altogether. It was enclosed by a temporary construction wall hemmed in by a chain-linked fence so that no one on the outside could see in.

Apparently, no one could get in, either.

"I told you to wait for me." Courtney appeared so soundlessly he jumped.

"Which way?" Grif said, not sparing her a glance. He felt like a lion pacing a cage, caught on the outside of the long, linked fence.

Courtney pointed the opposite way. "You passed the entrance. It's the section that's boarded, with a rendering of the new casino. It swings open to allow passage from the side street."

Of course. Chambers and his band of merry child-rapists wouldn't want to attract the attention of some annoyingly curious tourist. Yet he was still unprepared for the sight of a fleet of mostly foreign luxury cars once he'd passed to the other side. It looked, he thought, like the parking garage at the Ritz.

"Wow," muttered Courtney. "Vegas is filled with rich sickos."

The world was filled with them, Grif thought, wishing Nicole Rockwell were here to document it with her camera. "They could drive away in Pintos and it'd still be sick."

"Yeah, but this is just salt in the wound."

It was. You had to be birthed with a sense of entitlement to think you could get away with this. How many of these men were considered upstanding? They paid their taxes, went to church, built their companies . . . and raped someone else's child in their off-time. And they *did* get away with it. "Come on."

"I can't, Grif." She pushed some of the hair from her face when he turned, and sighed. "You know I can't."

Grif swallowed against the lump that rose in his throat. "She's in there, isn't she?"

Her answer was silence, a returned blank stare, and he knew that Katherine Craig—the woman who grounded him and moved him and was more chatty and energetic and deliberately blissful than anyone he'd ever met—was already surrounded by death-telling plasma.

Ignoring Courtney's heavy stare on his back, he broke into a jog. It wasn't going to be Kit, he thought, slipping into the building's shadows. Even if it had to be him.

From the outside, it looked as if jumbo construction trailers had been welded together to create a giant, enclosed octagon. It wasn't something that would go unnoticed—why would someone create a makeshift space in what was already a makeshift space?—yet the construction crews were long gone, and the abandoned hotel project was as dark and forbidding as an underground cave.

And of course, there was nothing left of the Marquis, where Grif had died. He didn't even try to picture the old resort. His was an old death, and had nothing to do with tonight. Besides, there was plasma purling in the sky, and the soft, effervescent waves were quickly narrowing into threads above the makeshift dwelling, and slowly sinking inside. He had to hurry.

Grif spotted, and ignored, the prominent and single steel door. No point in announcing his presence to the muscle undoubtedly stationed there. Toeing the shadows, Grif spotted windows on the conjoined trailers, all dark but for a small one that gaped wide. Too small and high for him, he thought, and looked instead for some sort of construction defect. A simple corner that hadn't been sealed tight, or a place of escape that only someone like Chambers would know about. He'd already proven he had backup plans for his backup plans.

Yet the walls were welded tight, not even a proper peephole to establish the layout inside, so Grif turned his back to the clustered trailers, and spotted the crane. It loomed near the rusting scaffolding of the abandoned hotel, and he might have considered it neglected, too, were it not for the shiny black Mercedes parked, nose-out, right behind it.

"Damned foreign cars," Grif muttered, but he was already connecting the dots—car to crane to ladder to trailers. Crouching low, he rushed the vehicle.

But there was no driver inside, only keys, which he naturally pocketed. At the very least, someone was going to have a hard time getting out of here tonight.

Leaving the car unlocked, Grif turned . . . and nearly threw a punch at the figure rushing him.

"What the hell are you doing here?" he asked, yanking her behind the giant crane.

Bridget Moore jerked away, and almost toppled backward. "You called me, remember? You wanted my help finding your girl."

He'd left two messages on her voice mail before heading to the graveyard. "If you knew about this place, why didn't you tell me before?"

"I didn't know. I called . . . my mother."

"Your long-estranged mother told you that Chambers was selling off Charlotte's virginity tonight?" Grif didn't believe it. Kit had claimed Mrs. Chambers was in such denial she was damn near comatose.

"No," Bridget—not her mother's daughter—shot back. "But she said this is where he comes for his boys' night out.

I'm the one who figured he was doing more than playing poker."

Grif jerked his head. "Get out of here, Moore. This is no time for revenge fantasies. Kit is in there."

Bridget grabbed his jacket as he tried to climb up into the crane, tugging him back down. "And so is a little girl who's scared out of her mind. I was."

"Don't try it. I don't trip over guilt." He began climbing again.

"You can't be two places at once," she called out, her whisper hushed but harsh. Grif paused before he could stop himself. Bridget hurried on. "You save the girl, and you might lose Kit. Or vice versa. Bet you won't be able to sidestep your guilt if one of them dies because of you."

Jaw clenched against a curse, he dropped back down. "And what if something happens to you?"

Her hard expression unexpectedly softened, and for a moment the girl she used to be peered from beneath the tough facade. "That's sweet, Shaw." Her eyes glittered in the dark. "But nobody's taking anything from me ever again."

Which Grif would be doing if he tried to stop her. Sighing, he tilted his head up. The plasma was thickening, and now swirled like fetid clouds above the trailer. "Come on."

Bridget followed close as they moved from machine to ladder, up and then over. Then they reversed, slipping down onto the trailer, and he was pleased when Bridget landed with no more sound than a cat burglar. She pointed to the entry hatch just in front of their toes.

Testing, Grif found it swung open silently, though he was still careful to lift it degree by degree. His power from Anne lingered, because even though no light filtered in or out, a steel catwalk popped below him like tiles in a Scrabble game. He entered, paused to be sure he hadn't been seen, then helped Bridget inside, only taking a breath again when she'd closed the hatch behind her. Crouching and silent, they looked around.

There was only one other figure up on the catwalk, and he was hunched opposite them, turned away, thick cables crowding the space in between. Fiddling with equipment, and intermittently putting his hand to his ear, he was clearly engrossed in whatever was being said over a wireless headset.

"Cameraman." Bridget pointed, and Grif saw she was right. The man had a shoulder cam, another propped on a tripod, while a third could be seen on the adjacent pathways. Yet it was the headset that bothered him most. One low word into that baby and everyone would know they were there.

Grif turned his attention to the room below, spotlit in pastel hues to appear oddly serene, like twilight emerging on a cool summer's eve.

But this was no day at the beach. Dozens of men flared around the makeshift room in spokes and cushioned chairs, each with a side table holding refreshments and a simple electronic paddle. The floor was carpeted in black, the walls draped in white sheers.

But the room's center was the real focal point. There, a platform stage sat draped in red silk, a four-poster bed centered atop, dripping with crystals and gold tassels. So there were lights, there were cameras . . . and there was the promise of action.

Plasma undulated over the sheer, silken walls.

"There he is."

Following Bridget's hard stare, Grif found Chambers at the

back of the room. His chair was identical to the others, but he'd elevated himself, like he was a statue or god. His shirt appeared blindingly white in the pastel spotlights, though that was because everyone else was in black. It made him look like nothing could touch him, and that alone made Grif want to punch him square.

Chambers leaned back in the plush chair, a gleam sparking in a gaze worn by spoiled four-year-olds and homicidal killers alike. He lifted a microphone, and smiled. "Before we commence the final bidding, I'd like to take a moment to welcome our first-timers. That's each of you seated in the front row. I think you'll agree, it's an exclusive club that you now find yourselves in, so don't be surprised to find your social network outside of this room greatly expanded. We, men of taste, men of the *same* taste," he clarified, "help each other. One final word of advice . . . make sure your electronic paddles are at the ready. Bidding tends to get . . . frenzied."

He laughed, and Bridget growled beside Grif, but the sound was drowned out by a loud buzzing. The cameraman whirled in their direction and for a moment Grif thought they were spotted. Bridget did, too; her tense limbs began to shake, but Grif put a hand on her arm, and could tell the moment she saw it. The camera wasn't pointed at them but between them, at a space in the rafters occupied only by a giant ventilation grille.

"Not a grille," he whispered harshly, his mouth gone dry.

"A cage," Bridget finished, and the cameraman punched a control panel at his side. Every gaze below lifted, fastening upon the black metal frame, though the interior was velvet-lined from top to bottom, its contents entirely obscured. It lowered slowly, no doubt to build anticipation, until it was suspended above the bed's center, and hovered there like a question. The plasma began to crawl across the floor . . . though that's not why Grif jumped. Something moved inside the cage. "Is that . . . ?"

"A woman," Bridget said tightly as the cameraman moved again, and the black velvet curtain fell away.

But Charlotte couldn't truly be called a woman, Grif thought, swallowing hard. Not by a long shot. Just as what she wore certainly couldn't be called clothing. But the silken restraints were meant to approximate both, snaking along her limbs to wrap up and around her torso, ending in a knot at her neck. One tiny nipple peeked from between the bindings, a pink petal flare against all the black and white, while one thigh lay exposed, revealing the full of her smooth bottom. Grif wanted desperately to take off his jacket and cover the child up.

But worse than the bindings, worse than the overt objectification, was the look in her eyes. As the cage slowly rotated, giving every man in the room a full and measured look, her stare was as blank as a doll's . . . and, of course, that's exactly what she was to them. A plaything to be toyed with, used, and discarded when they were done.

Charlotte's non-gaze remained locked above the heads of the gathered men, her body motionless even as her cage rocked. Crossing his feet at the ankles, Chambers lifted the microphone again. "Let the bidding begin."

Electronic paddles lit up all around the room.

"Jesus, Bridget . . ."

But she was gone. Grif had been so focused on Charlotte, he hadn't seen Bridget closing in on the cameraman and the control panel at his side.

Grif spotted the clouds forming even before she lunged. With a maddened cry, she didn't just bring the cage to a halt, she reversed its course. Jerking it back up and flashing a blade Grif didn't even know she carried, she gutted the man who had lowered it.

A gust of air rushed Grif, and from the corner of his eye, he spotted wings in the rafters. "Shit."

A Centurion. Glancing back at Chambers's confounded face, hearing the disgruntled murmurs from the men as Charlotte's cage continued to rise, he knew that more were coming.

Chambers was now yelling from behind his palm, causing the headset in the dead man's ear to go crazy with commands. *Get it fixed. Do it now.* But the cameraman was prone and twitching, and Bridget had eased back into the shadows. Grif didn't dare move, but pretty soon there'd be nowhere to hide.

Then Chambers surprised him. Instead of continuing to rant, he dropped from his small dais and crossed the expansive room until he was centered next to the bed. Though he cast a quick, irritated glance directly up, he replaced the frown with a wide smile, and leaned against one spearing bedpost. "We seem to be having slight technical difficulties, but at least your appetites are whetted. That's good. I was going to save this next surprise for after the bidding, a little something to make this night extra-memorable, but I see no reason to wait now. We have a very . . . special show tonight."

The microphone tilted in Chambers's hand, like an old crooner entertaining a rapt, admiring audience. And those gathered *were* rapt. "Now, you'll have to excuse our next prize for any unseemly behavior. She's never been this route before, but I have full confidence that she'll take to it quite easily."

Grif found himself leaning over the rail without even knowing how he got there.

"You should brace yourself for some rough play. She will
resist, and she will also be restrained, and hopefully she will
cry out. Let me assure you that no matter what it looks like,
she is a volunteer. She wants this. She needs it. And do you
know why?"

Chambers ceased pacing, and scanned the faces there like
they were gathered in a boardroom. "Because that, my brothers, is her raison d'être. Her role is to act as victim to your
conqueror. She is like a lion in the Coliseum, and being put
down is her purpose."

Then he nodded to the corner where the white panels parted
to reveal five men, shirtless and hooded, very much resembling
the gladiators that Chambers had likened them to. Entering
the room, they stood equidistance apart, hands folded in front
of them.

"Each of you has been preselected for this sport. You've all
shown yourselves as trustworthy in the past, so this is my gift
to you. Feel free to jockey for position. A little friendly competition always puts grit in your blood, and grants you the respect of your brothers who've chosen to watch. Perform well
for them, but remember, the five of you are ultimately a team."
He gestured again toward the door. "Now, shall we bring out
the prize?"

And the door, Grif thought, was proof that more rooms
lurked behind this one. Bridget was already working on free-
ing Charlotte, and she knew the way out. Meanwhile, the men
below would be occupied while he searched for Kit. Yet the
plasma plummeted to the floor as the door swung wide, and

though he already had one hand on the rungs leading out, Grif had to glance down.

Schmidt. First seen by Grif on a gas station's security monitor, last seen fleeing Tony's, there was now a bandage on his face where Anne's bullet had grazed his cheek.

Detective Hitchens entered next, and Grif huffed, surprised but not. He'd sensed darkness in the man at the stables, and would lay odds that he was the one who'd killed Paul.

Yet pulled along after them, wearing little more than mascara smeared beneath tear-filled eyes, was the woman that *Grif* had placed in danger again and again.

And now again.

Pow, Kit . . . right to the moon!

And she might as well have been on the moon. Another flurried rush of wings sounded in the rafters, and Grif knew Courtney was in. Sarge was right. No matter how hard Grif had tried, nothing had changed at all.

Grif's heart took up an ear-splitting thump, and his insides grew icy, same as when he'd landed on the Surface. Where were the decent men on this godforsaken mudflat? Where were the police, the Guardians . . .

He looked back at Kit and cursed.

Where was God?

CHAPTER TWENTY-SEVEN

Blindfolded again—and bleeding from the mouth where Hitchens had struck her—Kit was surprisingly coherent. It was as if the blow had brought everything into focus, and not just her vision but all of her senses. She felt the floor beneath her as she walked, different on the heel than the toe, just as the ache in her jaw from Hitchens's fist was different than the swelling in her lip, or the looseness of her tooth.

Though so much for no bruises.

Kit also knew the instant she and Hitchens were joined by Schmidt, and, of course, it would be him. Hitchens was just muscle and meanness, but Schmidt had intelligence and ambition, and was doubly dangerous because ruthlessness was attached to both.

"I should have raped you first," Schmidt hissed in her ear, arms sliding hard and rough along her exposed flesh. She

remained silent, but couldn't help the shudder that passed
through her already stiff limbs or the way her heart hammered
beneath his crawling fingertips. But she'd felt this fear before,
hadn't she? And Grif had been there then. So it was possible, if
she held out hope . . .

"No one to save you now, is there?" Schmidt said, reading
her mind, and because of that—or just because he could—he
yanked her head back by her hair and thrust his tongue in
her mouth. Kit gagged and tried to pull away, a futile movement which only elicited an unexpectedly high giggle. Then he
wiped her swollen mouth with the back of his calloused hand,
did the same with the tears tracking her cheeks, all while chiding Hitchens about marks, imperfections, and waiting until
the time was right.

Then the blindfold was ripped away and Kit was shoved into
another room that was alive with heat, pregnant with murmurs, and far scarier than the lonely cell she'd tried to escape.

Blinking and squinting, she tried to make sense of what she
saw. Then she wished she'd run faster.

Kit gasped, and futilely tried to cover herself while her mind
whirled. Who were all these men? And they were here for . . .
what? The girl? She caught sight of a bed, white and centered
on a sea of red silk, its four posters jutting into the air like
spears, while lights and cameras angled down from the rafters
above. Kit's vision swam, but her hyperfocus remained, and
she saw everything clearly.

It was there, in the way the men were eyeing her, in their
suits and ties, with champagne bottles and cigars at their sides.
It seemed impossible that anyone should wear such a dead expression, but they all did . . . right up until the moment someone to the left of her moved. Then those faces came alive.

Kit whirled to find five bare-chested men staring at her from beneath burlap hoods, each pair of eyes pinned on her with the same coldness as Hitchens and Schmidt and all the others who just sat there, watching.

Backing away, she eased from Schmidt's side, and this time his high giggle scraped along her spine like barbed wire. The room was otherwise stifling in its silence, and she fought back the scream clawing at her throat. They'd all like that.

"Before we start, we must go over the ground rules." It was Chambers's voice, but she had no idea where he was. Kit jerked her head, left to right, looking instead for a way out. "Wait—" she croaked.

"First rule?" Chambers continued, as if she hadn't spoken. "There are no rules."

"Wait!" Louder now, but still not her voice. Why couldn't she make herself heard?

"Have fun, boys."

And a buzzer sounded, like a bell ringing for a fight. Schmidt laughed again, but he and Hitchens remained flanking the door while the five hooded men each took a step in her direction. Kit tried to think, to open her mouth and say more, but her mind was tangled, her tongue useless, and her inflamed coherence had turned on her. She felt and saw so much that her entire body had gone numb.

The men spread out to make a net, driving her toward its middle. Kit couldn't help backing up toward the bed, even though she instinctively knew that's where they wanted her. That's where they'd attack.

In one last effort to make eye contact with someone, she finally found Chambers. He was sprawled at the back of the room, and almost looked bored, except his eyes were over-bright, and seeing that, she finally knew the truth: No one was going to help her.

Pack mentality had set in, and like Chambers, these men no longer saw her. Stripped of the rockabilly clothing that defined her, and the words that gave her a power equal to physical force, Kit had nothing. She wasn't a person to them, she was an object. And objects were there to be used.

Heart skidding, Kit considered running, cutting a path directly through the throng of heartless men. Surely no one would expect that. Yet she'd only taken two steps toward the aisle before one of the hooded men cut off the angle, again forcing her back.

Another attacker immediately feigned a lunge, and a few in the crowd applauded. Yet it was the lack of reaction that had the whimper rising in her throat. They'd all been here before, she realized. They'd done this to other women and gotten away with it.

And in a way, Kit thought, wiping at her face, I've been here before, too. Though it'd only been two men attacking her then. Not five.

And even one was too much. The tears welled and fell freely. "Please . . ."

But a backhand sent her sprawling to her knees. The force and anger of it seemed to surprise everyone . . . though it was the kick to her stomach that really brought the spectators to life.

"Do it again!"

And he would have if he wasn't shoved out of the way by a second, bigger, hooded man. Kit nearly thanked him out of reflex, but then his hand was around her throat and the crowd was suddenly cheering.

Spots danced before Kit's eyes as she clawed at his grip, and she barely registered the pain when her calves struck the platform. Her head bounced off one of the bedposts, but her attacker's grip loosened when a third man—or maybe it was the first—rammed him from the side.

Maybe they'd take out each other, Kit hoped. But her next breath carried the next moment, and all of Kit's remaining hope died with it. This man's hands were shaking, hesitant on her skin, though he still managed to use a gold tassel to bind her wrist to the bed. More strong hands jerked at her other arm, and as she stared at the bedposts, for the first time ever, she wished away the rest of her life. "Oh, God . . ."

Stars danced in her skull as she was slapped again. Then again. A roar rose from the crowd like a single voice, then another sole male cry raged above them all.

Oh, God.

He came directly for her, a faceless body rocking with aggression and purpose and, even through her unsteady vision, she saw the raw hatred. Why would someone hate her so much? Not that it mattered anymore, because this was the one. His fist was already cocked, and his eyes beneath the hood locked on her like missiles as he plowed down two other men on the way to her.

The crowd roared. The man did, too.

Kit closed her eyes and prayed it would be over fast. Then her left arm went slack and she screamed anyway.

Opening her eyes told her nothing. Three men were down, not moving. And what was that rocking just above her? An open cage?

More screaming—was it her? *No.* It was Chambers, and

Kit glanced over to see his face somehow looming and huge, though he remained at the back of the room. It was a microphone in his hand, she realized. That's what the noise was, and as another hooded man dropped, he screamed what Kit herself was wondering: What the hell was going on?

The last hooded man, the one who'd felled them all, turned to Kit. Fumbling at her wrist tie, she succeeded only in dragging herself lower, and she screamed as he lunged, but suddenly they were both flipped over the side, hunched and out of Chambers's view.

The amplified voice chased them over the edge. "Stop him!"

The man yanked off his hood.

And language flooded Kit again. "Grif? Grif! Oh, God! Get me out!"

His fingers worked against her restraint.

"Hey!" Hitchens's voice rounded the bed before he did. "Hey, buddy! You weren't supposed to injure the other—"

Grif spun just as Hitchens reached for his gun, and the blow had the weapon skittering across the floor. Rubbing her wrists, Kit raised her head. All eyes were back on her, but this time it wasn't five against one. This time it was her against dozens.

"I'll take those odds," she said, and freed, fueled by the sound of her own voice, she lunged for the gun.

Men scattered like roaches as she swung the gun around the room, but Kit didn't care. There was blood in her mouth and an ache in her ribs and every man fleeing had watched as she received both. Firing, she became one of them . . . but not quite. She chose her shots, aimed high. And searched for Chambers in the surging crowd.

She spotted him rushing a ladder that'd been obscured

behind sheers, but then gunfire from Grif's direction had Kit diving back behind the bed. "Grif!" She had to fight to hear her scream over the blood pounding in her ears.

"Stand up, Ms. Craig," boomed one sure, singular voice throughout the now-empty room. "Stand up, unless you want him to die."

"No, Kit! Don't—" Grif's voice cut off abruptly, a pained grunt curling at the end.

Kit stood. New chills broke out over her spine as she spotted Schmidt's fully extended arm, and the gun grazing Grif's temple.

"Do you know what you just did?" Schmidt's words were as sharp and even as teeth.

"Stopped you all from hurting women."

"You've stopped no one!" he roared, and he shook so hard she thought he'd fire for sure. But somehow he swallowed all of that hate and anger down.

Where did it go? Kit wondered. Where did a man put all of that inside of him?

"You can't beat me, Craig. I *am* the police. And here's what I'm going to say in my report. I found you here on an anonymous tip from a tourist—strange activity—and when I entered, you fired. Thank you for already providing the bullets."

"No. I—"

Schmidt raised his voice. "So I was forced to return fire. And now Griffin Shaw, a man with no records on file—very interesting, by the way—is dead. After using you as a human shield, of course."

"You're delusional. No one will believe that," Kit said, jerking her head at the mess around them. "And Chambers will turn on you."

But Chambers was already gone, and Schmidt's too-high laughter rattled through the empty room. "I'll kill him, too."

"So you're just going to kill everyone? Destroy the entire world on your way to . . . what?" She shook her head. "What are you after?"

"Only that," Grif said, sounding calmer, saner, than anyone had the right to with a gun pointed at his head. He cut his eyes sideways, as if tracking something that swirled and slid along the floor. "That's what those destined for the eternal forest do. They destroy. And in doing so, they teach the Third exactly how to treat them."

Kit frowned.

Schmidt cursed. "Jesus, Hitchens was right. You two really are weirdoes." He looked back at Kit. "Now drop your gun, and kick it away."

"No," Grif said, before her fingers could loosen. "This is a forty-five and he already fired five shots. He's only got one left."

"One will do," Schmidt snarled.

"Shoot him after I'm dead," Grif told Kit evenly.

Kit saw Schmidt's eyes narrow, still hard but less sure. "How noble. Letting the lady make the choice."

"You can do it," Grif said, ignoring Schmidt.

But Kit wasn't sure she could. And how many bullets did she have?

And how could she live if Grif died because of her?

She looked at him, eyes pleading for him to understand, then took a step forward. "Kit," Grif growled.

"Grif," Kit growled back, inching toward him.

Schmidt laughed, his swagger back. "She doesn't have it in her."

Angling toward Grif's other side, Kit raised her arms, sighting Schmidt's head. "Drop when I say so, Grif."

Both men's eyes flared wide, but it was Schmidt's voice that lowered. "I will chase you down."

"You can't chase everyone. Besides . . . I might not miss."

That did it. Schmidt redirected his aim. Kit found her trigger, too, but he was right, it was too late. She knew it even as she fired, and she jolted backward before the bullet struck, anticipating the hit. She smelled smoke, tasted tin on her tongue, and saw a flash, burning hot, then black, before her vision returned.

Schmidt was still there, yet he'd fallen and was now staring at her through the clearing smoke . . . or at something he found equally horrifying. He should have been looking down because a red pool grew beneath his chest as his limbs went slack. Kit's breath left her in a jagged exhale as she stared, but she couldn't hear it through the ringing in her ears.

"Grif!" She couldn't hear that, either, or his answer.

But she saw him. He was right *there,* somehow felled by the bullet meant for her, close enough to touch, yet like Schmidt, already drifting away.

The gun clattered to the floor as she dropped to her knees. "No!"

"Do you see it?" he asked, eyes wide on Kit's face and dazed.

"No. No blood." Not like Schmidt, not like a red pool he could drown himself in. "Where are you hit?"

"Not that. The plasma is gone. I think I did it . . ." His eyelids fluttered.

"Please, Grif," Kit begged, palming his stubbled cheeks. "Just hold on—"

But Grif's gaze had no hold left in it, and it floated before fastening somewhere on the ceiling. There it sharpened again. "The *girl*, Kit. She's in trouble . . ."

Kit looked up, and her eyes widened, too. Then she squinted. "Is that Bridget?"

And Charlotte, too. Both had seen what had happened below, but they hadn't left. Why?

"Chambers," Grif said, spotting him at the same time Kit did. "That's the only exit. He has a car waiting. But he needs . . ."

He needed Charlotte, Kit realized. She was the only real person connecting him to this night, this place. The others could be silenced, blamed, or explained away. "But Grif—"

He knew what she was going to say and shook his head, forcing away his pained wince. "Someone has to stop him, Kit."

She knew that. Else they'd never be safe. And all of it, including Grif's death, would have been for nothing.

"You're the only one left."

"Oh, God." Kit wanted to cry. Instead she bent foward and kissed his forehead, perhaps for the last time. Then, standing tall, the last one left, she bolted for Chambers.

Give me the tape."

Chambers's voice wafted down as Kit climbed the hidden ladder, finding her well before she'd hit the landing, though Chambers had no idea she was there. He was already squared off against his eldest daughter.

Daughters. Because Charlotte was tucked close to Bridget's left side, and while that side trembled, the knife glinting in her right hand remained steady.

"Drop dead," Bridget said evenly.

"You first," Chambers said and pulled out his gun.

Charlotte whimpered and covered her ears. "No, no, no . . ."

Bridget just shook her head. "You won't get away this time. I have the tape."

"I have the gun." Chambers stepped closer.

"Stop," Charlotte begged again. "Please."

Kit inched onto the platform, and moved into the shadows directly below the overhead exit. But now what? Kit looked down, saw Grif still splayed below, still staring. Tears tipped over her cheeks. What did he want her to do? What *could* she do? If she showed herself now, Chambers might spook and shoot them both.

"Besides," Chambers was saying, clearly feeling back in control. "You probably organized all this. You and Schmidt were running a prostitution ring out of the Wayfarer. You've been doing it for years."

The knife in Bridget's hand began to shake. "No one will believe that."

"You're a whore. Everyone will believe it." He jerked his head. "Now come here, Charlotte."

Charlotte automatically obeyed. Bridget gasped and reached for her, but only caught air, and Chambers straightened with a smile.

But Charlotte halted halfway between her sister and father. "Promise not to hurt her. No more killing. No more . . ." Her chin wobbled, then crumpled, and she couldn't finish.

"Of course, dear." He beckoned to her, and she took another step. Yet Kit knew that once he had Charlotte, there'd be no reason *not* to kill Bridget. She knew it, too, and without warning, she lunged for her sister. But Charlotte spooked and ran the opposite way, toward her father.

"Stop!" Kit revealed herself, with not a clue as to what she was doing, or would do next, only wanting to prevent the furied collision that had a child caught in the middle. Chambers half-turned, eyes widening when he spotted Kit blocking his exit, and he fired. Kit ducked, trying to make herself small, feeling her nakedness acutely as the bullet ricocheted off the catwalk, pinging like a deadly pinball.

Lashing out with the knife, Bridget screamed. Chambers whirled at the sound, but she struck him, managing to both avoid Charlotte and knock the gun from her father's hand. It skittered on the metal catwalk, then flipped to drop twenty feet, and clattered on the ground below.

Growling, Chambers punched her square.

"No, no!" Charlotte was screaming and covering her ears again, but Chambers reached out and jerked her by the arm, leaving Bridget knocked out, before turning to Kit. He looked like a bulldozer. "You can't stop this," he said, already walking, head lowered, eyes narrowed.

Kit whimpered, but held her ground. "Just give me the girl. You can go . . ."

"That's right," he said sharply. "I can go wherever I want, when I want, and with whom I want." And he was suddenly there, on her, hands around her neck, fingers squeezing. Kit groped for his hair, his eyes, his ears, wherever she could get a grip, and was pleased to hear his grunts and curses, yet the gray was moving in, her eyesight growing speckled, and somewhere far off, Charlotte was screaming again.

Then Chambers's head rocketed back with a sudden crack, his grip loosening as a foot flashed forward. A second blow from above had his entire body whipping away, and Kit shook her head, spotting him again just as he tried to right himself. The man always lands on his feet, she had time to think, but he was also tall, and top-heavy, and that was enough to cause his headlong flip over the low catwalk's side.

Covering her eyes, Charlotte screamed, but Kit watched him fall, his mouth open in shock, though for once he was silent. Even Caleb Chambers had no comeback for this one.

The bedpost missed his spine, but sank through his soft middle to thrust from his chest like a spear. He hung inches above the silky covers, his back slightly arched, his mouth gone slack. Kit reached for Charlotte and tucked the girl's head into her side so she wouldn't be tempted to look. However, Kit scanned the entire room below, eyes moving from Chambers and Schmidt, though not to Grif.

No need, with him standing beside her.

"How?" was all she managed as he put his arm around her and squeezed.

"Flesh wound. I'm wearing . . . something," he said, and Kit looked up into his face. He spoke calmly enough, but looked as dazed as she felt. "It was . . . a gift, I think. In my back."

He meant *on* his back. "Like Kevlar?"

"Like . . ." His voice trailed off, and he slid away, looking below. "Oh, no."

Kit peered over the short railing to where he was staring and felt her eyes go wide. "That's the woman from—"

"I know," Grif said, face drained of color, suddenly shaking. "I know."

And he raced to the ladder, and to the tall, black woman who was staggering, bleeding, and finally falling to her knees below.

CHAPTER TWENTY-EIGHT

Anne was still breathing when Grif returned, but the air rattled in her chest, liquid and low. Gently, he placed the powerful angel's head on his lap. "Oh, Anne. What happened?"

She laughed so that blood slipped from one corner of her mouth. "I was in the rafters. Wrong place, wrong time. Isn't that what you people always say?"

Grif looked up. He'd been outside, back on the building's rooftop when he'd heard the ricocheting gunshot. He'd thought then only of Kit's safety . . . but he hadn't known Anne was inside. The gunshot he'd heard go off from outside. It'd missed Kit . . . but found Anne.

"But I don't understand. You're a Pure. And your wings, the feathers protected me . . ."

"Of course. You can't kill what is Pure. But I am wear-

ing flesh . . . and I obviously didn't catch this bullet with my
wings."

No, her stomach was gaping wide.

Grif bowed his head. "Forgive me, Anne."

She surprised him by placing her fingertips to his lips, and
though they played there, there was nothing sexual in the
touch this time. "But this is amazing, don't you see? It's the
ultimate human experience. This pain is divine . . ."

But death was awful, Grif thought, eyes racing over her face.
It meant the demise of all those senses she craved. It meant
separation, loneliness, and losing those you most loved.

A corner of Anne's mouth lifted as she read his mind.
"Death is not the enemy, Griffin."

"It's the end," he blurted, even though he knew better, even
though he had wings.

"Wrong again. Death," she said, as her hand dropped away,
"is how you know you were alive in the first place."

Grif sat back on his heels, dumbfounded because it made
sense. Anne had been so greedy for every single life experience—
taste, touch, sound, sight and scent, even love and hate. Even
the negative ones like jealousy and rejection. Yet death, perhaps because of its finality, trumped them all.

"I'm glad to go," she whispered, seeing he finally understood. "Mortality is too exquisite for me."

Lifting his head, Grif gazed at the bodies of the two men
lying in small lakes of their own blood, then up at the two
women, Bridget and Charlotte, huddled above him, trying
to salvage what remained of their world. There were wings,
too, he saw, making out three pairs waiting in the steel rafters,
including Courtney, who leaned forward ever so slightly and

winked at him before returning to the shadows. Grif looked
back at Anne.

"So . . . Kit?"

She was by the door now, hands folded, watching them.
Watching *him*.

The Pure let her head fall to the side. Looking at Kit, she
sucked in a deep breath, searching for the plasma that would
mark Kit as doomed, before giving her head a small shake.
"I'm afraid that one . . . is as pure as they come."

Slumping, Grif dropped his head to Anne's shoulder, and
she patted it, briefly letting her fingertips play in his hair.
"There's one more thing. Your wife . . ."

Grif lifted his head.

"She never entered the Gates," Anne whispered, eyes shining too bright. "I know the name of every soul who passes
there. Evelyn Shaw was never one of them."

Grif swallowed hard, feeling tears well. "Incubation, then."

So Evie had anguished over her death, too. Too early, too
young, too soon. And all his fault.

"I'm . . . sorry."

He just nodded. "Thank you, Anne."

"Anas," she corrected, and with the last of her breath, added,
"Centurion."

Grif slid his hand over her smooth face, cupped her neck,
and pressed a soft kiss to her cheek. "Thank you, *Anas*."

Anas smiled slightly . . . and, a moment later, was gone.

You knew her."

Kit had been totally silent after they'd left the clustered
trailers. Bridget took Charlotte to her car to warm her and

call the police. But Kit had chosen to stay outside, shivering in Grif's jacket, watching him carefully. She'd seen the sadness on his face as the black woman passed away. She could mourn a needless death, too . . . but she still wanted to know why.

"Who was she to you?"

"Her name is Anas. She was . . . is . . ." He looked at her.

Kit gave a humorless laugh. "Just finish the sentence."

"An angel. A Pure."

Kit closed her eyes and blew out a long breath. More silence, and then, "Walk with me?" she asked, causing Grif's brows to rise in surprise. "Before the police and everyone arrive?"

He hesitated, but finally nodded. They wandered from the makeshift trailers, past the white elephant looming like a scar across the earth, and further into the night. Grif held her arm now and then, seeming to know when a stone or errant rubble lay in wait, but beyond that their contact was minimal, the conversation nonexistent.

When they reached a large tract of open dirt, just behind a small mountain of discarded rock, Kit stopped and turned to him. "Show me where."

"Where what?"

"The bungalows. Where Evie died."

"You believe me?"

"I could lie and say I do. But . . . come on, Grif. Angels? Wings? Centurions?" She shook her head. "But Evelyn Shaw was real. I saw a clipping about her, and I saw . . . a photo of you. My mind keeps telling me there has to be an explanation, but . . ."

"But?"

She folded her arms more tightly around herself, careful of her aching ribs. "But I want to hear yours."

Grif looked around, studying the dark like it was a map, but finally shook his head. "I can't tell where the bungalows were. I have a hard time—"

"With directions." She smiled tightly. "I know."

"Just so we're straight." Grif frowned, studying her face. "Are you mad at me or not?"

She softened a bit at that. "You just saved my life again, Grif. How could I be mad?"

"Then what are we doing here?" he asked, holding out his arms. "You want to hear me go on and on about something you don't believe? Something I know makes me sound crazy? Because it's kinda been a hard night."

Laughter bubbled from Kit, surprising them both. She felt like she hadn't laughed in forever. "I guess I just want to understand. To know something of the man who . . . Well, we made a good team, right?"

His jaw tensed, noting her use of the past tense, but he nodded once. "All right. You want to know about me? The truth?"

Not the easy answer, no matter how much she might want it, but the truth. "It would be nice, yes."

"My name is Griffin Shaw. My wife was murdered while I stood right next to her, and I couldn't stop it. I never even saw it coming."

Swallowing hard, Kit flashed on an image of her father dying years earlier, and understood a little better how something like that could cause this man's mental break. She nodded for him to continue, but Grif was staring blindly into the dark. She doubted he even knew he'd gone silent.

"For years," he began slowly, "I've allowed guilt and sorrow and regret to eat at me, and not just at me, but at my humanity. I couldn't get past everything I'd never change, I *wouldn't* move on. So I walked around dead inside instead." He frowned at that. "Funny how everyone knew that but me."

Kit didn't think it was funny at all.

"But then something happened that showed me I had it all wrong." Looking at her, Grif turned his back on the scarred terrain where his wife had died. "I thought I was alive in order to right old wrongs and get justice—or at least find out what had happened and why. But then a very wise woman told me that we're not supposed to just find the easy answers . . ."

Kit gave a half-smile, and finished for him. "We find the truth."

"And the truth, Kit? Is that there's really only one reason to be alive." He took her hands in his.

Shaking her head, she stopped him. She didn't need to hear it. She knew all about love. Lowering her head, she said, "You still love her."

Grif bent, forced her to catch his gaze, and wouldn't let her look away. "You told me you understood about loving someone. You said there's no getting over it, that no one can replace a spouse in your heart."

Kit nodded, because she *had* said that. Right now, though, she wished she hadn't been quite so understanding.

"But," Grif said, lifting her chin with his fingers, "you also said a person can carve out a new place in their hearts. For new people." His fingers splayed, gentled, and slid to cup the back of her neck.

"What are you saying?" she whispered.

"I didn't save you, Kit. You saved me."

He drew her close, and she closed her eyes as his arms encircled her, his scent—body soap and a hint of licorice and

Grif—washed over her. And it felt so good that she let herself be carried away, just for a moment, in the strength of those arms.

She could remember again later that he was crazy.

"You saved me," he repeated, kissing the top of her head. "You said I needed to move on from Evie's death. That I was afraid—"

"I'm sorry." She pulled back. "I shouldn't have said those things."

"But you were right," he said, holding her at arm's length, but still holding tight. "And you made me feel things I haven't felt in so long." He shook his head. "My wife is gone. I guess I've known that for a long time, but it was a catastrophe for me to admit it. Yet the line between a miracle and a catastrophe . . ."

Was a damned fine one.

She looked at him.

"What I'm trying to say is . . . I love you, Kit Craig." He said the words loudly, then said them again, even though she had fallen dead still. "I love you with all that's left of my heart, and with whatever time I have left on this earth. I love your twenty-first-century mind. I love the way you fight for what's right. I almost even love how much you talk."

She blinked at that, but he gripped her arms and carried on. "I think I love you for all the things that Chambers despised. You're flighty and contradictory. You're too cheerful. You're stubborn and, yeah, cavalier, and you never stop moving . . ."

"Are these still compliments?"

But he didn't hear her. "That woman you were asking about? Anas? She died desperate to feel what I feel for you now. This passion is a gift. It's a miracle. And it'd be a sin to throw it away."

"But Grif . . ."

"This is the only reason worth living at all. She died for this."

And gripping her arms hard, he poured himself into the kiss like his life really depended on it, like hers did, too. Kit dizzied immediately, a buzzing rising to claim her hearing, before whipping like an entire hive to short out her nerve endings.

She tasted dust and thunderbolts.

Fire flashed before turning to lava behind her closed lids.

Her blood pulsed with ozone and she scented rose petals on the air.

Swallowing hard, swaying, Kit pulled away. Not because she wanted to, but because she had to catch her breath. Her lashes fluttered exquisitely against her cheeks, and it took a moment to focus.

When she did, she gasped.

"Good God, Grif. You have wings."

"I know," Grif said. And his long-suffering sigh was the last thing she heard before the buzzing rose again, and Kit passed out.

CHAPTER TWENTY-NINE

Entering the station house, Kit couldn't help recalling the last time she'd been there, seated in the sterile, fluorescent surroundings, shocked into numbness by her best friend's murder. She gave the bank of chairs where she'd sat a quick glance, unsurprised to find that a new motley crew inhabited the spot. This place was an ever-revolving door of human drama, with all its folly and thrashing, but at least she wasn't the one who'd been sideswiped by fate this time.

Of course, Nic's death still shocked her to her core. The finality and the gross unfairness of it made her wish she could turn back time. So Kit chose instead to focus on its conclusion—Nic's murderer had been caught. Detective Hitchens wouldn't see the outside of a cage for the rest of his natural life. The investigation Nicole started had also turned out to be the paper's biggest headline yet, picked up by a nation that was by turns fascinated, dumbfounded, and repulsed that Caleb Chambers had been running young girls into the ground.

"Nic would have loved it," Kit murmured, earning a questioning grunt from the man who now walked with her, his hand placed firmly at the small of her back. That was something else that had changed, she thought, smiling up at Grif. This time she wasn't here alone.

"Come on," she said, spotting the open door at the end of the large bullpen where Dennis could be seen hunched over his desk.

But Grif pulled back just short of the detective's office, shoving his hands into his trouser pockets instead. "You go ahead. He's an old friend, and you trust him, right?"

She frowned, but nodded.

"Then go on." He jerked his head at the door. "And tell him . . . thanks."

A full smile bloomed at that. This man . . . this reticent, complicated, darkly sexy man could fight off murderers with his bare hands, but was confounded by the most basic of human relations. Well, Kit could help him with that. She had enough communication skills for them both.

Rising to her toes, Kit dropped a kiss on his cheek, as much to feel the stubble against her lips as to make him mumble and blush, then headed in to Dennis's office. She felt Grif's eyes on her back, and knew he'd settle himself atop the desk just outside, where he could still see her through the open blinds of the window. It was mildly unnerving—he said he wanted to be sure she remained protected and out of mortal harm—but it was also warming. It'd been a long time since someone had watched out for her.

Rapping on the open door, she stuck her head in the office, though she jerked back when she saw who else was seated there.

"Charlotte."

Still wispy as a colt, the girl gave her a hesitant smile. Yet she was clear-eyed, like she'd been getting sleep, and . . . something else, too. Self-possessed. At peace. Almost smiling.

"I can come back—" Kit began, but Dennis waved her in, gaze never shifting from his computer screen. Moving to his side, she put a hand on his shoulder. "I just wanted to stop by and say thank you. You vouched for me with the department and I've been able to get some great . . . What's that?"

Leaning over his shoulder, eyes also narrowed on the screen, she studied the video before drawing back, blanching when she saw herself appear. "He was really recording it."

Chambers had intended to capture the last moments of her life. The details of her intended death.

"Of course he was." Disgust on his face, Dennis paused the video with a rough slap. "But thanks to our budding detective here, that has turned out to be a great mistake."

Kit looked at Charlotte.

"I know a lot of those men," the girl explained, voice soft but even. "They came to the house for the . . . parties. I saw what went on there."

"Saw," Dennis agreed, pushing a paper toward Kit. "And told."

Kit glanced down to find the original e-mail transcript from a young girl . . . to Nic. Shocked, she looked back at Charlotte. "It was you? You're the one who found us through the Gregslist ad?"

Charlotte tucked a strand of hair behind her ear. "I knew it was wrong to send you to the Wayfarer, but I had no one to tell. Who would listen? And if he found out it was me—"

"You don't have to explain," Kit said. "I know . . ." *What kind of man your father was, and what he'd have done.* "I understand."

"I'm sorry about your friend," Charlotte said quickly, and her fragile composure shattered. "I never thought they'd . . . I mean, I didn't know . . ."

Kit knelt before the girl and put her hand on her knee. "Nic would have loved your bravery."

"That's not all," Dennis said, patting Charlotte's shoulder. "Tell her the rest."

Charlotte nodded. "Well, I heard things in that house. After my brothers and sisters were sent away, and I was isolated for . . . for grooming." She cleared her throat. "Well, you saw my mother."

Kit straightened. "Go on."

"So I'd wander. Sneaking, my fa—" She stopped, frowning. "He called it. But I heard him tell Hitchens to kill that man. Your ex."

"Paul," Kit said softly.

"I called the police—"

"There's a record of it in the call logs, and though it was anonymous, the caller mentioned Paul and Chambers by name . . . prior to Paul's T.O.D."

"But I was too late," Charlotte said, eyes cast down.

Kit shook her head. "Paul was blackmailing Chambers. Do you know what that means?"

Charlotte nodded, but Kit told her anyway. "It means you couldn't have stopped it."

"It means," Dennis corrected, "that we have a credible, viable, very brave witness."

Charlotte squirmed under the detective's praise, but lifted her eyes *and* her chin by a degree. Kit smiled.

"Strange thing, though . . ." Dennis's expression upended itself into a frown as he glanced back at his computer screen. "This tape skips a beat right when Jane Doe enters the room. We still have no idea where she came from, or who she really was."

"That *is* strange," Kit said, widening her gaze at Charlotte, before quickly changing the subject. "So do you think *they* knew what was going on?" she asked, jerking her head at the recording of the men circling the room.

"About the cameras?" Dennis huffed, and shook his head as he ran a hand through his dark hair. "Chambers has been getting away with this for so long I'm not sure they even cared. No one was ever outed before. It was like some big . . ."

"Rapists' club," Kit said, recalling how every head on the video turned her way, yet not one man had lifted a finger to help. Kit shuddered, then put it away, along with the memory of what was supposed to have happened next. It hadn't happened. And because of her—because of Nic and Grif and Bridget and young Charlotte the Brave—it never would again.

Linking his hands behind his head, Dennis leaned back. He was trying to look casual, but she saw the way his gaze darkened as it passed over the bruises on her neck. "Don't worry. I intend to identify every last one of them. Including those who were . . ."

"Hooded," she finished for him.

"There are other ways to identify a man. Especially with top-notch surveillance."

"Especially with a damned good friend on the job." Kit

squeezed Dennis's shoulder, and smiled down at him. "And what about your partner?"

Now his handsome face went dark. "Not my partner. Hitchens was in with Chambers. He'll go down for murder, attempted murder, and corruption. He's already confessed to running hookers as a part of his plea bargain. The thing that gets me though, is I *knew*." Frustrated, Dennis yanked at his hair. "Not what he was doing, not for a fact, but I could tell there was something off about him. And there was a look he'd get when around women. Around you."

Though the thought made Kit want to shudder again, she merely bent over and pressed a reassuring kiss on his forehead. "That's called your intuition, dear. If you were a woman, you'd have listened to it."

Charlotte giggled next to Dennis and Kit shot her a conspiratorial wink.

Meanwhile, Dennis glanced outside the office. "Yeah, well, right now it's telling me that if you don't back up at least two feet a certain someone is going to come straight through that window and over this desk."

Kit looked over to find Grif glowering. She waved, immediately cheered, but took a step away from Dennis anyway. No sense in pushing the buttons of a charmingly—and authentically—old-fashioned man.

"Anyway," Dennis said, once he deemed himself again safe. "The good thing is that the women caught in Chambers's and Schmidt's ring are now able to talk without fear of reprisal. The Church has even set up a program to get them mainstreamed again."

"Well, while the Latter-Day Saints clearly aren't all saints, they're not all Chambers, either."

"Don't have to tell me," Dennis said. "I was raised in the Church."

"Shut up," Kit said, drawing up straight and causing Dennis to grin sheepishly. He'd never mentioned it in all the years they'd known each other. "So should I call you Jack instead of Dennis, then?"

Dennis didn't laugh. "Believe it or not, this case has made this old Jack Mormon want to go back and visit the fold. I need something to . . . Well, it's just not an evil I'll ever understand."

And when people didn't understand something, Kit thought, they often turned to a system, and a group, to help make sense of it.

"What about you?" Dennis crossed his ankles. "All recovered?"

He said it lightly, but Kit saw the worry in his eyes. She shrugged reassuringly. "I rebound quick. Doesn't hurt that I got a fantastic byline and an exclusive story."

"Not to mention a guardian angel," Dennis said, jerking his head Grif's way.

"Oh, he's not a Guardian," Kit replied, with a smile. "Anyway, I have to run. I have an old mobster's funeral to attend."

"Ah, yes. Tony the Cobra. Have a pizzelle for me at the wake."

"Sure," Kit threw over her shoulder, before pausing at the door. "And listen, there's a barbecue blowout tonight. The Bender Boys are playing and Eddie Denning wants to show off his new hot rod. I know the girls would love to see you."

"You mean the weirdoes," Dennis corrected, and Kit raised a fist in mock attack. He held up his hands and smiled. "I'd love to come. I'll have to go home and change first."

"Damned straight," she said, giving his chambray and khakis a critical once-over. "Wear your creepers and grease that hair. I expect you to take me for a little swing around the block."

"My pleasure," he said, picking up a pen and lowering his head over his mounding paperwork. "Now stop flirting with me. Your fallen angel looks like he's going to come through that window."

Kit smiled widely, because it was true. Grif was in a smolder. But . . .

"He's not fallen, either."

"No?" Dennis looked up and cocked a brow. "What is he, then?"

Hand on the door frame, she shot her old friend one last grin. "Busted."

What an absolutely stunning day for a funeral."

The sun was bright, the spring was draining the snap from the retreating winter, and Kit had apparently decided to be thankful for the Now . . . even if she was twelve rows deep in a cemetery.

"What?" she asked in response to Grif's sidelong glance. "You want it rainy and storming just to match your mood?"

He snorted. "Not likely in Vegas."

And not convenient for the guests at Anthony "the Cobra" Prima's farewell bash, most of whom were hovering on the brink of their ninth decade, and shakily at that. Yet Grif had watched, baffled, as Kit drew a conversation out of everyone she met—complimenting one elderly woman on her vintage peacock brooch, sharing makeup tips with another—red lips apparently did wonders for any woman—while patting the hand of, and nodding agreeably with, a man who insisted they were related.

Yet even Kit's relentless cheerfulness couldn't disguise that most of the people gathered around Tony's humble grave would soon join their friend, more resigned to that and to saying good-bye to yet another peer than they were sad.

"Just think," Kit said, after the graveside ceremony was over and they had a moment alone. "Had you lived out your natural life, you might be here, too. Gnawing on your dentures. Hitting people with your cane."

Grif gave her a fish-eyed stare. "You finished?"

Sighing, Kit shook her head. "I'm sleeping with an old guy."

"Are you finished *now*?"

She then gifted him with such a wide smile that he couldn't help but smile back.

"Good. Then you stay here." He tried not to feel smug when her smile fell. "Try to pump some of these old-timers for info on Tony's relationship with the DiMartinos. I get the feeling they were still watching him, but I didn't get time to ask him about it before he . . ."

"Went to the old dago deli in the sky?"

Grif pinched the bridge of his nose, and sighed. "Just stay here. And remember, you still need to be safe."

"It can't get much safer than this," she said, and Grif had to agree. There didn't seem to be much to fear in this crowd. Yet he'd seen someone from across the shiny, flower-strewn casket, and he thought it might be someone he knew. Someone from before.

Glancing behind him, making sure Kit hadn't followed, he approached a wheelchair-bound man who had his back to the dispersing crowd as he gazed out over the expansive green cemetery.

"Joe?" Grif said, coming to a stop at the man's side. "Joe Pascuzzi?"

The man looked up, eyes thick with cataracts that made his gaze a blurry, diluted blue, but it was Joe all right. Beneath the wispy hair and paper-thin skin was the man Grif had known fifty years earlier—an associate of the DiMartino family, as made as a man could get.

"Who are you?" Joe asked, a frown rearranging his wrinkles into new patterns. "Are you my nurse? Where's my nurse?"

Grif's hopes plummeted. Joe's eyesight wasn't the only thing that'd gone.

"Never mind, old buddy," Grif said, though Joe had never been that. He turned away. "Have a good day."

"That you, Shaw?"

Grif froze. The voice had changed, the cadence and timbre stronger than before, and those watery eyes were suddenly fixed on him.

Grif knelt in front of him, and stared. "Sarge?"

"Who the hell else?" Joe's lips curled up as he stared down a passing woman. She hurried quickly on, as if she knew who Joe was . . . or used to be. "Think she's got a cigar?"

Grif shook his head. "First the bum, then the baby, now the old guy . . . what are you doing?"

Not-Joe glared back. "And you call yourself a detective? I can manipulate the very old and very young. People with a tenuous grasp on reality. Those closer to the Everlast than life."

"But Anas—"

"Yeah, I saw what happened to Anas. I ain't donning flesh just to bring your sorry ass back from this mudflat."

Grif shrugged. "She didn't find it so bad. Not in the end, anyway."

"That's right. And Anas was there on God's authority. Obviously, He already knew how it was going to go down with her . . . and you. His ways are mysterious."

"So I've heard," Grif muttered darkly.

Joe's expression hardened at that. "Hey, my job is just to deliver a message. The Host has conferred."

"And?"

"And it's unanimous. We have the death we needed on record. It's not the one we thought we'd get, but considering the good that will result from both Chambers and Schmidt being gone, the scales are again balanced."

"Which means?"

The milky blue eyes watched him carefully. "Katherine Craig may live."

Relief flooded Grif so hard and fast, he swayed. He had saved her? He hadn't killed her after all?

Sarge gave him time to digest that, then said, "We'd still like you to come back, though."

"That an order?" Grif asked, though from Sarge's—or Joe's—responding scowl, he knew it wasn't. Grif was still wearing flesh. Which, as Anas told him, meant he still possessed the gift of free will.

"I thought you might ask that," Sarge replied sourly, "and I already brought it up to the others."

That meant the Seraphim, Cherubim, and the Thrones. All in the first triad of Creation, higher even than the Archangels.

"And?"

"I explained to them all about your nightmares. About Evie. About the girl, too." Joe's eyes cut sideways, and Grif knew he was looking at Kit. "I also explained that you now possess some of Anas's immortality. Have you noticed your headaches are gone? Your breath comes easily? Your senses are stronger than they were the first time you were here?"

Grif had, though he thought it was just because he'd once again acclimated to flesh and the Surface.

Sarge shook his, Joe's, head. "She transferred Pure energy to you. She won't say how . . ." Leaning back, he frowned. "In fact, she's having a hard time saying much of anything right now—but it's as clear as a rainbow's promise. Purity lives in you, Grif."

Grif shook his head. "But that's . . ."

"Unnatural."

Grif was going to say "impossible," but the disgust in the Pure's voice rendered him silent. Sarge then sighed, Joe's thin chest falling concave. "What it means, Shaw, is that you can stay without the pain caused by cramming your soul into flesh and lungs that don't fit, even without a limit to your mortal years. You are something . . . new. You're an angelic human."

"So I can remain on the Surface? For as long as I want?"

"On one condition." He gripped the sides of the chair and leaned forward. "You have to help us in return. You got celestial power, so that means you're still a Centurion. You come when we call. You don't argue and you don't hesitate. We can use you for . . . special circumstances."

"How special?" Grif asked, wary now.

"Some souls get lost. Some are so wounded they flee their Centurion guides and hide."

Grif recalled hearing of the Lost back in Incubation but he'd never encountered one as a Centurion. No one he knew had.

"Let's just say we may have . . . use for someone like us on Earth," Sarge said cryptically before clearing his throat. "Maybe you can treat your Takes a little better now that you remember what it's like to live as well as die."

Grif nodded once. Point taken.

"In return, you may use your time on the mud as you please. Just . . . be careful what you ask for."

That was fine. Grif didn't want much. Just Kit. To still learn who killed Evie.

Who killed Griffin Shaw.

Looking away, Sarge inhaled deeply as he considered his surroundings. "Look at the trees, Grif. Look at this beautiful day. Look at the gorgeous woman staring at you right now like you're responsible for it all."

Grif did, and the day was immediately more beautiful because Kit was in it. Smiling hesitantly, she gave him a small wave, and his heart leaped at the thought of endless days with her in them. He smiled back.

"You know," Sarge said, watching them. "People treasure the moments in their lives because they know those times will soon be gone. A normal person like that girl over there focuses on the present because even if she doesn't acknowledge it, death still looms in her future."

But not for Grif. He was still angelic, and that made him different. Still, he was being given his long-awaited chance for justice. And though the Everlast had the Forest and the Third to exact punishment for such crimes, he couldn't just let it go.

"Don't be surprised to discover there are worse things to despair of than one's final days. You're out of sync with the natural world now. That will bring its own set of problems."

"No," Grif said immediately. "No, I'm fine with immortality."

Sarge gave a tight smile. "I didn't say you were immortal. I just said that you will live on until you, or someone else with free will, decides differently."

"So don't go throwing myself into oncoming bullets."

"Don't lose sight of why you're here," Sarge corrected gravely. "When there's time for everything, there's value in nothing."

But what did Sarge know, anyway? He'd never been born, or even worn flesh. He'd never experienced senses or death. Grif looked away. He'd also never had Kit Craig, girl reporter and newshound and rockabilly weirdo love *him* with a heart that was as vast as the Everlast. And that was purer than anything that lived in Grif.

"Yeah, well maybe I deserve this," he finally said, and perhaps that was why the day suddenly looked so beautiful. "She's the memories I don't have. She's the world I never knew."

She was the part of him he hadn't been able to access on his own. The part that had been Taken.

He turned back to the Sarge. "Can you understand?"

But Joe's brows were drawn low, and his mouth hung slightly open as he stared past Grif's shoulder. "Bring me my goddamned breakfast. I want some cantaloupe."

Grif sighed. It didn't matter. Even were Sarge still there, Grif doubted there'd be any understanding. So he patted Joe on the shoulder, and returned to the one thing in the world that did make sense.

Glancing up from where she sat alone, beneath an old oak, Kit dropped the dandelions she'd been fashioning into a halo. "Find an old friend?"

"Don't know if I'd call him that," Grif said, offering her a hand up.

She took it, then linked her arm in his once she was standing, as if they'd been walking like that for years. "What were you two chatting about?"

"Life. Death." Grif shrugged. "Small stuff like that."

"Oh, sure." Kit laughed, but didn't press.

Halting suddenly, Grif shoved his hands into his pockets. "Got a question for you, Craig. How 'bout walking this world with me for a while?"

Kit lifted a hand to shield her eyes from the sun, but it couldn't shield her smile. "Why, I think that'd suit me just fine, Mr. Shaw."

Grif leaned over so that the brim of his fedora took the place of her shielding hand, and kissed her long and hard, until a passing matron grumpily cleared her throat. Pulling away, Kit sighed contentedly. "My mind is spinning."

"'Course it is," he said, pulling her again toward the parking lot.

"I mean my world has been upended, too."

"Nah. Just clarified," he said, but his mind was spinning as well. "And so has mine."

"So we still make a pretty good team, huh?" She raised her voice as they reached her car and split. She'd left the top down in deference to the day, so caught his playful shrug.

"When we're not swinging at each other."

"Ah, well," she said, climbing in. "Where's the fun in that?"

"Always gotta be fun with you, Craig?" he asked, as they pulled from the cemetery lot.

"It certainly helps."

And Grif just smiled as they rocketed away, because she was right. It did.